STILL WATERS RUN DEEP

STILL WATERS RUN DEEP

NANCY ROSS

POOLBEG

This novel is entirely a work of fiction. The names, characters and incidents portrayed in it are the work of the author's imagination. Any resemblance to actual persons, living or dead, events or localities is entirely coincidental.

Published 2003
Poolbeg Press Ltd.
123 Grange Hill, Baldoyle,
Dublin 13, Ireland
Email: poolbeg@poolbeg.com

1 3 5 7 9 10 8 6 4 2

A catalogue record for this book is available from the British Library.

ISBN 1-84223-106-5

Cover designed by Slatter-Anderson
Typeset by Patricia Hope in Palatino 10/14
Printed by
Litografia Rosés S.A., Spain

www.poolbeg.com

About the Author

Nancy Ross is the only child of the well-known musician and songwriter BC Hilliam. After a career in the WRNS, followed by several high-powered secretarial jobs, two marriages and three children, she is now starting out on yet another career – writing!

To my younger son, James Hilliam Ross

PART ONE

CHAPTER ONE

Men with cameras pursued them. The people in the big house, peering from the side of the curtains, could see dark forms scuttling this way and that way, like hunting dogs with noses twitching. These people (only doing their job, some said) gathered in groups near the minister's country house, and some of them even attempted to clamber over the high stone wall which surrounded the estate. When, hampered by all the equipment they carried, they could not manage it, a ladder was produced from nowhere. They were joined by other groups – old people, young people and lots of children – who stood watching what was going on in bewildered silence. The inhabitants of the village of Broadleigh were proud to have their Member of Parliament living in their midst. Roderick Macauley was an important minister too, whose colourful personality was well known in the media and whose voice was often heard. Now they were beginning to wonder if he had let them down.

The press turned up in the most unexpected places: outside the salon in the village where Duibhne was having her hair done, and even in the grounds of the school which fourteen-year-old Robert Macauley attended. Robert's sister, Bridget, called the reporters "the rats" and said there were town rats and country ones ready to appear wherever you happened to be.

She was thinking of the town rats when she drew the curtains tightly across the front windows of her flat in the Fulham Road. She and her boyfriend, Silas, had just stepped into the flat, both breathing a little sigh of relief that no one had barred their way. No intrusive questions had been directed at them with a veneer of politeness. Silas had parked his car in the street and they had walked into the building, unmolested. The flat was on the third floor, overlooking Fulham Fire Station, and had been a twenty-first birthday present from Bridget's parents. She became accustomed to the sound of the sirens at any time during the day and night, and she found the activity at the station comforting, giving her a feeling of security. She liked standing at the window watching the firemen below hosing down a scarlet monster or playing football in the yard.

When Bridget was presented with the flat Silas thought they would spend their weekends and evenings painting the walls and ceilings. He imagined himself fixing tiles in the bathroom and getting exasperated in the process.

The pride in a job well done would make up for the aggravation. When he saw the flat for the first time, badly in need of renovation, that is how he imagined it would be. He and Bridget would follow the example of married or unmarried couples amongst their friends. He had not reckoned with the Macauley family however, and a few days after the flat had been purchased in Bridget's name an army of workmen moved in. When bestowing such a rich gift, undoubtedly a good investment, Roderick had said to his daughter: "It is all yours now and you can do what you please with it." Bridget and her mother shared the fun of the enterprise, ordering on the telephone and issuing instructions. It was probably thoughtlessness on their part that they did not consult Silas about anything.

He half-expected, half-hoped that it would be assumed that he would move out of his flat and into hers, but very soon realised this was not part of the plan, and he remained in his spacious, partially furnished apartment which he had always secretly considered soulless, and Bridget decided when she wanted him to visit her. At last her flat was completed, the thick pile carpets were laid and the interlined curtains hung in the windows. There was nothing more to be done.

"It's too early to close the curtains," said Silas. "You don't need to worry. Not even the firemen can see us up here."

She was unconvinced. She twitched the curtains together with an impatient movement, as if to attempt to separate herself from the world outside, a world where lights were being switched on in cars and houses, and everything appeared normal.

"Those hateful town rats have eyes everywhere," she said. "I can't even sit on the loo without feeling I'm being watched."

She went into the bedroom and Silas shuffled in after her. He watched glumly as she took a small suitcase from the back of the cupboard and put it on the big double bed. She started throwing clothes into it, banging open drawers and darting between the bedroom and the adjoining bathroom.

"Where are you going?" he wanted to know.

"To Pondings. I think Mummy needs me at a time like this."

There was no doubt about that. "May I come?" he asked.

She paused, a filmy item of underclothing floating from one hand. "Oh darling, you know I'd love you to come, any time, but now I think I should go on my own."

She did not appreciate how this small rebuff would affect him. He had first met Bridget when she was twelve years old, and he had known her and her family for all that time. Resentfully, he thought he must be entitled to share in the tribulations they were facing.

"Perhaps you are right," he mumbled, trying not to sound disappointed and pompous, and failing miserably. He made matters worse by adding, "You know best."

He watched gloomily as garments were shoved into the suitcase. He was familiar with all her clothes: they were dear to him, intimate. In went jeans, a bundle of T-shirts in various colours, a thick jersey and a skirt, suitable for the country, and a black dress in case she had to be smart suddenly. She poked shoes down the side of the case. Her make-up bits and pieces were chucked haphazardly into the flap at the top of the case. As she pressed down the lid, she looked at him, as if, at last, getting an insight into how he was feeling. If she had not felt so fed up herself she would have laughed at his lugubrious expression.

"You are being a bit silly," she accused.

He loved her, that was the trouble. All his adult life, and even in his adolescence, he had loved this one girl. It was a fact of life he had no wish to change. He was a young man who worked very hard in the City, earning a ridiculously large income for someone who lacked age and experience and made up the deficiency with flair and luck. There was a price to pay, and he sweated all day, jacket slung over the back of a chair, sleeves of a handmade shirt pushed up to the elbows, eyes fixed on a flickering screen. Almost constantly on the telephone. It was an unhealthy job, stressful, with long hours spent in the same stale atmosphere. The lack of fresh air and exercise showed: he had spongy pale skin, and he was heavy with the slightest suspicion of a paunch. Bridget, into healthy eating, tried to persuade him to eat salads and fruit, and to drink less alcohol, but he still grabbed quick snacks during the day, and in the evening, if he and Bridget did not go to a restaurant and he was alone, he could not be bothered to cook himself a proper meal.

He was the son of a canon. His parents lived in a redbrick house in the Midlands which had taken the place of a charming Georgian rectory, too big, too cold for sensible habitation. They moved when Silas was already at boarding-school, and he never thought of the 'new house', as he called it, as home. He was an only child, born when his parents had been married for some years and had given up the idea of having a child. He was a surprise which they never wholly accepted, although they would never admit it, even to themselves. They were a couple so bound together they had been perfectly content before the arrival of Silas. The advantages of having parents who loved each other so deeply were offset by an ill-defined feeling that he was an interloper in their lives. At the age of seven he was despatched to a boarding-school in the South of England, and this experience taught him how to deal with life on his own.

Silas knew his parents were proud of his achievements, but they had no understanding of the life he led in London. Of course they were aware of his association with the Macauleys. He had spent many holidays away from them because of that family, but they were unimpressed by the grandeur, uninterested. They read *The Daily Graphic*, so Silas supposed they would know about the latest debacle. He suspected they would not discuss it, even between themselves. It was their way to turn their faces against displays of weakness.

He sometimes indulged in a fantasy where his father was conducting the wedding service for himself and Bridget; his father dressed in his robes, and Bridget a vision in white; behind them, the Macauleys, pleased and happy. It was a dream, but a dream he hoped would come true one day. In the meantime he gathered riches in anticipation of that great responsibility.

"Do you want me to drive you to the station?" he asked. Although Bridget had a car of her own she was a nervous driver, and did not use the car in London. It remained at her home, Pondings.

"That would be nice."

She took a light jacket from the cupboard and threw it on top of the suitcase. Then she went into the small kitchen, dazzling with stainless steel and fresh paint, and opened the door of the refrigerator. She removed a small packet from one of the shelves and, as he stood in the doorway watching her, she chucked it in his direction. He caught it.

"Marks," she said. "You may as well have it."

At once he envisaged himself that evening, alone in his stark, impersonal flat, eating the whatever-it-was straight from a container tasting faintly of cardboard. He would have cooked it in the oven for the required number of minutes, then transferred it gingerly to a cold plate. Then, with a can of cold beer, he would sit watching the telly while eating and drinking. He was used to this familiar routine. Despondent, he watched her rummage in a kitchen drawer and fish out a plastic bag which she handed to him, and he put the packet into it.

Before they left she opened the sitting-room curtain a fraction and peered out. Street-lamps, traffic and lights and a few people walking along the pavement on the other side of the road.

"It looks peaceful," she said doubtfully.

"Of course it is."

He held her suitcase in one hand and the coat and the plastic bag in the other. She slammed the front door of the flat. She was carrying two empty milk bottles. They clumped down the narrow flight of stairs, and when they reached the bottom the automatic light went out. She shut the outer door, and was putting the milk bottles into a container by the step when the camera clicked. She blinked in the harsh white light of the flash, and instantly could see nothing but sinister black dots dancing before her eyes.

A voice came from the shadows. "Do you know if your father is going to resign, Miss Macauley?"

Another voice. "Are you going to see him this evening?"

"How is your mother taking it, Miss Macauley?" A female voice this time.

Bridget did not reply. She was determined not to insult herself or them by uttering the hackneyed phrase 'no comment'. Instead she shut her mouth in a thin line, and stood by the door of Silas's car looking disdainful and beautiful.

Silas whipped the keys from his pocket, and in no time at all they were both sitting in the car.

"Nice car, sir," called out one of the reporters as the engine roared into action. His face appeared in the window on Bridget's side, and she turned her head away.

"Sods," muttered Silas, driving too fast along the Fulham Road.

Bridget was shaking, whether from anger or fear he could not tell. He slowed down to a reasonable speed and put one hand over hers for a moment. "Don't let them get to you."

"How would you get back to London if you came with me?" she asked, suddenly very uncertain, vulnerable.

"Easily," he replied cheerfully, having thought that one out much earlier. "I'd get up at crack of dawn. No problem."

He glanced at her profile, so exquisite, like an alabaster sculpture, the straight Macauley nose, fair hair swept behind small, flat ears. Although he had known her for so long, he never tired of looking at that lovely face, and he never ceased marvelling at its perfection. Miraculously, it was his alone to love and cherish, for he knew that she had never known another man. He was her first and only lover.

She did not look as if she had done a day's work in

her life, yet she fancied herself a working girl. She was the owner of a small restaurant near South Molton Street. It was a sinecure, put in her lap by indulgent parents after she managed, with mediocre results, to get a diploma on completing a catering course. To Roderick it seemed perfectly natural for a proud father to give his daughter a restaurant to play with, and when the gift was made Silas had a hard time hiding his true feelings. He longed to protest about the unfairness, the absurdity of Bridget being given such a chance when others deserved it more. But she was thrilled, and he loved her, so he said nothing.

The restaurant was in a perfect position, not expensive, and always thronged with young people. The shoppers and workers turned down the little street leading to it for a quick lunch, and at night the couples gathered there for a healthy meal and a bottle of wine. Spirits were not served. Bridget gave it the name of Rocket. It was a little goldmine, but then Roderick would never have invested his money in a project that was not sure of success.

During the course Bridget had met a girl called Amanda Rhys. Amanda's parents owned a pub in the Cotswolds, and she planned to help them run it when she was qualified. When Bridget suggested she become a partner in Rocket it was too good an offer to refuse. Bridget had shown her father's business acumen in her choice of Amanda, for she had taken a management course as well as one in catering. Both girls were fired with enthusiasm and every available hour of the day was filled with designing the décor, planning the opening and then running the place.

Silas inwardly cursed Rocket as he hardly saw Bridget, she was so busy. Then he noticed the initial excitement had begun to wane, and she spent more and more time away from it. Secretly, he thought the wretched Amanda had made a bad bargain. She spent so much time keeping the place going, and Bridget took time off when she felt like it. She was still the boss though, and sometimes Silas heard her talking to Amanda on the telephone, giving orders in the clipped, brisk voice she used when she assumed her career-woman role. Silas thought it rather sweet.

He said, "It's much better that we drive to Pondings and you don't have to bother with the train. I'm happy with this arrangement."

Happy? He was deliriously happy when she murmured, "Thank you, darling."

"I haven't a toothbrush," he said, as if that mattered.

"Mummy will find you one. She keeps spares. I feel so much better now that I know you are coming with me."

It was music to his ears. Curiosity got in the way of his contentment for he longed to ask her what the reporters had wanted to know. What was the old boy going to do in this situation? Maybe Bridget herself did not know the answer.

She sat in the warm darkness of the car and thought

of her mother whom she loved, and wondered if she would mind Silas being there. No, she would not mind. She was understanding about most things, and knew Silas well and liked him. It was just that everything was so different at the present time, and it was hard to know how people would react. She thought about her father, who was lovable but tiresome. What a fool to get himself in this muddle! She resorted to a childhood habit and wished things could be the same as before it happened.

Her thoughts were interrupted by Silas, who made the most extraordinary suggestion.

"I suppose you would not consider marrying me?"

Bridget laughed aloud, anxiety forgotten. His rather pedantic way of expressing things never failed to amuse her. It was an unexpected proposal, for, in spite of having a good relationship, the idea of marriage had never come up before. Silas was a nice habit, but not someone you'd think of marrying, although she supposed he must be quite well off by now, and able to support a wife. Most of her girlfriends had had several boyfriends whereas she had had just the one. It was a bit dull, and she thought she should look further afield before deciding to settle down. The trouble was what to do with Silas while she was exploring the alternatives.

"You can imagine what the press would make of that," she said. "I don't think your timing is right."

"It might divert them from the main issue," he said hopefully.

"When I get married, " Bridget told him, "I want the

works. Fantastic wedding, heaps of bridesmaids, paid photographers – not snooper-rats lurking behind the bushes in the churchyard."

"I can understand that," replied Silas. After all, it was not so different from his own concept. "At least you have not given me a definite 'no' and you will think about it, won't you?"

"Oh, yes, I'll think about it."

"I'll ask you again when this business is over."

"Will it ever be over?" she sighed.

"It will be over very quickly," said Silas wisely. "You can be sure of that. These things are sorted out and forgotten in no time at all." He stared straight ahead wondering whether to say what he thought, then decided to go ahead and risk upsetting her. "I just can't understand what all the fuss is about."

"I don't know what you mean."

"Well, all this talk of resignation. Why should your father even think of resigning? It's a human weakness he has been guilty of. Aren't Cabinet Ministers allowed to make mistakes in their private lives?"

"It's very hard on my poor mother," said Bridget.

"Of course, we all know that, but that is nothing to do with her husband's place in the government." A pity, thought Silas, that Roderick was always spouting about family values. That must go against him. "If the worst came to the worst and he did resign, I'm sure, with his connections, he would soon find something else to interest him. He would be offered directorships, and many doors would be opened to him. No doubt he would get a peerage so he would have a voice in the House of Lords."

"But it would kill him not to be in the Cabinet," said Bridget sorrowfully. "It means everything to him."

Silas said nothing, but he thought: it will not kill him. He will survive, but what about his family?

"How is your mother coping?" he asked gently. Almost the same question the woman reporter had asked outside the flat.

"That's what I'm going to find out," said Bridget, and, for the first time, Silas wondered if his presence would be welcomed. It was tricky, and he would have to be tactful.

"Is your father going to be there?"

"I don't know."

As they left the London streets and purred along the motorway, conversation dwindled and Bridget fell asleep. She did not wake until the car turned into the long drive approaching Pondings. Ahead of them loomed the big house, and, as he had done so many times before, Silas marvelled at the magnificence of the place. Imagine being the owner of such a pad! There seemed to be a light blazing in every room.

He parked the car beside the wide steps leading to the front door. He carried her suitcase, coat and the absurd plastic bag and she pulled the bell. They could hear its shrill ring echoing through the house, and then the sounds of very slow steps coming nearer and nearer.

The door was opened by an old man – a very old man, white-haired and stooped. Bridget leaned forward and kissed him on a wrinkled cheek. Silas was not surprised at this – he knew the family and how every member of the household was part of it. That was Mrs Macauley's influence, and the old man had been in her father's employment in Ireland. In those days he had looked after the stables. Even when she was a young girl she had called him 'old Bell', not by virtue of his age but because he had a young son working in the stable with him, a young lad, barely in his teens, whom they called 'young Bell'. He had remained in Ireland but his father had come to England on Mrs Macauley's marriage, and had never returned to his homeland. He was a dear friend as well as an old retainer, and deserving of kisses from the children. Bridget's mother, although reserved with her acquaintances, was always warm-hearted with her servants.

"Is Mummy all right?" Bridget asked him.

"Your mummy is bearing up fine," said the old fellow. He had a melodic up and down Irish accent. "Sure, isn't that what we all expect of her?" He turned to Silas. "Good evening, Mr Tomalin. Have you a suitcase?"

"I was not expecting to come," Silas explained, "so I have brought nothing with me. Except this . . ." He handed over the bag containing the Marks & Spencer packet. "You can throw it away if you like."

"Not at all," said Bell, peeping into the bag. "Mary in the kitchen will enjoy that this evening." He went on, "You will have the same room as usual, sir, and I will see that it is made ready for you."

Bridget's mother did not give orders for them to be put in the same room, but she compromised. Silas always slept in the room they called the nursery. It was next to Bridget's bedroom, the room she had slept in when she was a little girl, and it was still full of all her childhood clutter, soft toys and china animals. Further down the passage was Robert's bedroom, Robert being Bridget's young brother. His room contained treasures which, on his strict instructions, had remained untouched since the day he went to boarding-school, ready for him to re-examine and gloat over when he came home for the holidays.

There were two other bedrooms in the nursery wing, now no longer used as they had belonged to the children's nanny (they called her 'Ma') and her son, Christopher. A third room, larger than the others, had been Ma's private sitting-room. The rooms were no longer occupied because, since the children had become too old to have a nanny, Ma had been given a cottage on the estate. As Robert was at school, Bridget and Silas had the nursery wing to themselves completely separate from the rest of the house.

The nursery was full of childhood relics and, in the presence of a rather moth-eaten rocking horse, a wooden fort and soldiers standing in lines on a shelf, Silas kissed Bridget. Then they went down the wide staircase together, hand in hand.

Mrs Macauley was sitting in the drawing-room.

Silas never failed to be impressed by this woman. Once he had heard someone say: "The daughter is a beauty, but she is not a patch on the mother." Loving Bridget as he did, he could not wholeheartedly agree with this observation, but he had to admit there was a breathtaking quality about Duibhne Macauley.

Of course he knew she was Irish, the daughter of an Irish peer, the Earl of Clonbarron, and sometimes he thought he could detect a very faint Irish lilt in her voice. Her beauty came from Ireland: the clear skin, almost unlined despite her fifty-odd years, the black hair with a smattering of white at each temple drawn back into a knot at the nape of her neck. Her face was narrow with high cheekbones, and the eyes – such eyes! A deep opaque blue under clearly defined arched eyebrows.

The long, slender neck and the delicacy of features seemed to accentuate the heaviness of her hair, as if it were a burden, as she sat on a sofa, head bent, stitching a canvas on a circular wooden frame.

When the schoolboy Silas had first started visiting Pondings on a regular basis, his mother, in an uncharacteristically curious mood, had asked him what Mrs Macauley was like, and he had replied in the idiom of the time: "She's cool." His parents had been mystified, but later he thought his youthful description had been just right. Duibhne Macauley was cool.

When she heard their steps she sprang to her feet in

one graceful movement. "How wonderful to see you, and what a surprise!"

The two dogs, Golden Retrievers, asleep in front of the fireplace, awoke to give them a welcome as well, tails swishing from side to side. One of them thrust a cold nose into Bridget's hand, and she went down on one knee, hugging the dog and loving him with all her being.

The room, like the woman in it, was elegant and restrained. Because it was still summer there was no fire burning in the hearth, but the whole effect was warm, inviting. Photographs of children at various stages of their development stood in silver frames on little tables. The sofas and armchairs were upholstered in soft colours, and the corners of the room were filled with massive flower arrangements. The rug in front of the fireplace was a Bokhari. Comfortably worn and faded, it had been the resting-place of dogs for many years. The walls were overshadowed by paintings in heavy gilded frames, mostly family portraits, without exception Clonbarron, and there were more of them in the dining-room. Expressionless, haughty faces stared down at them from another age, and Silas was familiar with them all.

They sat down and if Bridget and Silas felt awkward it was obvious that Duibhne did not. "I hope you children have not been bothered by reporters," she said solicitously.

"They were waiting outside the flat when we came out," Bridget told her, "but we managed to get away without saying anything. Horrid town rats."

"I'm so sorry," murmured her mother, as if apologising for their bad behaviour, as if she was to blame in some way. Then she went on to describe how they had waited for her to emerge from the hairdressers'.

"There is a photograph of me in *The Daily Graphic* with a scarf over my head. A perfect sight." She inclined her head in the direction of a long table by the door, and Silas was astonished to see the main daily papers laid out on it, neatly overlapping, as if they had never been looked at. Bridget walked over to the table and started leafing through them, and Silas joined her.

Although it had been a *Graphic*-exclusive all the national newspapers had reports of the story. The headlines were all too familiar. *'Macauley must go.' 'Millicent Jones tells of six years in the Minister's love nest.'* And there was a picture of Roderick leaving his flat in Eaton Place, ducking his head, and another of him, caught unawares and looking startled. Beside it was a photograph of Millicent Jones standing outside the house she shared with him for six years before she decided to reveal all to the press. At last they found the picture of Duibhne wearing the headscarf, yet still managing to look distinguished.

"We must talk about it, Mummy," said Bridget.

"Of course, darling," her mother replied serenely.

"You don't mind Silas being here, do you?"

"Not in the least. I look upon him as part of the family."

He exulted in his unique position. To be considered

by this woman as part of such a family was a privilege indeed. She was such a remote being he had never quite known, until now, how he stood with her.

Ten years before, Silas had been left at school over a long weekend because his parents had made other arrangements and could not have him at home. His father was attending a church synod and his mother a meeting associated with one of her many interests. It was not unusual for him to face long and boring days in an almost empty establishment. This time, a friend took pity on him.

"Come with me. I'm going to stay with a family I know. The chap is an MP – Roderick Macauley."

"Will they want me as well?"

"It'll be fine, you'll see. It's quite grand."

It was very grand, and at first Silas felt overawed, but Duibhne attempted to put him at his ease. He did not think Roderick noticed him particularly, but Duibhne was always kind. During the years the friend who had introduced him disappeared, but Silas remained, spending weekends with them and most of the holidays. When they went abroad he was asked to accompany them. He was Bridget's friend, she liked him better than anyone she knew, and with Robert he was like an elder brother. He was never a problem, had good manners, and the parents were anxious to please the children. For all these reasons he was accepted, but sometimes he wondered what it would be like to be an outsider in their midst, if the affectionate blue gaze of his hostess suddenly turned to steely disapproval. He knew it was possible.

Bridget asked: "Is Daddy coming home soon?"

"There is a possibility he will come this evening. He will try anyway. At this moment he is talking to the Prime Minister."

The significance of this rendered them speechless, and a silence ensued while they pondered on the fear such an interview must engender. At last Bridget ventured the question, "Do you think he will be asked to resign?"

"No, I'm sure that will not happen," said Duibhne. "Rod thinks the PM is reluctant to lose him. The whole thing will blow over. The newspapers write such rubbish, and they get everything out of proportion."

"What did I tell you?" Silas said to Bridget, forgetting that he had ever mentioned the possibility of resignation. He turned to Duibhne. "She fusses so . . ."

Bridget sat on the floor by her mother's feet. She took her hand and pressed it to her cheek. "Oh, Mummy, I'm so sorry this dreadful thing has happened . . ."

"Well, the most important thing is that we must give Daddy all the support we can. He needs it."

"But six years . . . how can you bear to think of him being with that woman for all that time?"

Duibhne's voice was gentle, comforting. "You must remember, my sweet, he spent the inside of the week in London, away from home, away from me. Can you imagine the loneliness of the flat, returning from the

House to darkness and emptiness, sometimes late at night? I should have stayed with him, but I chose to stay here because I love this place. It was selfish of me."

"He must have been out a lot," said Bridget with the practical logic of the young. "Didn't you notice when you telephoned him in the evening, and he was not there?"

Duibhne sighed. Of course she had noticed. She remembered the answerphone with its recorded message *'I'm sorry I am unable to answer your call . . .'* Over and over she heard those words until she made a decision not to call him any more. She would wait for him to call her, and this he continued to do, conveying always his love for her and for the children from whom he hated to be parted. If she had suspicions she banished them from her mind, in the belief that if she did not think about something it would go away. Years before she had adopted that philosophy. Now she knew it to be a delusion.

Silas asked, "Why did that woman talk to the press at all?" They never called Millicent Jones anything but 'that woman'. "Surely it was in her best interests to keep quiet?"

"Now, there is something 'they'," Duibhne meant the press, "have not got hold of yet. At least, I don't think they have. I know about it because Rod told me." She lowered her voice as if imparting a great secret. "I had a pair of Ferragamo shoes which I found uncomfortable. I put them on one side for Bell to take to the charity shop.

They had never been worn, and Rod thought that woman would like them. Goodness knows what put that in his head, but anyway next time he saw her he gave them to her. The poor lamb thought she would be pleased, but she was anything but pleased. She has dainty little feet and is very proud of them, and I have clodhoppers, size seven." She extended a long narrow foot to prove her point. "She was insulted. I expect it was the thin edge of the wedge."

"I expect it was," said Silas kindly, not believing a word of such an absurd story. He glanced at Bridget, and she raised her eyebrows.

They went in to dinner, a fairly subdued meal with old Bell hovering over them like an anxious mother hen. Even in the mild weather the dining-room was chilly. The French window into the garden was open, and the curtain stirred in the draught. The gloomy portraits and heavy furniture made the room dark. Food was never over-plentiful at Pondings, and Silas often rose from the table feeling hungry. Tonight's offering of cauliflower cheese and fruit from a bowl set in the middle of the table was hardly satisfying, and he reminded himself that they had not been expected. Munching on a bread-roll he wondered idly how the immensely tall and muscular Roderick fared with such Spartan rations. Perhaps, as well as other favours, Millicent Jones provided hearty meals. He knew that Bridget and Robert were used to scrounging food from the kitchen.

Bridget broke the silence by saying: "I must go and see Ma. How is she?"

"She's fine," her mother replied, "and her garden is a dream."

Thank God I'm leaving early in the morning, thought Silas. At least I'm spared seeing Ma. Ma and her son, Christopher, gave him the creeps. To his mind, Ma was the one flaw in the perfect Macauley set-up – although now he must admit to Roderick Macauley being flawed, but in a recognisable way.

Roderick did not come after dinner. They trailed back into the drawing-room, and sat and waited for him to ring with news about his talk with the Prime Minister. Their thoughts were concentrated on the telephone, and when it remained silent their spirits dropped and conversation lapsed. Silas suggested they watch the news on the television, but Duibhne was reluctant, no doubt fearing their name would be mentioned, and dreading it. Eventually, they decided to go to bed.

"He hasn't been able to get to a phone," said Duibhne.

Bastard, thought Silas.

Later he lay in bed in the nursery, a double bed thoughtfully provided by his hostess. Bridget had stayed downstairs to be with her mother for a while. In the semi-darkness he could discern the outlines of the rocking horse and the fort and a doll's house by the window. Somehow they gave him a sense of security and permanence. He felt himself drifting into sleep, and when Bridget slipped into bed beside him he wanted to make love to her, but he was too damned tired. Years of closeness to her made him understand she felt the same – not tired in her case, but a little depressed, not in the mood for sex. They wrapped their arms around each other and went to sleep.

During the night Silas woke just long enough to hear the tyres of a car crunching on the drive beneath their window. He heard the front door slam and then footsteps in the hall below. There was the murmur of voices and sounds of activity.

The master of the house had returned.

CHAPTER TWO

Silas was awoken by the alarm in his wristwatch. He was a light sleeper, and the tiny, high-pitched sound forced his eyes open instantly. He stared into the darkness trying to get his bearings until he remembered he was in bed with Bridget. It would have been very easy to relapse into the warmth of slumber again, but he knew he must resist the temptation. Bridget's head lay just below his chin, and one of her arms was stretched across his chest. Carefully, reluctantly, he extricated himself from the soft embrace. She murmured when he gently changed her position, but she did not waken.

Quietly, he got out of bed and crossed the room to the window. He drew the curtain to one side and looked out. An early morning mist was swirling across the velvet lawn, and pinpricks of dew sparkled on the grass. Here, on this side of the house, the garden swept down to a row of poplars at the bottom, outlined black against a dark blue sky. Very soon it would be light, and already the birds had started greeting the day. He thought of the traffic beginning to pile up on the motorway, threatening to delay his journey into London. Suddenly he realised he had not got the essentials of life: laptop, filofax, papers – all in a despatch case in his flat. He would have to call in on his way to collect them. He began to feel anxious.

Hastily he brushed his teeth with the toothbrush Duibhne had given him the previous evening. She had supplied him with a disposable razor too, but, feeling his chin with the palm of his hand, he decided not to use it. There was no time to shave. He did not have a heavy growth of beard, and he thought that no one would suspect he had not shaved that day. It occurred to him that he could not recall a time when he had gone to work in a shirt he had worn the day before.

He searched in the clutter of bottles and jars on Bridget's dressing-table until he found a comb. He dragged it through his straight brown hair, and, glancing in the mirror, decided he would pass. Then he crossed to the bed and bent down and kissed Bridget on the cheek. She slept.

He crept down the wide oak staircase, uncarpeted so that every step creaked as he put a foot on it. A glimmer of light filtered through the heavy curtains of the window by the stairs. It was a tall narrow window taking up two thirds of the staircase. Somewhere in the house a clock chimed five times. He felt the strangeness of it – he was the only person awake in that big house. When he reached the foot of the staircase he realised he was wrong in that assumption.

He saw a shaft of bright light coming from a room to the right of him, the room which he knew to be Roderick's study. The man must be up at this ungodly hour. He cursed inwardly, and wondered if he could somehow steal past the door without being spotted.

"Silas!"

Too late, he had been seen.

He went into the room, smiling. Roderick Macauley was sitting at his desk, his giant frame encased in a Barcelona chair. There were papers strewn in front of him, and a light behind him shone on his fair hair, a faded thinner version of his daughter's hair, now, as Silas knew, fanned out on the pillow of the bed in the room above them.

"It was so good of you to come, Silas," said Roderick. "I know how hard it is to make an early start." He had never been so charming. He removed his half-moon spectacles and laid them on the top of the desk, as if affairs of state must take second place to this chance meeting. "Divvy has told me what a tower of strength you have been. I'm very grateful."

Silas mumbled something about it being 'nothing at all', at the same time feeling that precious time was eluding him. Surely Roderick must see that he wanted to get going as soon as possible? No one got up at that time of the morning without a good reason.

For some reason he did not quite understand he felt unnatural in Roderick's presence. It had always been so. He had an illogical feeling the man was mocking him, an underlying conviction that he did not take him seriously, attached no importance to him whatsoever, this in spite of the pleasant manner. Silas, who was holding down a good job, earning an outrageously high salary for a young man of his age, ought not to have felt uneasy about anyone, but with Bridget's father he felt his self-esteem ebbing away as he spoke.

Roderick, no doubt unaware of the effect he had on his daughter's lover, went on to say, "I suppose, Silas, old man, you would not consider coming down here again this coming weekend? I know it is a bit soon for you to make the journey again, but I would be most awfully grateful if you could manage it. We have planned to go to the village fête in Broadleigh on Saturday. Robert has an exeat so he can come with us. We shall ask him to bring a friend along, but it will still be a family gathering. You understand?"

Silas thought he did understand, and he nodded.

"If you come I know Bridget will come too." Roderick gave a little snort of laughter. "Your presence is my guarantee of her being there. You know how she is not keen on these county occasions."

He laughed outright this time, showing perfect white teeth. It was the laugh of a man secure with his place in the world. How does he do it? thought Silas, almost resentfully. For, in that family, only Bridget showed real distress about what had happened. She was aware of the degradation of the whole sorry business and that her parents' marriage was imperilled by it. Silas suspected that the fourteen-year-old Robert might be a bit cut up about it as well, for publicity about a parent was amusement value for schoolboys, especially if the boy involved was in his first year. Yet, Duibhne and Roderick presented a calm exterior, as if it was a very small difficulty they had to face.

"Thank you, I'd love to come," said Silas in what he hoped was a firm voice. A childish reason for his gaucherie was that he never knew what to call Roderick, who, on one occasion, had suggested he call him Rod. Roderick he could have managed, but, so far, Rod had proved impossible.

"I'll be here on Friday evening," he said, and again, "Thank you."

"I look forward to it."

"Please excuse me. I have to go. The traffic . . ."

"Of course, of course." Roderick put his spectacles back on his nose, and once more bent his handsome head over the papers on his desk. Silas knew he was dismissed and hurried to his car, exulting that he would be seeing Bridget again so soon, and this time he would be arriving on Friday so they would have the whole wonderful weekend together.

The roads were clear until he reached the outskirts of London, and he was able to think about Duibhne and Roderick. What sort of relationship did they have? It was a mystery that always intrigued him. There seemed to be a sort of separated togetherness about them. In Roderick's case it was hard to tell the difference between the public figure and the real man. It was apparent that Duibhne admired her husband hugely, and she was the perfect wife. Perfect except that he had sought companionship elsewhere. She had an old-fashioned, rather endearing way of addressing him as 'dearest'. 'Does that suit you, dearest?' she would say when they were making plans, or 'Whatever you think best, dearest,' when a decision had to be made.

It was very different from his own parents who, as he knew, loved each other deeply – he had to concede they had hit upon the right formula for a happy marriage. They bickered affectionately all the time – the canon had been known to call his wife 'an interfering old besum' and she was constantly telling him he was an 'old fool'. They could say anything to each other without fear or uncertainty. It was a relationship founded on years of trust and respect.

Silas telephoned Bridget that evening. "I'm coming down on Friday."

"Really?"

"Your father invited me. He wants us to go to the Broadleigh fête."

"Oh, so boring. He knows I hate that sort of thing. He's up to something."

"You may be right. How did the interview go . . . you know, last night?"

"Absolutely fine. All is forgiven. Very understanding."

Of course it was the expected result. All the rumours of resignation had emanated from the press, wanting a good story. There had never been any doubt about the outcome. Now all that remained was the repair of a damaged marriage.

"I'm staying here for the week," Bridget said. "The restaurant will have to manage without me."

On Friday when he drove to the house he felt he had never been away. Bell opened the front door and took his case. "Wonderful to see you, sir. They are all waiting in the drawing-room for you."

Duibhne was sitting in her usual position in the corner of one of the sofas, tapestry in hand, and Bridget was sprawled in a chair flicking through the pages of a magazine. The dogs were lying nearby as their usual place on the rug had been commandeered by two boys, sitting cross-legged on the floor, playing a game of cards.

When she saw Silas Bridget leapt to her feet and flung her arms around his neck.

"I'm so glad to see you!"

It was gratifying, but, knowing her as he did, he could not help thinking that this show of affection was the result of boredom. After several days at home she was in need of a diversion.

He was grateful that Roderick was not at home. A good thing about visiting Pondings was that the master of the house was seldom there. It was much easier without him, and Silas enjoyed dinner with Duibhne, Bridget, Robert and his friend whose name was George Simkin. The boys were lively and chatty, and regaled them with stories of school life and the absurdities of the masters. It was a very happy evening, and Silas looked at Duibhne to see if she was showing signs of strain, but her face only radiated amused contentment.

During the previous week the press had half-heartedly pursued their campaign. The Prime Minister had given Roderick a reprieve; it was up to them to prove it was a wrong decision. They were leaving the Minister and his family alone for the time being, and concentrating on Millicent Jones who supplied them with a never-ending fund of information. *'I loved him and lost him, says Millicent'* was one headline, and *'Millicent knows how to make him happy'* was another. The reportage had no substance and was the last gasp of a dying story.

The sun shone brightly on the morning of the Broadleigh fête. A little breeze stirred the tent flaps, and small fluffy clouds scudded across a blue arc of sky. Roderick, who had arrived home late on Friday night, towered above everyone else, personifying his nickname 'Atlas' which had been bestowed on him by fellow Members of Parliament or by the media, time having blurred the original source of the name. There were numerous cartoons of him, clad like a boxer in the ring, displaying muscles or carrying weights bearing captions which reflected the topics of the day: Taxes,

Reform, and, when he became Health Minister, NHS. The originals of the cartoons had been purchased, neatly encased in narrow black frames, and now hung in the downstairs cloakroom at Pondings.

He strode among the people, his wife, family and friends hovering behind him. He clasped the hands of old ladies who gazed up lovingly into his face, he spoke cheerily to all the villagers. He'll be kissing babies next, thought Silas. Roderick's personal friends, the county gentry, greeted him with slightly embarrassed smiles, uncertain about what was the right thing to say in the circumstances, as if speaking to someone who has suffered a bereavement, not knowing whether to mention it or not. Silas was amused, however, when a military-looking man slapped Roderick on the back, and shouted in his ear, "All well now? Plain sailing from now on, what?"

Bridget and Silas managed to break away from the entourage, and the fête provided them with entertainment for about an hour. Silas shot at a moving target and failed to win a goldfish, and they entered all the competitions and raffles and spent a lot of money in a good cause. They met young friends, and stood chatting in the sunshine, all eyes hidden behind dark glasses. They were happy, having spent a very satisfactory night together. They felt comfortable with each other, a good team, and, having been a team for so long, the initial excitement and anticipation had dissipated. Now the only difference that lay between them was that Silas wanted to marry Bridget, and she was unsure of her feelings and what she wanted from life.

At last, Roderick, having bestowed his munificent goodwill on all the locals, was ready for lunch. He cast an eye about him, wondering if he had misjudged the situation. Everything seemed very peaceful. The picnic place was chosen, and two rugs were placed beneath a giant oak tree. The expensive hamper was removed from the boot of the car. All the usual delights were produced in plastic containers: chicken legs, quiche and salad. Plates were taken out of leather straps, knives and forks laid on a table covered with a cloth. Later there would be strawberries, and Silas was certain Roderick would bring out a bottle of champagne. Under normal circumstances there would indeed have been champagne, but Silas did not know that before they set out Roderick had instructed Bell to take it back into the house. "We'll drink that this evening."

They started with soup from a thermos. Duibhne always made a speciality of the soup, heavily laced with brandy, and it was handed round at all outside activities. She said it reminded her of her hunting days in Ireland when her father had often given her a sip from his flask, to help keep out the cold.

Robert and his friend George were provided with their own thermos of soup, undiluted with alcohol. Robert was his usual ebullient self – he took after his father in temperament – but poor George had lost the sparkle of the previous evening and was consumed with shyness. Duibhne did her best to put him at ease, but he replied in monosyllables to all interested enquiries. Like Silas, he had difficulty knowing how to address Roderick, and the fear that he might have to do so rendered him speechless. It was easier in the old days when public schoolboys called the fathers of their friends 'sir'. George could not remember whether Robert's father was Sir Roderick or Mr Macauley, and he did not know what he was Minister of – Education, Environment, Transport? Rather than be caught out not knowing he played safe and said nothing.

Duibhne was pouring the soup into cups when the man approached. He was dressed in the uniformly correct rather shabby tweed jacket, and he lifted his cap and addressed Roderick. "Excuse me, sir, I am from *The Daily Graphic.*" He waved a card in the air to prove it. "Would you object to my taking a photograph of you and your family?"

They had not noticed the camera, and Silas rose to his feet, his immediate reaction being to see the fellow off, although he half understood the reason for his presence. Roderick quietly restrained him, a hand on his shoulder forcing him to sit down again.

"Delighted," he said, stretching his long legs on the ground, in front of his wife who was kneeling on the rug, poised with the thermos. He looked the embodiment of the happy family man. She smiled her gracious smile. In spite of themselves Bridget and Silas found themselves smiling also. Obligingly, the two boys grinned broadly at the camera.

"Fire away," said Roderick, his face lighting up as if by command.

"That's good," said the man. "Great." *Click, click.* The whole incident so open, so friendly, so different from the hitherto cloak and dagger encounters with the press.

"Thank you, sir. Thank you, madam." Ingratiating, he asked the names of the 'young people'.

"My daughter, Bridget," said Roderick, waving a hand, "and her friend, Mr Silas Tomalin."

"T-O-M-A-L-I-N," interrupted Silas, for people were apt to spell his name wrongly.

A little impatiently Roderick continued, "This is my son, Robert, and his friend George Simkin."

The man wrote all this information down in a little notebook, and then left, again raising his cap, saying he hoped they would enjoy the rest of the day. After he had gone only the boys discussed what had happened, wondering if they would see their names in the newspaper.

Suddenly, no one had any further interest in the fête. When they had finished eating Duibhne started putting the dirty plates and cutlery into the hamper, and closing the lids on the remainders of the food. "Do you want to stay, dearest?" she asked her husband.

He thought for a moment. "Another half hour."

"Come on, Silas," said Bridget briskly, "let's walk about."

They walked past lines of parked cars, and stopped and watched miniature dogs being judged. Bridget put her hand in his. "It make me sick," she said, referring, as he knew, to the incident during lunch.

"Yes," he agreed. "I knew it was going to happen." It was almost true. That early morning encounter with Roderick had convinced him something was in the air, but he was not certain what it was.

"Shall we make an excuse and return to London tonight instead of tomorrow? You could stay at my flat."

He was delighted with the idea, which Bridget presented to her parents on the way home. "We've just remembered we have to go to a party tonight." She and Silas were crammed in the back seat with the boys, and Roderick was driving, Duibhne beside him.

"You do not 'have to go' to a party," Roderick pointed out. "You are not compelled to go."

"Very special friends. Sorry, Daddy."

"There are so many things I want to discuss with you. Rocket, for instance."

"It's your fault I have not been there for so long," she retorted.

"You make me feel very sad when you say that," he said. "I am able to be at home so little. I was looking forward to this weekend with all the family."

"We've been with you today," she said, on the defensive.

"You know exactly what I mean," he said reprovingly.

"I hoped you would be here tomorrow as well. Sunday, a quiet day. It is so disappointing."

God, this is awful, thought Silas.

"And your mother was looking forward to it too, weren't you, darling? Like me, Mummy was expecting you to stay until Sunday evening."

"I don't mind in the least," said Duibhne firmly. "Of course you must not let your friends down."

Her magnanimity had the effect of making them feel guilty. There is always a party somewhere on Saturday night, thought Silas, trying in his mind to justify their action. His main objective was to remove Bridget from this uncomfortably contrived family solidarity. Ordinary scruples were no longer involved. He was prepared to lie if it meant making their escape.

Back at Pondings, Bridget said, "I'm sorry, Mummy."

"Please don't say anything more about it, darling," replied her mother. "I have the boys to keep me company." Presumably, she would have her husband as well, but she seemed to have forgotten this for the moment. Silas thought he detected a slight note of irritation in her voice, like the smallest ripple on a calm lake.

The ripple had gone when she said, "I have lots to do, you know. And I shall have to get the boys back before lock-up on Sunday evening."

She turned to her daughter and fixed her with a very straight blue gaze. "However, I must ask you to keep your promise and go and see Ma before you leave.

She is expecting to see you sometime during the weekend."

"Of course," said Bridget. "I wouldn't dream of returning to London without seeing her. You know that."

CHAPTER THREE

Bridget loved Ma dearly. If she had ever troubled to analyse the love she felt for this woman she would probably have concluded it was because Ma was so straightforward. There were no challenges to face in Ma's attachment to the children, no doubts or pretences. Bridget felt that Ma loved Christopher, Robert and herself, and there was no room for anyone else in her existence. No friends, no family except themselves. A man must have figured at some time in her life, but it was hard to imagine what sort of man he could have been.

Sometimes Bridget thought her mother was too good, too considerate of everyone around her. It set her apart from ordinary mortals. She felt there was a little bit of her mother she could not reach, but Ma offered the whole of herself – unreserved love for her three children, as she called them.

There were endearing flaws in Ma's character. She was

stubborn and could lose her temper. She and Bridget had fought many battles, especially when Bridget was a rebellious adolescent, but the conflicts had all been resolved by a show of affection on both sides.

Bridget and Robert took their troubles to Ma, for they could be sure of her whole-hearted attention. She had nothing else to think about, so it was easy for her. She did not organise her life, but lived haphazardly from day to day, apparently without fear of the future or regret for the past. They never thought of discussing personal problems with their father. It was unthinkable. He had no time for the trivial anxieties of his children. Duibhne and Ma had brought up Bridget and Robert between them, and Ma had taken on the greater part.

She was the person who bathed them when they were small, took them for long walks, bouncing the push-chair along rough country lanes. She ferried them around in her old ramshackle car and, when Bridget was older, collected her late at night from disco parties. When Bridget came out into the night air it was comforting to see Ma in her car waiting for her, knowing she would never complain about the lateness or the inconvenience.

Bridget had earlier memories of Ma tucking her into bed and kissing her goodnight. Then she would leave the comforting light on in the passage so that the little girl could see it before she went asleep. Her mother would come in, smelling delicious, and would bend down and touch her cheek with her lips. Slipping quietly away, switching off the light on the landing. Not purposefully

– it was just that she did not understand the routine. Bridget would lie in the darkness until she heard Ma's heavy footsteps, coming to switch it on again.

One of Bridget's fondest memories of her childhood was the room in the nursery wing they called Ma's room. The nursery was for playing in, but Ma's room was for living in, and was familiar, unchanged for as far back as she could remember. Now it was unoccupied, but the old furniture was still there and the television, and Bridget liked to go in there sometimes and sit in Ma's comfortable chair.

The big window on the south side looked out on to the lawn, the same view that Silas had seen in the dawn light from the nursery next door. The fire in Ma's room was surrounded by a fireguard, a heavy cumbersome thing with thick brass bars and a small triangular leather seat at each corner. It was wonderful perching on one of the corner seats, so near to the warmth of the fire which was lit promptly at ten o'clock every morning during the winter. Ma told the children that the fireguard had been in Duibhne's nursery in Ireland, and the pictures on the wall came from there as well. One was a scene of woodland fairies by Margaret Tarrant, another was of Jesus surrounded by children of all nationalities, the black children looking the same as the white children except for the colour of their skins. There was another picture of a collie dog sitting amongst a lot of chickens in a farmyard. When Robert was away from home he thought of that picture.

One wall of Ma's room was filled with a bookcase, from floor to ceiling. Some of the books belonged to the children, but most of them were Ma's own. She was an avid reader. In the centre of the room was a table where they sat for meals. The food appeared on a tray, carried up the stairs by Mary, the cheerful daughter of the cook whose name was Bridie. These women had worked for Duibhne for years and were devoted to her, but Bell, the butler, went even further back and had a special regard for his mistress.

A local lady called Mrs Hughes came in to clean, and Thursday was her day for 'doing' the nursery wing. Christopher was always particularly happy on Thursday because he and Mrs Hughes got on like a house on fire, and Christopher had long disjointed conversations with her (stopping her from getting on with her work, she said).

Bridget went away to school when she was twelve years old, and it was only made bearable by the letters she received from Ma. Her mother wrote to her, and her father rarely, but Ma could be relied upon to write every day. Sometimes only a few lines, sometimes a message from Christopher, just a scribble or two laboured letters 'HI'. When it was Robert's turn to go to preparatory school at the age of eight Ma protested he was too young. His only joy in that hostile world was the daily letter from home. Not much news, just a report on the welfare of the dogs, cats, rabbits and hamsters, left in Ma's care.

Duibhne was always anxious that Ma should join them

for meals in the dining-room, especially when the children were away. Invariably she refused, but what outsiders did not realise was that Duibhne came to Ma's room on the many evenings when Roderick was not there, and the two women had their supper on trays while watching the television.

If there was a dinner party Ma was asked to attend. She never did, but instead came downstairs for a drink before dinner. She always wore the same black dress, no jewellery, and her frizzy hair stuck out from her head like a coarse brush. She was painfully shy, and stood in an ungainly way, clutching a glass of sherry and staring straight ahead. People did not know what to make of her. They tried talking to her, but there was little response. No one knew her real name – she was just Ma. When it was time to move to the dining-room she slipped away without anyone noticing.

In Broadleigh she was regarded as an eccentric. The villagers liked her though, and stopped to exchange greetings and casual remarks when she was out walking or shopping. She retreated when it looked as if someone was trying to get close to her. They grew to respect her desire for privacy. They said amongst themselves that she only cared for Bridget and Robert and, of course, her pathetic son, Christopher. This was not true. She cared deeply for Duibhne.

"Do we have to go?" Silas asked as they drove away from Pondings.

"You don't want to?" Bridget sounded surprised. "Don't you like Ma?"

"Ma is all right," said Silas, "and I know you think the world of her. It is Christopher I find hard to take." Seeing Bridget's expression, he added hastily, "I know it is wrong of me, but I can't help it."

"It's understandable," said Bridget, nodding. "A lot of people feel the same way. You are not the only one. I suppose I see him differently because I have known him all my life." She smiled. "He is so sweet."

"Does he ever become aggressive?"

"Never. He has the loveliest nature. Good will towards everybody. And you must agree there is nothing repulsive about him. He does not drool or unzip his flies in public. He is a perfect gentleman."

"I suppose it is the near-normality of him that I find disturbing," said Silas. "Who knows what is going on in that deranged mind of his? What sexual fantasies or murderous thoughts?"

"I don't think so," replied Bridget. "I think his poor mind is just floating, with a few, very few, random thoughts struggling to the surface. And those thoughts, whatever they may be, are completely harmless."

"Certainly his mother has a cross to bear, having given birth to a son like Christopher."

"She does not look at it in that way. She adores him. He is the reason for her existence, especially now that Robert and I are away most of the time."

He parked his car on a patch of grass by the side of

the narrow lane outside the cottage. There was a wooden gate and a path leading to the front door. They did not get as far as ringing the bell: the door was opened at once.

One of the things that Silas found slightly disconcerting about Ma was that she was undoubtedly a lady. She had been the children's nanny and Silas would have felt happier about her if she had behaved like one, but she never had. He had never had a nanny – a clergyman's stipend does not run to such extravagances – but he had a preconceived notion of what that sort of person should be like. Certainly not this tall, angular woman with wiry hair and a brown leathery face. She was dressed in a tweed skirt and what looked like a man's checked shirt, the collar undone showing a scrawny neck. On her feet she had brown flat-heeled shoes. She kissed Bridget, and took Silas's hand in a strong grasp.

"How lovely to see you both! Come in." She had a low gruff voice with an underlying accent which Silas had never been able to identify.

Inside, her cottage was a shambles: books and newspapers strewn everywhere, coats thrown over the arms of chairs, odd shoes lying on the floor. The sitting-room, with a fireplace taking up almost the whole of one wall, was crammed with oversized furniture, everything covered with a thin layer of dust. The dust seemed to be in the air, and had solidified on the windowpanes so that the room was dark. Incongruously, porcelain figurines, ladies in sprigged dresses, gentlemen in flowered waistcoats, colourful birds and animals, were perched on every available space: the chimney piece, the windowsill and in an alcove by the fireplace. Where did all these things come from? Silas wondered. They seemed so out of keeping with Ma's unromantic character. The dingy walls were covered with pictures, mostly oil paintings of horses. Horses of bygone days, with flared nostrils and arched necks. What possible interest could they hold for Ma? And where had they come from? He must remember to ask Bridget about them. Ma and Christopher had moved here straight from the nursery wing which had contained few of her belongings. Presumably, Roderick had presented her with the cottage as a token of gratitude for many years of faithful service. Had he also given her a sum of money which she had spent at the local auction sales? The contents of her little house looked as if they had come from an auction room.

The other thing that intrigued Silas was her name – Ma. She had never been called 'Nanny', always Ma. It had a parental ring to it which was appropriate as she regarded all her charges as her children, and often referred to them that way. Perhaps the name 'Ma' had originated with Christopher who found it easy to say.

"Go into the garden," she said. "You will find Christopher there. I'll make tea and we'll have it outside. It is such a lovely day."

As Duibhne had said, the garden was a dream. Ma had got to work on it as soon as she moved into the cottage. It had the cluttered charm of the house, but, unlike it, was full of colour, fresh air and sweetness. Not an inch of space was wasted, and beyond the crowded herbaceous border there was a small orchard flanked by a vegetable patch. Ma laboured in the garden many hours of the day, as could be seen by her rough sunburnt hands and broken nails.

Christopher was sitting on the grass in the shade of a Catalpa tree that stood in the middle of the lawn. When he saw them approaching he scrambled to his feet.

"Hello," he said to Bridget, and to Silas, "Hello."

Bridget put her arms around his waist and laid her fair head against his chest. Silas felt a shudder somewhere in the pit of his stomach. How could she?

Christopher was tall and very dark. Like many handicapped people he was inclined to heaviness. His thick black hair was streaked with grey and he wore spectacles. It was difficult to estimate his age, but Silas knew that he was in his thirties. He was dressed in old-fashioned grey flannels, a short-sleeved shirt and, on his feet, socks and sandals.

When Bridget hugged him he made unintelligible sounds, looking over her head at Silas, smiling his vacuous smile. He smiled a lot – at people, at animals, at everything that caught his eye in the strange isolated world he inhabited. Suddenly, his lifted his hand and started stroking her hair in a funny awkward way that made Silas's blood freeze. "Pretty," he said.

'Pretty' seemed to be his favourite word, and he used it over and over again as the three of them strolled around the garden. He touched the flowers lightly with his fingers as if he loved them. He had a shuffling walk, and lacked coordination so that he sometimes stumbled, and, when he did, Bridget took his arm.

By the time they got back to the tree Ma had set up a flimsy table, and on it was a tray laden with everything for tea. A home-made cake, uncut, reposed on a plate, as if she had baked it in anticipation of their visit.

"Looks good," said Bridget.

"I expect Robert and his friend will come sometime during the weekend, and they will polish it off."

Silas had to admit it was a cheerful tea party. The affair of Robert Macauley and Millicent Jones seemed very remote from this country garden, although he knew that Bridget had discussed the unhappy business with Ma.

Now they talked of less serious topics. Ma was a little constrained with Silas, but he recognised this was her usual manner with anyone outside the family. Over the years he had become closer to her, and she was almost natural with him, but not quite. With Bridget she was completely at ease, and they laughed together from time to time. Somehow, it was strange to hear Ma laugh and, when she did, Christopher joined in too, and she looked at him with loving indulgence.

When he was not laughing, Christopher was very engrossed in wolfing down wedges of Victoria sponge. He left bits of cake on his chin, which worried Silas, but Ma made faces at him and he wiped the crumbs away with his hand. Then he lurched to his feet and shook more crumbs off his trousers, looking at them, in turn, for their approval.

At last, it was time to leave. It was getting late, and the evening sun filtered through the branches of the tree, laden with big fat leaves. Shadows fell across the lawn, and it was very still, very peaceful, with only the noises of nature – buzzings and distant cooings.

"This is such a wonderful garden," said Bridget. "I hate to leave it."

"You know we love to see you at any time."

"We love. Yes, we love!" cried Christopher. He was examining a ladybird crawling on his hand.

"He's crazy about ladybirds," said Ma.

Silas tried to say goodbye to him, but he got no response. Christopher was too occupied watching the ladybird to notice him. The tiny creature progressed from the back of his hand to his wrist. For the first time, Silas noticed his hands, manly well-shaped hands with dark hairs on the wrists. Christopher twisted the hand with the ladybird on it, this way and that way, bending his spectacled eyes closer to it. He was not aware of Bridget's quick kiss on his cheek.

"He's miles away," explained Ma apologetically.

CHAPTER FOUR

The girl standing outside the mews house thought how charming it was. It was squeezed in between other little gems similar to it, situated in a neat little square. As she stood on the steps leading to the blue front door she became conscious of eyes, peering at her from behind the curtains of the neighbouring houses. It was understandable. There had been a lot to interest them during the past week. The perfect symmetry of the front of the house was marred by a very modern contraption on the wall by the door. When she rang the bell, a voice crackled on the intercom, "Who is it?"

"Delphine Blake."

"Oh, it's you. I'm coming down."

She heard the clicking of high-heeled shoes on the tiles in the hall, and the door was opened by Millicent Jones.

She came out on the step and looked from left to right. "I expect they are snooping as usual."

When they were in the hall, she slammed the front door. "I won't be sorry to leave that lot in the square – nosey buggers."

Delphine Blake was a reporter on *The Daily Graphic*. The newspaper prided itself on giving its readers the information they wanted without being too vicious in the process. Delphine was over the moon when she was given the story of the Minister's long affair with Millicent Jones. It was the first assignment of any importance to come her way and she was certain she would make a good job of it.

When she was told that she was to follow the story, the first thing she did was to telephone her mum and dad in Croydon. Then she telephoned her boyfriend, Tim Shaw, who worked for a weekly publication called *Hey!* and he was suitably impressed.

That was over a week ago, and since then Delphine had visited Millicent several times. The two women had become sort of friends. Delphine stopped calling her Mrs Jones (she was divorced from Mr Jones) and Millicent called her Delphs. She was called Delphs by everyone except her parents, for she had decided long ago that Delphine was not the name for the smart career woman she aspired to be, and she would have changed it if she had not known how upset it would make her mother. She compromised and called herself Delphs. It was she who had recorded Millicent's words when she said, "I know how to make him happy". She had gone on to say, "He does not love his wife", but Delphs had not used that phrase. There was no need, for she was well aware that the wife is always the loser in these matters, the public siding with the mistress every time.

Now she knew that the picture of the Macauley family having a picnic at the village fête, taken by a colleague, was intended by her editor to bring the whole episode to a moralistic conclusion. All is forgiven. Loyal wife stands by husband. Prime Minister turns a blind eye. Story over. It was the policy of the *Graphic* to show their readers that they had family values at heart.

Delphs thought she should visit Millicent one more time. It seemed to her that she ought to explain that there was no blood left in the pitiful saga. It was drained white unless Millicent chose to write a book about her life with the Minister. The visit seemed a polite thing to do, as she had been very cooperative, and, anyway, Delphs could not help rather liking the woman. Secretly, however, she deplored the betrayal which, even if Roderick deserved it, his family did not.

Roderick had rented the house in the mews during the six years they knew each other. Now he was refusing to make any more payments. Not surprising since she had sold him down the river. Delphs was of the private opinion that Roderick had been cooling off, and that was why Millicent had decided to inflict punishment before punishment was inflicted on her. The story of the Ferragamo shoes had been magnified in importance, although it was true that Millicent was paranoid when it came to anything concerning Roderick's wife.

The two women went into the immaculate kitchen, and Millicent filled an electric kettle from a shiny tap. "Instant?"

"Yes, please. Have you decided where you will go?"

Millicent's voice must have irritated Roderick sometimes. "I've found a flat in Drayton Gardens," she said. "Everything I want. And unfurnished. I'm having my own furniture this time." Nothing in the house belonged to her, except her clothes and a few personal possessions.

"Are you taking everything from here with you?"

"You bet I am. When I'm settled I'll flog it and get my own stuff." She could afford to be extravagant with the money she had obtained from the *Graphic*. Her indiscretion had paid off.

There was something cosy and basic about Millicent. For one thing, she was not in the least good-looking, although striking in a brash way. Her face was all mouth, with a little stray tooth sticking out on the side, where it ought not to have been. Delphs wondered, why didn't she do something about it? Perhaps one of her lovers had said he liked it, so it had stayed. Her figure was top heavy: big breasts and spindly legs. She was justly proud of her legs, and, of course, her neat little feet in high-heeled shoes.

After her recent behaviour it would be absurd to describe her as a warm-hearted woman. Yet Delphs felt that tenderness was there, hidden, but with her sort of woman there was no outlet for it. She thought she could understand why Roderick had risked his political career and his marriage in order to spend time with her over a period of six years. She was sexy, in the earthy, rather vulgar way men appreciate, and she dressed well. She was probably a good cook.

Delphs almost asked her if she would be lonely in the flat in Drayton Gardens. She decided not to because it seemed cruel. They went into the sitting-room, and drank coffee from mugs. Delphs noticed a copy of the *Graphic* lying on the coffee table between them.

"I think there is nothing more to be said about this story, Millicent," said Delphs at last, after a melancholy silence. "These things are a nine-days' wonder, you know, and it will soon be forgotten."

"Do you think she will stay with him?"

Delphs thought it was hard for Millicent to ask that question. "Very likely. But even if they divorce it will only be a small paragraph."

She noticed the *Graphic* was open at the page showing the picture of the smiling group.

"Look at them!" cried Millicent, her voice rising. "Cheshire cats!" A red-painted fingernail swooped down on to the photograph, and she demanded, "Who is that shit-bag?"

"That is Silas Tomalin, boyfriend of the daughter, Bridget. The two boys are Robert Macauley and a friend from school."

"Oh, I know Robert." She looked closely at Duibhne and admitted, "She photographs well, the Snow Queen."

Delphs was looking at Roderick. Long legs stretched out on the grass, head at just the right angle for the camera. Everything working out as planned – you had to admire his ingenuity. "Good old Atlas," she said. "He is good-looking. There's no doubt about that. Do you miss him?" She could not help thinking that if a man like that shared her bed for six years, and then everything came to an end, she would miss him.

"You're kidding," replied Millicent, without conviction. "He wasn't all that great. What man is? She can keep him."

There was a pause while Millicent considered her uncertain future.

"Someone like me," she said at last, "hasn't a chance against a woman like her. Let's face it, she is the daughter of an earl, worth a packet, and, if that isn't enough, she's good-looking as well. It isn't fair."

"She can't be feeling very secure at the moment," Delphs pointed out.

"Oh, all that security nonsense means nothing to her. Position, a suitable marriage, beautiful house, satisfactory children, they are the things that matter to someone like her. She hasn't lived – Rod said it time and time again. Real life hasn't touched her."

It was too late for Delphs to get out a notebook and jot down the words of wisdom. The moment had passed and anyway she had heard them before.

"Good luck," said Delphs, as she took her leave. It was unlikely that she would ever see Millicent again, but she said kindly, "Keep in touch."

"I will, love. Thank you for all you have done for me. You have told the truth and that is all that matters. My conscience is clear."

Mine too, thought Delphs. For what do we live but to make sport of our neighbours? Someone had said that, she could not remember who it was, but it seemed to her that the *Graphic* provided the sport in the kindest way possible.

"Where are you off to now?" asked Millicent. "Back to the office?"

"No, I'm going home to see my mum and dad."

"Lovely! Have a nice time."

She accompanied Delphs to the front door, walking ahead with little short steps, absurd heels clopping the floor. Under the bright ceiling light in the tiny hall she looked middle-aged and lonely, as if all the confidence and bravado had melted away leaving an unsure frightened woman.

Her sad image remained with Delphs on the drive to Croydon. Disquieting, like a portent of what her own future might hold.

With a sense of relief she parked the car outside the familiar suburban semi-detached house. It was good to be home again, through the gate and along the concrete path with the neat little strip of garden on each side. It was safe, unchanged.

Her parents were proud of their only child. She had done well at school, had been to university and now had a good job. They boasted that she had never given them a moment's anxiety. She had sailed through the teenage years without problems, and now she had a steady young man who met with their full approval. Of course they knew that times had changed, that there were alternatives these days to the long engagement and eventual marriage which had been the norm when they were young. However, they both hoped for that outcome.

As soon as she arrived and embraces and kisses were exchanged, her mother poured some sweet sherry into minuscule glasses, and put them on the little round silver tray her husband had won at the bowling club. Mr Blake had been a solicitor's clerk and was now retired, happy to spend his days tending his flowers and vegetables, watching the box or just sitting. He was sitting now, in his special chair by the window, green cardigan buttoned over his fat stomach, feet in carpet slippers.

"You've been busy, my girl," he said. Loyally, he read the *Graphic*, although he was not politically in tune with the views of that newspaper, and he had followed the story of Roderick Macauley and Millicent Jones.

"Yes, Dad, but it's all over now."

"I'm sorry the Prime Minister gave that man another chance," said Mrs Blake, a small birdlike woman who liked to air her opinions. "It's more than he deserves. Sets everyone a bad example, that's what I say."

This was exactly what the *Graphic* wanted from its readers – the views within the family. On the home front Delphs found it extremely irritating. "Oh, I don't know. Perhaps he was unhappy with his wife. They say it takes two to break up a marriage."

"They may say that," retorted her mother, "but it is not true. One person can do it very easily."

Delphs laughed. "I expect you're right, Mum."

"She's always right," said her father."

"Women who break up families," went on Mrs Blake, warming to her theme, "are guilty of a crime, and should be punished."

"Maybe they are punished. It is hard for them too." She did not want to talk about the Macauleys and Millicent Jones. She wanted to leave all that behind her when she came home, to try and blot out the memory of the expression on Millicent's face when she left her, the look of utter desolation. "The story is finished," she reminded them again.

"And you don't want to talk shop," said her father with more understanding than his wife.

"That's right." The firmness in her voice fell upon deaf ears. There was no stopping her mother now.

"That wife of his is a good-looker," she said. "Always was. Of course I remember her from years back when she was mixed up with that other business."

Delphs took a sip of her sherry. Let her get on with it, she thought, she will soon tire of it.

"She was a young girl then, and a perfect picture."

"What was it all about then?" asked her husband, knowing what was expected of him. Mrs Blake gave a sigh of pure satisfaction. She had a captive audience, and that was very pleasing, and she detected that even Delphine was beginning to show interest.

"Well, it happened in America," she said. "But it made the English papers as well because her father was a lord. An Irish lord he was. I remember what the papers said about him – 'Lord Claughessy goes to the aid of his daughter.' There were pictures of him – long and lanky he was, like a bloomin' daddy-long-legs, getting into the aeroplane to take him to America. He was scared stiff of flying, but he had to get there in a hurry because his daughter was in trouble and needed him." It was a dramatic story, and she sat back in her chair and looked at them in triumph when she had finished.

"But Mrs Macauley is the daughter of the Earl of Clonbarron," said Delphs, "or was. He's dead now." She had a vague recollection of hearing about the case her mother was talking about; reporters are expected to have photographic memories about things like that. "It must have been over thirty years ago," she murmured, "and it was a different set of people, Mum."

"Long before you were born," chipped in her father who always forgot the age of his daughter, and could never believe she was a woman in her thirties.

"It was not!" cried Mrs Blake, getting excited and exasperated with the two of them. "It was the actual year you were born, Delphine. I was trying to think of a name for you, and that girl's name took my fancy. It was so unusual and your father and I like unusual names!"

Mr Blake, anxious to keep the peace, said nothing.

"Then I decided that no one would be able to pronounce it, let alone spell it."

"So you chose Delphine instead," said Delphs dryly.

"I don't know why you dislike it so much. It's a lovely name, and you are a silly girl not to like it. Even now, I don't know how that other girl's name is pronounced, but I recognised it as soon as I saw it in the *Graphic*."

"It's pronounced 'Divna'," said Delphs slowly, the nucleus of a strange idea beginning to form in her mind.

They talked of other matters until it was time for her to go. They tried to persuade her to stay, have a meal, watch a programme on the television, anything to keep her with them. But she wanted to be on her own, she wanted time to think.

"You don't believe a word I say," said her mother reproachfully as they walked down to the gate to see her off.

"As a matter of fact," said Delphs, "I do believe you. And I intend to look into it, and I will let you know what I come up with."

The next day, after working hard all morning, she telephoned Tim. "Meet me for lunch today?"

"I'm a bit pressed . . ."

"It's important. Please."

They met at a small eating-place in Fleet Street,

swarming with members of the press and the legal profession. Delphs secured a corner table, set aside from the others, and ordered a glass of white wine for herself and a lager for Tim.

When he arrived, she said, "I've chosen this table because I don't want anyone to hear what I'm saying."

He was amused. "What's up? Have you discovered the identity of the fifth mole?"

He was sandy-haired and freckled, five years younger than Delphs, and they had been a couple for three years. He did not want to share a flat with her, as he believed cohabitation without marriage destroyed relationships. He was full of odd ideas like that, and Delphs loved him for them. He did not like working for *Hey!* as the policy of that magazine was against his principles. He was not interested in rich people being photographed in their luxury homes, but he was ambitious and realised that his present job would eventually lead him to something more rewarding.

They planned to marry one day, but marriage was not particularly important to either of them. They both had careers that interested them, and Delphs had no desire to settle down to domesticity and motherhood. Sometimes she had misgivings when her mother reminded her that her childbearing years were slipping away at an alarming rate. She did not share these feelings with Tim. A man would never understand.

After they had ordered lunch, he said, "What is this all about?" He could tell she was nervous.

She made him wait until the food was in front of them. Then she leaned forward. "Tim, do you know about something that happened over thirty years ago, involving the daughter of Lord Claughessy?"

He thought for a moment. "It rings a bell."

"Well, that girl is the wife of Roderick Macauley. I don't know how I could have been so blind, and I don't know how it could have escaped the notice of all the other people covering the Macauley affair."

"Probably because it's not true. Mrs Macauley is the daughter of the late Earl of Clonbarron. You have written that enough times, God knows."

"Lords have a habit of changing their names, Tim. They inherit other titles. When all this happened in America the Earl of Clonbarron, Duibhne's father, was called Viscount Claughessy. His elder brother was the Earl, and he relinquished the title and went to live in the States, calling himself plain Mr Shannon. Shannon is the family name. Duibhne Macauley was Duibhne Shannon before she married Roderick. When Mr Shannon died, his title passed to his brother, Viscount Claughessy. After he died, it went to a nephew in Australia, or something of the sort, losing the Irish connection. You cannot get rid of titles that easily, Tim. They survive, even if you don't want them."

"So Mr Shannon didn't have a son to take it on?"

"He did have a son, but he died before his father. In any case, he would not have inherited the title as he was illegitimate. The story of his birth reads like a Gothic novel. His father had a love affair with gypsy girl, and they lived together in a hovel in the west of Ireland. She died giving birth to a boy whom his father named Bartley. Bartley is another family name. Lord Clonbarron fled to the States, taking the child with him, no doubt to escape the scandal. He settled in Oregon and bred horses."

The food remained untouched in front of them. They were too engrossed to eat.

"And the boy?" Tim asked.

Delphs produced a folder containing photostat copies. "There is very little about Bartley in these clippings from American and English newspapers. His death was reported in the local Oregon weekly, but we can't tell much about him from that. After all, he was unimportant, the son of a wealthy bloodstock owner, Tom Shannon. He had one moment of fame, and that was all. The American papers did not grasp the relationships in the case, and the English papers did not dig deep enough to find out."

"Until now," said Tim. "You are beginning to find out now."

"There was interest in her though," Delphs went on, "and in her father. Here is a picture of him taken before he flew to the States to be at his daughter's side in her hour of need." She handed Tim a copy of an old newspaper photograph showing an immensely tall man, head down, climbing the steps of an aeroplane. "That photograph appeared in both English and American editions. This one of her is from an American newspaper."

Tim took the other photograph and studied it

closely. It showed a young girl with the gaunt figure of her father on one side, and a short dark man on the other. The caption underneath read, *Miss Shannon with her father, an English lord, and her attorney, Mr Felix Goldberg.* Above the photograph were the puzzling words, *Good luck, Debbie!.*

The face of the girl stared back at Tim over the years. A frightened face. "It's a lovely face," he said.

"It still is."

"What put you on to this?"

"It was something my mother said which made me start thinking. I made these copies from old records this morning, and I was able to track down the American papers as well. The task was made easier because my mother, bless her, remembered the exact time when it happened. What was not so simple, however, was finding out what happened afterwards, and there I must admit defeat. You know how these stories are kept on a back burner until something new happens and the interest is revived? Not in this case. As far as I can tell it is not mentioned again, anywhere. I spent hours this morning looking for references to it, but even after researching over a period of five years I came up with nothing. Zilch. It looks as if the press, like the family, swept the whole thing under the carpet, and forgot about it."

"I agree it is very strange," said Tim, "but sometimes momentous events supersede all other news stories. For instance, when Kennedy was shot there was no room for anything else. Everything was concentrated on that one item of news, nothing else was of any interest." He was still studying the photograph held in his hand. "Poor little Dibna, or whatever you call her." The picture made no connection in his mind with the wife of Roderick Macauley.

"Divna," Delphs corrected him. "It's pronounced Divna."

At last, she picked up a fork and dug it into her salad. "The Americans had difficulty with her name too. They gave up trying to pronounce it and called her Debbie."

PART TWO

CHAPTER FIVE

Duibhne Shannon was born at Clonbarron House, County Limerick, Ireland, in the four-poster bed in which most of her forebears had been conceived and had entered the world. Her mother, Lady Claughessy, had longed for a baby, but her yearning was tempered with other considerations: pride and inheritance. She wanted a son. She hid her disappointment from her husband who would not have understood it. He was delighted with his daughter and believed her to be the turning point in a series of dramatic events.

Lord Claughessy was christened with a fine array of names: Charles Bartley Shannon. And Charles Shannon he was known to family and friends until the death of his father which occurred while he was in the army during the Second World War. Like his brother, Tom, he never rose from the ranks, and it was to his credit that in spite of his background he was popular with his fellow soldiers. Soldiers, when they like someone, give him a nickname. When word went round that Shannon was now to be known as Claughessy, immediately he was given the name of Claw. The name stuck, probably because it suited him so well. He was birdlike with a nose the shape of a macaw's beak, an elongated stooped body and stork's legs. He was absurdly different from his elder brother, Tom, who was short and stocky with reddish hair and a snub nose, the image of his father. Claw was such a maverick it was generally acknowledged in Limerick that he must have been born on the wrong side of the blanket.

Both boys had an idyllic childhood at Clonbarron, parents who adored them equally, hunting, shooting and a succession of tutors to educate them until they were old enough to go away to school. They were close in age and did everything together, including enlisting for the army at the beginning of the war. They were poor soldiers, but felt it was their duty. Tom, particularly inept, was given the task of looking after the horses in a cavalry regiment, the only job he was fit for, and Claw served in North Africa for a short time. When their parents died within a few weeks of each other there was no one left at Clonbarron to care for an already run-down estate.

Before the end of the war both brothers received a compassionate discharge so that they could return to Ireland and sort out a desperate state of affairs. Clonbarron had somehow survived the Troubles but did not fare well in the Second World War. Tom and Claw returned to find their old home in disrepair and the gardens a wilderness. Their mother had been proud of the gardens, but there was nothing to be seen of their former glory, just a tangled mass of weeds and undergrowth. Trees had been hacked down for firewood, and vandals had smashed nearly every window in the house. It was a damp shell and squatters inhabited some of the rooms. They were soon flushed out by Tom brandishing a shotgun.

The first priority for the brothers was the purchase of thoroughbred horses for the stables, and a Mr Bell was employed to look after them, with half a dozen lads working under him. This expenditure meant that they cut corners on other matters which required urgent attention. For instance, the yard was not an impressive sight. There was a permanent muckheap in one corner, and in the winter months this became an evil-smelling slurry. The stable doors had once been painted green, but the paint had worn away and the frames had rotted. The lads and horses walking around the yard stirred up the thin layer of gravel on the ground, which turned into sticky mud, freezing into a hard crust when the frost came.

A few improvements were made to the house, but not enough. Clonbarron was a Georgian mansion, surrounded by many acres of fields, sub-divided by low, grey stone walls. The long bumpy drive, peppered with potholes, led to a half circle at the top, where, in an earlier age, the carriages had waited. Wide stone steps approached the front door from both sides, flanked by ornate wrought-iron railings. The door itself was a massive affair with a fanlight above.

On the other side of the door was a vast hall, and the dankness assailed the nostrils of anyone entering. It was gloomy and cold, overpowered by dark heavy furniture. An oak settle was hidden beneath piles of clothes, and the floor was cluttered with riding-boots and wellingtons, thrown on top of each other in an untidy heap. On the wall there were lines of stiff macintoshes hanging on hooks. There was a special room for such things, but it seemed convenient to leave them where they were.

The walls of the rest of the house were decorated with patterns of spreading damp, and large buckets were at the ready in the long passages to catch the drips from the leaking roof. The two bachelors seem to accept these unfavourable conditions, but it was to this house that Tom decided it was time to bring a wife.

Tom was now in his late thirties, and had been involved in several amorous adventures. Despite his unprepossessing appearance (he was not distinguished-looking like Claw) he was attractive to women, although it may have been his title that appealed to them.

At a race meeting at the Curragh he spied Miss Kathleen O'Connor. She was the daughter of wealthy parents who lived in grandeur in Fitzwilliam Square in Dublin.

Tom was ecstatic. "Isn't she the most beautiful creature?" he asked his brother.

Claw agreed. "An ornament," was how he described her.

Tom stayed at the Shelbourne Hotel in Dublin in order to further the romance. While he was there he accosted a couple of little bellhops working in the hotel with the words, "Want to be a jockey?" It was the ambition of every undersized youth in Ireland, so they accepted at once.

Without difficulty Tom gained admittance to the O'Connor home, and charmed Kathleen's parents. After a decent pause, he showed their daughter a ruby ring lying in a bed of faded blue velvet. He explained that the ring had been given to his mother by the famous Potoski family in Russia. Tom had been told the story many times, how the carriages were driven into an ante-room of the palace so that when the guests stepped out there was a covering over their heads. He described to Kathleen, as his mother had done to him, the long dining-table where the dazzling silver and crystal competed with the diamonds adorning the ladies. And when the lady guests were elegantly seated, they found a favour by each place setting, wrapped in plain white paper and tied with coloured ribbon.

"And my mama's gift was this ring, and I want you to have it and be my wife."

As well as being romantic, Tom possessed the arrogance of the aristocrat. He did not think for a moment that the lovely Kathleen would refuse him, but that is what she did, very politely, very firmly. Her mother was devastated, for it is not every day the Earl of Clonbarron proposes to your daughter. She thought Kathleen had been very foolish. It was not as if she was a young woman – she was twenty-six, and it was unlikely that another chance like that would come her way. She expressed her feelings so strongly that Kathleen herself began to wonder if she had made a mistake.

"He is too short," was her excuse. She neglected to mention he was the wrong brother.

Tom returned to Clonbarron, taking with him the two lads he had acquired in Dublin, handing them over to Bell for training. His failure to win the hand of Kathleen did not cast him down for very long, and the field was open to Claw. The whole procedure was repeated, staying at the Shelbourne, visiting the house in Fitzwilliam Square, except that when he asked Kathleen to marry him she accepted. If she was surprised when he presented her with the ruby ring, recounting at the same time the history attached to it, she did not show it. They had a magnificent wedding in Dublin and a honeymoon in the Lake District which was 'abroad' in Claw's eyes. Since the war he had not wanted to travel far afield.

He took his new wife to Clonbarron where his brother, Tom, was head of the household, even though he did not assert his authority. Kathleen hoped it was a temporary arrangement, for she did not like living in her brother-in-law's house which was cold and uncomfortable, and not her own to do with as she liked. She was horrified at the state of the place, but she was in an awkward situation because she had not reckoned with Claw's intense love for Clonbarron. Also, she discovered there was a stubbornness in her husband's nature which was hard to overrule. Kathleen loved Claw and she had married him for love, so she decided to make the best of things, for the time being at any rate.

It helped having a mutual love of hunting. Going to meets, arranging for horses and horseboxes to be at the right place at the right time, occupied them on most days of the winter months. Then there was their interest in the racehorses which Tom trained. There were race meetings to attend and, in the evenings, they went out to dinner with friends or had people to dine with them. Kathleen acted as hostess for both brothers, and she soon became part of the local scene and was much admired for her beauty and poise.

One evening, Lord Clonbarron, returning from a day's hunting, spied a tinker girl splashing her bare feet in the puddles of a country lane. Undeniably, Tom had style; he lifted her up on to his horse and, with her frail body straddled in front of him, he rode home.

The girl's family did not regret her leaving their midst, but they felt money could be made from the escapade and, with this object in mind, they hovered around the big house, and eventually set up camp, caravans, horses and the general trash they carried with them, just outside the main gate of Clonbarron. Sometimes one of them would venture into the grounds, and when Claw saw one of the 'swine' (as he called them) he fired his gun in the air, and had the satisfaction of seeing the trespasser scuttle away.

Life became intolerable for poor Kathleen.

"Tell Tom to get rid of her," she pleaded with her husband, encouraged that he was as outraged as she was.

The girl was inarticulate, and unpleasant odours surrounded her. Her dark hair was matted and filthy. Perhaps Tom had a Shavian notion of teaching her to speak correctly and cleaning her up at the same time, but it was a hopeless task. No one, not even he, could make out her gibberish, and she did not understand about washing. However, a faint impression of a pretty face could be seen through the grime, and there was no doubt that Tom was sexually besotted. He spent hours in the biggest bedroom in the house, his bedroom, making love to her in the carved oak four-poster bed. His groans and shouts could be heard by everyone, and sometimes the girl escaped down the back stairs to the kitchen where one of the servants would give her food, which she wolfed down like a hungry animal.

Claw realised that something had to be done. His fastidious wife kept her distance from the lovers, but one day she passed the girl on the stairs and saw, with one shocked glance, that she was pregnant. The fact that Kathleen yearned for a child, and so far she and Claw had not managed to conceive, made the situation even more poignant. She became hysterical and, with a heavy heart, Claw approached Tom and told him that he and Kathleen would have to find somewhere else to live.

Tom was well aware that his own behaviour was reprehensible, and decided a fair solution was that he and the girl should leave. It was hard to know whether it was his sister-in-law's icy looks or the proximity of the tinker relations which made him take this step. Perhaps he intended to return to his home one day when his passion had subsided.

The lovers went to an empty dwelling on the estate, a tumbledown whitewashed bothy, unheated and damp. The girl would have been better off in one of the caravans owned by her father or uncles, or sitting by the great fires the tinkers made in the evenings. She stayed because she was frightened to leave, and she died in that terrible place giving birth to a son.

Tom drove to the house of the doctor to get help, but he was too late. When the two men arrived at the cottage they found the girl lying on the stone floor in a pool of blood. The baby, attached by the cord to his mother, was wriggling like a small fish. Tom, transfixed, stood and watched the doctor kneel down and examine the girl whom they both knew to be dead.

"The child," he managed to blurt out, "will the child live?"

Later, the tiny creature was put into his large hands, and he was overcome by a feeling of responsibility and love. Tears filled his eyes.

The news spread like a forest fire throughout the county. There was gossip in the pub and in the village shop, and the topic was discussed at every dinner party, the story becoming more dramatic each time it was told. The tinkers were in a vengeful mood, the men taking up a menacing stance on either side of the gate. Their keening could be heard all through the night. It was all too much for Kathleen who felt she had landed in an alien country.

"I'm going home to Mother," she said.

"Please, please stay," pleaded Claw. "It will pass. It can't last for ever."

Tom, looking at both their faces, thought the time had come for him to disappear, and, like many Irishmen before him, he decided the United States of America was the answer to all his problems. He hired a nursery maid to look after his little son, and booked a passage for the three of them to travel to New York on the Queen Mary, sailing from Southampton. Early one morning, without being seen, he drove away from Clonbarron.

His ticket was made out in the name of Mr Shannon, for, in defiance of the rule that an illegitimate child cannot inherit, he had decided to renounce his proud title.

And plain Tom Shannon he remained until the day of his death.

CHAPTER SIX

The departure of Tom was an answer to all Kathleen's prayers, and she was convinced, despite the entailment, that Clonbarron belonged to Claw from then on. While Tom had been in residence she had not been prepared to spend any of her own money on the house and estate, but now she wanted to make it a place where they would be proud to live for the rest of their lives.

The first thing that she organised was an agent, and Mr Kendrick arrived from England. He was a studious middle-aged bachelor who was given accommodation in the lodge cottage, the place least affected by water seeping through the roof.

"Is it really necessary to have an agent?" asked Claw plaintively. "We have never had one before."

Kathleen, in command, assured him it was, but, discreetly she asked Mr Kendrick to consult her husband before making any decisions about improvements to the place. It did not take him very long to appreciate the problems, and soon he had mustered an army of roofers, plumbers, decorators and gardeners.

Claw was full of admiration. "What a fellow," he said. "He's turning the place upside-down." He was particularly impressed when Mr Kendrick managed to obtain rent payments from tenants who had not paid rent for years. Tom, and his father before him, had been lax in collecting monies owed.

There was a general feeling of hatred towards the agent, and a stone was hurled at his car when he was driving along one of the lanes. Being English did not add to his popularity. The tide turned in their attitude towards him when it was realised that he was bringing work into the neighbourhood, and also plans were being made to renovate the rundown cottages where the tenants lived. He installed Bell into a newly done-up stable house, and work was done on the stables and yard to make them presentable. He did not always get credit for the innovations he made. For instance he persuaded Claw to provide warm sweaters and breeches for the stable lads to wear when they rode out on a cold winter's morning. These boys of small stature were paid five shillings a week if they behaved themselves. Neither he nor Tom had ever thought of giving them anything else. When they misbehaved Tom had no scruples about giving them a good hiding, but Claw could never bring himself to do this. Life improved for them when Lord Clonbarron went to America.

"God bless you, sir," they said when Claw handed them the clothes.

He was near to tears when Kathleen told him she was expecting his child.

"Oh, my darling," he said, trying not to betray emotion which he had been taught from childhood never to show.

He worried about her all the time, and was relieved when a few months into her pregnancy she was advised to give up hunting. If there had not been so much to do she might have been irritated by this advice, but she busied herself around the house, lumbering from room to room, all swarming with workmen, clutching swatches of material and wallpaper patterns to her enlarged stomach. She felt no joy in pregnancy. Although looking forward to the outcome, the actual state filled her with vexation.

Her irritation was increased when a letter arrived from Tom, posted in Eustace, Oregon. He enclosed a list of items he wanted sent to him.

"We are not going to do that," said Kathleen. She and Claw were sitting having breakfast in the morning-room, the only room as yet untouched by workmen. She threw the list down on the table in disgust. "He's asking for so much," she said. "There will be nothing left."

Of course, this was nonsense. Clonbarron was crammed with paintings, furniture and artefacts. Tom's requests would make very little difference.

"Everything belongs to him," Claw pointed out. "If

he wants it he must have it." He tried to comfort his wife by saying, "He must be planning to stay out there, or he would never trouble to do this. It is good news, really."

Giant crates were shipped to Portland for collection. They contained furniture, paintings (Tom favoured portraits of horses rather than ancestors although there were a few of those as well) and his mother's collection of Meissen porcelain.

The renovations to the house were nearly completed when Duibhne was born. In the big bedroom everything was changed: fresh paintwork and wallpaper, new curtains and hangings for the four-poster bed. Kathleen even threw out the furniture which she felt had been tainted by the former occupants. Fashionable modern pieces were ordered from Heals in London, painted dark turquoise and heavily embossed with gold leaf. She threatened to get rid of the bed because of its associations, but her husband demanded it remain where it was.

Claw was overjoyed at the direction his life had taken. He looked forward to the birth of his child and he was proud of his wife who had transformed Clonbarron to its former brilliance, so that it was now like it had been years before when his mother had presided.

Before the birth a midwife was installed in a nearby bedroom, and the doctor was summoned in good time. It was an easy birth, but Kathleen soon discovered she was devoid of maternal feeling. It did not matter as

Duibhne was at once put in the charge of a nanny who had come from England. For some reason, hard to understand, it was fashionable to have an English nanny. An Irish girl called Eilish was employed as a nursery maid. Apparently it took two women to look after one small girl.

Nanny was a stout elderly woman with white hair scraped back in a bun, kept in place by white hairpins. She had been nanny to the offspring of some very grand people, and she dropped their names in the conversation whenever she could. She enjoyed reading the glossy society magazines, and pointing out her charges to the admiring Eilish. "He used to wet his bed," she would say of a prominent political figure, or "She was a very bad eater," when they were looking at the picture of a young girl engaged to one of the Royals. Nanny crackled and her black sensible shoes squeaked. With the servants she was a soft-voiced tyrant, and her orders were obeyed. The fact that, like Mr Kendrick, she was English made her even more formidable.

Everything ran smoothly in the nursery, and Kathleen could resume hunting with a clear conscience. She did not know that Claw, who had been brought up by a nanny and knew the breed, was in the habit of crossing the periphery and, perching his long body on the extreme edge of the leather corner seats of the fireguard, he would watch his daughter having her bottle. Sometimes, he extended a finger which he put into the tiny hand, delighting in the strong grip. Two bright blue eyes would stare into his face. Nanny approved of Claw. His behaviour, in her view, was right and proper for a father. "Not like the other one," she confided scornfully to Eilish.

Kathleen's indifference to the child altered when Duibhne started to walk, and talk in a beguiling way. She was a pretty little girl, much admired by her mother's friends. At about this time Kathleen decided she must have a son, if any heirs of the wretched Tom were to be kept away from Clonbarron. Claw often had to remind her that there was no reason why Tom should not remarry and decide to come home.

"Why don't you write and ask him if he intends to stay there?" she asked, knowing as she spoke that her request would never be granted, but it would be nice to know where they stood. There had been no word from Tom since they had arranged to send so many of his belongings to the States. He had not bothered to acknowledge their safe arrival and, as Claw never wrote letters, it looked as if all contact between the brothers had been lost.

When her mother became interested in her, Duibhne started seeing her parents twice a day. Before breakfast, when she went to their bedroom and played on the big bed, and after tea when she was brought into the drawing-room. She played bears on the floor with her father and hide and seek behind the sofas before Nanny or Eilish collected her, promptly at six o'clock. During weekends she went with her parents to visit friends or go to a local point-to-point. The Limerick Show was an annual event and a family outing.

Duibhne was five years old when something happened which was to change her life completely. She was an only child, for Kathleen and Claw had not been able to repeat the miracle of her birth. In later years she was to remember the day quite clearly. It had started by Claw coming to the nursery and telling Nanny that his daughter was to spend the morning with him. He had gout and was hobbling, one foot encased in an old slipper.

"Her ladyship is hunting," he explained, "but I have to stay at home because of my bloody toe."

Nanny sniffed, she was good at sniffing, and this was to indicate that she did not like swearing in the nursery. Claw took no notice and he and Duibhne went, hand in hand, into the drive at the front of the house, to say goodbye to Kathleen.

She looked superb in an immaculately tailored hunting-coat and breeches, white stock, shiny black leather boots and a bowler perched on top of a neat chignon.

The sight of the two figures gave her a qualm of conscience. "I don't like to leave you," she said.

"Of course you must go," said Claw, wincing from the pain in his foot. "The little one and I will have a lovely time together."

"Yes, go, Mummy," said Duibhne, who always enjoyed time alone with her father.

The prospect of a day's hunting was too hard for

Kathleen to resist. "Well, if you insist . . ." she said. She kissed them both, reaching up to Claw and bending down to her little girl. Afterwards they felt there was a lingering fondness in her kisses. It was a cold crisp day and Claw stood, holding the small hand of his daughter, watching his wife get into the chauffeur-driven Buick. They saw her gloved hand come through the window to wave before the car was driven down the drive, and out of sight. An hour earlier the horsebox had set off for the meet, and her mount would be ready for her when she arrived.

The hand through the window was the last glimpse Duibhne had of her mother, and the recollection of that hand remained with her always. An irate farmer had put a wire across a gap in a stone wall. He was angered by the gentry ploughing up his fields in their pursuit of the fox. Lady Claughessy galloped straight into the wire, and gave an ear-splitting high-pitched scream as she became aware, too late, of it being there. It was her last utterance. Immediately, a host of people gathered around her body, and someone caught her horse which had stumbled to its feet. The doctor, one of the riders, gave the assembled crowd his terrible verdict. The master ordered everyone to go home: hunting was over for that day.

They were such a devoted couple people wondered how the bereaved husband would cope with such an all-enveloping grief. For days he closeted himself in their bedroom, refusing to see anyone. Then one day he emerged, and after that coped with the sorrow in his own way, an unexpected way, but then Claw often did the unexpected thing. He turned to his child, and from being a nanny's girl she became a daddy's girl. It was touching to see his lordship walking hand in hand with the little creature, and she went everywhere with him.

He taught her to ride, riding alongside her little pony on a leading rein. He insisted on Mr Kendrick taking her out in the car to follow the hunt, so that if they stopped in a covert he could wave to her. At the end of the day he would give his horse to a stable lad to trot home, and then he would climb in the back of the car with her. It was a terribly boring day for a child, and Mr Kendrick, a kindly man, would think of games for them to play such as 'I spy' and 'I packed my grandmother's bag'. A picnic at noon provided a diversion.

When Claw had a dinner party he allowed Duibhne to come downstairs, and she sat on his knee at the head of the table, until the glow of the candles and the shining silver and glass made her eyes droop. Then Da (as she called her father) would press a bell by his foot, and a very disapproving nanny would appear to shake her awake and take her off to bed.

When she was eight years old she started cub-hunting, and when she was ten she went out with the Limerick hunt accompanied by Bell. At the age of twelve she was considered old enough to go alone. It was evidence of the contradictions in Claw's character that although he lived in constant dread that something bad would befall his treasure, he had no reservations about her returning alone after a day's hunting. On many winter evenings she and the pony would walk miles along the deserted country lanes, often wet and weary, Duibhne longing for the moment when they clip-clopped into the stable yard, and a boy would take the pony from her for a rub down and a feed. The moment she jumped to the ground her duties were over. Everything was done for her. Although his wife had died in the hunting-field, Claw could not find it in his heart to believe that hunting was a dangerous pastime. Hunting was in his bones, and as precious as life itself.

Claw had an army of advisers, Limerick ladies who took it upon themselves to help the poor lonely man in the upbringing of his daughter. Mostly he thought he could get on very well without them, but he was too polite to say so. But sometimes he listened to their advice.

One day he summoned Mr Kendrick to his side. "I'm told I should get a governess for Duibhne. What do you think?"

Of course Mr Kendrick had no thoughts on the subject. He knew that a local lady came in to teach Duibhne from time to time; certainly it did not seem to be a very permanent or satisfactory arrangement for a child who, at that time, was approaching seven years old.

"I suggest we advertise," he said. "Would you like me to put a notice in *The Times*?"

Claw was relieved that the problem was solved so

easily. When a week later Mr Kendrick appeared with a file full of replies, he was amazed to see how many people had answered the advertisement.

Claw read each letter very carefully, and finally chose one from Miss Glenda Pinkerton. She had an address in Bournemouth, and Claw had been taken there for a seaside holiday when he was a boy and he thought it a magical place. He did not bother himself with her qualifications – he just handed over the letter, and said, "Ask her to come here on a month's trial."

Glenda Pinkerton had been governess to a family in England, and had been given the name of Pinkie. When she arrived at Shannon airport she was met by a man whom she assumed was her employer. Only after half the car journey and an awkward conversation on both sides did she discover this was not the case.

"I'm so sorry – I'm the agent. You will meet Lord Claughessy of course when you get to Clonbarron."

"Can you tell me something about the child I am to teach?"

Mr Kendrick was enthusiastic. He had a very soft spot in his heart for Duibhne. "I'm sure you will have no difficulties there. She is a charming child."

"And her mother? The letter did not mention her mother."

He explained the circumstances, and this silenced Pinkie for some time. She sat in the car reflecting on the interesting fact that her employer was a widower. It added an exciting quality to the job.

When she was introduced to Claw he took her hand and smiled at her. It was the smile that had captivated Kathleen and the Limerick ladies, and Pinkie basked in the sunshine of it. When he introduced her to his shy little daughter she felt she had come home.

It was inevitable that Nanny disliked Pinkie from the start, and no one was better at making her feelings plain. Poor Pinkie thought the antagonism was directed at her personally, but she was wrong, it was directed at anyone who came within the hallowed circle. Pinkie's life was made miserable by Nanny's silences, Nanny's disapproving sniffs, Nanny's way of never directly addressing her or referring to her by her name.

When Pinkie entered the room she interrupted whispered confidences Nanny was sharing with Eilish. These were stopped abruptly when she was seen. Straightforward rudeness she might have been able to deal with, but it was more subtle than that.

"You had better behave yourself, " Nanny warned Duibhne, "or she will be after you."

Pinkie had breakfast, lunch and tea in the nursery, but she dined with Claw. She was included in all family outings and treated like family. When he asked her to call him 'Claw' she felt it was an honour. Being with him was very natural and easy; there were no difficulties in finding things to say to each other. He was utterly devoted to Duibhne, and privately Pinkie thought there was something a little unnatural about his all-consuming love for the child.

Sometimes Mr Kendrick joined them for dinner, and then the two men talked of estate matters, and Pinkie was left out. She liked Mr Kendrick who, surprisingly, remained Mr Kendrick, and she never called him by his Christian name which remained a mystery. Once she told him about her problems with Nanny, which she never mentioned to Claw.

"A lady with a very narrow life," he said seriously. "No wonder she cannot see beyond her own horizon. What has she got in life besides Duibhne and Eilish and the company of other nannies?" Pinkie did not find his words helpful. She felt he was speaking for them all when he spoke of narrow lives.

It was a lonely existence, but Pinkie was sustained by a secret dream that Claw would fall in love with her. It was not impossible for she was a good-looking woman with a respectable middle-class background.

There was speculation about their relationship, but Claw was oblivious to the gossip. He simply did not think of her in a romantic way. He regarded her as a friend, and he got it into his head that she was clever, which she was not. It seemed as if he had resigned himself to a life of memories, and the ambitions of Pinkie or any of the Limerick ladies were wasted on him. He was happy in his own way, living at Clonbarron and visiting England twice a year (travelling by ferry from Dublin) to go to Royal Ascot in June and to the Newmarket Bloodstock Sales in September.

Despite her deep affection for Duibhne, Pinkie

decided that her daily dose of petty tyranny from Nanny had become intolerable. She resolved to leave Ireland and return to Bournemouth. She gave it another month. During that time Nanny was struck by a municipal dust-cart while walking in Limerick on her afternoon off. She was taken to hospital with severe injuries to one leg which was to leave her with a limp for the rest of her life. Eilish went to visit the patient, and reported she was 'very low'.

Pinkie was uncertain whether she should call in at the hospital to see Nanny. There was no reason for her to be charitable. She had not yet told Claw of her decision to leave, and the accident gave her a brief respite. Life in the nursery became serene and peaceful. One afternoon, on impulse, she purchased flowers from a florist in Limerick, and, armed with these, she went to the hospital.

She was shocked by Nanny's appearance. She was in a private room (by courtesy of Claw) and lay in a narrow bed, her leg held in the air by a pulley. It was a frightened old woman who managed to give Pinkie a wintry smile, thereby dispelling all the hostility the other woman held for her.

"Go and ask the nurse for a vase," she said in her usual autocratic way, when she saw the flowers. When Pinkie had arranged them, and put them on the locker by the bed, she was rewarded with the words, "They are lovely."

Pinkie sat in the chair by the bed, and told her about Duibhne and how much the child was missing her. "Do you think you feel well enough to see her?" she asked. "I know she would love to come, and I can bring her any time you say."

"That would be ever so nice," Nanny replied. "It gets lonely."

"I'll come again," said Pinkie.

After that visit she went every afternoon, and sometimes she took Duibhne with her. On one of the visits, when she was leaving, Nanny called her back. "Thank you, Glenda," she said.

Pinkie returned to Clonbarron with a heart full of joy, for she knew the conflict was over, the battle had been won. There was no need to leave her lovely little Divvy, no need to discard for ever the imaginary world which occupied her thoughts before she went to sleep. Her dream of fulfilment with Claw remained intact.

Nanny was in hospital for a month, and welcomed news from home. Pinkie told her how Duibhne, sitting at the nursery table, had coloured a picture for a competition in the *Limerick News*. It was a picture of Father Christmas delivering presents, and she had painted the red of his cloak, never going over the lines, and the bright green of the tree behind him, and all the decorations and gifts tied up with different coloured ribbons.

"She won!" announced Pinkie. "And she has received a letter saying she is to collect her prize from the cinema."

"Oh, dear," said Nanny, "what are we going to do about that, Glenda? She can't go, can she?"

"You think not?" asked Pinkie, worried.

"It would not be right," said Nanny decidedly.

But when Claw was told of it he thought it perfectly right that his daughter should collect her prize.

"It is most rewarding," he said, "and I do congratulate you, Pinkie, on this achievement. Do you think Divvy is going to turn out to be one of those artistic women? A painter or something of the sort?"

"No-o, I don't think so . . ."

The manager of the cinema was very pleased to usher Lord Claughessy and Pinkie into two front seats. The presentation was before a showing of *Annie Get Your Gun* which the Clonbarron party did not wait to see. There was a ripple of applause as the little figure walked on to the stage, wearing clothes a size too big for her (ordered from Harrods by Nanny), white socks and Start-Rite shoes.

"It was all right," Pinkie assured Nanny later. "It went very well."

Pinkie had the use of the car, and she drove Nanny home from hospital. On the way she told her that Mr Kendrick was getting her compensation for the accident. "He thinks it will be about a thousand pounds."

"A thousand pounds!" exclaimed the old lady. "Well, fancy! And I know what I shall do with the money, Glenda dear. I shall buy myself a diamond ring with part of it. I have always wanted a diamond ring. My young man was killed in the First World War, you know, before he could give me one."

So Nanny came home from hospital, and eventually purchased the ring which she wore on the middle finger of her right hand, for to wear it on the engagement finger would not have been the correct thing to do. When she saw her friends, Nanny St Patrick, Nanny Cloverdale and Nanny Kildare she had the satisfaction of knowing that none of them had a diamond ring, sparkling and catching the light, like the ring on the finger of her right hand.

It was small compensation for the accident which had taken the stuffing out of her, and she was content to nod by the nursery fire, and allow the faithful Eilish to wait on her. When Duibhne was twelve years old, Nanny retired to her native land, to spend the rest of her days in a comfortable home for the elderly, paid for by Claw. Pinkie wrote to her, and went to see her when she visited England.

Pinkie formed the opinion that Duibhne was growing up in a very restricted environment. By this time she was considered old enough to act as hostess for her father. When Pinkie asked her what the grown-ups discussed at the dinner table, she replied, "Horses, foxes and the form book."

Pinkie was dismayed and contrived to fill her young charge's head with English history, English literature and the history of art. Irish history did not feature in the curriculum. She sent to England for books about the great painters.

"If only we could visit the famous galleries," she

sighed. "Oh, for a chance to go to Paris, Rome and Madrid!"

She tried to make Claw understand there were gaps in his daughter's education, but he did not know what she was talking about, and travelling abroad was out of the question. It meant boarding an aeroplane, and he could not envisage that for himself or any member of his family. He thought it an experience they could all do without.

Pinkie's endeavours did have some effect, however, and this became evident to Claw on Duibhne's fourteenth birthday when he asked her what present she would like from him.

"Choose anything you like, my darling."

"I would like the sketch by Constable."

He looked at her, his expression a mixture of pride, admiration and surprise. Solemnly, he marched into the morning-room and removed a small picture from the nail on which it was hanging. He had not noticed it particularly before, but he knew what it was and the fact that she wanted it pleased him.

Duibhne hung the picture over her bed, and, although there came a time in her life when she was parted from it, she was later reunited with it, and always loved it. It was a peaceful drawing of the outskirts of London, before traffic and suburbia took over from the rural aspect. A tree in the foreground reminded her of one at Clonbarron, and when she looked at the scene she thought of her father removing the sketch from its usual place, and handing it to her.

As for Pinkie, she felt all her hard work had been rewarded. She had a definite place in Clonbarron; she was a woman with power. The servants obeyed her, her pupil adored her, and she still had thoughts of higher things to come.

CHAPTER SEVEN

As Duibhne approached sixteen Pinkie decided that she should take O-levels.

"Are you sure?" said Claw when she mentioned the matter to him. Years earlier he and Tom had both taken the School Certificate, and had not been able to scrape up a pass between them. In consequence, he distrusted all examinations. However, another side to his character made him regard academic prowess with unreserved admiration.

"I'll think about it," he said. Pinkie knew that meant he was going to consult his female advisers.

"There is no need to involve any of them," she said resentfully. Over the years she found it increasingly annoying that Claw turned to this band of women when he had doubts about the correct way to bring up his motherless child. Pinkie felt sufficiently in control herself without their meddlesome interference.

The Limerick ladies replied in one voice that O-levels were an essential part of a girl's education. Of course their daughters had been sent to boarding-schools where such things were dealt with on the spot (they had advised him to send Duibhne away, but he had resisted such a terrible suggestion). They shook their heads, and said, with the wretched Pinkie at the helm, there was little chance of the dear girl getting good results.

Claw turned to Pinkie, "What shall we do? Forget it?" He half-hoped she would say 'yes'.

"Of course not," said Pinkie briskly. "I'll find a way for Divvy to take the exams."

She discovered that Duibhne would have to attend a proper school for two weeks, so that she could take the O-levels under correct supervision. After many telephone calls, letters exchanged, and with the kind help of Mr Kendrick, arrangements were made for Claw to accompany his daughter to England, and there she would stay at a girls' boarding-school in Ascot where she would sit for a series of examinations in various subjects. It was all very exciting, and Pinkie expected and hoped that she would be asked to go with them, but it did not occur to Claw to include her.

The possibility of flying was not even raised, and Mr Kendrick drove them to Dublin where they boarded the *Princess Victoria.* Father and daughter shared a cabin on the nightmare journey. It was the first time Duibhne had been away from Ireland, and it was not an experience she would remember with pleasure. A terrible storm blew up during the night, and the creaks and groans, the constant movement, up and down and from side to side, made them sick with fear. Privately, Duibhne thought flying must be preferable to this.

A hired car waited for them on the other side, and Claw drove to Ascot. By the time they drove into the entrance to the school, an imposing grey stone building, they were exhausted.

The headmistress was a kind woman with a soft voice and soft grey hair. She greeted them warmly, and instructed a young teacher to show Duibhne where she had to go. Claw was about to shuffle after her, but he was quietly restrained.

And what of Duibhne at the age of sixteen? She possessed the first tremulous signs of beauty. A pale skin, blue eyes and clearly defined black eyebrows. She had never been told she was pretty, so she had no reason to believe it. When she was dressed for hunting, in that uniform that makes the plainest woman attractive, she was breathtakingly lovely. In everyday clothes she was dowdy. Her tweed skirts were too long, with uneven lumpy hemlines, and Pinkie favoured sensible brown shoes for her, and ankle socks. Her magnificent hair was twisted in one heavy plait. The girls at the school in Ascot looked at her with fascinated horror when the young teacher introduced her: "This is Duibhne Shannon, and I want you to help her as much as you can."

From the moment she entered the school Duibhne

knew that she was different. It was a shock. *'Like a doe in the noontide with love's sweet want, as the companionless Sensitive Plant,'* she felt rejected. All this, and the terrifying prospect of exams as well.

The headmistress was pleased to welcome the daughter of Lord Claughessy to her school, and she was touched when she heard that he was staying at a local hotel for the full two weeks of the examinations. "You must not worry," she assured him. "Duibhne is in good hands here. We will look after her."

Of course he did not believe her, and was constantly walking into the building and being a positive nuisance. He was seen wandering in the corridors, looking for his child. His presence was usually heralded by a group of giggling girls, standing in a corner, watching him. The headmistress tried to explain to him, politely, that other parents were not permitted to visit the school at all hours and so often.

One day when Duibhne was speeding along one of the passages, lost as usual, she saw the tall figure of her father, ahead of her. She rushed to him and, putting her arms around his waist, exclaimed, "Dearest, dearest Da!" She became conscious of stifled laughs from two girls who were walking behind him. She was dismayed. Never in her life had she thought of her father as an object of mirth, but these silly girls seemed to think so. One of them said to her later, "Why is he always here? Can't he bear to be parted from his little girl?"

Duibhne shared a bedroom with four other girls. A

nice room with chintz curtains and pretty bedspreads. One of the girls had a teddy bear sitting on her pillow, and there were photographs of parents, brothers and sisters standing on the lockers between each bed.

The girls sprawled on the beds, chattering and laughing, leaving Duibhne out of their conversation. They talked a great deal about boys, and one of them read a letter she had received. The ending, which was *'With best love, Tim'*, produced gales of merriment. When she had finished reading it, the girl tucked it in her bra. Duibhne was completely mystified by their behaviour.

They tried to be friendly, but she did not want their friendship. It was during this stay in Ascot she learnt that with one straight disdainful look she was able to quell their silliness. It had an instant effect, like a blind being drawn over a sunlit window. She was left alone, which was a bittersweet victory. It was a stratagem she was to employ on rare occasions throughout her life.

In the evenings they changed into smart frocks, dusted powder on their faces and smeared their lips with lipstick before going downstairs. Duibhne had no experience of powder or lipstick, and Pinkie had not thought it necessary to pack anything for her to wear in the evening.

She was asked to attend a class called Music and Movement. The girls made up a sort of ballet, in this case *Romeo and Juliet*. The accompaniment was supplied by a teacher playing the piano. They gestured and pointed their toes, waved their arms and swayed to the tinkling music, appearing to enjoy every moment of the improvisation. Duibhne was very relieved that, as a visiting pupil, she was not expected to take part.

At the end of the evening, before they all trooped off to bed, they were admitted to the headmistress's room. They sat in a circle around her chair, and she read to them. The book she was reading was *A Tale of Two Cities* and Duibhne was enthralled. It was the only part of the day when she felt happy.

She did not understand the school rules, and, after a while, no one troubled to explain them to her. She had difficulty in finding her way around, and it was a miracle that she managed to find the right room each day for the examinations, which were written under the sharp eyes of an invigilator. Duibhne would sidle in, just in time, and sit at a small desk, something she had never done before (the nursery table was used for lessons at home), faced with printed and blank sheets of paper. It was to Pinkie's credit that she managed to get five O-levels.

At last it was over, and time to return to Ireland. Duibhne had mixed feelings about the whole experience. She thought about the girls and their easy happy friendships. Pinkie was her only real friend. They had thought her stiff and priggish when really she was just ill at ease with them. Two weeks of their society had not been long enough to break down barriers, and perhaps if she had stayed longer with them she would have discovered the secret of having fun.

Claw was thankful to go home. He had not enjoyed staying in an hotel and he was not used to being reprimanded, even in gentle tones, by headmistresses. He noticed that his daughter was more subdued than usual, but he attributed this to the strain of taking exams. He could not know that for a short time she had glimpsed another life, a life where young girls, like her on the threshold of maturity, had laughed together and talked intimately about subjects of which she was completely ignorant. Being away from home had unsettled her, and she could not analyse her feelings.

Pinkie noticed the change in her. "What is the matter, dear?" she asked.

"I don't know."

She is growing up, thought Pinkie tenderly. She loved her and worried about her as well. She hoped she had told her the right things in preparation for adulthood, but she felt a spinster in her forties was not the ideal person to talk to a young girl. Claw was hopeless, she decided. He appeared not to have noticed that Duibhne was unfolding, changing gradually from his awkward little cygnet into a swan.

Pinkie did not feel forgiving towards Claw, as she considered he had slighted her by not asking her to accompany them to Ascot. Her dreams did not survive the rebuff (although she knew in her heart it was unintentional) and, now, when she laid her head on the pillow, sleep came at once. No longer did she indulge in her particular bedtime story, of love, honour and triumph over the ladies. After ten years it was a loss to give it up, but, like Duibhne, she had changed. The face that looked back at her in the mirror had grown older, and reflected her doubts and uncertainties. She envisaged years ahead of her, living under the same roof as Claw, close, but with a distance between them. Was this all that life had to offer her?

A diversion occurred in the shape of a message from England. Pinkie's father, a widower, living in a seaside bungalow, had suffered a stroke. She must go to him at once. Claw was full of concern, and Mr. Kendrick was instructed to arrange everything so that Pinkie's journey to Bournemouth was as stress-free and comfortable as possible. Money was pressed into her hand, in case she needed extra cash while she was away. She felt cherished. Duibhne was distraught. Of course she was sympathetic, but she implored Pinkie not to be away for too long.

Comforted by such warm displays of affection, and knowing that as long as she stayed in Ireland she could always be sure of security and a good home, she travelled to Bournemouth. There, a different scene awaited her. The bungalow was cramped, overheated, crowded with hideous furniture. Pinkie had lived in a very different world for so long it was hard to step back into the old one. The kitchen irked her, with its old-fashioned gas stove, and the space under the sink hidden by a curtain. Her bed was hard and unyielding.

She sat beside the frail old man, holding his cool

bloodless hand. She spoke to him endlessly, trying to raise a sign of recognition.

"I'm here, Father. Glenda . . . don't you know me?"

It was hopeless. He slipped away from her. She had heard the expression 'he just slipped away' so many times, and it was true. He was gone in a moment when she turned her back on him to get him a glass of water. 'A happy release' was another expression that came to her mind. The usual clichés about death and loss were repeated over and over again, as cups of tea and sandwiches were passed around after the funeral.

It was a relief when Frank Grainger, the bank manager, crossed to Pinkie's side, and said cheerfully, "Your father and I had some good games of golf together."

Grateful, she murmured, "Thank you."

"Please tell me if there is anything I can do to help."

"Well, I shall have to sell this bungalow," said Pinkie, "and there are a few investments. I shall need help about those."

Tentatively, Frank came up with a suggestion. "Perhaps you would have dinner with me at the Crown one evening, and we could talk about these matters?"

She looked at him. He was not good-looking or distinguished, but he was a pleasant man. Solid and dependable.

"I'd like that very much," she said.

She dressed to go out with him, knowing that she looked quietly elegant. It was the first time she had been out with a man for many years. She found her mother's jewel box, and she put on stud diamond earrings, and pinned a small diamond bar-brooch on to her plain black dress. She felt like an independent woman, and she noticed the admiration in Frank's eyes. It was a long time since anyone had looked at her in that way, and it was happening to her, making her fantasies about Claw seem foolish and unreal.

During the meal it was inevitable they should talk about his problems as well as her own. He was a widower, and lonely. His married daughter was a joy to him, and he was proud to be grandfather to two dear little girls, but they lived in Cornwall, and he saw them infrequently.

It took many weeks to wind up her father's estate. Letters from Duibhne begged her to come home. Home. It was her home, her only home, but it assumed a remote quality. She tried to describe it to Frank, but he had never been to Ireland, and his knowledge of stately homes and their occupants was limited. However he enjoyed listening to Pinkie (he called her Glenda) talking about Claw and Duibhne. He knew they were important to her.

"Divvy must be like a daughter to you," he said.

Pinkie knew it was not so, and although there had been a time when she hoped for the stepmother's role, she had never thought of stepping into Kathleen's shoes. Sometimes she wondered if Duibhne would have been different if her mother had lived. From stories she heard from Nanny, Kathleen did not sound a maternal sort of person. At least Pinkie had supplied the woman's love that was missing from Duibhne's life.

When probate had been granted she said to Frank, "I have to go back. They need me."

Then he told her that he needed her too. He asked her to marry him, and she accepted.

She returned to Ireland, clutching this great secret to her breast. When she arrived at Shannon airport, and Claw and Duibhne were there to meet her, she felt sure they would guess at once, but they were unaware of anything different about her, just happy to have her back.

"Oh, I've missed you so much," cried Duibhne, tears in her eyes. The unrest she had felt during the last weeks showed in her face.

"You are so thin!" said Pinkie, concerned. She noticed the high cheekbones were more defined than before, and, when she put her arms around her, the girl's body was fragile in its slenderness.

She did not know how to tell them her news. She put if off for several days, until an anxious telephone call from Frank made her decide to speak.

"Married!" exclaimed Claw when relating the tidings to his female friends. "To a bank manager! Do you think he is her intellectual equal?"

Duibhne told Pinkie that she was happy for her. Without ever being told, she had always sensed that Pinkie was a woman who desired marriage. Years before, Pinkie had taken it upon herself to tell her charge the facts of life, realising that Claw was not equal to the task.

The girl had asked, "Have you done it?"

Pinkie had replied, "Sadly, no."

Thank goodness she will not die without doing it, thought Duibhne. It seemed to her the worst possible fate.

She and her father went to England for the wedding. Pinkie was surprised that Claw agreed to make another journey, but she had not reckoned with his loyalty and deep affection for her.

The bride wore ivory satin instead of white in deference to the fact that Frank had been married before. His granddaughters were small bridesmaids, and Duibhne was the tall gawky one walking behind them. Pinkie had chosen apricot-coloured flounced dresses for her attendants. Duibhne's arms stuck out like sticks from the ruffled sleeves, and her beautifully formed breasts were hidden beneath a fichu of apricot froth. She felt terribly unhappy, and on the edge of tears. Pinkie's bank manager was not what she had expected. He was short and rather stout, and had a bristly moustache. Surely Pinkie would not like doing it with him?

She dreaded the parting. For ever, she thought. Nothing would be the same again. All the women in her life had left her, her mother, dear old Nanny, and now Pinkie.

At the reception she stayed close to her father.

Pinkie wanted the most precious people in her life to get on with each other, but she had to accept the truth that poor Frank found it impossible to carry on a conversation with Claw. There was a murmur of interest when Lord Claughessy rose to his feet, a towering figure wearing a morning coat which had belonged to his father, and was too small for him. It did not matter that he made a very poor speech.

Pinkie clasped Duibhne close to her, with mixed feelings of joy and sadness, then they left for their honeymoon, and Claw and his daughter were able to wander back to their hotel and prepare for the journey home. Bournemouth had been a disappointment, and Claw insisted it had changed since he was a boy.

At Clonbarron the days passed into weeks and the weeks into months. Most of the young people had left Limerick, although they returned from time to time to visit their parents. The sons of Claw's friends took Duibhne out, to the races, to a point-to-point or a hunt ball. They found her aloof, and one of the young men jokingly called her 'the iceberg'. She heard about it, and it did not help.

Claw's advisers told him that she should have a season, go to London, live in a flat in a good area like Queen's Gate, be presented and go to parties. One of them even offered to act as chaperone.

Duibhne gave way to despondency, and the idea of going to London did not dispel her gloom. She did not enjoy dances in Ireland, so why should she enjoy them anywhere else? She dreaded the thought of being manipulated by a woman she hardly knew. It did not happen. Somehow the scheme was shelved and forgotten; possibly Claw's lack of enthusiasm was to blame. Duibhne was relieved and sorry at the same time. She did not know what she wanted.

Darkness settled around her. In the winter the monotonous regularity of her days was broken by hunting and exercising her pet greyhound, Little Chancer. Letters from Pinkie conveyed happiness, but anxiety about her. She was hostess at dinner parties given by her father, where the talk was of killing foxes, and the guests were old and boring. She tried to stifle her yawns, but longed for everyone to depart so that she could go to bed.

Then something happened that promised to disrupt the routine. One morning, at the breakfast table, Claw found by his plate a blue air-mail envelope. He tore it open, and read the contents, then he handed the letter to Duibhne, exactly as he would have done if Kathleen had been sitting beside him instead of his daughter. It was his first communication from his brother, Tom, in nearly twenty years.

Tom Shannon wrote from the States saying that he and his son, Bartley, intended to visit them.

CHAPTER EIGHT

Claw was not happy about the impending visit, but, if Tom wanted to come home, and as Clonbarron was his home in respect of ownership and entailment, there was no way he could be refused that privilege. In ordinary circumstances he would have welcomed the prospect of seeing his brother again after such a long parting, but the circumstances were not ordinary. Claw was very apprehensive, and hoped it was only a visit, as Tom had stated in his letter, and not something more lasting and permanent. He never wrote letters, but he instructed Mr Kendrick to reply on his behalf and tell Tom that he and his son would be welcome.

Duibhne was in transports of delight and anticipation. At once, she wrote to Pinkie to tell her the exciting news. At last the slow tempo of her days was given a jolt, and an event was about to happen that would give her a life, rather than just an existence.

Of course she was familiar with the story. Even after so many years the dramatic events that took place before she was born were still common knowledge in Limerick.

She and Pinkie had talked about it many times, and wondered about Uncle Tom and the mysterious Bartley. They formed the romantic notion that being of 'Romany' stock he would look like Heathcliff.

Preparations were made for the arrival. A few older people on the estate (Bell was one) remembered the Earl and shook their heads, as if to say no good would come of his return to Ireland. Explanations had to be made and instructions given, and, standing in the stable yard, Claw delivered a short speech to his servants: Ronane the butler, Nonie, the cook, Bridie, the maid, Bell and his son, and everyone else who happened to be around and prepared to listen. He asked them to call his brother Mr Shannon. "That is the name he wishes to be known by."

"So, what are we to call you?" shouted a cheeky stable lad.

"My lord," replied Claw shortly.

"My Lord is up there," replied the boy, pointing at the sky.

Claw was vastly amused, and told the story many times over.

Tom was not to occupy his old room with the four-poster bed, as Claw slept there now. Instead, he and his son were given rooms in the west wing of the house where the roof was sounder, and it was not so damp. Since the death of Kathleen, Clonbarron was gradually returning to its previous state of decay, this in spite of Mr Kendrick's best efforts to keep it in good shape. He had a hard task trying to persuade Claw to spend money.

Duibhne and her father went to Shannon airport to meet the guests, if that was the right way to describe the two exiles. She was on the right track when she dreamed of Heathcliff. The nineteen-year-old Bartley, or Bart as his father called him, was a tall thin young man with olive skin and heavy brows. His eyebrows met in the middle which made him look as if he had a permanent frown. Duibhne remembered how Nanny had told her that men with eyebrows that went straight across like that were not to be trusted. Under a thatch of dead black hair were eyes of a surprisingly clear blue, and his chin had a deep cleft. The image was flawed in one particular, the blue eyes were short-sighted, and Bart wore spectacles. It was slightly disappointing, for who could imagine Heathcliff with glasses?

It was a poignant moment when the brothers clasped hands. At one time they had been so close; now they studied each other's faces, and both decided the other had aged. Claw regarded Tom with a mixture of amazement and horror. Indeed, he was a strange sight, dressed like an American from the Mid-west, even to the cowboy boots with heels (no spurs, Claw noticed) and a dreadful scarlet peaked hat on his head. Claw half-expected Americanisms such as 'Hi, how are you doing?' to come from his lips, but when Tom spoke his voice had not changed. He was busy issuing orders to everyone near him, "Carry this, if you please!" and "Get a move on there, I'm in a hurry!".

He had a way of standing very still, stocky short legs apart, with his right hand upraised, fingers wide apart and straight in the air. It was a small gesture which seemed to result in instant obedience. Duibhne was fascinated. She had heard how Uncle Tom used to purloin the bellhops from the Shelbourne Hotel, bribing them with promises of fame and fortune, and bringing them back to Clonbarron to work his racehorses. Now she could picture the technique he must have used, calling them to follow him with an imperious wave of his hand. When one of the airport officials had carried the heaviest bag to the waiting car, he was dismissed with a nod of the head.

"Look at the stuff he's brought with him," whispered Claw to his daughter. "Is he planning to stay for good?"

On the way home Tom talked incessantly about the Morgan horses he was breeding in Oregon. "They are the best," he said, "the best."

It was hard to tell how he felt about being in his own country once more, whether he was moved by the sight of the moist green fields and the soft Irish rain falling like a mist over the hills.

The boy, for he was only a boy, stared out of the window at the countryside.

"Do you like it?" Duibhne asked curiously.

"It's much like Oregon, but we have proper mountains at home." He had a pronounced American accent. ("It does not suit him," Claw was to say to her later. "Anyone can see he's bog Irish.")

When they had settled into their rooms, which seemed to suit them well (no comment was made about Tom's old bedroom), Bart was taken on a tour of the house. Family portraits and treasures were pointed out to him, and it made Claw very nervous.

"What sort of house have you in America, Tom?" he asked.

His brother whipped out a wallet from his coat pocket and showed them an aerial photograph of a modern house, like four white cubes stuck on each corner of a square, bright-blue swimming-pool in the centre.

"The stables are over here," Tom pointed out a row of smaller white cubes, "and they are spick and span. My yard is like a show ring all the year round."

When he saw the stable yard at Clonbarron he was scathing in his criticism of it. "What a hell hole," he said. "I don't know how you stand it, Claw." He said this many times over, as he stumped around, peering into the stables and scowling at the lads who stood open-mouthed, staring at him.

Perhaps he hoped to get a rise out of his brother – it had always been good sport in the old days – but it was not forthcoming. All Claw wanted was to be allowed to stay in the home he loved, and it comforted him to hear

Tom slanging everything at Clonbarron and boasting about his house in the States. He watched him anxiously, in case he showed any signs of wishing to return to his roots. He did not think the boy was favourably impressed with Ireland, but it was hard to get an opinion out of Bart. Duibhne thought he was shy, but her father attributed his silence to sullen arrogance.

The local gentry and the farming community were eager to meet Tom, having heard all about his past indiscretions. Many people had only heard the story, and had moved to Limerick after the events occurred. But his reputation lived on, and if the stout little man wearing odd clothes did not live up to the legend, they did not mind. They were enchanted when he turned up at Leopardstown races wearing a Stetson. They knew he was the Earl of Clonbarron even if he chose to forget it. Invitations arrived by the dozen, and the brothers were out nearly every night.

Bart declared he hated dinner parties, and Duibhne, who agreed with him, was happy to stay at home so that he was not left on his own. It was the polite thing to do, she explained to her father.

Most evenings, the two of them sat down to dine together in the sombre dining-room with its heavy furniture and family portraits, blackened by time. Ronane waited on them in the slapdash manner he adopted with them because they were young and did not matter, and when they had finished they went into the drawing-room where the curtains had been closed and the fire lit.

Because he was silent and awkward, like herself, Duibhne felt at ease with him. She tried to draw him out, to persuade him to talk about his childhood in America. She wondered how much he had been told about the circumstances of his birth and his mother. To while away the long hours they spent together she taught him a game called Spite and Malice. It was a card game for two people involving luck and skill, and Bart was a quick learner. He was also, she soon discovered, a bad loser, but she did not hold that against him.

During the day they went out riding together, and there was no doubt that Bart was perfection when it came to riding a horse. He was very confident, very restrained, and even his uncle had to admit, a joy to watch.

Claw distrusted him from the start. There was a sly deviousness about him he did not like, and he looked slovenly and unshaven all the time. It was a relief that he showed no interest in hunting. He would not have been proud of his nephew in the hunting field where sartorial elegance was the norm. Tom, on the other hand, thoroughly enjoyed his days out with the Limerick, and once with the Scarteen. On these days he did not sport his strange attire, and dressed like everyone else. He had discovered his old hunting clothes in a trunk in the attic, and made great play of the fact that they still fitted him.

At the dinner parties they attended, and from time

to time held at Clonbarron, he joined in the chatter as if he had never been away. He knew all the local landmarks; nothing much had changed, so it was easy for him to slot into hunting talk which was the same as it had been twenty years earlier. It alarmed Claw to see him so much in his element, cigar held between splayed fingers, sipping port and charming the company. The ladies were half in love with him, and Claw had the terrifying thought that he might fancy one of them and be persuaded to stay.

While the brothers were being entertained, Duibhne and Bart entertained each other. They went for walks together across the fields, accompanied by Duibhne's greyhound. Little Chancer, who had once been a champion, was now a pet, thereby disproving the theory that racing dogs cannot become house dogs when they retire from the track. She held him on a long rope until they were in the open country, then she freed him, and off he went like a grey streak. Bart was interested, and said he would like to have a young greyhound to race in the States.

One day, walking along the lane near the entrance to Clonbarron, they saw the tinkers. They had been in the same place for many years, and buried in time was the reason they had settled there. Mr Kendrick had tried to move them on, but they resolutely remained. As Duibhne and Bart approached they looked up and stared at them. They were sitting around a big fire, as was their custom, surrounded by rickety caravans and makeshift dwellings put together with pieces of wood and corrugated iron. The ground was littered with their possessions: old prams, pots and pans and remnants of clothing draped over the bushes. The children were half-dressed, barefooted and dirty, the women huddled in shawls.

"Do they wander from place to place?" Bart asked.

"No, they seem to stay put. This lot have been here for as long as I can remember."

"Why doesn't your father get rid of them?"

"I don't know. Perhaps it is not that easy. I think they have rights."

He stood and looked at them, and then he said, "They are probably my relations."

"If they are, you should speak to them."

She said it as a sort of dare, not expecting him to take any notice of the suggestion. To her surprise, he walked up to a man, older than the others, and said, "I am Lord Clonbarron's son."

The man removed a pipe from his mouth, and bared his discoloured teeth in a smile. He spoke, but they could not understand a word he said.

"They speak their own language," explained Duibhne, "but they understand what you are saying."

The old man called another man over, a giant of a fellow, and started talking to him, pointing at Bart all the while. The big man went to a caravan, and collected a short thick stick which was leaning against a door. He came back with it in his hand.

"Have you any money?" Duibhne was beginning to

feel nervous. She said to her companion, "I think that is what he wants."

Bart produced a five-pound note from his pocket.

"Too much," she said.

"No."

He handed the money over to the older man, and smiled at him. It was the first time Duibhne had seen him smile. The old man seemed pleased with the unexpected windfall, and walked over to a woman, wrapped in a red blanket, and showed the note to her, with a gabble of explanations. She looked up and favoured Bart with a toothless grin.

"Are they poor?" he asked Duibhne, as they walked away.

"Some people say they are very rich. They have chosen their way of life. It is their heritage. I'm sure they are not poor like some people in Irish villages who are hungry and cold."

That evening, after dinner, when they were sitting in front of the peat fire, she said, "You are very untidy-looking, you know. You make me think of the tinkers we saw this afternoon."

"That figures."

"Why don't you cut your fingernails? They are very long, and dirty as well."

"I don't know."

"And your hair. You ought to get your hair cut."

He was silent, and she wondered if he was offended. But, when she looked into his face, he did not look annoyed, so she continued. "Will you let me cut your fingernails?"

"Okay."

She skipped out of the room, gleeful. For the first time in her life she was flirting with a boy, teasing him, and she was enjoying every second.

She returned with a little leather manicure set that Pinkie had given her one Christmas, and she sat on the floor in front of his chair, and took one of his hands. Very carefully, she cut the nails on that hand with her little scissors. She liked holding his hand in hers, it was a thin bony hand, faintly clammy to the touch. She took time removing the grime from beneath the nails with an orange stick, and then smoothing the nail ends with an emery board. When she had finished he examined his fingers closely.

"Better," he said.

She turned to the other hand, and gave that a manicure as well. "That's done," she said, and kissed the back of it, very lightly. "I don't think I dare attack your hair. I am not expert enough and would make a mess of it."

"You might," he said.

"I'll take you to Limerick tomorrow," she said, "and one of the Miss Dooleys will wash it for you." The Miss Dooleys were two maiden ladies who owned a hairdressing salon in Limerick and, as they had the monopoly, did a roaring trade. Their shop was always crowded and, so as not to keep other people waiting, the women often left with the rollers still in, hidden under a scarf. They brought them back on their next visit. Miss Shelagh Dooley did the sets, and as she could only do one style, it meant that the heads of the Limerick ladies tended to look alike. A few favoured gentlemen were allowed in the salon for a short back and sides, and the elder of the sisters, Miss Moyna, performed that task in an adjoining room, separate from the main salon.

"I don't like the sound of that," he said, pretending not to be pleased with the attention.

As Duibhne was sitting on the floor, she leaned against one of his knees. Soon, she felt his hand come down and touch her shoulder. She became acutely conscious of his hand resting there.

"Why were you so long getting the scissors and things?" he asked.

She explained, "I had to go to the other side of the house, to my bedroom."

"Which side of the house?"

"Do you remember yesterday I took you into the old rose garden, with the statue in the middle?"

"I think so."

"My bedroom overlooks that garden."

"Where does your father sleep?"

"We took you into that room the first day you were here. With the big four-poster bed – you can't have forgotten!"

"Where I was conceived," he said.

She did not know how to reply to that. Conception was not one of the subjects she and Pinkie had ever discussed.

"I expect a lot of people were conceived in that bed," said Bart.

The brothers returned early that night, and surprised them. Duibhne rose quickly from her position on the floor.

"Couldn't stand another minute," explained Claw. "We felt so damned tired we could not keep our eyes open."

"Come on, Bart," said Tom. "Bed!"

Claw stayed behind for a few moments longer to talk to Duibhne. He was worried about her. It did not seem fair, leaving her to entertain that oaf every night.

"I'm afraid you must be very bored, my darling. If neither of you will come with us, what can I do?"

"I don't mind, really I don't."

"I can't think what you find to talk about. It must be terrible for you."

"It is not as bad as you think."

He kissed her on the forehead and said, "It can't last for ever. One day they will both be leaving us." He did not have an inkling of the effect his words had on her. She felt that time was racing along too fast.

After her bath that night, she studied her naked body in the long speckled looking-glass in her bedroom. She cupped her breasts in her hands, and then pressed her palms against her flat belly. She looked at herself from the front and from the side, and dusted herself with talc, another gift from Pinkie. The fine white powder hung in the air, and settled in a film on top of the dressing-table. Then she brushed her hair until it shone, and put on a clean nightgown, smelling sweetly of fresh air and soap.

When she was in bed, she lay looking at a shaft of light slanting across the room. It came from the light in the passage outside her room, which she had left switched on.

She wondered if he would come. She imagined that he would wait until everything was completely quiet. The tiniest sound made her heart beat faster, until she realised it was only the creaking bones of the old house. The floorboards groaned for no apparent reason, and the wind made sad noises as it penetrated the gaps in the windows.

The minutes turned into hours, and he did not come. The desire to sleep overcame her disappointment and, in the manner of the young, she pressed her cheek into the pillow, and slept.

CHAPTER NINE

During breakfast the following day, Duibhne felt Bart's eyes upon her. Blue eyes, behind the glasses, watching every movement she made. She was embarrassed, wondering if she had misunderstood his intentions on the previous evening, and thinking that she had behaved in a forward fashion. His penetrating gaze made her uncomfortable, as if he could read her shameful thoughts.

"Shall we go and see the horses?" she asked.

He nodded.

They went into the stable yard where a young man was mucking out. "This is young Bell," she said, "the son of Mr Bell."

The boy laid aside a pitchfork and doffed his cap.

"Mr Bartley is from the United States of America," she said.

"I heard that, Miss."

Bart was silent. He had nothing to say. They looked

at the horses in the stables, then she nodded and smiled at the boy, and they walked through the archway and across the drive to a field where the mares came to the fence to be patted on their velvet noses and nuzzled under their chins.

"They are so beautiful," said Duibhne. "Don't you think they are beautiful?"

He did not bother to answer her question, but he looked around him and said, "All this belongs to my father."

She was stung by the implications behind the statement. "I know," she said, "but Uncle Tom does not want it, and we do." She glanced at him. "So, what does it matter?"

He shrugged. "It does not matter to me," he said. "The house is creepy, and the stables are a mess. It is very different from our place in Oregon."

"There are lots of yards around here which are very neat and tidy, " she said, on the defensive. "You need not think everything is America is so perfect. I agree our yard is a mess, and I don't know why it has always been like that – there seems no way of changing it."

"Your father will not spend money on something that does not belong to him," said Bart, and she knew that he must be echoing words that Tom had said to him. "He is a mean guy."

"Da is not mean," she retorted, her eyes filling with tears. She was so upset by the direction the conversation had taken that she did not speak another word to him.

Acutely unhappy, she felt somehow he had managed to gain the upper hand, to be in command.

Silently they walked back to the house, and it was he who spoke next, "Tell me again, where do you sleep?"

Her heart pounding, she took him along the path encircling the house until they were standing outside the east wing. "That is my room," she told him, pointing to a window above them. "Pinkie, my governess, used to sleep in the room next to mine – that is her window on the left. Now she has gone, no one sleeps there, it is empty."

He stood looking at the window, rocking on his heels. "I see," he said. "I'm glad you have told me, as I didn't understand what you meant last night. It is such a big place."

"Isn't your father's place in Oregon as big as this?"

"It's big, okay, but small compared to this."

She was sure he would come that night. She lay between the sheets, very still and straight, listening for his step on the landing. As before, she had left the light on in the passage so that he could see his way to her room.

When she saw his dark form in the doorway, she whispered, "Shut the door."

She had no idea what to expect, she only knew that it was something that had to be done, and she had chosen Bart to do it. She could not exist forever without knowing what it was like.

She trembled when he climbed into the bed beside

her. He put his arms around her and kissed her hard on the mouth, his tongue forcing her lips to open. He threw back the bedclothes and she lay on her back, shaking. She noticed, in a detached way, that he was not wearing his spectacles. He took them off at night? Roughly, he pulled the nightgown over her head, so that she lay naked, defenceless. He peered at her, and she heard him draw in his breath sharply. She felt his body against hers, relentless, and, it seemed to her, in those agonising seconds, tearing her tender flesh. Absurd, incongruous thoughts tumbled in her mind – that Pinkie had not told her it would be painful, but then she would not have known, would she? All their talks had been before her bank manager came on the scene. Oh, Pinkie, are you happy with your bank manager?

Bart lay by her side, panting, the sweat pouring from his body. Not a word was spoken between them. As soon as he had regained his breath he got out of the bed, and left. She realised then that he must have pattered along the corridors from the other side of the house without any clothes on, and she wondered if anyone would see him on his way back.

She was wide awake, thinking about what had happened. She turned on the bedside lamp, and found there were bloodstains on the bottom sheet. She would have to tell Bridie that she had started her 'visitor' in the night (this was the name Pinkie had taught her to use when she was having a period). Pinkie, like Nanny before her, had left her. That was the trouble with nannies and governesses: they were impermanent people to take into your heart and love.

Truthfully, she had to admit she had not enjoyed it, that mysterious function so important to men and women in their pursuit of happiness. It had been over so quickly; surely that could not be right? She must have been a disappointment to him or he would have stayed longer, and that fear made her sad, so unbearably sad that she buried her face in the pillow and wept.

Weeping has to stop sometime, and she controlled her sobs and put on her nightgown. What would Da say if he found out what she had done? He would not be pleased, she was sure of that. Strangely, mixed with her shame was the conviction that she would like to try it again. There was a quality about the whole experience that made her long for it to be repeated. She fell asleep with that thought in her mind.

The following evening, the brothers stayed at home, an unusual occurrence. Perhaps they had become weary of dinner parties and late nights. Instead of the scraps Nonie cooked for the young people, a proper dinner was served. A bottle of claret and a bottle of port were brought up from the cellar, and the candles in the silver holders were lit.

Claw, carving the pheasant, looked up from the sideboard and enquired, "What sort of food do you eat in Oregon, Tom?"

"We go in for Mexican cooking," said Tom.

"Humph!" Claw made no further comment except to mutter something that sounded like, "Too hot for my liking."

Claw noticed that Duibhne was pale, and staring at her plate. He felt contrite because he had left her too long with her boorish cousin. The boy seemed to be in a sulk about something. His presence put Claw in a bad temper which lasted all evening.

Duibhne anguished about Bart's feelings for her, and whether her ignorance and immaturity had put him off. She made the mistake of thinking that he was a man of the world, which he was not. He was a boy.

He did come to her room that night, and stayed until the early morning light outlined the edges of the curtains. He did not speak, but he kissed her on her mouth, on her neck and on her body. She was ready for the hard thrust, and this time it gave her a feeling of pure pleasure and release. A peculiar sensation that travelled to every part of her, even to the tips of her toes. She tried to hold on to the glorious feeling, making little cries when she felt it was slipping away. It escaped her, and the tears coursed down her cheeks. Bart licked the tears with his tongue, and she pressed her lips against the little hollow at the base of his throat, and whispered, "I love you." He did not respond by saying he loved her, but she did not mind. She knew it was his strange silent way. When he got out of bed to leave, she held him back. In the early morning light she could see his young body, desiring her. He fell upon her, and the whole wonderful business started again.

During the afternoon of the same day they took Little Chancer into the fields and let him loose. Then their knees buckled and they sank to the grass, making love beneath a blue sky with a skylark soaring above them. The weather changes rapidly in Ireland, and soft rain began to fall on them, but they did not notice. The dog returned from his mad skirmish around the field, and stood by them. It was raining in earnest now, and the greyhound's coat was wet and shining like the pelt of a baby seal. They attached the rope to his collar and allowed him to drag them home.

They were drenched when they got back to Clonbarron, and explained to the two brothers that they had been caught in the rainstorm on their walk.

"Hot baths!" ordered Claw. A hot bath was his remedy for all forms of dampness. After hunting it was essential to immerse oneself in hot water without delay. In his view standing about in wet breeches was an invitation to illness.

He and Tom went into the morning-room where tea was laid out for them on a little table in the bay window. The sun reappeared from behind a black cloud and cast its rays across the lawn and into the room. There was a white Irish linen cloth on the table which was set with the Rockingham tea service and a silver teapot. The sun was warm on their faces, as they sat in two comfortable wing chairs which were covered in faded material, chosen by Kathleen many years before. Claw found himself thinking about her, as he often did, and wishing things had been different.

Upstairs, Duibhne and Bart found the house quiet, and there was a stillness about the empty passages, as if everyone was asleep. They went to their respective rooms to fetch dry clothes, and then met again in the corridor outside her room. At any moment a servant might appear, but they took a risk and bathed together in Duibhne's bathroom.

The bath took an eternity to fill, bulbous and vast, standing stolidly on ball and claw feet. The hot water bubbled out of the brass taps at a slow pace, and when it was halfway up, to the level of the green marks below the taps, they took off their wet clothes and climbed in. They sat facing each other at opposite ends of the bath, making the soaping of each other's bodies an excuse for further touching. Then, wet and slippery, they lay on the cold black and white tiled floor, and made love.

Some time elapsed before they changed into fresh dry clothing and made their way downstairs.

"We thought you were never coming," said Tom. "What on earth have you been doing all this time? The tea will be stone cold. Claw, ring for more."

"There is no need," said Duibhne. She felt light-headed, glowing, and her skin tingled. She felt sure they must see a change in her, notice her flushed face and bright eyes. She longed to reach out and touch Bart. She contented herself with looking at him while her father poured out two cups of tepid tea.

She thought, I shall remember this moment for ever: the ageing brothers sitting in the sunshine, the white tablecloth and the silver teapot on the stand and Bart looking at her with all the longing she felt herself.

He spoke. "It's been a great day." It was the closest he would get to a declaration of love.

"I'm glad to hear it," said Tom, "for it is your last in Ireland. Tomorrow we leave. I have the tickets."

"Oh, no," cried Duibhne, stricken.

"I'm afraid so," said her uncle. "I've had enough. I want to go home."

He had always been a man to make a speedy exit.

Praise be to God, thought Claw thankfully.

CHAPTER TEN

On his last night at Clonbarron Tom was busy packing until the early hours of the morning. He had brought so much luggage with him, and had acquired more during his stay. He had visited a tailor he knew of old, living in the nearby village of Hospital. Tom had forced the man out of retirement, and persuaded him to make breeches and suits for him which he now had difficulty in stowing into his suitcases. His son helped him with the almost impossible task, and there was no chance of escape.

Duibhne, lying awake, was thinking, he must come. Dear God, make him come. The praying, pleading went on all the night, with no sleep, and, when the morning came at last, she saw in the mirror a girl with lank hair and puffy eyes. She splashed cold water on her face, and went downstairs to face the family.

All through breakfast a tired and irritable Tom

fussed about the journey ahead and about the bad weather which he thought might prevent them from taking off. Bart was silent and morose, and did not look at Duibhne. Claw was trying to conceal his elation. He even had kindly feelings towards Bart now that he knew he was leaving them for good, as he hoped.

He drove them to Shannon airport through the driving rain. The brothers sat in the front of the car, Duibhne and Bart in the back, not speaking, not touching. They could not move because of the luggage piled all around them, squeezed into the back when there was no further room in the trunk.

"My God, what a country," exclaimed Tom, looking through the window at the grey sodden landscape. "I'm glad to leave it." He did not mention that he was returning to Oregon, a state renowned for its heavy rainfall.

When Duibhne said goodbye to Bart, leaning forward to kiss his cold cheek, she whispered: "Please write."

On the way home the weather changed. The sun came out, and there was a sharp clean feel to the air. "It's good," said Claw with satisfaction. "Our home will be our own again."

"But you liked Bart, didn't you?" asked Duibhne. She felt impelled to speak his name, and that morning she thought she had detected a softening in her father's attitude towards the boy.

"Not to be trusted," was Claw's decided reply. "He

has the shifty ways of his tinker forebears. Breeding tells."

After a week Duibhne started intercepting Sean, the postman, as he pedalled his bicycle along the drive. Every day she took from him a bundle of letters, with the excuse that she wanted to save him the trouble of delivering them himself. Mostly they were dull business letters addressed to Mr Kendrick, and nothing arrived from America.

Another anxiety assailed her. Surely the result of so much passion must have entered her body, and was, at this moment, creating a new life inside of her? In the privacy of her bedroom she examined her breasts in the looking-glass, and decided they looked swollen. She pressed her hands against her flat stomach, and wondered if awesome changes were taking place within. She agonised over what terrible fears the future might hold for her. In fact, the worry made her even thinner, and Claw noticed, and enquired, "Are you all right, my lamb?"

Her eyes filled with tears, and she longed to blurt out the truth to him. She must tell someone, and surely he would understand? In her heart, she knew that he would not understand, and would be heartbroken and bewildered. It was as well she did not put him to the test, for, soon after, the dreadful uncertainty was over. The blessed relief was tinged with sadness, as if her last tenuous link with Bart had gone.

Each day followed the last with a terrible sameness. She rode her horse before breakfast, exercised Little

Chancer, and managed to persuade her father to allow her to take driving lessons.

Pinkie wrote cheerful letters from Bournemouth. Married life seemed to suit her, and she was learning to play bridge. Duibhne wrote back, and, although she mentioned the visit of Tom and his son, she did not tell her old friend of her love for Bart. She tried to write it, but she could not find the right words. By now she had stopped hoping for a letter from him, and she steeled herself to accepting the truth: he was not going to write to her. In her mind she made excuses for him; after all, her father never wrote letters. Her kindly consideration for Sean's welfare came to an end, and she no longer went to meet him as he puffed up the drive.

Claw had recently formed a friendship with a widow called Lady Elizabeth Down. She became a frequent visitor to Clonbarron, and was forever airing her opinions and making her presence felt. Because of her influence a few improvements were made; the roof in the east wing was repaired at last, and new curtains appeared in the drawing-room. She was a tall, ungainly horsy woman with a loud voice and buck-teeth. Duibhne's indistinct memory of her beautiful dead mama made her wonder how he could possibly admire such a woman. It was difficult to assess how far the relationship had progressed. There was an innocence about Claw that made it hard to remember that he had once been married and fathered a child. Resentment of Elizabeth added to Duibhne's troubles.

She tried to put her feelings into words when she wrote to Pinkie: *I do not care for Elizabeth Down. She is very bossy and Da seems to be completely under her spell. She demands things and she gets them. Do you remember the comfy old sofa in the morning-room? It is gone, to goodness knows where, and another ugly thing is in its place. I expect she has given instructions for our sofa to be destroyed.*

Since writing the above, I have discovered the stable lads have the sofa in their rest room, so they are lucky!

If she comes to live here I don't know how I shall endure it. I am determined to make it clear to her how I feel.'

No doubt Pinkie knew her ex-pupil well enough to recognise the meaning behind the last sentence. Her answer came quickly, but was no comfort. *'I'm sure your father has been very lonely all these years,'* she began (now that she was married it was easy to say), *'Perhaps you should show a little more understanding? Do try to find some good qualities in the lady; I am sure if you look carefully you will find them. The sofa was in a bad state, you must agree; the springs had gone and it was very uncomfortable.*

It sounds to me as if you have not got enough to do. I'm sure there are courses in Limerick which might interest you. French conversation, for instance. Your French is very shaky. Or, what about classes in embroidery? You used to love making things when you were a little girl, and there must be someone who could teach you how to work tapestries and do fine needlework. Think about it, dear. I am so glad you are learning to drive, that will make a big difference in your life. I don't know what I would do without my car . . . '

This was not what Duibhne wanted to be told. Her dislike for Elizabeth was intensified when she noticed that she called her father 'Charles'. It was the name he had not used since before his army days. Perhaps it reminded him of his youth, for he appeared to like it. His daughter thought it was just another irritating hold the woman had over him, a special name that no one else used.

In despair, Duibhne threw Pinkie's letter in the wastepaper basket, and sat down and wrote to Tom Shannon.

'Dear Uncle Tom,

Since you left I have felt very much at a loose end, and it has made me think I would like to travel to other parts of the world, instead of staying in the same place for the rest of my life.

Please may I visit you for a while? I know it is a lot to ask, but I so want to come. If you are agreeable I will ask Da to give me the money for the ticket.

With love to you and Bart,

Divvy.'

She wondered if she should say that she would ask Da to provide her keep while she was with them, but decided that it sounded insulting. When the letter was posted, she felt guilty and excited in turn. She started to waylay Sean again, and, in a few weeks, was rewarded with a blue airmail envelope. It was addressed to Claw, and she put it beside his porridge plate on the breakfast table.

With a beating heart she watched him slit open the envelope with a knife.

"Tom has written asking you to go and stay with him in Oregon. Surely you will not want to go?"

"I do, I do!" cried Duibhne. "It would be so good for me to travel! You know you went abroad when you were young."

"To France, just the once," he growled. "Never as far as America, and my time abroad during the war did me no good at all."

"I cannot stay at Clonbarron for ever, much as I love it. Please, dearest Da, let me go!"

"I'll talk to Elizabeth," said Claw, "she will know what to do."

"Oh, do we have to ask her? Couldn't we work it out ourselves?"

She might have felt more charitable towards the lady if she had heard her reaction to Claw's plea for a decision about the invitation.

"Of course the child must go," she said. "There is nothing here for a girl like her; all the young people have moved away or gone to England. This is a wonderful opportunity for her, and will help with her shyness."

Claw did not know his daughter was shy, but reluctantly he asked Mr Kendrick to write the letter to Tom Shannon and make the necessary arrangements for the journey.

He flatly refused to allow her to fly, so Duibhne travelled to England on the dreaded ferry (a calm journey this time and almost enjoyable), then by train to Southampton where she boarded the *Queen Mary* bound for New York.

She travelled first class, and when she entered her cabin she found flowers and a note from her father: *'One month only, love Da.'* The sight of the flowers almost reduced her to tears – it was so unlike him to think of such a thing (she did not guess that they had been Elizabeth's idea). Standing in the luxurious cabin with its private bathroom she felt very much alone. Travelling on her own was daunting for a girl who had never been further than Ascot, and then accompanied by her father.

When she ventured into the dining-room she found that she was seated at the Captain's table. She met a group of rich Americans, middle-aged husbands and smartly dressed self-assured wives, who were enchanted by the beautiful girl, and were kind to her. Also, sitting at her table was a famous film star. She and Pinkie had seen him many times in the days when they used to go to the cinema in Limerick. Here he was, sitting next to her, large as life and looking every bit as handsome as he did in the films. It was very strange seeing him in the flesh, and even stranger when later he tapped on her cabin door.

Despite his fame and good looks she was not tempted, for she was loyal to one person. She explained this to him, firmly, but with charming good manners, and he found her ingenuousness delightful. The voyage took five days, and, as she refused to sleep with him and there was no one else on board to interest him, he occupied the time in telling her how she should dress, how she should do her hair (he refused to allow her to have it cut) and giving her lessons on the dance floor.

He was very attentive, much to the amusement of the other passengers, and, without him, Duibhne might have been bored, for a liner is not the most entertaining place for a young girl. Instead, she found she was enjoying herself. When they docked at New York he insisted on accompanying her to the station. He kissed her gently on the lips before she climbed on to the enormous train which was to take her westwards. Suddenly, a man leapt from the crowds on the platform and took a photograph of them. It was her first experience of such a thing, and it made her nervous. She imagined the picture would appear in some newspaper, but she never saw it. She never saw the film star again either, although she followed his career with interest, and his marriages of which there were many.

The train stopped at Chicago, and she had to break her journey for a whole day before boarding another train at six o'clock in the evening. Wandering around the city by herself made her feel very lonely, and it was a relief to settle into the sleeping car in the evening. The journey to Portland, with its beautiful and majestic scenery, was very long, and she spent most of the time sitting in the open observation coach at the back, getting smuts on her face from the engine. The rugged country flashing by gave her a headache, and the sheer grandeur of it made her long for the green simplicity of Ireland.

At last the train ground to a stop in Portland station. She had arrived, but there was no one there to meet her. All Mr Kendrick's cleverly worked out plans had ended in this disaster. She was on a bustling railway station, surrounded by people scurrying this way and that way, in a strange country where she did not even know how to operate a payphone. Tom must have either made a mistake in the date or forgotten all about her.

She did not know what to do. A woman noticed the young girl, sitting on a big suitcase, close to tears. "Can I help you, honey?" she asked.

Duibhne explained the situation, and managed to find Tom's telephone number in her bag. The woman took it, and went off to telephone.

After what seemed an interminable delay, Tom arrived in a truck to pick up his niece. Loftily, he called out "Thanks!" in the direction of the woman who had given up so much of her time and had insisted on staying with Duibhne until someone came for her. Her case was hauled into the back of the truck.

As she climbed in beside her uncle, the girl said to the woman, "Thank you so much. You have been very kind . . ."

"You're welcome. Have a good holiday!"

Tom gave no reason for not meeting the train, but he explained that Bart was busy breaking in a colt and had been unable to come.

He drove through Portland, a busy crowded city with wide streets and big department stores. When they reached the outskirts Duibhne noticed that most of the houses were made of wood. As they turned on to the freeway, Tom said, "Look behind you and you'll see Mount Hood."

It was the first time she had seen a mountain of that size, topped with snow gleaming in the sunshine. "Does anyone climb it?" she asked.

"Oh, yes, it's an easy climb. I have done it several times, with a guide of course. There is a cabin at the peak where you can spend the night before making the descent the next day. There is a story that someone struggled to the top, collapsed on the bed in the cabin, and, when he awoke in the morning he found there was a bottle of milk left for him outside the door!" He laughed. Duibhne liked his laugh, unaffected and masculine. She began to warm towards him, and feel more relaxed.

"Has Bart climbed Mount Hood?"

"Never. Not interested."

They reached a part of the freeway where the traffic thinned out, the four lanes becoming two. On one side of them was a range of hills covered with dark coniferous trees, on the other an expanse of green, with an occasional house standing by a river, which, like a long grey snake, disappeared from view and then reappeared again. "The Willamette," said Tom. At one point the river was wide enough for them to see the logs clustered on the water.

"It is so green," said Duibhne wonderingly. "I did not expect it to look like this. It is like Ireland." It was so different from the granite wilderness she had viewed from the train.

She must have said the right thing, for Tom looked pleased. "Nowhere like it in the country," he told her with satisfaction. "It's the rain that does it. Oregon has a hell of a lot of rain, and it makes everything lush and green. You are right, like Ireland. That's why I chose to live here." He laughed again. "Hardly worth your coming all this way, is it?"

CHAPTER ELEVEN

Duibhne expected a house that was so modern on the outside would be modern on the inside as well. She did not know that when Tom Shannon hired an architect to design his house, at the same time he wrote a letter to his brother, requesting that certain things from Clonbarron be sent to him in Oregon. As Tom was the rightful owner of Clonbarron and everything in it, and Claw merely a younger son with no rights, the request had to be complied with, and he and Kathleen sadly collected the furniture, paintings and porcelain on Tom's list (more a demand than a list) and arranged for their shipment to the United States.

When, eighteen years later, Duibhne stepped into the cool white interior of Tom's house, it was like coming home. The stately Lady Mary Claughessy (1712 to 1772) adorned one white wall in the entrance hall, and Duibhne knew that her husband, Viscount

Claughessy (1716 to 1798) was in the dining-room at Clonbarron.

There were many paintings of horses in Tom's house, and Claw had hated parting with these. Horses standing stiff and immobile, as if they never moved, held by the cardboard-like figure of a stable boy dressed in livery. Horses galloping, legs splayed, and shiny chestnut mares standing beside their foals in bright emerald fields, with Clonbarron somewhere in the background.

In the sitting-room of Tom's house there was a long shelf which was completely covered with pieces of porcelain, standing in line. Duibhne thought they looked unhappy in such surroundings, but later she learned they had belonged to Tom's mother, and were very precious to him.

The cumbersome furniture looked awkward too, as if it did not belong. In Clonbarron everything seemed so permanent, settled in for hundreds of years, the tallboys and dressers standing as if they had been on the same spot for ever, forming a barrier against goodness knows what sort of dry or wet rot.

Tom had thought of calling his stud farm Clonbarron, but, perhaps realising that he could not reproduce his childhood home in another culture, he called it Shannon instead. He was only interested in breeding now, and had no horses in training, having decided to give up racing when he left Ireland.

Duibhne was nervous about seeing Bart again. She

wondered whether those few weeks in Ireland had been as important to him as they had been to her. He would realise the reason behind her visit, and perhaps he would feel he was being trapped into a relationship he did not want. When Tom whistled for someone to take her suitcase from the truck, she thought he might come, but a boy appeared and carried the luggage to the room assigned to her.

Her bedroom looked out on to green wasteland with mountains in the distance. It seemed as if they were miles away from anywhere. There was not a house or a farm in sight, and when she ventured into the corridor in order to look out of the window facing the opposite direction, the view was the same.

As she came down the stairs, she saw Bart in one of the soft leather chairs, reading a newspaper.

"Hello, Bart."

He did not get up, but said, defiantly American, the one word, "Hi."

So with these words they greeted each other, and then could think of nothing more to say. For this Duibhne had travelled a great distance to be by his side.

It was better that night when he came to her room. It made all the waiting, the anguish, worth while. She was worried that Tom would hear them. They did not have a corner of the house to themselves, as they had at Clonbarron.

By the time Duibhne came down to breakfast the next day, Tom and his son had left the house. They were gone all day, and on the days after, so it was lonely. There were only two ways of getting beyond the long dusty track, the truck and an ancient Dodge motor car. Tom and Bart usually commandeered the Dodge.

It would have been unbearably lonely for Duibhne if it had not been for Magda Angelo.

Magda was the unexpected addition to the Shannon household, and Duibhne wondered why neither Tom nor his son had mentioned her existence during their stay in Ireland. It was extraordinary that her name had never cropped up in their conversation, and there seemed to have been no communication with her. On the first evening, Duibhne observed the woman hovering in the background, and when they went into the dining-room for the evening meal, she dished it up, and then sat down at the table with them.

Duibhne wondered if she was a servant, but then Tom said, "Divvy, this is Magda, who is my love, and puts up with me," and she realised she was not a servant.

Magda came from New Mexico, the daughter of a well-to-do restaurant owner who had lost patience with her because she was shy and gauche, and no help to him in his business. She had met Tom sixteen years before Duibhne came to stay with them, and had been his mistress all that time. It was difficult to understand the attraction between these two very different people, the rotund aristocratic horse-dealer and the quiet retiring woman.

Duibhne, a shy person herself, found shyness in others understandable, and she set about trying to break down the defence Magda put up against anyone who was not close to her. It looked as if that meant everyone except Tom.

Magda had been the only woman in that household for so long, cooking delicious meals for Tom and Bart and the stable hands, and it seemed to Duibhne she must welcome female companionship.

Gradually, very gradually, Duibhne perceived that she did welcome it. The walls of reserve surrounding this strange fascinating woman began to crumble. In her low husky voice she told the girl that the town of Eustace lay about fifteen miles away. It was the nearest place of any size, and the stud manager drove her there once a week to get provisions. He would take Duibhne as well, if she cared to accompany Magda.

They shared the passenger seat of the truck, as Tom and Bart were using the Dodge. They bumped all the way to Eustace, holding on to each other for support. Duibhne was not impressed with the town which was desolate and garish. The office blocks were all the same, the gas stations festooned with coloured flags, and the houses, made of wood, dark and dreary with identical verandas in front of each one.

The manager, whose name was Virgil, parked the truck in a parking lot, and the three of them trooped into the supermarket, picking up trolleys on the way.

"Goodness," said Duibhne when she saw the

supermarket, the shelves laden with tins and the fruit and vegetable section bulging with produce. "Limerick has nothing like this."

"This is small compared with most," Magda told her. "Eustace hasn't a big population so the shops aren't up to much. The best stores are in Portland." She hurried along the lines, checking her list very efficiently and, in a short time, the trolleys were filled to overflowing with everything they would need for a week, including bottles of spirits and cans of beer.

Tom and Magda had few friends, which was strange remembering all the invitations he had received while he was in Ireland. At home, after dinner, he was content to spend the rest of the evening in his special chair, purloined from Clonbarron, and punctuate his television-watching with gulps of whisky. Usually he was fairly drunk by ten o'clock. Duibhne could not recall him drinking so much at Clonbarron, but perhaps he got drunk at the dinner parties he attended – no Limerick hostess would be surprised at that. Bart drank quantities of canned beer, and sometimes he was as fuddled and sleepy as his father, and as boring to the two women who sat with them, occasionally exchanging a sympathetic little smile.

Duibhne kept assuring herself that things had not changed between her and Bart, but part of her was looking forward to the time when the month was up. How would she feel about parting from him again? It disturbed her that no words of love ever passed his lips.

"My father has spent a lot of money getting me here," she complained to Magda, "and for what? I am more isolated than I was at home. They do not even allow me to ride their precious horses."

"There is the pool –"

"I can't spend all day in the pool," Duibhne interrupted impatiently.

"You are feeling homesick?" asked Magda. "I think perhaps you look forward to returning to Ireland?"

"I don't know."

It was true, she did not know. She had come to this godforsaken place so sure of her love for Bart, and of his love for her. She would have travelled anywhere in the world to be near him. Now she was not so certain about how she felt. Even their lovemaking had lost some of the magic and become almost a habit. He came to her room nearly every night, silent, demanding, departing in the early hours without saying a word to her, leaving her feeling dejected and full of doubts. She had no one to talk to about her fears for the future, about her unsatisfactory present. Although by now she was getting on very well with Magda, she did not know her well enough to confide in her to that extent – that's what she thought anyway, having never known anyone in her life with whom she could be completely open.

In a few days' time she would be starting on the journey home. She thought of Claw's message exhorting her to stay in America for one month only. When she first read it she had thought it inconceivable that she would be returning so soon. Her thoughts had been muddled, but at the back of her mind she hoped she would stay with Bart for ever. She even had a little daydream in which she wrote to her father and told him that she was marrying her cousin.

There was a reason behind her sense of despondency and her slight show of irritation with the ever-kindly Magda. By this time, she believed herself to be pregnant. Her last escape had made her complacent, and she did not think it would happen to her. She was ignorant of birth control; Pinkie had not considered it necessary to instruct her on that score, and Bart was not interested. They were not close enough to discuss such matters.

Tom and his son talked of her departure, neither seeming to care very much, just discussing ways and means of getting her to Portland Station to catch her train. The day came nearer and nearer, and Duibhne began to panic. She knew that she must tell Bart, and she did, late in the evening after Tom had stumbled off to bed, followed by Magda.

She took a deep breath, and said, "I think I am going to have a baby." Both Pinkie and Nanny had considered the word 'pregnant' unladylike, so instinctively she did not use it.

A dark flush suffused his face. He looked at her with disbelief which quickly turned to anger. "You stupid bloody bitch," he said.

The reply stunned her. She, the beloved child, protected all her life, had never expected to hear such words levelled at her. She stared at him, open-mouthed, feeling she could not breathe, that she would faint.

At last she managed to say, "Surely you love me a little?"

He did not answer her question.

"What shall I do?" she asked pathetically.

"How should I know?"

They sat on the edges of their chairs, facing each other. Bart's hands hung limply over his knees, and he stared at the carpet, head down. He looked a picture of misery, and Duibhne suddenly felt sorry for the trouble she had brought upon him. She put out a hand to touch his arm, but he shrugged it off.

"It is not my fault," he said at last. "You had best go home."

"You know I can't do that."

"Why not? Your father will look after you."

She thought of Lady Elizabeth Down, and the suggestion seemed even more impossible. She could not imagine telling Claw, and how he would receive such news.

"It would be a scandal," she said, "and anyway I do not want to leave you."

"Well then, we had better speak to my father. He will know what to do." He was relieved that he was about to pass the burden on to someone else's shoulders. For the first time Duibhne noticed how young he was.

"Do you think that is a good idea?" she asked doubtfully.

But already he was at the foot of the stairs, shouting, "Dad! Come here a minute, will you?"

Tom came at once, still fully dressed.

"What's the matter?" he demanded, looking suspiciously from one to the other.

Bart pointed a finger at Duibhne who had slumped in her chair. "She's pregnant."

"Yours?" roared his father, and Duibhne, even at such a moment, was fascinated to see his face redden, as his son's had done, and upstanding blue veins appear on his forehead.

He did not wait for the answer to his question. He said, "You bloody young fool, you've done it this time, boy!"

Duibhne did not know what he meant, but she could see that his fury had made him almost apoplectic. Like so many men of his generation he did not care to remember his own sexually colourful past, and was intolerant of any behaviour he deemed to be beyond the pale. He was continually ranting on about the 'decadence of the young people of today' and the 'falling off of moral standards'.

"She can't stay here," he pronounced. So far neither he nor his son had addressed Duibhne by name. Now Tom spoke to Bart only, as if Duibhne was not there. "Magda and I are not having that. It's not the sort of thing she would put up with for a moment, I can tell you that. You must write to Claw and tell him his daughter is returning in foal, due to your crass stupidity. That is the only thing you can do."

Bart was surprised. He had thought his father would sympathise with him, and blame the girl. Now it seemed as if it was the other way round. He knew all about his gypsy mother and the dismal hovel where he had been born. Tom had no right to sit in judgement on him, and he resented it.

"I don't want to do that," he said. "I'll find somewhere for us to live."

Duibhne rejoiced to hear these words. She got out of the chair and stood by his side, slipping her hand into his. She felt the pressure of his fingers.

"I'll find another job too," said Bart defiantly.

"Oh, no, you won't," said Tom. "I can't afford to lose you just because of that pasty-faced whore. You will come to work here as usual and, with the money you earn, you will have enough to live on."

It was remarkable that neither father nor son considered the possibility of Duibhne having an abortion. Tom and Claw were lapsed Catholics and Bart had no religion at all. The Catholic tradition went back centuries in the Clonbarron family. At one time a small chapel adjoined the house in Limerick but it was now derelict. The brothers had been brought up to go to Mass and the faith was in their bones. They decided to abandon it when they returned home after the war, and they told each other that they had only kept it up in the past for their mother's sake. With her death they could do as they pleased. But it was hard to go against the principles they had been taught to respect. Abortion was a mortal sin, and, although he would never admit it, Tom still regarded it as a sin.

"I'll ask Virgil to look out for a rented place for you both," he said. He was more himself, more composed.

Bart looked quite pleased; he rather liked the idea of having somewhere of his own. Duibhne felt her world was crashing down around her, and she was powerless to do anything about it. As long as she lived she would never forget her uncle calling her a 'pasty-faced whore' and she felt very far removed from the gentle loving atmosphere at home. She wondered if she had lost it for ever.

"I hope you have remembered you are first cousins," went on Tom, almost flippantly. "The child of such a union will probably be an imbecile."

It was his parting shot before he stumped off to bed.

CHAPTER TWELVE

Duibhne wondered what Magda would say to her when she saw her the next morning. She knew she would be in the kitchen, and she found her there cooking bacon and eggs in a big frying-pan. The men had already been fed, and had left to attend to their various duties. The big kitchen was full of cooking smells and the aroma of hot coffee.

Duibhne sat on the edge of the wooden table and watched Magda. She did not expect her to comment on something which, no doubt, had been imparted to her on the previous night when Tom climbed into bed beside her. She was wrong, for Magda, turning the eggs over (once-over-easy the men called it) and then transferring them to two plates, said, "I hear you are not leaving us after all."

"No, I'm not. You know the reason?"

"Yes. I don't know whether to say I'm sorry or

happy for you, it depends on how you feel about it. Perhaps you don't know yourself." When there was no response, she said practically, "Do you want breakfast?"

"No, thank you."

Magda added slices of crispy bacon to the two plates, and said, "Take these to the boys in the dining-room, and then we'll have some coffee in here." Tom and his son always ate in the dining-room, and the men sat down to meals at the big kitchen table.

Duibhne took the two plates and put one in front of Bart who did not look up, and one in front of Tom, who, to her surprise, half-rose to his feet. He said kindly, "Thank you, Divvy, Did you cook for us?"

"No, Magda did, as usual."

His unusual display of gallantry made her feel intensely embarrassed. She wondered if he was remorseful for his rudeness to her on the previous evening. She had no intention of forgetting it, however hard he might try to ingratiate himself with her. She hurried away, without looking at either of the two men.

She and Magda drank the steaming coffee, sitting at the kitchen table. Duibhne felt chilled, and warmed her hands on the hot mug. The smell of the empty frying-pan on top of the stove nauseated her. She felt humiliated, sick at heart and terribly alone.

"Bart will not marry you," Magda interrupted the silence in a matter-of-fact voice. "they never marry. It is against their principles."

"Not even when there is a child?" asked the girl.

"Not even then. I don't want to be unkind, my dear, but I think it best that you know what to expect." She had never talked so openly before and Duibhne sensed there was a new feeling of kinship between them, as if the turn in events had wiped out the old constraint.

"Tom and I had a child," went on Magda, "a girl. She died when she was two months old. A cot death."

"I'm so sorry."

"I can talk about it now," she said, but Duibhne was sure this was the first time she had done so. "Her name was Mary. Before she was born I tried to convince Tom that it was the right thing for us to get married, but he bore a grudge, you see, because Bart could never inherit. He did not want to take the risk of having a legitimate son who would have a claim to the title and leave Bart out." She paused. "After Mary died I did not bother any more. What was the point? We just carried on as we had done before."

"It sounds to me as if he behaved very selfishly," said Duibhne.

"Obstinate more than selfish, I'd say," replied Magda. "He pretends that the title means nothing to him, that he prefers being plain Mr Shannon, but actually, the whole family pride bit means the world to him. He is a strange mixture, my Tom."

"But that has nothing to do with Bart," Duibhne argued. "He could marry without affecting anything." She could not help feeling that Claw would be more understanding if she and Bart were married.

"He follows his father in all things. Tom is against marriage, so Bart is as well. My advice to you is to get in touch with your Da, as you call him, and go home. There is no happiness for you here."

"Bart is the father of the child I am going to have. We must stay together."

"Bart is too young for fatherhood," said Magda decidedly. "He has not the character for it."

Duibhne felt the tears come to her eyes. Magda noticed, and touched her hand. "Oh, my dear . . ."

"I'm staying," said Duibhne stubbornly. "I hope to make a success of things."

"That being the case," said Magda, removing her hand, "I think I should take you to see a doctor. You want to find out whether this is a fuss about nothing, don't you? It could be a false alarm."

"I don't think so," said Duibhne slowly. "I don't think I'm wrong. I feel different, special. I am unhappy about the dreadful mess I have got myself into, but, at the same time, I don't want anything to change. It is hard to explain."

"I think I know what you mean," said Magda. "I knew almost at once when I was having my little girl, and the feeling of fulfilment never left me all through my pregnancy, and stayed with me after she was born. For once in my life, I was completely happy."

"It is so sad," said the girl. "How did you cope with such grief?"

"Not well, I can tell you," replied Magda frankly. "It

was touch and go between Tom and me and, for a time, neither of us thought our relationship would survive such a battering. I stayed because I thought he needed me, and I'm glad I did."

Virgil instructed the head stable boy to take them to Eustace in the truck. He could not take them himself, as Tom had given him the Dodge with orders to find somewhere for the young people to live. The nightmare drive was made even more uncomfortable because the boy drove too fast. Clinging to each other, the two women implored him to slow down, but he took no notice. He knew that no one in Mr Shannon's establishment would punish him for reckless driving.

Observing her greenish pallor, the doctor said, "Not feeling too good, eh?"

"No." She was thinking of the return journey, dreading it.

He examined her. "It's early days, of course, but I don't think there is much doubt. I'll let you know the result of the test, but I'm pretty sure it will be positive."

Later, when he was behind his desk, and she was seated in front of him, she noticed that he was quite old. Thickset, with a thatch of snow-white hair, the sort of hair most American doctors seem to have when they get close to retirement.

He looked sharply at her over half-moon spectacles. "Are you pleased about this, young lady?" He knew she was unmarried.

"Yes," she replied truthfully.

"Good. My name is Dr Heinrich Leroy, and I want you to come and see me in a month's time, and every month after that. My receptionist will arrange the appointment. Don't forget to come."

"He is a nice man," said Magda, as they walked away from the Medical Arts Building. "I think he will look after you well."

At last they got back to Shannon. Duibhne climbed out of the truck and staggered into the house. She made straight for the downstairs cloakroom, her stomach churning, and leant over the basin fighting off waves of nausea. After bathing her face with cold water she felt better.

"That's the last time we go to Eustace in that terrible truck," pronounced Magda. "It is bad for the baby, all that bouncing about." She was behaving like a mother towards Duibhne, anxious, solicitous.

While they had been away Virgil had found them a place to live. "Sounds all right to me," said Tom. Duibhne could tell there was not going to be much choice about it.

"She is too tired to go anywhere today," said Magda firmly, "They can look at it tomorrow."

The apartment was about ten miles from Shannon on the shore of a large lake, Lake Trevelyan, named, as Duibhne was to learn later, after one of the early explorers of the region. The house on the lake belonged to an elderly widow, Mrs Mactaggart, who let the bottom floor in order to supplement her pension. Her part of the house was approached by rickety wooden steps. In front of the house there was an unmade road the width of one car, then a tangled mass of bulrushes merging into the lake.

The ground-floor apartment had a fair-sized veranda on the lakeside and two doors, one inside the other: a mesh door on the outside and the entrance door within. The mesh door was a protection against mosquitoes, a problem in that environment. Always, Duibhne was to dislike the mesh door, and find it sinister and frightening. When someone rang the bell, and the inner door was opened, all that could be seen was a dark shadowy figure on the other side of the netting.

The inside of the apartment was furnished throughout in brown and orange. These two colours were predominant in the carpet which swirled in the main room, and then flowed into the bedroom. The colours appeared again in the curtains, unlined, and in the rough material of the upholstered armchairs. A flight of steps led to a cellar where a thin layer of water lay on the stone floor. It smelled of stale air. "I should keep the cellar door closed," advised Virgil hastily, shutting it and locking the door with a key. He was showing them over the apartment on his own. Tom had not wanted to come and Magda was cooking the evening meal. There was no sign of the owner of the house.

The kitchen provided all the basic needs. A small electric stove. A refrigerator. An old cracked sink with a wooden draining-board, soft with constant use. An off-balance table leaned drunkenly against one wall, with two plastic-topped stools beneath it. Under the sink was a shelf for cleaning materials, and there was another for the pots and pans. On one side of the kitchen was a glass-fronted cabinet containing an assortment of thick glasses and chipped china. Below, a drawer (which Duibhne found out later was forever sticking) full of cheap cutlery, battered wooden spoons and odds and ends. The kitchen had one window looking out on to another unmade road at the back of the house, with a dark forest of trees behind, and another, very small one, looking out on to the lake.

The bedroom was quite large with a double bed covered with a chenille bedspread (brown again). Next door was a bathroom and, as it was so small, they went in separately to look at it. The bath was stained, and so was the lavatory basin. Duibhne turned away from the sight of the lavatory and, instead, looked beyond, into the bedroom, and the view from the window. The lake was a dark blue expanse, shimmering with silver lights, the spruce-covered mountains behind it.

"It's lovely," she breathed.

"Okay?" said Virgil, much relieved, and, turning to Bart, "Okay?"

"I guess so."

They went back into the living-room where there was a television set and, surprisingly, a large print on the wall of a loch in Scotland, with the name AJ Andrews, Glasgow, in the corner.

"I'll fetch Mrs Mactaggart," said Virgil, and they heard him open the two doors and bound up the steps outside.

Duibhne and Bart stood silently in the depressing room, far apart and with nothing to say to each other.

Mrs Mactaggart was a shock. She looked like a witch, with long white straggly hair and wild eyes. With a sinking heart, Duibhne realised that this was to be her only neighbour in that out-of-the-way place. The old woman signed the contract with a spidery signature – *Florence Mactaggart* – and Bart signed as well. The apartment was theirs.

Duibhne wrote to Claw telling him that she was not coming home. It was a difficult letter for her to write. Hard to explain the circumstances, but she told him everything with frankness and humility. Perhaps she deviated from the absolute truth when she wrote, *'I am very happy. Please do not worry about me.'* She went on to tell him about her new home, situated by a beautiful lake. She tried not to think of the anguish her letter would cause him.

It was summer and, although the wooden house was always in the shade, the water sparkled in the sunshine and, in the evenings, the mountains reflected the blaze of the setting sun, and became like giant scarlet embers against the darkening sky, casting a red glow on the shimmering water. Looking at such dramatic beauty Duibhne could not help but feel hopeful.

She and Bart settled into a sort of routine. He went

off to work for his father every day, in the second-hand car Tom had bought for him. Duibhne borrowed cookery books from Magda and tried to make interesting dishes for him to eat when he returned in the evening. Duibhne was not alone very much during the day because Magda was usually there. She bribed Virgil to drive her over in the early afternoon, picking her up again in the evening, so that she was back at Shannon in time to cook the dinner.

One day she arrived on her own, driving a bright yellow Volkeswagen Beetle, the little car owned by almost every housewife in the United States. "I came under my own steam," she announced proudly. "It is mine, all mine. I bought it today. I thought I must have a car of my own in case I have to come to you in a hurry if you need me."

It was amazing that she had never thought of buying a car for herself before. She was a woman of independent means, but Tom did not like her to have freedom: he wanted to be in charge. She had gone against his wishes because a new excitement had opened up for her. Her whole life, her existence, had become centred on Duibhne and the unborn child. Tom was still there, of course, very important in her scheme of things, and she was determined that she would continue to make him happy. The new car meant that she could juggle her time between visiting Duibhne and being there when Tom came home in the evening.

The hot steamy days of August merged into

September, and then the rain began to fall in earnest. Before, it had come in little spurts; now it fell relentlessly, pattering on the wooden tiles of the roof, pitting the blue surface of the lake, and a permanent grey cloud settled over the mountains. The water lapped almost to the edge of the steps, forcing its turbulent way through the barrier of rushes. The trees beside the house dripped with lichen, crawling over the trunks and into the branches. Like a cancerous growth the lichen spread everywhere, disfiguring the paths and hiding the light.

Bart became increasingly impatient with Duibhne. Lying in the bed beside her, he cursed the swollen stomach which got in his way. A pregnant woman held no charms for him, and he was not looking forward to the arrival of the baby. He stayed away for a night, telling her that he was needed at Shannon. She was terrified, lying alone in the bed, unable to sleep. The child inside her was active, as if aware of her fears. She could not find a comfortable position. And, when at last she slept, she awoke in the morning to the sound, audible through the thin boards of the ceiling, of Florence talking to herself. Sometimes she watched her, dressed like a bag-woman, with down-at-heel, old-fashioned boots, wandering along the shoreline, picking up bits and pieces and putting them in a sack.

"You can't leave me in this place alone at night," she pleaded with Bart. "Not with that crazy woman above, muttering to herself. Please, please don't stay away again."

He promised he would not, but a few days later he did not return at the usual time.

The following day Magda came to collect Duibhne to take her to Eustace for her monthly check-up. Dr Leroy noted the girl's anxious appearance, the hands twisting in her lap. The lovely face had hollowed cheeks.

"Feeling all right?" he asked, looking at her over his glasses.

"Yes."

"Happy?"

"It's a bit lonely where we live," she explained, "but Magda comes to see me." Dear Magda, sitting in the waiting-room, ready to take her back.

He continued to look searchingly at her.

"It rains so much," she said, feeling something was expected of her.

"Well, you ought to be used to that," he replied. "From what I hear Ireland is a terrible place for rain."

"It's different," she said. She thought of soft Irish rain, making the grass even greener and sweetening the pure fresh air.

"Is that fellow of yours looking after you?" asked the doctor suddenly.

Immediately, she knew what track he was on, and she gave him the look, the look which indicated so clearly, enough is enough, the subject is closed.

"Of course," she said icily in answer to his question.

"That's what I like to hear," he answered heartily.

"Not too long to wait now, my dear, and we will be in the business of having ourselves a baby."

Bart did not return that night, and she telephoned Shannon and spoke to Tom. He told her that Bart was not there and he did not know where he was. The following morning, after an almost sleepless night, she came out of the apartment and stood on the veranda, looking at the lake swathed in mist. She became aware of Florence, standing on the steps.

"Your man is with another woman," shouted Florence.

Duibhne stood perfectly still. For a few seconds she was unable to move her limbs, then, very slowly, she turned and went back into the apartment, shutting the dreaded mesh door and the main door behind her.

Once in the living-room, she peered out of the window, and she saw the old woman had moved down the steps, and was standing outside looking at her. Standing in the rain, silhouetted against the leaden sky.

CHAPTER THIRTEEN

When Bart returned home that evening Duibhne was not in the usual place in the kitchen, cooking a meal for him, nor in the living-room which was the next room he marched into. He found her in their bedroom, lying on the bed. She was flat on her back with the bump uppermost, all too obvious for his liking. He was trying to forget that very soon he was to become a father, and that mound reminded him of the fact. The prospect of the imminent birth filled him with dread, and he did not try to disguise his feelings. He felt that fate had dealt him an unkindly blow and that Duibhne had brought him nothing but grief. Fervently, he wished he had never laid eyes on her.

"What in God's name is the matter with you?" he demanded.

She sat up, and proceeded to tell him what Florence had said. "Is it true?"

"You can believe it or not," was his reply, "but how would that old harridan know what I do? She never moves from this place."

It did not escape her notice that he had not denied the allegation. She became almost hysterical. *"I hate it here!"* she shouted. "It's horrible, wet and damp and unhealthy! Not fit for a child. I don't want to stay another minute."

"We haven't a choice, have we?" he retorted. "Because of you and that bloody brat you are about to produce we have to stay here, whether we like it or not."

"You can't mean that," she cried, desperate now. "You must be pleased about the baby! Say you are pleased!" She buried her face in her hands and her body shook with sobs.

"Is there anything to eat?" he asked.

"No."

She looked up and he hit her upturned face a sharp stinging blow across the cheek. It was the first time he had struck her and it gave him pleasure. So much pleasure that one of his rare smiles spread across his face. He noticed the redness appearing on her tear-stained face and he was glad. He went outside, slamming the doors behind him. He climbed into the car his father had given him, and he drove away. He told himself that he was justified in leaving as she had not cooked for him.

That night an eerie light hung over the lake, making it look like an old-fashioned sepia-tinted photograph. Dark, threatening clouds hung over the mountains.

Then came the thunder, and the lightning zig-zagging across the sky. Years before, Nanny had taught her to count between the flashes of lightning and the crashes of thunder, and if you reached five that meant the centre of the storm was five miles away. Now, lying trembling in her bed, there was no time to count as the room reverberated with an ear-splitting explosion, and at once was filled with dazzling light. She feared the house would tumble down around her, and she prayed the storm would go away.

Towards the morning, as the storm rumbled into the distance, came another anxiety, pains in her stomach. She tried to take no notice of them, and thought perhaps they were the result of fear, but they came back, each time more severe, and closer together. The baby was not due for another two weeks, so surely it could not be that?

At six o'clock, when a hush had fallen after the storm, she decided to telephone for help. Over and over again she dialled the number of the hospital and then of Shannon. Nothing. The line was dead.

She climbed up the insecure steps to Florence's part of the house, holding on to the shaky handrail. She banged on the door and the old woman opened it a crack.

"I'm having my baby," she shouted, "and I can't get help on the telephone."

"Storm has blown down the lines, I reckon," said the woman flatly.

"What can I do?"

"I ain't no expert at delivering babies," said Florence.

"Please go and get someone," pleaded Duibhne in desperation. "You must help me!" She leaned against the doorpost as another pain engulfed her, stronger and harder than before. Dear God!

"Ain't nothing I can do, " said Florence, trying to shut the door between them. "You get that man of yours to help you!" She managed to close the door.

Duibhne eased herself down the steps, holding on to the banister. As she entered the apartment she was struck by the silent unfriendly atmosphere of the place. It was hostile, and the only form of communication, the telephone, mocked her with its uselessness. She thought of Bart's mother, giving birth on her own, and she wondered if it was going to happen to her.

She tried the telephone again, knowing that there would be no response. There was nothing more she could do, and she sat at the table waiting for the terrifying unknown to happen. Suddenly, the leaden silence was broken by a sound, the welcome sound of a car drawing up outside. It was Magda, worried because the telephone lines were out of order and she could not contact Duibhne.

It took but a second for Magda to appreciate the situation. She supported the girl to the car, no time to pack a suitcase. Duibhne could not bear to sit on the car-seat, and slid into the well at the front. Magda locked the door and they set off. Although Duibhne knew that Magda was frightened out of her wits, she could not forbear from giving shouts of pain from time to time. At last, they arrived at the entrance to the hospital, the hospital they had chosen because it cost less money than any of the others and because Duibhne, being pregnant, could not be insured with the Blue Cross until after the arrival of the baby.

A wheelchair was produced and she was helped into it. As they trundled her along the corridor, the waters broke. In the delivery room, they laid her on a table and placed her feet in stirrups. She was offered a mirror, placed at the end of the table, so that she could watch the birth but, in terror, she declined it. As she looked up, she saw a row of faces, looking down at her from a gallery.

"Who are they?" she gasped.

"Students," said the young man who had been called to deliver the baby. "Do they bother you? I can send them away."

"No, no," she said, "let them stay. They don't bother me."

She was beyond caring. Nothing mattered any more, not even the infant they held up for her to see, red-faced, screaming and undeniably masculine.

Of course there was no sign of Bart. Even that fact did not concern her. She closed her eyes and they took her to a clean white bed in a ward.

"Thank you," she managed to say to one of the nurses before she went to sleep.

"She is so beautiful," said the nurse to her companion,

as they straightened the bed. "Have you ever seen anyone so beautiful before? And that wonderful English accent!"

Later, they told her it was a pleasure to look after her because she wanted her baby. For the few days she was in the ward she felt cosseted and surrounded by kindly faces. The girls who came to that hospital, some of them barely in their teens, were not, on the whole, happy with motherhood. Duibhne could hear them screaming when they were in labour and, later, crying into their pillows, after their babies were born. She tried to block out the sound, and instead listened to the bleating of the babies as they were trundled along the corridor in their little cribs on wheels. Nearer and nearer they came, at feeding times, and one of the little creatures, baa-ing like a lamb, belonged to her.

She examined the perfect features of her newborn son, the nose, the pursed tiny mouth, the ears lying flat against his neat head. She looked at each miniscule finger in turn, and held his little hand to her cheek. He was an entity for which she was half-responsible, her own special miracle. She did not know that her wonder was the same wonder Claw had felt when he had visited the nursery to see his daughter being given her bottle.

Magda brought Bart to the ward to see his son. Had she prevailed upon him to come? Duibhne could not be sure. She had not seen him since he struck her on the face, and that seemed a long time ago. There was nothing to show for his action of that evening and it was as if it had never happened. He stood at the end of the bed, a callow youth, awkward, ill at ease. She felt almost sorry for him. She asked him to look at the baby, lying in the crib beside her bed.

"Do you like him?" She tried to keep the anxiety out of her voice.

"He looks okay."

"He is wonderful!" cried Magda. "Look how sturdy he is, and his eyes! He looks as if he is taking everything in, and he is only one day old!"

"Has he a name?" asked Bart.

"Bartley," Duibhne told him. "I want to call him Bartley, if you approve of course. It is a family name, and both his parents are Shannons."

"Do you want to hold him, Bart," Magda asked, leaning over the crib.

"I guess not," said Bart. "I would be scared of dropping him. He looks so small."

Mother and child left the hospital after three days. As is the custom in the States, a nurse carried the baby to the waiting car. Magda was at the wheel, and Duibhne, sitting beside her, was handed the baby, wrapped in a shawl. The nurse stood on the pavement, waving to them as they drove away.

All Bartley's needs were provided by Magda. She purchased his first clothes, his diapers, his cot, and, with difficulty, at Duibhne's request, his pram. Only in the city of Boston do American babies have prams. A push-chair, for when the baby was older, was the rule in

Oregon and, during the wet cold months of winter, the babies stayed indoors. When Duibhne took her new baby out in his English-style pram, the neighbours peeped round their curtains at the strange sight. Some days, when it was not raining, the pram could be seen standing on the veranda. Florence came down the steps to look at him, and she pronounced him "a swell little guy".

Tom came over to view his grandson, and he was visibly proud. He gave Duibhne a hundred dollars to help with expenses. During his visit he went out of his way to be charming, and Duibhne almost found herself warming towards him.

A social worker who introduced herself as Barbara Mills called at the apartment. She weighed Bartley, and almost echoed Florence's words when she said he was "a great little guy". She shook a small bell by his ear, and his little body made a convulsive movement.

"He's not deaf, that's for sure," she said, laughing.

She turned to Duibhne. "How are you feeling, honey?"

"I'm fine, thank you."

"You look rather tired, so call in on Dr Leroy and ask for some vitamin pills." She handed Duibhne her card. "And don't hesitate to call me if you have any problems."

Before she left, she looked about her. "This is a lonely place for a new mother. Do your find it so?"

"Yes, a bit."

"Is your fellow supportive?"

"Yes, of course."

Like Dr Leroy, Barbara Mills was given the look. She

had never encountered anything like it before, as most of the people she visited were only too anxious to impart all their worries to someone who was willing to listen. She said hastily, "Well, I'll be off, then. I'll call again in two weeks' time."

After she had gone, Duibhne stood at the door and watched her car disappearing down the lane. She wished Barbara Mills had stayed longer, and she knew that if she had been more friendly, more forthcoming, she would not have left so abruptly. For some reason, she rejected people who tried to get close to her, to help her. Magda was the exception; she was endlessly grateful for the kindness that woman had shown to her. It was different because she knew that Magda needed her and Bartley, that they gave her as much as she gave to them.

Suddenly, standing alone, she felt depressed, homesick, and she thought of Ireland and her father.

"Oh, Da!" she said aloud, as if he could hear her over the miles of land and water that separated them. A mist had settled over the lake and covered the mountains so that they were dark ominous shadows.

As usual, it was raining.

CHAPTER FOURTEEN

In Magda's eyes Bartley was the best baby in the world, and she marvelled at his equable disposition when she came to see him, which was almost every day. She did not like to be parted from him or his mother for any length of time.

"Doesn't he ever cry?" she asked.

Duibhne replied truthfully, "Yes, he does cry."

The trouble was that he cried on a regular basis, every evening from about six o'clock onwards. This was the time when Bart was likely to be at home, when he wanted to be fed and did not enjoy listening to his son raising the roof. It was as if somewhere in Bartley's small frame there was a clock which told him when to start crying and when to stop. It interfered with Duibhne getting the supper on the table and, even if she managed to prepare it in advance, Bart had to eat it alone. He complained, and Duibhne got flustered. No doubt her anxiety was transmitted to the baby through the special bond that is between a mother and child.

She tried everything she could think of to quieten him, lifting him from his cot, rocking him, walking up and down with him on her shoulder, cuddling him, giving him an extra bottle and even, in desperation, propping him up with cushions on the chair in front of the television. Nothing she did made any difference. After a peaceful day with Magda, when everything was well ordered and right, Duibhne did not know how to face the uproar of the night.

One evening, when Bartley was expressing his disapproval in the only way he knew, they heard Florence crashing down the steps, and then banging on the outer door. "Are you killing the kid?" she shouted.

Duibhne burst into tears.

"For Christ's sake!" Bart was shouting himself, it was his immediate reaction to the sight of tears. He went to the inner door, and opened it a crack. They could see Florence's dark form on the other side of the mesh, menacing.

"There is no need to worry, Mrs Mactaggart, the baby is well. Just go off home, will you?" She stood there a moment, hoping he would come out and talk to her face to face, and when he did not she went away, and they heard her going upstairs.

Duibhne continued to weep. Once started she could not stop, she felt so tired and a failure. As if in sympathy, the baby bellowed lustily, a strong healthy roar. Later, he would fall asleep, utterly exhausted, waking again at two o'clock in the morning.

"You are one hell of a mother," said Bart. "The old woman is right. It does sound as if he is being tortured. Don't just stand there, do something!"

She took her hands away from her tear-streaked face and looked at him.

On the way home, Bart had stopped at one of the taverns just off the freeway. The tavern was the American equivalent to the English pub, but there the similarity ended. These places were dark and gloomy, bearing names like The Feathers or The Queen's Head. Some of the proprietors attempted to make them look authentic, with brasses, fake fireplaces, cheap prints and oak settles. They failed to get the right atmosphere. Bart had visited one of the taverns, but he was not drunk. He had taken just enough alcohol to make him feel aggressive and ill-used by life.

Prompted by such feelings, his fist shot out, and he struck the weeping girl with his knuckles. It was a man's blow, and his closed fist caught her straight in the eye. Before, when he had hit her, it had been a glancing blow, and the redness it caused had soon disappeared. He knew that this time it was different.

Magda was very distressed when she saw Duibhne. By this time the eye was completely closed, and a yellowish bruise had spread over one side of her swollen face. She had tried dabbing it with cold water, but there was no disguising it. No disguising who had caused the injury either. Magda had no hesitation in telling Bart that she would report the incident to his father. Bart knew only too well what his father's reaction would be. A gentleman does not strike a woman, whatever the circumstances. Fearing his wrath, Bart implored Magda not to tell him.

"Why not?" she wanted to know.

"Please . . ."

"You seem less brave, all of a sudden," she said scathingly, "although you were brave enough when it came to lashing out at poor Divvy. It takes a man like Tom to deal with someone like you."

"I'm sorry," he said, humbly for him. Turning to Duibhne, he said, "I promise it will not happen again. You have my word."

"I don't think you should mention it to Uncle Tom," Duibhne told Magda. "He will only get upset and worried. It was partly my fault it happened. I was being feeble and stupid. The old woman upstairs gets on my nerves, always watching us."

Magda knew about Florence, and had seen her crone's face peering from the window above. "Very well, I'll say nothing this time," she agreed, "but it's more than you deserve, Bart."

He was tremendously relieved and, after Magda had left, he asked Duibhne to put off seeing Dr Leroy until the bruise had faded.

Winter had finally set in now, but, although there was snow on the higher ground and on the mountains, it had not settled near the lake. Often it was too cold for Bartley to sleep in his pram on the veranda, but on crisp sunny days he was out there, with a net over his pram in case of stray cats. Florence disapproved, and called out, "That little fellow will die of cold," but Duibhne ignored her.

The trees dripped and there was a constant smell of damp and decay. The wooden structure of the veranda became wet to the touch, soft and pulpy.

One day, Duibhne saw a rat crouching in the corner. It had sleek wet black fur and small bright eyes. It was probably a water-rat come in from the lake in search of food. It did not frighten her for she was used to rats – there were plenty of them in the stables at Clonbarron. However, she told Bart, "We must get rid of it. It could spread infection and harm the baby."

He wanted to appear helpful, for the bruise was still very visible on her face. That evening he came home with a gun, lent to him by his father. "If you see the rat again," he said to Duibhne, "and I am not here, shoot it." He laid the gun on a small table leading to their bedroom.

She was not at all concerned about it lying on the table. She was accustomed to seeing guns at home in Ireland, left carelessly in all sorts of strange places. Her father liked to have a gun in an accessible spot so that he could take a pot shot at a rabbit, if he saw one sitting on the lawn. Moreover, he had taken his daughter out shooting many times, and she was a good shot. She was sure she would kill the rat, given the chance.

Bartley's cot was in the bedroom all day, but at night, just before they went to bed, they trundled it into the living-room. They devised this arrangement because Bart found the baby's movements and little snuffles disturbed his sleep. Having only the one bedroom in the apartment was a drawback.

Duibhne began to realise that she welcomed the nights Bart did not come home early; she even got used to the times, and they became more frequent, when he did not come home at all. He took no interest in his child, and made her feel that Bartley was an encumbrance he could do without, and she was always trying to quieten him so that Bart did not become enraged by his crying. The more she tried to pacify him the louder he bawled, and the angrier Bart became. She felt torn apart by them both.

It was a relief to be on her own so that she could deal with her fractious baby in her own way. Even listening to the mutterings of the strange woman on the floor above was preferable to listening to Bart's constant complaints. She telephoned Barbara Mills and told her the problem, and Barbara assured her there was nothing unusual about it and recommended Gripe Water, which helped. Magda insisted that she visit Dr Leroy and he prescribed vitamin pills because he thought she was too thin. Nothing escaped his sharp eyes, peering at her over the half-moon spectacles, and she was glad the bruise on her face had disappeared.

The evening after she had seen the doctor in the afternoon, and after kind Magda had ferried her and

Bartley home, and then driven off, Duibhne sat in the big chair, trying to comfort her baby. He had started crying as soon as they entered the apartment. She put her hand on his stomach which the colic had made like a tight little drum. Suddenly, she felt him relax, and the crying stopped. She held her breath as he lay in her arms, gazing into her face with an intense stare. His blue eyes, unwavering, looked at her closely as if seeing her clearly for the first time. She kissed his soft downy head and presently his eyes closed, and he was asleep. It was like a miracle and she sat for a long time, holding him and loving him.

Her thoughts turned to her father, as they often did, and she wished he could see his grandson. In the blessed silence she had a feeling of great contentment mixed with melancholy. At midnight, she laid him gently in his cot, and then went into the bedroom, leaving the door open. She crawled into bed, immediately falling into a wonderful deep sleep.

An hour later, she was awoken by Bart. She heard the familiar sound of the two doors banging, and she listened to him crossing the room beyond, hitting the cot on the way, and then lurching around the bedroom, bumping into the cupboard and cursing. She pretended to be asleep when he climbed into the bed beside her. His arm fell across her body and he mumbled some words, but sleep overtook him before he could do anything. Carefully, she removed the arm, then turned on her side and went to sleep again.

Promptly at two o'clock, Bartley began to make little whimpering noises, which soon turned into vigorous cries. He was hungry. Duibhne lay steeling herself to throw the warm bedclothes aside, and go to him. Suddenly, the form beside her heaved itself out of bed and staggered out of the room.

Bart was going to the baby! She listened to him walking across the creaking floor, and into the living-room.

She hear him say, "Stop that fucking noise, you little bastard!"

Like lightning, she leapt out of bed and into the next room. She was too late. Bart had grasped the infant by the back seam of the garment he was wearing, and was banging his head on the side of the cot.

She could not scream, no sound would come from her mouth, but she managed to take the baby away from him. Bartley lay still in her arms, no crying now, and a livid mark was already appearing on his small head.

"It was an accident," said Bart. He was staring at the limp little body and there was real fear in his eyes. As was his way, he left the scene, slamming the doors behind him. She heard him drive off with a crashing of gears and squealing of tyres.

Duibhne telephoned first for the ambulance and then to Magda. After what seemed to her an eternity the ambulance arrived and behind it, Magda's little car. Duibhne was able to whisper to her the gist of what had happened before she climbed into the ambulance, holding the inert baby. She was aware of Florence, standing on the steps, watching as usual.

At the hospital, a nurse took Bartley away from her, and she was asked to wait in the hall. There were long benches and, as she sat down on one of them, she saw Magda coming through the swing doors. She came straight over to Duibhne and, sitting down beside her, said very firmly, "You must tell the truth about what happened."

"Won't Bart get into terrible trouble for hurting the baby?" Instinctively, Duibhne's hand went to her cheek, no longer painful.

Magda did not reply. Privately, she thought no punishment was bad enough for Bart.

"The baby will be all right, won't he?" Duibhne asked anxiously. She could not worry about Bart and his troubles at such a moment.

"Babies are tough," Magda reassured her. "I'm sure he will be fine."

"He was so quiet in the ambulance," Duibhne told her, "so still, so beautiful." She thought of her lively child, suddenly hushed, lying in her arms without moving or opening his eyes. The memory filled her with terror.

Neither of them could speak after that. The two women sat in silence on the hard wooden bench, listlessly watching people coming and going. Their minds were too full of fearful thoughts to make conversation. There was activity all around them, accident cases arriving on stretchers, nurses in crisp blue and white uniforms and doctors in white coats bustling about dealing with the casualties which entered in a steady stream. None of these people spoke to them. A black cleaner appeared with a mop and bucket, and they lifted their feet so that she could swill the floor on their side of the bench.

At last, a young nurse approached them and Duibhne was asked politely to follow her. She was taken into a room where a woman wearing a light blue suit was sitting at a desk, a middle-aged woman, grey-haired and rather stout. Does she work during the night, Duibhne thought, and then realised that it was nine o'clock in the morning. She and Magda had been sitting in the hall for nearly six hours. The woman had just arrived at her office, was straightening her skirt and settling into her chair, ready for a new day. This was her first assignment.

"My name is Mrs Holmes," she said. "Please sit down, Mrs Shannon." It was the first time anyone had called Duibhne Mrs Shannon, and she corrected her at once. Mrs Holmes nodded her head.

"Is my baby all right?"

"The doctor has examined him, and we will get a report soon. What is the name of the social worker who has visited you?"

"Barbara Mills."

Mrs Holmes wrote it down, and then asked for the

father's full name, the mother's full name, the address where they lived, Bartley's name and the date of his birth. It seemed to take an age for her to get all these facts on paper, then she looked up and said the words Duibhne had been dreading: "Tell me what happened."

Duibhne took a deep breath. "I put Bartley on a chair while I went into the kitchen to warm the milk for his bottle. He must have rolled off the chair and on to the floor."

Mrs Holmes studied the notes in front of her. "What sort of chair is it?"

"A big armchair."

"I see." She looked at Duibhne, a very straight direct gaze, as if summing her up. The girl knew her story was not believed, and she could no longer hold back the tears.

"Where you alone in the apartment when this happened?"

"Yes." She tried not to sob.

"The father of the child, where was he?"

"He was working away from home that night."

With a sad expression on her face, Mrs Holmes regarded the weeping girl. Like others before her, she could not help noticing the lovely face, still lovely despite exhaustion and despair.

"I want you to think very carefully, Miss Shannon. Did you, or anyone else, do anything to harm the baby?"

"No."

"By accident, say?"

"No."

There was a pause while she wrote something down on the paper in front of her. Then she gave a little sigh, and said, "Well, you go and wait for the doctor's report. I hope it is good news."

"We are keeping Bartley under observation," said the young doctor, who appeared on the scene after Duibhne and Magda had been waiting for another two hours. "As he is so young, and in no danger, we do not think it is necessary for you to stay with him." His look softened when he saw the stricken faces of the two women facing him. "I suggest you return tomorrow to see how he is progressing."

There was nothing further for them to do but walk out of the hospital, and across the road to the car park. When they were sitting in the car, Magda said, "He told us Bartley is in no danger. That is a comfort."

She stayed with Duibhne at the apartment for the rest of that day and then for the night. She telephoned Tom and told him that was her intention. He wanted her to return to Shannon, but she was firm in her resolution to stay by Duibhne's side.

"There is no room in that place," he complained. "Where will you sleep?"

She and Duibhne shared the big bed, but neither of them could rest. In the early morning, Magda pattered into the kitchen and prepared hot drinks for them both.

"We must stop worrying," she said. "It does no

good. I'm sure he will be all right." She tried to sound confident, but they were both too frightened to sleep.

They went back to the hospital, and this time they were taken to the Nursery Ward, a large sunny room, the walls decorated with furry animals and coloured balloons.

"He's in the corner," said the nurse. "He's a darling baby."

Bartley lay in a cot, padded on the sides. He was asleep, and there was a large lump on the side of his head. Magda thought the lump on his head was the most awful thing she had ever seen in her life, and she turned her head away from the sight of it.

"We think there is no lasting damage," said the doctor they had seen on the previous day, "but it is hard to be certain with such a young child."

"May we take him home now?" asked Duibhne.

"I'd like to keep him here a bit longer. What about taking him home tomorrow?"

"I see."

"I'm sorry. I know it's disappointing for you."

"You must come and stay at Shannon," said Magda as they walked back to the car. She did not think that Tom would put up with her being away for another night. He had telephoned her again that morning, raging about her absence, and also the absence of his son who was nowhere to be seen. "I don't want you to stay alone in that place."

"But what about Bart?" said Duibhne. "Suppose he goes home and finds no one there?"

"We will drop in at the apartment and leave a message for him, if that makes you happy. Personally, he is the least of my worries."

When she was sitting beside Magda in the little car, Duibhne covered her face with her hands. Head bowed, in a muffled voice, she asked the question she had asked so many times, "The baby will be all right, won't he?"

She turned to Magda for reassurance, and Magda provided it by saying, "He is being well looked after, and you acted quickly and efficiently." She almost added, 'And that will be in your favour', but decided it would only prompt Duibhne to ask questions she could not answer without frightening her even further.

Magda was convinced the unpleasant episode was not over; she was sure there would be repercussions. She was appalled that Duibhne had lied to save Bart and, in her view, it was misplaced loyalty, and later she said as much to Tom. He did not agree. He cursed his relations, and the problems they had foisted on him.

"Damn Claw and his bloody girl," he muttered to himself, as he went to get the truck. He was gone for two hours, searching for his son. When he returned at last, unsuccessful, the three of them sat down to a silent meal. Duibhne knew that her uncle was seething with rage, but she could not worry about him; all she could think of was the frail little body lying in the hospital cot.

The next day they were allowed to take him home.

"You feel confident about looking after him?" Mrs

Holmes asked Duibhne. She had been summoned to her office once again.

"My friend will help me," she answered. "We are staying with her for a while."

"I would like to meet your friend," said Mrs Holmes, and she and Duibhne walked into the hall where Magda was waiting. Duibhne introduced them and they shook hands.

"Bartley has been x-rayed," said Mrs Holmes, addressing Magda. "The swelling has gone down, but please let us know at once if you are not happy about him. For instance, if he sleeps more than usual, or if you have difficulty in waking him."

Magda thought, 'The Social Services are going to watch Divvy like a hawk after this, and it isn't fair. She has done nothing.'

Everybody was kind but Magda knew, and perhaps Duibhne suspected, that the kindness was tinged with mistrust. A nurse appeared, carrying Bartley in a shawl. His blue eyes were wide open.

"Oh, the dear!" cried Magda, her eyes filling with tears.

The nurse started to hand the bundle over to her, but she said, "No, no," indicating Duibhne, "this is the mother."

After they had been at Shannon for two days, Tom found Bart walking along the road, not far from the house.

He stopped, and held the door of the truck open for him, and Bart jumped in. "You are needed," said Tom shortly. "I am short-staffed as it is, without you doing a disappearing act."

At Shannon Bart was treated as if nothing had happened. Tom did not want to hear anything said against his son, and Duibhne and Magda realised that to ignore the incident was the only possible route for them.

Bart said that he and Duibhne and the baby should return to the apartment, and Duibhne agreed with him. She sensed that Tom resented their presence, and he made it plain that he thought Magda spent too much time with her and Bartley.

They went back. They hardly spoke during the car journey. He was thinking of the mess he had gotten himself into, and she was getting used to the idea that she no longer cared for him. Both felt there was no escape from the bonds which held them together.

It was a cold November day. The leafless branches of the low hanging trees brushed the top of the car as they turned into the lane and the wheels sank into the mud. There was no movement on the lake; it was as flat and shiny as a sheet of black oilskin.

Florence had heard the car and was standing in her usual position on the steps.

"Baby okay now?" she called out.

"Yes, thank you," replied Duibhne.

Bart carried Bartley in his carrycot (the latest gift

from Magda) and Florence watched the little family until both the doors were closed. Then, shivering in the cold, and mumbling to herself, she went back to her part of the house.

CHAPTER FIFTEEN

Duibhne did not complain any more when Bart was away, sometimes until the early hours of the morning, sometimes all night. She was never lonely during the day because Magda spent so much time with her. Tom did not like it, but Magda impressed upon him that it was her duty to keep an eye on them. After all, she was always at home to cook an evening meal for him.

Barbara Mills visited the apartment more frequently than before. Magda was well aware that she was working under the aegis of Mrs Holmes. As she had rightly predicted, Duibhne was under surveillance. Fortunately, she did not suspect anything and welcomed Barbara when she came to see her. As for Barbara, she could find no fault in the way Duibhne looked after Bartley. She had never met the elusive Bart.

"You hardly see him any more?" asked Magda. They were both sitting on a rug on the floor in front of an electric fire in the living-room, and Bartley was lying between them.

"It doesn't matter," said Duibhne. "I would rather not see him."

It had been a good day. Magda had arrived in her little car at about ten o'clock, and they had decided to get away from the enervating atmosphere of the lake, and make for the mountains. They had climbed higher and higher, following a sign which said, *'To the View Point'*, but when they reached the top, and Magda had parked the car in a half-circle on the edge of a sheer drop, they found the famous view was shrouded in cloud.

They sat in the car and ate sandwiches, which Magda had brought with her, and hot soup from a thermos. The soup reminded Duibhne of her hunting days in Ireland, and she told Magda of the soup laced with brandy which Mr Kendrick had to hand when a long cold day came to an end. Magda said, "I did not think of that! This is just plain ordinary soup."

Duibhne let Magda give Bartley his bottle because she knew it was a joy for her and, between them, they managed to change his diaper in the back seat of the car, stowing the soiled nappy in a plastic bag. Then Duibhne got out of the car and walked about, her feet scrunching in the snow, carrying the baby in her arms. He was wrapped warmly in blankets, and had a woolly hat on his head which kept slipping over his eyes, making them laugh.

"Don't go near the edge!" cried Magda.

Bartley's cheeks were beginning to get very red, so they decided to go home. Magda made Duibhne wait with the infant while she carefully reversed and turned the car. Then they got in and started on the downward journey. It was more tricky than the ascent, and the car slithered from side to side on the icy track. Magda felt very nervous, and wished they had never embarked on such a perilous drive, but Duibhne was young enough to think of it as an adventure. However, they were both relieved when they were on the freeway again.

Duibhne knew that Magda had taken the place of Pinkie as her special friend. She wrote to Pinkie and sent her photographs of Bartley, and Pinkie replied and told her about her happy life with Frank, about the new house they had bought in Bournemouth and about the new friends she had made. It all seemed very remote from Lake Trevelyan.

The deep affection she once felt for Pinkie had been transferred to Magda. They knew the love was there, it was understood, but they were both too shy to express it. Magda was aware of the age difference between them. She had a motherly or elder sisterly attitude towards the girl, but Duibhne did not realise this as she had never had a friend of her own age, and did not know what it was like.

She was almost happy, resigned to life in this strange place. Bartley was a good baby, taking his bottle greedily, making sad little mewing noises from time to time, but not often. His lusty bawling was in the past. When the two women in his life, his mother and Magda, gave him his bath, his blue eyes seemed to look past them.

"He is different," said Duibhne. "We let him down, and he knows it."

"He had a shock when he was very little," said Magda, "and it will take time for him to get over it."

She thought he had changed. It was as if he had lost hold on life, and had distanced himself from them, and from the world which was still so new to him. She told herself that it was ridiculous to have such fanciful thoughts, and his mother must not be allowed to share them for a moment.

"He is still very young," said Magda, "and his eyes cannot focus on us yet. In a few weeks he will be smiling at us, and splashing in his bath."

She looked at him lovingly, lying on his front on the rug. His legs were sturdy, and he was trying to lift his head, like a little turtle.

She said to Duibhne, "Have you thought about going back to Ireland?"

Of course Duibhne had thought about it, and she knew in her heart that her father would welcome her and her child. It was a sense of failure that held her back and also the fact that she did not know what the situation was at home. For all she knew, Claw and Elizabeth could be married by now. She wrote letters to him, but he never replied. The lack of response did not worry her, but sometimes she wished he could be a bit more like other people, people who answered letters and kept up with their family.

"It might be the best thing to do," Magda was saying.

"But what about you? You would miss us if we went away." She knew how important they had become to her.

"Oh, yes," said Magda slowly, stroking the baby's silken head with one finger. She would miss them more than words could say. She thought how colourless her life would become without them.

"If only you could come with us!" sighed Duibhne.

"I could never leave Tom."

"Not just for a visit? You could come with us on the journey, and stay with us for about two weeks, say?"

"Not even that." Apparently, she had forgotten that Tom had left her when he and Bart visited Ireland. Then she asked, "Have you a return ticket?" Neither of them mentioned Bart as a reason for staying.

"I think the time ran out months ago."

"Do you need money to get another one?"

"I have money," said Duibhne awkwardly. Each month Mr Kendrick sent a cheque to her bank in Eustace, and the money was converted into dollars. It showed that even if he did not write letters, Claw still thought of his daughter. She explained this to Magda.

"But Bart pays the rent out of his wages?"

Duibhne was embarrassed. "Well, no. As a matter of fact, I pay the rent."

Magda was shocked. "Tom has no idea of this."

"Please do not tell him," pleaded Duibhne.

"There is nothing to keep you here," said the older woman firmly. She was glad she had brought the matter into the open, so that it could be discussed freely in the future, and eventually a decision made. Now, she decided to let the subject rest for the time being, and give Duibhne time to think about it.

She looked around the room. "You have done wonders with this place," she said.

Duibhne had replaced the curtains with thicker ones in a warm colour, to keep the draughts out in the cold weather. She had thrown rugs over the armchairs so as to hide the hideous covers, and purchased a few cushions. In the centre of the table stood a large jug containing dried leaves she had collected in the fall, and sprigs from the hedges, covered in bright red berries.

"I haven't been extravagant, as you can see," she said, smiling, "I don't want to put money into the pocket of the old woman upstairs."

Magda's eyes were still slowly taking in the changes to the room. They settled on the little table by the bedroom door.

"What is that gun doing there?" she asked sharply. She had never noticed it before, almost hidden by scarves and gloves, left carelessly where they had been dropped. It was unmistakable though, long and shiny, and in Magda's eyes, menacing.

"It's Uncle Tom's gun," Duibhne explained. "We

have our own pet rat here, you know. I saw it one day on the veranda. I hope to take a pot shot at it if it returns, or Bart will."

"I don't think you should leave it lying around like that."

"If it worries you, I promise to ask Bart to take it back to his father. Anyway, we have seen no sign of the rat again."

Magda almost suggested taking the thing back herself, but she did not like the idea of carrying it to the car. She disliked firearms, and she was surprised that a sensitive person like Duibhne would have such a potentially dangerous weapon just lying on the table, as if it was the most natural place for it to be.

"I must go," she said. "I want to get back to Shannon before dark."

Duibhne came to the door with her, carrying Bartley. The sky was overcast, with threatening black clouds and a few drops of rain beginning to fall.

"I'll see you tomorrow."

"Thank you for a lovely day."

"I enjoyed it too." Magda bent her head and kissed the baby's soft cheek. "Goodbye, my precious."

It was nearly midnight when Duibhne began to think of going to bed. Bartley had been given his last bottle of the day, and was securely tucked up in his cot in the living-room. He was not asleep, his blue eyes staring straight ahead of him. One tiny hand was extended by his face, and Duibhne put her forefinger into the little palm, but he was too sleepy to grasp it.

She had just moved into the bedroom when she heard the mesh door being opened, then a key being inserted in the lock of the inner door. She stood very still. It was unusual these days for Bart to return so early.

"Who is it?" she called, trying to keep the fear out of her voice.

The light clicked on in the next room. "Who do you think it is, you stupid cow?"

She walked into the room, and saw Bart standing by the door. He looked terrible, unshaven and bleary-eyed.

"You're drunk," she said.

"What if I am? It's not surprising, is it? It's no joke living in this hole with you and the kid. No wonder I drink."

"Don't feel sorry for yourself," she retorted. "No one feels sorry for you."

"You've made sure of that, haven't you, baby? Endlessly complaining about me to my father's mistress. I tell you, I'm sick of that ugly bitch coming here every day. It's my place, and I forbid her to come any more."

It was an empty threat, and he must have known it, but he continued in the same vein, threatening to 'tell his father' and saying Magda was a 'meddling cat'.

"You're mad," said Duibhne. "You can't forbid her to do anything. You can't stop her coming here."

"You'll see."

She played her trump card. "Perhaps it will not

matter any more. I'm thinking of going back to Ireland, and taking Bartley with me."

He stared at her, and she could not tell from his expression what his emotions were at that moment, but she knew that he believed her. He swayed towards the cot, and stood looking into it.

"Keep away," warned Duibhne, an edge to her voice.

He laughed. "It's like that, is it? I am not going to be allowed to have anything to do with my own son."

"You have lost that right."

He moved away, as if obeying her instructions. "It is my child," he said, his voice becoming a whine. "I want to hold him. I have never held him."

The baby was wide awake now, making little noises and sucking his fingers.

"Not now," she said, and then more kindly, "Later – of course you may hold him later. Not now, because you have been drinking and may drop him."

"Drop him!" He repeated her words. "I may drop my bastard son. Let's see if I drop him . . ."

He moved towards the cot. She was never to know what he would have done. Afterwards, she wondered if he was sincere in his wish to hold the baby in his arms. Now, she felt she dare not take that risk and, as his hands went out, she felt for the gun, lying on the table beside her. Perhaps if she had not had the recent conversation with Magda, she would not have remembered it was there, and the event which took place within the next few seconds would not have happened at all. As it was, her hand reached out and she felt the cold metal beneath her fingers. All she could see was his hands delving into the cot, and she pointed the gun at him which had the effect of making him start back. A look of savage anger passed over his face, and she knew instantly that if she lowered the gun she would be putting herself and her child in danger.

She fired accurately, and the bullet hit him in the neck. She saw the look of surprise on his face as he spun back, blood spouting from a terrible hole in his throat. His back met the wall, and she watched in fascinated horror as he slithered slowly down its surface. His blue eyes stared ahead, grotesque, behind spectacles spattered with blood. Then as if in slow motion, he toppled forward, face on the floor, his body in a crumpled heap against the wall. Blood was soaking into the carpet, then spreading out from beneath his body.

Bartley began to cry, his cries louder and stronger than they had been for weeks, and, putting the gun back on the table, Duibhne lifted him out of the cot, and held him against her shoulder. Then she walked to the telephone, which was by the bed in the next room. She laid the baby on his back in the middle of the bed while she dialled the operator, and asked to be put through to the police.

A woman answered. "What number are you speaking from?"

Duibhne gave her the number. "Someone has been shot," she said.

"The address where you are at present, please."

Slowly and clearly, Duibhne gave her the address.

"Is that a child crying?" The voice was sharp.

"Yes, it is my son. I will attend to him when I have finished talking to you."

The woman's voice changed, her brisk tone became mellifluous. "Don't worry, honey," she purred, "wait there, and someone will be with you in no time at all."

"Thank you very much," said Duibhne politely.

CHAPTER SIXTEEN

The American newspapers soon latched on to the strange aloof character of the woman behind the shooting. Some reports referred to her as 'The Ice Maiden' and others as 'Lady Cool'. There was confusion about the titled and non-titled people involved in the case, Americans being apt to run into difficulties when it comes to titles. The name Duibhne caused another problem. No one knew how to spell it, let alone how to pronounce it. Only the short account of the incident in the English newspapers got it right. Finally, defeated, some reporter in Oregon hit upon the idea of calling her Debbie. It evoked the girl next door, good-looking but sad, misunderstood. It seemed to fit poor beleaguered Duibhne.

Fifteen minutes after she made that momentous telephone call to the police, the Sheriff's Department squad car arrived at Lake Trevelyan, closely followed by an ambulance. Because of recent heavy rainfall the lake had encroached upon the drive in front of the house, and there was not enough space for two large vehicles. Eventually, the ambulance parked in front, and the squad car down the little lane to the left. There was much shouting of directions, and bright lights pierced the darkness. Florence, who had been cowering in her kitchen since she heard the shot, now appeared and took up her usual stance on the steps.

Duibhne was perched on one of the cheap wooden stools in the kitchen, waiting for the police to arrive. She had shut the door of the living-room adjoining, as if to block out the terrible sight it contained. Bartley had continued crying for a few minutes, then he stopped and went to sleep, his head tucked into her neck.

She could see through the little window that there were people clustered on the veranda. Someone hammered on the door. Averting her eyes, she hurried through the living-room and opened the doors. There were three police officers, one of them a woman, and they seemed to fill the dark little space between the doors. They pressed against the wall so that the ambulance men could get by. Then they followed Duibhne, still carrying the baby, into the kitchen, and shut the door, as she had done.

The woman police officer was severe-looking, youngish with her hair tied back with an elastic band. She wore a sort of Baden Powell scout hat, tipped forward over her eyes, with a leather throng at the back looped on the top of the knot of hair. Without speaking, she took the baby from Duibhne and he started to cry again. She began to bob him up and down, in an ineffectual way, to quieten him.

They stood in an awkward group until there was a knock on the door, and they saw the two ambulance men standing there. One of them said, "There is nothing for us to do here."

Duibhne noticed that one of the police officers had a triangular gold band on his cap, and she wondered if that meant he was more senior than the others. He seemed to be the spokesman for the other two, and he said, "In that case, I'll have to call for extra men and a photographer. Forensic as well will have to come. I'm sorry, but it means you waiting here for a while."

"Okay," said the man, "we'll wait in the ambulance as it's so crowded in here. In the meantime we'll try and move a bit further forward, otherwise there will be no place for them to park."

The police officer was already talking into a walkie-talkie, giving orders, carefully pronouncing the address.

When he had finished he turned to her. "You shot this man, ma'am?"

"Yes." It was the first word she had spoken since making the telephone call, and she was surprised that she had any voice at all, and that it sounded so normal.

"He was your husband?"

"No, my cousin."

"His name?"

"Bartley Shannon."

"Your name, please."

"Duibhne Shannon."

That was the first difficulty. He murmured, "Cousins," and asked her to spell her first name. He relayed this information into a little device he held in his hand.

The lights of the ambulance shone through the windows as it moved to make way for another car, driving very fast. There was a screeching of brakes but, although there was a great deal of noise, sirens were not sounded at any time. More uniformed men piled into the room, and spilled into the kitchen. There was hardly room for anyone to move. One of them said, "It's muddy out there."

Duibhne noticed that one man was dressed in an ordinary suit. He was short and stocky, with a pugnacious look. He marched straight into the living-room, and then returned to the kitchen almost at once. He pointed a finger at Duibhne. "Has she been in there since it happened?"

The police officer who had asked her the questions looked at her enquiringly.

"Only to let you in," she said. Suddenly, she felt very frightened. The walls seemed to be closing in on her. She sat down again on the stool.

The man said, "Don't worry your pretty head, lady. We're just doing our job." Then he turned to the police officer, and said, "Well, what are you going to do about it?"

The man answered firmly, "I am about to make an arrest." He looked at Duibhne from a great height, and said, "My name is Lieutenant Sam Bendozzi. You are under arrest for first-degree murder." He nodded to one of his companions, who handcuffed her wrist to his. In contrast to the belligerent attitude of the other man, she felt he was almost sympathetic. She was right, he did feel sorry for her, and later he was to say to one of his colleagues, "It's not every day I arrest a dame like that. She was a real classy broad."

Lieutenant Bendozzi issued instructions for Duibhne to be taken to the booking room. "I'll be along later," he said.

Gradually, people were leaving the apartment, although some stayed behind – photographers and forensic, she imagined. The side of the room where the body lay was crowded with people. The woman carrying Bartley, who she had managed to calm, walked ahead through the two doors, and climbed into one of the waiting cars.

Duibhne went in the second car, sitting in the back seat with the silent man to whom she was handcuffed. A police officer and a driver were in front. As she climbed into the car, she heard Florence shout from the steps, "I should never have let you into my house!"

They skidded through the mud in the lane, and Duibhne, peering through the window, saw the water of the lake shimmering in the lights of the car. She would never see it again. At last they reached the freeway. The windscreen wipers were working at full speed. "Jesus, what a night," remarked the driver.

The booking room was in the Police Administration Building in Eustace. It was furnished with a row of hard-backed chairs and a desk. Nothing else. The man walking beside Duibhne released the handcuffs, and sat down on one of the chairs. She was told to sit beside him.

Behind the desk sat a woman, stony-faced, the harsh electric light and the white walls giving her the appearance of someone who had never seen daylight or sunshine. At her command, Duibhne removed the gold watch from her wrist (it had been Kathleen's) and a signet ring bearing the family crest, her only jewellery. As she handed over the watch, she noted the time, twenty minutes past two.

The woman, eyes fixed on her the whole time, bent forward and removed a small plastic bag from a drawer in her desk.

"Have you any other jewellery?"

"No."

"Any money on you?"

"No."

"Have you false teeth?"

"No."

She put the watch and the ring into the bag, then rummaged in the drawer again, never casting her eyes down for a second, until she produced a label with a string attached. She wrote on the label and tied the string around the bag. Then she handed Duibhne a form and a pen, and asked her to sign. "Your belongings will be kept safely," she said.

A man entered the room carrying a large camera. Duibhne was asked to stand in front of a thick dark curtain which looked as if it was covering a window. Front-faced photographs were taken, and then side views. It was quickly done, and the man nodded at her as if to say 'thanks', and left.

Now I am a criminal, she thought, and she imagined the photographs, with a number beneath, and her face looking as she was feeling, bewildered and frightened.

The straight-faced woman rang a bell. It was a clear strident sound in that almost empty room, yet Duibhne had not seen her press a button. By her feet, she wondered, like Claw used in the dining-room at Clonbarron when he wanted to summon the butler?

A policewoman entered at once.

The man sitting beside Duibhne rose to his feet, nodded to the woman behind the desk, and left the room. It was all done like a clockwork sequence.

Duibhne was escorted down a long corridor, through a swing door, and into another corridor. A door was opened and she found herself in a cell. It was, as she knew, the inevitable conclusion of a nightmare night. A steel door clanged behind her.

The feeling of unreality was, in a strange way, a help to her. It was as if she was watching herself from a distance, a girl acting a part, not herself at all. The remote disembodied sensation was accentuated by the square white cell, and she seemed to see a tiny figure in the centre of it, herself, standing alone under a light in the ceiling which was enclosed in a wire cage.

The door had a small rectangular opening in it, covered with a sliding panel which could be drawn back from the outside. In a corner of the room was a washbasin, and beside it, a lavatory. There was a narrow metal bed with a red blanket lying across it. She lay on the bed and wrapped herself in the blanket. She felt deathly cold and could not stop shaking. She heard steps outside the door, then a click and the light above her dimmed and became a faint glow.

Somehow, the rest of the night passed, with frequent interruptions when the panel was drawn back, and a torch was shone into the cell, the bright light aimed at her figure lying on the bed. She managed to control the shivering, and even slept uneasily for a little while. She knew that she must have slept because she was awoken suddenly by shouts and groans from the cell alongside hers, and she became very apprehensive.

She realised it was morning when the door was opened with a key, and a tray was placed on a small shelf just inside the room. It was breakfast, consisting of a plastic cup containing coffee and a plastic plate upon which reclined a waffle with a piece of bacon reposing on it. A plastic knife and fork, an envelope of sugar and a small carton of milk were also provided. Later, she heard the key in the lock again, and a black hand reached around the door, and the tray was taken away.

She had no way of telling what time it was. She sat on the bed or lay down on the top of it, and the hours passed very slowly. She had drunk the coffee at breakfast, but had not eaten the food. When lunch appeared, she was hungry and she ate it.

The feeling of unreality she had experienced the night before had left her. Now, it became very clear to her where she was, and what she had done. She thought of Bartley, and wondered where he had been taken.

As it was winter, the darkness began to fall early. She could just make out the sky through the small window, fractionally open behind four bars. A little cold night air came through the crack.

Suddenly, the door was opened wide, and a large woman stood in front of her, a bunch of keys fastened to a belt around her ample waist.

"Come with me."

She was taken into a small white box, for that is what it seemed like to her, a shoebox with straight white sides, and no shadows cast by the electric lighting. In the middle was a table and three chairs. Two men were seated on two of the chairs, the other was empty. By the door, on another chair, sat an impassive expressionless policewoman, straight-backed, hands folded in her lap.

One of the men got to his feet. Duibhne was embarrassed because she felt a mess. She was still wearing the skirt, blouse and cardigan she had been wearing when she was arrested. She had washed in the little basin – a flannel, soap and a towel had been provided – but she felt unclean. She had not been given a brush and comb and her hair was untidy, and her body sweaty with fear. She felt at a disadvantage with the man standing in front of her, so spruce and smelling faintly of aftershave. He was a small man with very dark, soft hair.

"My name is Felix Goldberg," he said. "I have been asked to represent you."

He nodded at the other man who was still seated at the table. "You remember Lieutenant Bendozzi, Miss Shannon?"

"Of course."

"Please sit down." He was excessively polite.

"Lieutenant Bendozzi is here to take a statement from you. What you say now will be recorded." She noticed there was a small black object in the middle of the table. She sat down, and Felix Goldberg sat down too, opposite her, looking at her very intently.

"I must impress upon you to tell the exact sequence of events during the night Bartley Shannon was killed. Please do not withhold any information."

She took a deep breath, and began her answer at once. She desired very much to get this part over. "Bart came home at about midnight which was unusual as he often returned home in the early hours of the morning, or not at all. At first I was not sure it was him, and I called out, 'Who is it?'"

She paused, and found herself staring into the

velvety brown eyes of the lawyer. The harsh glare of the room emphasised every feature of his face: the prominent nose, the slightly greasy olive skin and minute black specks on his chin and upper lip. I must be dreaming, she thought, why am I sitting here, with this man?

He prompted her. "What was his reply?"

"I don't remember," she said. "He was drunk. Rather, he had been drinking. I could tell that at once."

"Was he very drunk?"

"No, I suppose not very drunk. He said he wanted to hold the baby, take him out of his cot. I told him he must not do that as he might drop him."

"You thought he had drunk too much to be trusted with the baby?"

"Yes. When he insisted, I took the gun from the table and I shot him." She had said it, the words she had dreaded to utter had been said. What must they sound like? He did not do as I wanted, so I shot him.

"Was there another reason you thought he might harm the baby?" With his lawyer's instinct he hit upon the right question to ask.

"Yes, because he had done so before. Bartley was taken to the hospital in Eustace with injuries he received from his father. He was in hospital for two days. Oh, I know now I should have told the truth about what happened, but I thought Bart would get into terrible trouble for harming the baby. I tried to make excuses, but I'm sure they were not believed. It seemed the right thing to do at the time."

"Please, will you tell me why there was a gun in your apartment?"

"I saw a rat on the veranda, sitting in the corner, and I thought we should try to destroy it, if it appeared again. My Uncle Tom, Tom Shannon, that is Bart's father, lent us the gun."

Lieutenant Bendozzi leant forward and switched off the recording machine. "It is an interesting gun, sir," he said to the lawyer, "with two triggers and a top lever. I have never seen anything like it before. It was loaded with cartridges when it was fired."

"It was my father's gun originally," said Duibhne.

The Lieutenant switched on the recording machine again.

"You are experienced with guns, Miss Shannon?" He asked the question this time, and Felix Goldberg leaned back in his chair, and listened.

"Yes."

"After you fired the gun at Bartley Shannon, what did you do?"

"I telephoned the police."

"At once?"

"Yes."

"You knew he was dead?"

She shivered. "Oh, yes, I knew that."

"So, you reckon it was about ten after twelve when you fired the shot?"

"About that time."

"Thank you, ma'am. A statement will be prepared

setting out what you have told us. You must read it carefully and, if it is correct in every detail, you will be asked to sign it."

He recited the date and the time of day into the machine, and then he switched it off. He addressed the lawyer, "I'll leave you now, sir. Do you want to be alone with your client?"

"Yes, please."

Lieutenant Bendozzi nodded at the silent woman sitting in the chair by the door, and they left together. The door closed behind them.

Felix Goldberg said, "Tomorrow morning, on your behalf, I am going before a judge to ask for bail. If bail is granted you will be allowed to leave here, but you will be ordered to remain in the State of Oregon until the date of your trial and thereafter. Your uncle, Mr Tom Shannon, has agreed to pay bail of one hundred thousand dollars, and had instructed me to act for you."

"It is very generous of my uncle," she said.

"It is." The significance of the gesture struck them both at the same time. He looked at her, his eyes full of compassion.

His evident sympathy was too much for her, and she buried her face in her hands. Her shoulders shook and tears fell through her fingers.

"Miss Shannon," he said, his voice soft and gentle, "I must explain to you, the grim place where you spent last night is called a twenty-four-hour holding cell, and I hope you will only have to endure one more night there. As soon as I have obtained bail you will be released." He sounded confident.

"It's not that," she cried. "It is the awful thing I have done. I deserve to suffer."

His heart sank. It would not be easy defending a young woman who was consumed with guilt.

She wiped away the tears on her cheeks with the back of her hand. "What about my baby?" she asked.

"Ah!" He was on easier ground with that question, which he had anticipated. Bending down, he picked up a briefcase by his feet, and he put it on the table in front of him. He opened it, and began riffling through the papers in it until he found the one he wanted. "At present Bartley is with . . . let me see . . . Mrs Betty Freeman. She is a registered child-minder, and he is in good hands."

"Why can't Magda look after him? She is used to taking care of him, and she loves him."

"Magda is Miss Magda Angelo?" he asked. When she nodded, he said, looking at the papers again, "I see your social worker, Miss Barbara Mills, is to visit Miss Angelo tomorrow morning. Beyond that, I can tell you nothing."

He got to his feet, very neat, very correct in his dark suit. It struck her that he did not seem like an American.

"I hope the night will not cause you too much distress," he said, looking at her gravely. He thought for a moment, and then told her, "It is important that the charge is changed to one of manslaughter. If you are convicted of first-degree murder it will be very serious for you."

Her eyes were swimming with tears. She is so beautiful, he thought, what a tragedy! His words must have made some impact though, as he hoped they would, for she looked frightened as well as sad.

"You realise what I am saying, don't you?" he persisted. "You understand the position?"

"Yes, I understand."

"I shall leave you now, but I shall be back tomorrow, I hope with good news." He thought how trite the words sounded. How could any news be good for her?

He looked around the door, and the woman waiting outside came in.

"Goodbye, Miss Shannon," he said, holding out his hand. She took it.

"Goodbye, Mr Goldberg, and thank you."

CHAPTER SEVENTEEN

When Barbara Mills arrived at Shannon, she wondered what sort of reception she would receive.

The dark foreign-looking woman who opened the door seemed ill at ease, and looked as if she had been weeping.

"Miss Angelo?"

"Yes," said Magda, "It's Barbara Mills, isn't it? Come in, but I'm afraid you will find Mr Shannon in poor shape. This terrible tragedy has upset him dreadfully."

"Perhaps I should not intrude on his grief," said Barbara. "Really, it is you I have come to see. Could I speak to you alone?"

"No," said Magda decidedly. "I think you should talk to Mr Shannon as well." As she led the way, she said, "You know that he has put up the money for Divvy's bail?"

"Yes, I do know that, and I think it is very magnanimous of him."

She was shown into the white living-room, and a figure heaved itself out of one of the leather chairs. Barbara saw the puffy face, misty eyes, somehow so poignant in this bull-like little man.

"I'm so sorry," she said, deeply moved.

He clasped her hands, and then reached for a big red handkerchief in his breast pocket, and unashamedly mopped the tears from his cheeks.

"They were both too young," he said. "Too bloody young. My son was only nineteen – twenty, I forget. Too young to take on the responsibilities of a family, that's for sure. It was bound to end in disaster."

Magda gently took his arm. "This is Miss Mills, darling," she said. "You remember I told you this morning she was coming?"

"Of course," said Tom. "Sit yourself down, Miss Mills."

"Barbara, please."

"Sit down, Barbara."

When they were all three seated, he went on. "I blame myself. They should have stayed here, but I thought they would be better off in their own home, with the baby."

"We both thought that," said Magda loyally.

"They had no money problems," said Tom. "Bart kept his old job, working for me." The mention of his son's name produced noisy sobs and vigorous blowing of his nose into the red handkerchief. When he had recovered himself, he looked straight at Barbara and said, "It's a bugger."

In normal circumstances, she would have been amused, but it was not the time to smile at the eccentricities of the English. For she regarded this strange man as a member of the English aristocracy and, being American, did not appreciate that the Irish have an aristocracy as well. The Scots, yes, with their kilts and castles, but she tended to think all Irishmen were Yellow Cab drivers or janitors.

"I'm sorry to bother you in the midst of such grief," she said, becoming more business-like, "but I wanted to talk to you about your grandson, Bartley Shannon."

"Where is he?" asked Magda eagerly.

"He is with one of our foster parents, Mrs Freeman. You need not be concerned about him, he is being well looked after."

Magda's hands were clasped as if in supplication. "Please, please could I care for him, here in his grandfather's house?"

"Of course that is a possibility that has been considered," said Barbara. "Mr Shannon is Bartley's nearest relative in this country, after his mother, so it would be perfectly in order for him to take responsibility for the child at a time like this." She added hastily, "We hope it will be a temporary arrangement."

There was a long pause. Barbara looked intently at the two people whose lives had been thrown into disarray by circumstances they could never have foreseen.

Tom bent his head, and stared gloomily at the floor.

He was aware that Magda's eyes were upon him, and that after all the years she had devoted to him, loving selfless years, he was being tested. A selfish word now, a reference to his age, his desire not to be encumbered, and all would be lost. He knew it, and he did not wish to lose Magda.

So he spread his fingers in that characteristic gesture of his, and pronounced in a voice that could not be disobeyed, "The boy is my grandson, and of course he must come here, and Magda will look after him."

Barbara Mills was impressed, and she promised to put the wheels in motion at once. When she got back to her office, she telephone Felix Goldberg and told him what Tom Shannon had said. "He is absolutely determined," she said, "and Miss Angelo seems an efficient lady and obviously adores the child. Of course we will have to look into the background, but it should be fine."

"Great news!" said Felix. "I think it will make all the difference to my client's peace of mind. Am I allowed to tell her today?"

"I think you may," replied Barbara. "That poor girl needs all the cheer she can get."

It was late when Felix went to see Duibhne. A great deal had happened that day and he had been busy. Darkness was beginning to fall in the small town of Eustace, and the lights were being switched on in the cars, in the houses, in the streets.

He wondered how she had been during her second night in a cell.

"I hope she managed to get some sleep," he said to his companion in the car, a large shadowy form huddled in the seat beside him.

"God," came the voice out of the dimness, "it doesn't bear thinking about."

After Felix had left Duibhne on the previous day, she had been escorted along a narrow corridor. They met another uniformed woman who leant against the wall to allow them to pass. "See you in the canteen, Fay?"

The policewoman called Fay replied, "Give me half an hour while I settle in Her Royal Highness."

She took Duibhne into a shower room, and told her to take off all her clothes. She was given a bar of soap, smelling faintly of disinfectant, and ordered to wash her hair with medicated shampoo which Fay mixed for her in a plastic jug.

Duibhne stood under the shower and the tepid water on her body and in her hair felt good. She soaped herself and it was a relief to be clean again. She noticed that Fay was watching her very closely, and it made her feel slightly uneasy. She caught her eye and looked away.

"Hurry up," said Fay. "It's nearly time for me to go off duty. I don't want to be here all night." She threw a towel to Duibhne who started to dry herself with it.

"Can't I get some fresh clothes from home? These are so awful."

"Not worth it. I'll give you a clean pair of panties – that will have to do for now."

She produced an old-fashioned hand mirror and a brush and comb. She held the mirror so that Duibhne could see to do her hair.

When she had combed it through, Fay held a hair-drier in her hand and dried it for her. "Pretty hair," she commented when she had finished. She opened a cupboard, and put everything she had used in it, hairbrush, comb, mirror, shampoo, jug, soap, hairdrier, and then she locked the cupboard door with a key from her belt.

"Get moving," she said.

Surprisingly, before the door of the cell was closed with a clanging shudder, Fay gave her another red blanket. "Sweet dreams," she said.

Later, food on a tray was put through the aperture. Ground beef in gravy, a dollop of potato and a fried tomato. Beside it on another plate was a piece of apple pie and a slice of cheese. Duibhne was hungry and she ate it all.

The previous night had been a few hours; this one encompassed the whole evening as well, and the evening was a busy time. Listening to the shouts, expletives, the clash of steel and footsteps running (or, more frightening, walking slowly) she was almost glad of the locked door. At least she was safe.

She got as close as she could to the little window to breathe in the fresh night air coming in through the bars. When the whole place had quietened down and the middle light had been dimmed, she decided it was time to go to bed. She took off her cardigan as a token gesture to the night, and she wrapped herself in the two blankets and lay on the bed.

She willed herself to sleep. She desired sleep above all things, and she forced herself to escape into a dream about Pinkie who was visiting Oregon in order to see Bartley.

She awoke when the torch was shone into her face, but immediately went to sleep again, hoping to resume the dream where it left off. But the dream refused to recur, and instead she dreamed of a sleek wet rat, sitting on its haunches, looking at her with little black eyes.

The next day seemed interminable. Many times she wondered if Mr Goldberg had forgotten his promise. She could not bear the idea of spending another night in that place. The lights had been turned on in her cell and in the corridor when Fay came to fetch her.

"Wanted in Visitor's Room!"

Felix jumped up when she came in. The place was deserted; normal visiting hours had long since passed. Despite the shower of the day before she still felt unclean. She was conscious that the collar and cuffs of her blouse were grubby.

"The judge has granted bail in the sum of one hundred thousand dollars," he told her. "As I told you, your uncle has agreed to pay your bail, but the judge made one stipulation." He paused, as if reluctant to continue. It had to be done though, so he said, "The condition of your bail is that you do not see your son until after your trial."

She was silent, and could not trust herself to speak. In her most depressed moments during the day she had not imagined this would happen.

He knew he had dealt her a cruel blow, and he tried to soften it by saying, "I promised you good news, Miss Shannon, and here it is. Miss Barbara Mills has recommended that Bartley be looked after at Shannon by Miss Magda Angelo."

"I'm very glad to hear that," she said, and managed to reward him with a faint smile.

"I thought you would be, and now you are free to leave here and waiting in the hall is someone I'm sure you will be happy to see."

He took her arm and they walked through the door and into a big hall. The policewoman who had accompanied her to the Visitor's Room faded into the background. Suddenly, there was the sense of being free once more and, sitting on a bench, was Claw.

"Oh, Da!" She laid her head against his chest, and wept into his suit.

"You are making a damp patch," he said, stroking her hair. He looked over her head at Felix. "Thank you," he said. "What next?"

Felix whipped out a gold pen and a little notebook. "I have to come and see Miss Shannon as soon as possible," he said. "There is a lot we have to discuss. Where are you staying?"

"We have rooms in a little place on the outskirts of Portland. It is called the Log Cabin. Here is the address." Claw produced a card. "Come whenever you want."

"Oh, Da!" said Duibhne again. "How did you get here so quickly?"

"I flew," said Claw proudly. "Nothing to it. I can't think why I was so squeamish before."

Felix took Duibhne to the room where she had been taken on her arrival, and her watch and ring were returned to her. No sign of the stony-faced woman, but instead a smiling girl who wished her luck as the items were handed over to her.

"Be prepared for a shock when we leave here," said Felix looking at Claw.

"I've already come across them," Claw replied. "They were hovering around when I got on my aeroplane. Can't we leave by the back way?"

Duibhne did not know what they were talking about.

"Better not," said Felix firmly. "It's as well to have them on our side. We don't want to antagonise them at this juncture."

Claw nodded. He was always ready to listen to a voice of authority.

With her father on one side, and her lawyer on the other, Duibhne faced the cameras and the bright lights.

A cab was waiting for them, and, as they stepped

into it, one of the pressmen called out, "Good luck, Debbie!"

That was the caption he used, above the photograph of her startled face: *Good luck, Debbie!*

CHAPTER EIGHTEEN

The months that followed her release were difficult ones for Duibhne. There were many empty hours in which to regret the past and feel anxious about the future.

She and her father decided to remain at the Log Cabin because it was not well known and it was conveniently situated just out of town. The people who visited it were mainly travellers breaking their journey for just one night, and not interested in their fellow guests.

It was a fairly depressing place, and had a curious smell which, as Duibhne discovered, emanated from the wood; it was almost wholly constructed of half-timbers. Claw managed to do a deal with the management, and paid handsomely for all the rooms on one floor, a room for himself, one for his daughter, a private bathroom and a room where they could sit and watch television. They ate their meals in the hotel dining-room downstairs.

Felix was a frequent visitor. Very soon they were on first name terms, and an affectionate understanding grew between the three of them. Felix was a busy successful man, and he and Magda provided their only links with the outside world. Magda came, armed with photographs of Bartley and stories about him. Tom did not come, although Claw had sorted out with him the payment of the bail money. It was a source of sadness for Duibhne that the brothers did not meet for she knew they had a lot in common. But Tom was nursing a grievance, and his feelings were so bitter that Felix decided not to call him as a witness. Stubbornness on both sides resulted in Claw and Duibhne never seeing Tom again.

Felix was anxious that Duibhne should know exactly what she was facing, and sometimes he thought she did not appreciate the gravity of her situation. She did, but it was not in her nature to reveal her feelings. She knew he was being kind when he tried to explain everything to her, but she found the prospect of the coming trial almost unbearably oppressive, and she was not interested in the process of the law.

She was restless, and there was nothing to fill her uneasy days. Wandering around Meier and Frank, the big department store in Portland, did not amuse her, and she was always afraid of being recognised. Everyone bustling around the big city looked so normal. Not one of them, she decided, had been accused of first-degree murder. When she went to

Portland on her own (Claw refused to accompany her) she would return to the hotel feeling more depressed than before, and she would telephone Felix at his office, and ask, "Are you coming this evening?" and invariably the answer would be "Yes".

Another reason for Duibhne's discontent was anxiety about her father. Claw was like a fish out of water in the States. He did not begin to understand the American way of life, and Americans on the whole (even Felix at times) found him a baffling character. He failed to disguise the fact that he yearned for Ireland. He fell upon the letters that arrived from Mr Kendrick, and read them over and over again, although they were never answered.

When Felix came to dinner he was asked, after an indifferent meal, to play a game called Spite and Malice. It was a card game for two people that Duibhne and her father had played for many years. She taught Felix the rules, and he enjoyed that part, but he began to dread Claw's usual request for a game. One game led to several more, and Claw was happy to play well into the night, writing down the scores on a little pad.

Duibhne came to his rescue by saying, "Felix does not want to play, Da."

"Really? Why didn't he say so, then?"

Felix did not tell him it was because he was too polite to refuse. The problem was solved by Fletcher, the black porter at the hotel. He agreed to play with Claw for a dollar a game, and during Fletcher's free time they played game after game. They got on very well together, and the only time during this waiting period Duibhne heard her father laugh out loud was when he was with Fletcher.

Claw seldom stepped foot out of the Log Cabin; it was as though he thought everything outside was hostile and should be avoided. He spent most of his days watching black and white movies on the television or playing cards with Fletcher. One day he received a letter from Lady Elizabeth Down telling him that she was marrying Sir Thomas O'Neill, a Baronet from County Cork.

"Oh, Da, I'm so sorry," said Duibhne when he told her.

"No need to be," he replied. It was difficult to tell how he felt about it. Had things been different he might have married her but, as it was, he was never to marry again, living at Clonbarron, with memories of his beautiful Kathleen, until the day he died.

At last, after months of waiting, the date of the trial was set.

It took place in an ornate panelled courtroom, an enormous Stars and Stripes flag much in evidence. After some time the jury was selected, six men and six women, and two men in reserve. There was an elderly white-haired man who owned a hardware store, a hairdresser, an accountant, a schoolteacher, a woman who called herself a child-carer, a widow with a grown-up family, a dental technician, the manager of an open-air cinema, a PT instructor, a garage mechanic, the owner of a restaurant and a retired car park attendant. There were two black people in the group, the retired car park attendant and the accountant. They sat in two rows looking eager and interested. In a long trial the jury becomes increasingly dispirited and listless, but this was an undefended case, and not likely to continue into another day, so the attention did not flag.

The Prosecution Attorney was a man called Matthew Stennart. He was a handsome fellow with a shock of curly grey hair and an aquiline nose. He would have looked distinguished had it not been for his short tubby frame. His case was that there was insufficient evidence to prove that Bartley Shannon ever struck the defendant or that he was responsible for injuring his infant son. His contention was these injuries were inflicted by Duibhne Shannon and that she murdered her lover without provocation, probably after a domestic tiff.

Lieutenant Bendozzi gave evidence about the arrest, and the police doctor confirmed that death must have been almost instantaneous. Bartley Shannon had been dead for about fifteen minutes when the ambulance men arrived at the apartment. He had been shot in the neck with one bullet. One by one, the police officers and the ambulance men were questioned. Then came the forensic evidence and photographs of the body were handed to each member of the jury. It all took a very long time.

Matthew Stennart called Mrs Fern Holmes who

testified that the baby, Bartley Shannon, had been brought to the Gibb County Hospital in Eustace in the early hours of the morning with head injuries. He was examined immediately by Dr Stephen Bradley who advised keeping the baby in hospital under observation. Mrs Holmes produced her notes, which were handed to the members of the jury who examined them in turn, and it could be seen that she had written on the admission form, 'Injuries inflicted by Mother? Father?'

Mr Stennart said, "I see that you have written 'Mother' first. Does that indicate that you thought it the most likely possibility?"

"Objection," said Felix, getting to his feet. "You are leading the witness."

"Sustained," said the Judge.

Duibhne, sitting at the table next to Felix, thought how different he was in the courtroom, and she could hardly recognise the gentle soft-spoken man who had visited them so often at the Log Cabin.

"Let me phrase it another way," went on Mr Stennart. "You did not believe Miss Shannon's explanation of the accident, that the baby rolled off a chair?"

"No, I did not."

"You thought she was lying?"

"Yes."

"Why was that, Mrs Holmes?"

"The injuries were too severe for a fall of that nature."

When questioned by Felix, Mrs Holmes said, "I

came to no conclusions as to how the baby received the injuries, but I was not satisfied with the explanation. Miss Shannon told me the father was not present at the time of the accident, but I did not believe her. Because of that my suspicions must fall on both of them. Hence the question-marks in my notes."

Said Felix, "If you were suspicious that this baby had been maliciously injured by one of his parents, why did you do nothing about it? Surely making a comment on the admission form was not sufficient in a case of this sort, where the welfare of an infant was at stake?"

Mrs Holmes looked down at her hands folded in her lap. Felix regarded her intently, and eventually she raised her head. "I liked the mother," she said. "She was very distraught, and I was sure she loved her child. She . . . well, she was a child herself. Very young. When I met Miss Angelo I was reassured. She seemed a competent older woman, who would keep an eye on them."

"What do you think about that decision now?"

"In view of what happened, I suppose I was wrong not to take the matter further."

"No further questions," said Felix.

Duibhne studied the judge. He seemed old to her, and distant. As he was not wearing robes and a wig he looked no different from anyone else, but she could not help noticing that he seemed to have no interest in her whatsoever. He never glanced in her direction. The members of the jury, on the other hand, stared at her whenever there was a gap in the proceedings. When they all trooped out for a lunch-break, all their heads were turned in her direction.

After lunch, Dr Stephen Bradley was the next witness. He said the baby had a large swelling on the left side of his head. He was barely conscious when admitted to hospital, and the x-ray showed slight bleeding within the skull. There was a colourless discharge from the ear on the left side which was not an unusual symptom in a head injury of this sort. Such symptoms could be dangerous, but, on the other hand, could clear up quickly with no ill effects. It was difficult to predict the outcome of a severe blow to the head sustained by such a young child.

Felix asked him, "Could this blow have been inflicted by hitting the baby's head against the slats of a wooden cot?"

"Of course."

"That person would have grasped the baby and then repeatedly hit his head on the side of the cot, in a frenzy?"

"He would have to be out of his mind to do it."

Mr Stennart got to his feet. "You mean he or she would have to be out of his or her mind to do it?"

"Yes, I do mean that."

Florence Mactaggart was called to the stand. If Duibhne had been capable of being amused at such a time, she would have been diverted by Florence's changed appearance. This was her great moment and she had prepared herself for it. She was wearing a green silk dress, and her hair had been blue-rinsed and coiffured for the occasion.

She said the Shannons were bad tenants, and she soon regretted taking them into her house. He drank too much, and she neglected her child. "She hadn't a notion how to look after a baby."

Felix questioned her closely about her assertion that Bartley was neglected. "Are you saying that he was dirty, uncared-for in his appearance?"

"No, he looked tidy enough."

"I understand that Miss Angelo visited almost every day. Did you observe that from your upstairs window?"

"Yes, I saw her coming."

"And she helped Miss Shannon with the baby?"

"I suppose so."

"The baby's washing, for instance – was that hung on a line at the back of the house?"

"Yes."

"Every day?"

"Most every day."

"So, when you talk of 'neglect', Mrs Mactaggart, perhaps you are referring to the baby crying a lot?"

"Why, that baby hollered so much that one night I came down and asked them if they were killing it."

"Have you had much contact with small babies, Mrs Mactaggart?"

"No."

"Well, if you had, I am sure you would agree they do cry a great deal, especially when they are very young."

He then talked of her claim that they were bad tenants.

"They did not pay the rent on time?" he suggested.

"Oh, no, they always did that."

"You mean, he did?"

"Well . . . she paid it to me."

"So, when you say they were bad tenants you do not refer to non-payment of rent, but to something else. You were disturbed by their radio, perhaps, or the television on too loud?"

"No."

"Just the noise of the crying baby?"

"And him coming in at all hours," said Florence, "and shouting at her . . ."

"No more questions," said Felix, and Matthew Stennart realised it had been a mistake to call Florence Mactaggart as a witness for the prosecution.

The gun was produced in court. "It is an English gun, your Honour, called a Purdey. We are not familiar with it in this country."

"What is it used for?"

"It is a sportsman's gun, your Honour, for shooting duck."

"I think you mean pheasant," said the judge with a self-satisfied smile. "In England they shoot pheasant." He made a note of it, as if it was of the utmost importance. There was a polite titter from the jury.

God help us! thought Claw, watching this pantomime from his seat just behind his daughter. My old gun. Tom had no right to it. Must be worth a packet. What does that old fool know about guns?

"Why did they have a gun in their apartment?" asked the judge, still scribbling.

Mr Stennart said, "I understand Miss Shannon saw a rat on the veranda of the apartment. The gun was lent to her by Mr Tom Shannon, father of the deceased, Bartley Shannon. It was shipped from Ireland to this country with various possessions belonging to Mr Shannon."

Nonsense, thought Claw, he must have just taken it at some time. I always wondered what happened to it.

"That was over twenty years ago, your Honour."

"I see," said the judge, still writing. "So it was not used for the purpose it was intended?"

"No," said Mr Stennart. "As far as we know, the rat never reappeared. When the gun was fired the bullet penetrated the throat of the deceased. If it had hit any other part of his body he would probably be alive today. One bullet killed him. I have no doubt that if Miss Shannon had seen the rat she would have destroyed it."

Felix leapt to his feet. "The fact that Miss Shannon is a good shot has never been in dispute," he said angrily.

Magda Angelo was the most important witness for the defence. Felix had thought of calling Barbara Mills next, but decided against it, and called Magda instead. She looked pale, and it was obvious that she was under great stress. For a shy reserved person like her, it was a terrible ordeal.

She testified that Duibhne was loyal to her lover,

Bartley Shannon, and because of her loyalty she lied when asked about the injuries to her baby. "I asked her not to lie," said Magda, almost in tears, "but she thought Bart would get into awful trouble if she told the truth."

She said that she had known the deceased since he was three years old. She watched him grow into a strange introspective young man, idolised by his father. She sometimes thought Tom Shannon was too indulgent with his son. He was young for his years, and she and his father were of the same opinion that he was not mature enough to take on the responsibilities of fatherhood. Tom thought by making the young people live on their own, they might grow up enough to face the future as well-adjusted parents.

"They were both too young," said Magda sadly. "That was the trouble."

She had seen Duibhne's face after he had struck her, and she was horrified. "It was a vicious attack; the side of her face was swollen and badly bruised and one eye was completely closed."

Magda told how the girl had put off going to see Dr Leroy because she did not want him to ask any awkward questions. Here again, she had been loyal, misguidedly, in view of later events.

"Please tell the court your recollection of the time when the baby was injured," said Felix.

"Divvy telephoned me in the early hours of the morning, and I came at once. When I arrived the ambulance was already there. I got a brief look at the baby, and he was lying still, his eyes half open. At first, I thought he was dead. Divvy went in the ambulance with him, and I followed in my car. I never thought for one moment that she had hurt him. I knew it was Bart. When I got to the hospital the baby had been taken away, and she was there, sitting on her own. I said to her, 'Tell the truth,' but unfortunately, she didn't take my advice. She was a wonderful mother, and loved her baby. Of course she didn't hurt him."

"You realise we have only your word for this?" said Felix. "You are the only person who saw the injuries which you say were inflicted on Miss Shannon, and the only person who can vouch for the fact that she shot him because she thought he was going to harm her child, as he had done on a previous occasion."

Magda put both hands on the rail in front of her, and leaned forward. "I understand that," she said, "and I know I am under oath and have sworn to tell the truth. Bart behaved badly because he was young, and frightened by the situation in which he found himself. He felt trapped, and drank too much because he was sorry for himself. The drink made him act in an unforgivable way. This terrible thing happened because Duibhne thought he was going to harm her baby – again. It is a woman's instinct to protect her child at all costs." She broke down and sobbed.

The jury watched her distress, and it was plain, from the expression on the face of each person sitting there, how their minds were working.

Felix Goldberg's closing argument could not better Magda's final words. He kept his speech short so that the jury would not forget the impact her words had made. Matthew Stennart realised that Magda Angelo had successfully quashed any thought of a verdict of first-degree murder.

After the judge's summing up, the jury retired for a short time. When they returned the judge said, "Ladies and Gentlemen of the Jury, have you reached a verdict?"

The foreman (the white-haired owner of a hardware store) handed an envelope to the judge, who opened it and read aloud the contents: "We find the accused guilty of manslaughter."

The judge looked at Duibhne for the first time, and said: "I sentence you to five years imprisonment."

CHAPTER NINETEEN

In most people's lives there comes a time when circumstances force them to move out of the circle of family and friends, and into the company of complete strangers. It happens, for the first time perhaps, when a child goes to school, that never-to-be forgotten moment when the person you most care about turns and walks away from you. It happens when a stay in hospital becomes necessary, an operation or an illness, leaving the individual vulnerable and alone, at the mercy of doctors and nurses unknown to them.

It happened to Duibhne Shannon that late afternoon in summer when firm hands guided her from the courtroom and, suddenly, everyone had left her. Her father, Felix, Magda, the sad and sympathetic faces of the jury, all gone in the space of a few seconds.

She was bundled into a bus and sat with other silent downcast women, all making the same journey: to Gibb

County Jail, Eustace, Oregon. Only it was not called a jail, but the Correctional Facility for Women. In the same vein, the cells were referred to as rooms, despite the fact that they were undeniably cells and therefore places from which there was no escape. The canteen was the dining-room, and the units which accommodated the prisoners were called houses. Despite these niceties, the women prisoners were issued with baggy trousers and tops bearing the words *Gibb County Jail, Eustace, Ore.,* followed by a long number. No pretensions about that message, for all to see.

Duibhne was told that she could not have visitors until she was medically cleared, and not before seventy-two hours had elapsed since her admission. Being medically cleared meant medicated showers and shampoos, urine tests and strip-searches, morning and evening. She found the strip-searches particularly degrading.

She was issued with two pairs of the baggy trousers, two tops stamped with her number, tennis shoes, three pairs of white woollen socks and three sets of underclothing. The rule was a complete change of outer clothing once a week, underclothing and socks were changed every two days. Two sheets and one pillowslip were changed weekly, and everything went to the prison laundry. Bundles were left in the corridor on Monday morning for collection.

Duibhne was given all this information as soon as she arrived. No time was wasted in telling her how her life was to be regulated during the next five years. The prisoners (but they were called 'residents' not prisoners) were allowed to walk along the corridor, through a door and across a concrete yard to another house where they had meals. In the dining-room there were separate tables, each table accommodating six women, and residents were forbidden to talk to people sitting at other tables. They queued up with plastic trays for their food.

Duibhne's room had a bed, a desk, and a lavatory and sink in one corner. There was a radiator which in winter was always just warm. The heavy door had the usual slit with the sliding section outside. A small window, placed high, looked out on to the drive approaching the building. The room was like the one she had been in before, and she remembered Felix saying, "The grim place where you spent last night is a twenty-four-hour holding cell. I hope you will only have to endure one more night there." Her present cell, although larger and cleaner, was just as grim, and she thought: How can I bear to live here for five years?

On the second day she was taken to see the Warden. A policewoman sat in a chair beside her throughout the interview. The Warden was a charming-looking woman, middle-aged and comfortably plump. Her expression was serious and compassionate as she studied the beautiful weeping girl sitting in front of her. Duibhne sobbed uncontrollably; everything seemed unbearably bleak at that moment.

"Come now," said the Warden. "It's not as bad as all that."

She waited until Duibhne pulled herself together and became more composed, then she said, "When you leave this room you will be given a form, and I want you to write on it the names of the people you wish to visit you. Miss Angelo, of course, and your father, and I suggest your lawyer as well. In due course you will be able to see your little son, but you will have to fill in another form for that privilege." She paused. "I'm afraid there are a great many forms to complete in this establishment, it has to be that way." She sounded almost apologetic.

What is she doing in a job like this? thought Duibhne. In the midst of her misery the room and its occupant seemed like an oasis of kindness, and the woman sitting silently beside her was the only reminder of the harsh unsympathetic world beyond the door. A quick glance around revealed floral curtains at the windows and family photographs on the desk, standing beside a vase of flowers. Although it was obviously an office, with filing cabinets and an electric typewriter on a table in the corner, it had been made to look quite homely.

"My name is Mrs Stockdale," went on the Warden, "and I am here to help you in any way I can. If you want to see me, put your request on a form, and an appointment will be made for you." She looked down at a file on her desk. "You will be moved from your present room in A House to another in B House. This will be a larger room which you will share with another resident."

"Please may I stay on my own?" asked Duibhne.

"I'm afraid not," replied Mrs Stockdale and, for the

first time, there was an edge of authority to her voice. "Believe me, you would find that very lonely. I have taken care in choosing the girl with whom you will share a room, and I am hopeful it will work out well for you both." She sounded like a headmistress of a girls' boarding-school. She went on, "You will be working in the kitchen. Can you cook?"

"A bit." Duibhne remembered the few occasions she and Pinkie had ventured into the kitchen at Clonbarron to make flapjacks or pancakes on the griddle. And, later, there had been her more ambitious efforts when she had followed recipes given to her by Magda, when she wanted to impress Bart.

"Well, there is no elaborate cooking done here, and of course you will start with mundane tasks like peeling vegetables. However, in time, you will be given more interesting things to do. You will be paid for this work, fifty cents an hour, and the money will be put into your bank account here. You can save it, or withdraw it if you wish to spend it in the shop. Have you been shown the shop yet?"

"No."

"You can buy things like shampoo and soap there. Sanitary towels are provided free. Tampons are not allowed." She gave a little sigh, and Duibhne wondered how many times she had explained these rules and regulations. It must have become a tedious task for her.

"I see," she said.

"As well as the job in the kitchen," continued the

Warden, "you can learn a skill while you are here. Is there anything that interests you particularly?"

"What sort of thing?" she asked.

"For instance, you might like to learn another language. We have volunteers who come here and teach for us. Our ladies – " Duibhne supposed 'ladies' was a variant of 'residents', "– learn pottery, woodwork, bookkeeping, secretarial work and a great many other skills. Have you any idea what you would like to do? It is important you do not waste your time while you are here with us." She made it sound like a holiday.

Duibhne thought for a moment. At last, she said, "Could I learn to embroider? I remember there was a woman in Ireland who made wonderful embroidered pictures, and she worked tapestries as well, in gros point and petit point. If you don't mind, I should like to learn how to do that."

Mrs Stockdale was surprised by the request, which had never been made before. However, she promised to do her best and suggested, or rather issued the order in her firm gentle way, that Duibhne attend needlework classes in the meantime.

"The other thing I have to tell you," she said, " is that Barbara Mills, who made the arrangements for your baby to be looked after by Miss Angelo, has agreed to visit you once a fortnight. She is taking a special interest in you, so I am happy to agree to this. I know you will find her sensible and helpful."

She gave a little nod to the policewoman sitting in

the chair, and it was obvious that this was a signal that the interview had come to an end. As Duibhne was escorted from the room, she noticed another woman, a 'new commitment' as a recently admitted prisoner was called, waiting, with a policewoman by her side, to go into the Warden's room.

Duibhne tried to focus her mind on the visit of her father and Felix. It was the only event to look forward to in her utterly hopeless existence. At last it was the day when she would be allowed to see them. Then a twenty-dollar note was stolen from one of the women. The residents were not allowed to carry money, and when the culprit was asked to own up, no one came forward. This resulted in the whole of A House being gated for that day, which meant that they were not allowed to see any visitors.

Duibhne thought her heart would break. She asked permission to have a bath, and once she was sitting in it she allowed herself to cry. Tears of self-pity rolled down her cheeks. Time in the bath was limited to ten minutes, and very soon there came a hammering on the door and she was ordered to come out.

"Cheer up," said one of the guards, "you'll be able to see your family tomorrow."

The Visitor's Room at the Correctional Facility was vast and barn-like, with a long table down the centre which was sectioned off into areas like telephone booths, with the residents sitting on one side, and the visitors (limited to two) sitting on the other.

Felix had thought of letting Claw go alone on this first visit, but then he thought the older man would almost certainly get lost wandering around the big building, so he decided to accompany him.

The hostility between the two men was very apparent, even to Duibhne. Claw thought his highly paid attorney had let him down badly. He could not believe that his daughter was going to languish in jail for five years. He had expected her to get off. She had shot a bounder, who deserved to die, and he had anticipated taking her back to Ireland with him.

Over and over again, Felix tried to explain that the verdict of manslaughter was a victory, and he could not have hoped for anything better. The fact that Claw seemed unable to grasp this simple fact was very exasperating. Also, he told him that a sentence of five years does not necessarily mean that length of time; with good behaviour it could be much less. His words had no effect: Claw obstinately refused to listen to any argument. The usually even-tempered Felix wanted to say to him, 'She has committed a heinous crime, goddam it,' but the words remained unsaid. He would have said them to anyone else, but he realised that Claw was different to other people. Also, like many before him, Felix had rather enjoyed the adulation, the near hero-worship the man had once evinced for him. Now that was all gone and, without any consideration into the matter, Claw had withdrawn his trust and regard.

Both men tried to put these emotions to one side when they saw Duibhne. It seemed to Felix that in the few days since the court hearing she had become thinner, finer. Her appearance moved him deeply, to a depth far beyond the ordinary feelings of a lawyer for his client. She was working in the kitchens now, and wore a light blue overall, and her hair was hidden beneath an absurd white cap. The place she had just left was hot and steamy and Felix observed, with a stab to his heart, the little beads of sweat on her brow and on her top lip. As soon as she had seen her visitors she would return to work.

It was too much for Claw, and he started to weep, noisily as his brother had done, pressing a handkerchief to his eyes. His sobs had the effect of making his daughter resolute. She put her hand across the table and touched his hand for an instant. They were allowed that much bodily contact.

"Please, dearest Da," she said, "it is not too bad here at all. I am settling in very well, I promise you." She looked at the lawyer. "Felix, when you leave here, I want you to persuade my father to return to Ireland. Please do that for me." It was as if she knew that he would do anything for her. "It is the only way. He cannot go on living at the Log Cabin on his own. He would be unhappy, and I would be unhappy thinking about him."

Claw said, "I cannot leave you, my darling."

"Yes, you can, and you must. You know how often

we have said that time passes very quickly. It will pass quickly for me here, and I can only bear it if I can think of you at Clonbarron, waiting for my return. Please, please go home."

Back on a more realistic level, Felix said, "I think I should tell you that I intend to file a Notice of Appeal for a shorter sentence. The Appellate Court has six months to reply. They can confirm the conviction, reverse it or order a new trial."

"Oh, what is the good of all that talk," demanded Claw angrily. "It does not help us, now."

"If you do return to Ireland," replied Felix with dignity, "you can rest assured I will do all I can for Duibhne."

"Of course," she said, "we know that, dear Felix, and we are grateful. Promise me, Da, you will go home as soon as possible. A visit like this is lovely, but it is upsetting for both of us. I shall cope much better if I know you are back at Clonbarron."

She knew by the resigned expression on his face that she had won her point. He stumbled to his feet, as if anxious to get the leave-taking over.

"Magda is coming to see you on the next visiting-day," Felix told her, "and, of course, I shall continue to come whenever I can." He felt his life was going to revolve around those visits.

Duibhne watched them leave, the tall shambling figure of her father and the dapper little lawyer. At the door, Claw looked back at her, and raised his hand.

Sadly, but thankfully, she realised it was a gesture of farewell. In that emotionally charged moment she tried to imprint his precious face on her mind. She was touched when she saw Felix take his arm, and help him from the room.

CHAPTER TWENTY

Everything in prison moves more slowly than in the world beyond the high gates. There are many hours, days, years to fill, and no necessity to hurry their progress. Three months elapsed before Duibhne was moved. Once again she asked to remain on her own, and, once again, she was refused.

Two police sergeants marched her along corridors, across a quadrangle and into another house. She carried all her belongings with her in a drawstring bag.

Then Duibhne met the young woman who was to share her life for some time to come, for, despite his optimistic promise to Claw, Felix would be unsuccessful in his plea to the Court of Appeal.

Hazel Chamberlain was in her twenties, small and fair. When Duibhne was shoved into the room, she was kneeling by a drawer beneath one of the beds, stowing her clothes into it. She looked up and smiled, and got quickly to her feet. She held out a hand in welcome and Duibhne, feeling awkward, took it.

"I hope it's all right that I have taken this bed," said Hazel. "There's no difference between them."

"Of course it's all right," said Duibhne stiffly.

"I suggest you put your things in your drawer," said Hazel, "and that will make us feel so cosy and at home."

Duibhne looked at her sharply. She was not sure, but she thought she detected irony in the last remark.

Emptying the drawstring bag took less than a minute, and then the two girls sat on their respective beds, and looked at each other. There were two hours to fill before they went to supper at six o'clock.

Duibhne thought, this is not going to work (she could not guess that this was the only time she would experience the feeling) and she did not know what to say.

Hazel broke the silence. "I have been sharing a room with a much older woman. We got on, but we didn't have much in common. She has gone home now, I'm glad to say."

"Home!" said Duibhne. "It's hard to imagine."

"Where is your home? England?"

"No, Ireland."

"There's a rumour going around that you are a countess, or something of the sort. Is that true?"

"No, it is not true," said Duibhne shortly.

"I'm sorry. I didn't mean to upset you. People get weird and wonderful ideas in this place. Nothing else to think about, I guess. You mustn't let it worry you."

There was another silence between them, an oppressive silence, for there was no escape. No way one of them could just walk out of the room.

Duibhne looked about the room. As before, a corner was sectioned off for a lavatory and a small washbasin, but this time there was a folding screen which could be drawn across for privacy. Two desks, like shelves, were attached to the wall on one side, and there was a built-in radio above one of them. She had been told that there were two bathrooms along the passage, both containing lavatories, and these could be used, after obtaining permission, at allotted times during the day. At the other end of the corridor was a recreation room where there was a black and white television set. The room was always unpleasantly full of smoke – even the guards lit up in there.

The two women sat in silence and the walls closed in on them, forcing them to get to know each other, to create a pattern for their future life together which would be tolerable to both of them.

Hazel sighed. "I think that I should start by telling you why I'm here," she said, "otherwise you will be for ever wondering what I did to deserve this punishment."

She had been an intern at the Portland University Hospital. Her parents lived in one of the English-style houses on the hill behind the city. These houses were considered rather grand, and only the very rich could afford them. Hazel was a loving daughter, clever and popular. Everything in her life was good.

One night she went to a party and had too much to drink. She knew she had drunk too much because when she was driving her car back to her apartment, she found herself laughing, laughing aloud to herself, with no one else to hear. Afterwards, she remembered thinking that if a police car drove alongside her and forced her to stop, she would have a hard time keeping a straight face. That did not happen, but a woman with a child in a push-chair stepped out into the road, in front of Hazel's car.

The woman was at fault, and perhaps Hazel would not have been able to avoid her even if she had been completely sober, but she was not sober and, on that night, she was responsible for the deaths of two people.

The jury in their verdict took into account the fact that the child's mother had also been drinking. She had been to a party at a friend's house, and had taken the child with her. He was asleep in the push-chair which she thrust ahead of her into the road, in front of the oncoming car.

"That little guy," said Hazel sadly, "was at the mercy of two drunk women, and he didn't have a chance."

She had been sentenced to ten years imprisonment. Duibhne was amazed. It did not seem fair that she had been given five years for what seemed like a more serious offence. She told Hazel about Bart and the baby.

"I can't understand why I only got five years," she said. For the first time she was beginning to see things in proportion.

"Drunken driving," said Hazel. "Judges are very unforgiving about that, quite rightly." She added wisely, "Also, you had provocation. It makes a difference."

Eventually, the bell rang for supper, and the two girls joined the stream of women making their way to the dining-room.

Hazel had been at the Correctional Facility for six years. Duibhne, the new girl, marvelled that she had remained so sane. Like her, she was employed in the kitchen at first, but now worked in one of the offices. She was allowed to continue her medical studies, as far as it was possible to do so, and her desk was always covered with papers and books. She spent a great deal of time reading and writing, and Duibhne envied her this occupation.

She was able to advise Duibhne about prison life. According to her, the worst aspect of a community composed almost entirely of women was the lesbianism. "Some of them are just sad," she said, "but some of them are frightening."

She predicted that before long Duibhne would be receiving 'kites': forbidden love-notes, pressed into her hand or pushed under the door.

Hazel said, "On no account report these to the Warden or anyone else. It's creepy, but you have to put up with it, and say nothing. Telling tales to the authorities immediately puts the person doing the telling in danger. Terrible danger. This place may seem to be run on regulated lines, but there is an undercurrent of frustration and anger amongst the women, and it comes to the surface from time to time."

The Warden had acted with understanding and wisdom when she put Duibhne and Hazel together. They were kindred spirits, and they soon organised a routine which they followed in the confines of the cell in which they spent so much of their time. They took it in turns each morning to swill out the room with the mop and bucket provided for the purpose. Blue linoleum covered the floor of their room and the passage outside. Duibhne called it 'the sea beneath their feet'. The one who did the cleaning had the bath. Ten minutes was the time allowed for a bath, and that included the scrupulous cleaning of it after.

Their sleep was interrupted every night by heavy footsteps along the passage, the metallic rattle of the grid being drawn back and then the merciless glare of the flashlight, moving up and down and across the room. This happened every hour during every night and, when it did, the girls murmured in their sleep and automatically raised a hand to indicate their presence. People who live above an underground or in the shadow of an aerodrome become accustomed to the noise, and hardly notice it. That is how it was for Duibhne and Hazel; the clanging of the keys and the harsh light was a brief interlude in the blessed relief of their dreams.

Magda came to visit her, and brought her news of the baby. So far she had not been given permission to bring Bartley to the Correctional Facility, and Duibhne thought this very unreasonable, and could not understand the delay. Magda told her that Tom had accepted the situation although he took no interest in his grandson, and had forbidden her to mention the name of Duibhne or her father. He still grieved for his son.

Magda's visits always left Duibhne feeling depressed. "How can you face living here for so long?" she asked Hazel. They stayed in their room in the evening, hardly ever venturing into the smoke-filled television room except to see the news.

"I welcome it," said Hazel frankly. "The worst time for me was before my trial when I was living at home with my mother and father. I wanted to die, but I did not have the courage to kill myself. I told myself that it was because it would upset them so much, but that was not the whole truth. I was just plumb scared. There was a part of me that wanted to live. It is right that I stay here after what I did. Any discomfort I have is less than I deserve, and that makes me feel better."

"An atonement?"

"No, not an atonement. Nothing can atone for what I have done. Don't you feel that, Divvy? Isn't your mind confused with fears and doubts?"

Duibhne thought about Bart moving towards the cot. To pick up his son and hold him proudly, loving him? She would never know. She remembered only her hand on the trigger, pressing it. The recollection was so awful that she hid her head in her hands in an effort to block it out.

"That's what I mean," said Hazel, understanding at once. "This is the only place for such memories. It is called a place of security and that is what it is, a security from a living hell. When I leave, I hope to go back to medicine so that my life is not wasted and I can do some good, but I shall never forget my years here, or the reason for them. It will be with me until the day I die, and it will be with you too, Divvy. We can never escape the remorse, but at least we have been given a breathing-space to learn how to live with it. That is what prison will do for us."

Duibhne had never heard talk like this before. Reasoning, discussion and argument had never been part of her existence, and she began to suspect that Claw's chatter about hunting, shooting and the form-book was very limited. No wonder he had been at a loss when staying at the Log Cabin; he had no reserves to call upon. She thought about him a great deal, lovingly imagining him at Clonbarron, and hoping he was happy. She received no letters from him, and did not expect any. In fact, she received no mail at all (Pinkie had not been told of her whereabouts) and Hazel found this surprising.

Life was amazingly busy. The hot tiring work in the kitchen, the needlework class which was an euphemism for the excruciatingly boring task of sewing on name-tapes for the new commitments, and every night sitting in the poorly lit cell, talking, talking. Urine tests, the dreaded strip-searches, the two inches of open window behind bars through which they could see the trees and the sky. She and Hazel walking round and round the quadrangle for fresh air and exercise. This was their life, and day followed day quite quickly.

Once a fortnight Duibhne was visited by Barbara Mills who was astonished that she was accepting everything so well. And there were viisits from Felix, still working for her early release, and in love with her. "Be thankful you don't love him," said Hazel. "How impossible that would be!"

They got to know each other's visitors. Hazel's kindly parents gave Duibhne a cheerful wave as they came into the Visitor's Room, and saw Duibhne sitting further down the table from their daughter.

One day the Warden summoned Duibhne to her room, and told her that a lady called Mrs Smythe had volunteered to teach her embroidery. "She is coming a long way," said Mrs Stockdale, "and it is very good of her. I think you will like her – she is English." She looked at the girl with a little smile. "You look different, more relaxed. You seem to have accepted the life here. Do you get on well with Hazel Chamberlain?"

"I like her very much," answered Duibhne eagerly. "We have become friends."

She realised that never before in her life had she had such a friend. Not even the beloved Pinkie had given her companionship like this. She loved Magda, but it was a different sort of friendship. She and Hazel talked about everything, and they shared jokes. Jokes had not formed part of her relationship with Pinkie or with Magda. They teased the police staff, who took it in good part, so far and no further. The guards liked a 'good laugh with the girls' and the same premise applied to the other residents. It took a long time before a happy solution was reached of being familiar, but not too familiar. Getting on with everyone was tricky, and there were some strange people about.

Most of the residents had a healthy respect for Hazel, and she was protective of Duibhne. "Stay close to me, baby," she said, "and you'll come to no harm."

However, sometimes the unexpected happened. A woman heard that Hazel had been responsible for the death of a child. She came over to her table in the dining-room, which was against the rules, and shouted, "Murderer!" and, at the same time, emptied a cup of hot coffee into Hazel's lap. It scalded the tops of her legs, but she did not complain, only became despondent and tearful. "That's the sort of thing that makes me think I can't go on," she said.

Duibhne looked forward to the embroidery lessons. Mrs Stockdale told her that Mrs Smythe would come once a week for an hourly session. "I'm afraid you can only work when she is with you – and, of course, a guard. She tells me that a pair of sharp scissors is an essential, so that means no stitching in your room. That is the rule."

The Warden had gone to a great deal of trouble to secure the services of Mrs Smythe. A friend had told a friend, who had told someone else, that a volunteer was needed to teach embroidery to an inmate of Gibb County Jail. It sounded special and Mrs Smythe accepted the challenge at once. The lesson was held in a section of a large room where the voluntary teachers and their pupils met once a week. The classes varied in size and Duibhne was the only resident who received individual attention.

"I wonder why Mrs Stockdale has done this for you?" asked Hazel, with a familiar gleam in her eye. "It smacks of privilege, don't you think, Divvy? But surely that cannot be – in our democratic country? I can't help thinking that the Warden would not have done this for any of the other residents. Can you explain it?"

"No, I can't."

Mrs Smythe was a comfortable lady with pink cheeks and a rather sad expression. Duibhne soon learnt the reason for the sadness. She was homesick. Her husband had emigrated to the States ten years before. He was a physicist, perfectly satisfied with his decision to leave England, and impervious to his wife's feelings about the move.

She spoke with a slight Devonshire accent, which was charming, and she had steadfastly resisted the intrusion of Americanisms or American inflection in her speech. In her eyes nothing in the States could compare favourably with the English counterpart. The weather was not as good as English weather (too predictable) and the people were not as genuine as English people.

On her first visit to see Duibhne she brought with her an example of her work. She had made a little book for her first grandchild, illustrating the old nursery rhymes. Each picture was composed of hundreds of minute stitches, the colours graded in different shades of silk thread. It was exquisite.

"I can never do anything as beautiful as this," said Duibhne, slowly turning the parchment-coloured linen pages.

"Of course you can, my dear," said Mrs Smythe. She was thrilled to be teaching this beautiful girl, so distinguished-looking and obviously high class. If she had known her pupil was the daughter of a lord, she would have been even more impressed, but this information was not given to her.

She taught Duibhne how to incorporate petit point in a gros-point tapestry, the birds and the flowers worked in smaller stitches – no patterns allowed, and the designs worked straight on to the canvas. She was an expert, and the hour they spent together once a week went very quickly. In return for the tuition she received, Duibhne talked about digestive biscuits, Marmite and mince pies at Christmas time.

"She is more a prisoner than I," Duibhne told Hazel, "for I shall go home eventually, but she has no alternative but to stay here. Her husband must be a very insensitive man not to realise how unhappy she is."

"Hasn't she a daughter and a grandson who live near her?"

"Yes."

"Well, she wouldn't like to leave them. I bet my bottom dollar that if her husband died, and she had the opportunity to return to England, she wouldn't take it. It's hard for people with a heart in two countries."

Duibhne was promoted in the kitchen, and was now allowed to help with the preparation of meals. Mrs Stockdale offered her the chance of working in the filing room, a responsible job which involved secrecy, but she refused it. She had got to like the group of women who worked in the kitchen; there was a camaraderie there which she thought she would miss if she moved to another department.

Especially, she liked the Head Cook who was a vast black woman called Grace. Grace provided Duibhne with stories which she recounted to Hazel in the evening. The filing room sounded dull by comparison, but it had the advantage of being cool. The kitchen was airless, and stiflingly hot, and the sweat ran down Duibhne's back beneath the blue overall. It was a relief when the shift was over, and she could take off her cap, and shake the wet hair clinging to her head.

The fifty cents she earned mounted up, and she seldom took money from her account. She was given a little book, and she liked watching the money accumulate. She had never worn make-up, so the only items she purchased from the shop were deodorants, soap and shampoo.

"Why all the saving?" asked Hazel, who tended to

spend money on silly things like bath salts, scent and endless packets of Lifesavers. "Who are you saving for?"

"For Bartley, I suppose."

"But surely Bartley will be looked after? Your father will see to that, won't he?" Hazel became a bit sharpish when talking about Claw, and Duibhne was aware of this, and tried to avoid mentioning him too much.

"Of course," she said.

It was hard to explain, even to someone as understanding as Hazel, for Hazel had not had a child. She could never understand the terrible overpowering need to do something for a child who has been taken away from you. Duibhne felt helpless in her longing to express her great love for Bartley. She was not allowed to hold him in her arms, to press her cheek against his soft cheek; all this had been snatched away from her. All she could do was to save the fifty cents an hour she earned in the kitchen, and watch it mounting in her little book.

CHAPTER TWENTY-ONE

Duibhne thought about Bartley so much, and it angered her that she had not been given permission to see him. Photographs and stories were of small comfort when she could not be with him and touch him. Magda told her that Dr Leroy was taking a special interest in him (it seemed as if everyone took a 'special interest' in Duibhne and anyone connected with her), and she took him to the surgery for a check-up once a month. Apparently, Bartley was a healthy child and the only ailment he had ever had in his short life was croup when he was a year old.

Hazel was sympathetic and indignant for Duibhne. "Everything moves at such a snail's pace here," she said. "When was the last time you spoke to the Warden about it?"

"Six months ago, and she promised to do something then. I suppose I shall have to fill in a request form to see her again."

"Why don't you mention it to Magda? Perhaps she could help."

"Oh, I'm always mentioning it to Magda," said Duibhne impatiently, "and nothing happens."

"Well, what about Felix? Now, that's a good idea. If anyone can influence Mrs Stockdale he can, and he'll welcome the chance to do something for you. This is a practical way of showing his devotion to you, and better than just making sheep's eyes at you across the table in the Visitor's Room."

Duibhne laughed. "You are ridiculous!"

"You know as well as I do that he longs to sweep you in his arms, and take you away from all this."

"Oh . . . really!"

"Yes, really, and I am as jealous as hell. I wish I had an ardent lover coming to see me. Much as I love Mom and Dad and Aunt Nancy, they're not exactly romantic."

"You can share Felix if you like," said Duibhne generously, "I'll ask him to put in a request to see you next time."

"No, thank you," replied Hazel. "You keep your love life to yourself, Lady Divvy. I don't want any of your leftovers."

"The trouble is that I saw Felix yesterday," said Duibhne, "so now I have to wait another week before I can see him again." She frowned, and then her face lit up as she came up with a solution. "I know, I'll telephone him!"

"Oh, is that such a good idea?" Hazel was suddenly

worried. The telephone queue was notorious. Any arguments, any fights usually emanated from that line of restless women waiting for their turn to use the telephone which was on the wall in the corridor. Tempers were frayed and emotions ran high for some of the women waiting to speak to a husband or lover. It was significant that a male police sergeant always stood guard at the end of the telephone queue.

"It will be all right," said Duibhne. "I telephoned Magda once, and nothing dreadful happened. The trick is not to speak for too long – that is what enrages them. I can be very quick saying what I want to say to Felix."

She had to wait until evening, as the time for using the telephone was between six and seven o'clock. Grace was ahead of her, so she had someone to talk to, and Grace told her she was going to talk to her little boy who lived with her sister. Behind Duibhne was a girl with the unlikely name of Joy. Joy was bad news, and Duibhne wished she was not so close. She slouched against the wall, chewing gum. Chewing gum was against the rules, and she was still wearing her cleaner's uniform, also against the rules, the strings hanging loose, her hands thrust in the pockets.

Grace was on the telephone, talking to her son. Because Duibhne was next she kept the conversation short. "Mommy has to go now, honey. You be a good boy and do what Angel tells you." Angel! Duibhne tried to picture Grace's sister who rejoiced in the name of Angel.

Grace put down the receiver and Duibhne, smiling at her, moved to take her place.

"My turn," said Joy, stepping in front of her.

"No, it's not," said Duibhne quickly. Hazel would have been cross with her for making that reply and, as soon as she made it, Duibhne realised her mistake. The golden rule was never to argue, never put up a fight, however unfair the situation – especially when dealing with a tricky character like Joy.

"I tell you, I'm next," Joy shouted, "and don't you look at me like that, you fucking stuck-up bitch!"

The women in the queue behind her started to move back, and the sergeant made his way to the front. Duibhne stood and stared at Joy, rooted to the spot. She was paralysed, and could not summon the power in her limbs to step aside, to let the woman have her own way. She knew what she had to do, but she was incapable of moving.

The next moment she felt a sharp stinging sensation in her shoulder. The knife was aimed at her chest, but was diverted by Grace, whose enormous bulk had sprung into action. Strong black arms caught hold of Joy, and pinioned her arms to her sides. The knife fell to the floor with a clatter, spinning across the shiny blue linoleum. The sergeant was there, clamping the handcuffs on Joy's wrists. In seconds, two other men appeared and she was led away.

Duibhne looked with interest at the blood seeping through her top, first of all covering the words *Gibb*

County Jail and then spreading to *Eustace, Ore*, and her number below. It was strange how dark it had become and how tired she felt. Thankfully, she laid her head on Grace's ample bosom. The woman was murmuring to her, but she could not hear what she was saying. It just seemed to her as if she was sinking into a comfortable warm blackness.

She was put on a stretcher and taken to the Infirmary. She awoke to find herself in a bright airy room containing six beds. A sister and a nurse were always on duty, and there was a resident lady doctor who looked after the patients in all the houses. The kind sister held Duibhne's hand while the doctor stitched up the wound. It was a deep gash. "You were lucky," she commented.

"I was foolish," said Duibhne.

"Well, you are making up for it now by being very brave," said the sister.

The atmosphere was different in the Infirmary, unofficial and ordinary. Her shoulder throbbed, but they gave her pain-killers. It was quite pleasant lying in bed with two pillows for her head, which was a luxury. She was relieved the other beds were empty; evidently nobody was sick in B House.

The only other time she had been in hospital was for Bartley's birth, and this was much the same sort of ward, except there were bars on the windows. The window opposite was much bigger than the one in the room she shared with Hazel (a small square above their heads) and, as it was level with her bed, she could lie and gaze at the sky and the tops of the trees swaying in the wind. She was content to lie and just look out of the window. She felt she had no strength left in her body.

She was allowed visitors, and as long as they were on the list and kept to certain times, the request forms were waived. Felix was the first person to come, and he was visibly distressed when he saw her. Her face was very pale, and one shoulder was swathed in bandages. The hand of her good arm lay on the coverlet, and he covered it with his own hand, something which would not have been tolerated in the Visitor's Room.

"You might have been killed," he said.

She whispered, "I was trying to telephone you when it happened."

His heart lifted. "Why?"

"I wanted to ask you to speak to the Warden about my seeing Bartley. I want to see him so much."

"Of course you must see him," he said. "When you are strong again, Magda will bring him."

"Why not before that? Why not here?"

"It may be against their wretched rules. I'll try to arrange it," he said, echoing the words the Warden had used. "Leave it to me. I'll do all I can."

"Thank you," her voice trailed into a sigh, as if she was too weary to go on. She turned her hand over so that she was clasping his fingers.

"You are not well," he said. "This has been a terrible shock for you, and it will take time to get over it."

She admitted, "I worry about Joy. I keep expecting her to walk in."

He looked around the room. "You are alone here at night?"

"Yes, I don't like it much. At first I was pleased that the other beds are unoccupied; now I wish I had some company. Of course I know the night sister is not far away, and I can ring the bell if I want her to come. I'd be fine, if only I could stop thinking about Joy."

"She's miles away," said Felix, squeezing her hand. "She has been transferred, so you will never see her again. There is an enquiry going on about how she managed to get hold of a knife, and hide it in her overall pocket." He frowned. "In my view they are far too lax in this establishment. All that psychological mumbo jumbo the Warden is so keen on . . . I don't approve of it if it jeopardises security. There are too many women in here who do not deserve the kid-glove treatment." He shuddered, "Anything could have happened . . . "

He had nightmares, waking in a sweat having dreamt of Duibhne lying in a pool of blood. He thought her too fine a person to be subjected to such horrors, and yet the lawyer in him acknowledged that she was serving a sentence for manslaughter. There was no getting away from that fact.

He looked lovingly at the small wan face lying on the pillows. She looked very defenceless at that moment, but he knew there was steel in her make-up – he reckoned her aristocratic forebears had given her that. And that thought reminded him of Claw, and he asked, "Do you want me to get in touch with your father about this?"

"Good heavens, no!" she said, and he was glad to see her smile. "He might take his life into his hands and board another plane. Felix, do not tell him. It would alarm him, and the story would become exaggerated in the telling. Really, it is only a small matter, and I shall be better in no time. I'll probably have a very small scar to show for it."

"You'll have to tell people you got it in a skiing accident," he said.

The wound did not heal quickly and she took a long time to regain her strength. Magda was concerned when she came to see her; she had not expected her to look so frail.

"I was hoping you would bring Bartley with you," said Duibhne.

"I'm sorry," Magda replied. "I haven't been given permission yet, and don't you think we should wait now until you are completely better? The bandages might frighten him."

"The bandages might frighten him," repeated Duibhne wonderingly. "Of course, you are right. He does not know me, does he? He must think you are his mother."

"No," said Magda firmly. "He doesn't think that. You forget how little he is."

She loved Duibhne, but she was beginning to think

that everything to do with the girl presented a problem, and the incident with the knife was just the latest in a series of perplexities. She remembered Tom's words as he went off in search of his son: "Damn Claw and his bloody girl." Of course, she did not feel that way, but sometimes she looked back regretfully to more peaceful days. Life at Shannon with Tom and the baby was not easy for Magda.

Mrs Stockdale came to visit Duibhne. She was ushered into the ward by the sister, and treated with great respect. Duibhne realised that she was honoured by the visit (Hazel would regard it with suspicion, she was sure) and she felt like a soldier in bed, lying to attention when the General stopped to talk to him.

She had always seen the Warden sitting behind her desk. Now, she saw the whole of her, a plump woman with fat legs. She wore a bright blue suit, the skirt tight over her stomach and hips, and high-heeled shoes looking as if they hurt her, the sides digging into the flesh around her ankles. She sat on a chair next to the bed, and Duibhne relaxed.

"I hope you're feeling better," said Mrs Stockdale.

"Much better, thank you."

"I am told the food is excellent in the Infirmary."

"Yes, it is very good," answered Duibhne who, having worked in the kitchen, knew that the food sent there was the same as the food sent to the canteen.

"And you have had visitors, I hear."

"Please, may Hazel be allowed to come and see me, and Grace? Grace saved my life."

"Hazel has already put in a request to come and see you, and I shall suggest Grace does the same."

"That is very kind of you." Duibhne wondered if it was the correct moment to broach the subject of Bartley, and decided it was.

"Mrs Stockdale," she began, "I am so anxious to see my son." She rushed ahead with the next sentence before the other could say anything. "Magda, the lady who is looking after him, thinks we should wait until the bandages are off, and I agree with her. But after that . . . may I see him? Please?"

"I'm sure you may," said the Warden, "and in any case you cannot return to your room until the wound is healed, and children are not allowed to visit the Infirmary. Those are the rules, but, when you are better and back in your house again, then we will arrange for you to see your little boy. How old is he now?"

"Eighteen months."

"Still a baby," said the Warden thoughtfully.

She got to her feet. The visit was over. "I hope you make a speedy recovery," were her parting words.

For some reason, Duibhne thought, she is not at ease. There was an expression on her face that she could not comprehend. When Hazel arrived, accompanied by one of the guards, she told her about it.

"If she was fazed," said Hazel, "it is probably because one of her ladies behaved in an unladylike manner. Attacking someone with a knife does let the old place down, you know. She can't be happy about it."

"Of course that must be the reason." It was wonderful seeing Hazel again. "I've missed you," she said.

"I guess you haven't missed me as much as I've missed you," said Hazel seriously. "At least you have been living in the lap of luxury, while nothing has changed for me, except there is no one to listen to my garbage. I can't tell you how bored and lonely I am without you, so, for God's sake, get better soon and return to the happy homestead before I go completely nuts."

After she had gone, Duibhne lay quietly, watching a bird which was perched precariously on the topmost twig of the tree outside her window. Backwards and forwards it teetered, battling with the wind, until suddenly it abandoned the balancing act, and flew off. Free.

Pictures came to her mind of her father, Clonbarron, Pinkie and Nanny, Hazel's visit and the little plant in a pot she had brought, purchased from the shop and now standing on the locker next to the bed. Then she thought of Bartley, and how she would be seeing him soon. Very soon.

She closed her eyes, and let her thoughts drift in an unconnected way, on the edge of sleep. For the first time in many months she felt almost happy.

CHAPTER TWENTY-TWO

For a week after the knife attack, Duibhne was overcome by a lassitude which made her content to lie still in bed, and look out of the window. Then she began to feel well again, and the long days and nights in the Infirmary became almost unbearably boring.

On the days when she had no visitors she turned to the sister or young nurse for conversation, but there was none forthcoming, only the daily enquiry about her bowel movements. She suspected they had instructions to be attentive to the needs of the patients, but not to become too friendly. This was the attitude adopted by the guards in the prison block, although they did not always stick to the rules.

She wished someone would join her in the ward. The days seemed interminable, and she looked forward to the nights when she could sleep the time away.

She read. One of the trusted ladies ran the library,

and she arrived with a trolley loaded with books. She was supposed to come twice a week, but that did not satisfy Duibhne's demands who read at least one book a day. So the library lady came as often as she could without incurring the sister's displeasure. On one of her visits, Duibhne implored her to stay and talk to her.

"I can't tell you how deadly it is here on my own," she said. "Couldn't you stop a few minutes?"

The woman sat on the bed. "I don't suppose anyone will notice if I wait here a while."

She told Duibhne that she was sixty-two years old, and the girl told her, with sincerity, that she did not look it. It is a strange fact that people do not age prematurely in prison. They lead such an even uneventful life, away from ordinary anxieties, that their youthful looks are preserved well into old age. The woman sitting on the side of Duibhne's bed had a tall spare figure, and dark hair, cut very short.

Duibhne asked, "How long have you been here?" It was the stock question the prisoners asked when they met for the first time, usually followed by another question about the length of the sentence.

"Fifteen years," replied the woman. "I think I should be released in a year's time." She introduced herself; her name was Bernice Cooper. "What sentence did you get?"

"Five years," said Duibhne.

"That's nothing," said the woman. "It will soon pass. A short time like that doesn't change you. You can come out, and forget it ever happened. Now me, I was forty-seven when I came here, and I have grown old in this place. God knows what I'll do with myself when I leave. I'll be too old to get a job, that's for sure."

Fifteen years! Duibhne thought, what on earth could she have done to deserve such a stretch?

In common with most of the residents, Bernice was only too anxious to recount her story, and in Duibhne she found a willing listener.

Bernice was an only child and, after the death of her father, she lived with her mother in the family house in Portland. The mother became increasingly disabled with rheumatism, and was eventually confined to a wheelchair. Bernice had a job as a waitress in a diner, which was hot tiring work. She returned home in the evening to a querulous old woman, endlessly grumbling about her unhappy lot, and ungrateful for the care her daughter took of her.

It was a relationship tainted with bitterness. Over and over again, the mother taunted the daughter about her unmarried state, about the fact that she was in her forties and no man had desired her. Nothing Bernice did was right. Her mother did not like the food she cooked for her, she accused her of selfishness and neglect, and resented her going to work, although she knew in her heart that if Bernice stayed at home they would not be able to manage. They could survive financially and continue to live in their home because of the meagre wage Bernice received.

"I was in prison," she said, "long before I came here."

Their unsatisfactory life together continued, and the only change in the dreary monotony of their existence was a deterioration of the old woman's health. She developed a heart problem, and was prescribed pills. Every morning, before she went to work, Bernice put the pills under three down-turned egg-cups, standing in a row on the kitchen dresser, so that her mother would be sure to take the right number of pills at the right time of day. Under the first egg-cup was the morning dose, under the next the lunch-time one, and the last two pills of the day were under the third egg-cup. That way no mistakes could be made. The doctor had said the heart pills were very strong, and they must follow the instructions on the label.

One day a man called Charlie White came into the diner. He sat alone, an unprepossessing man wearing a grubby raincoat. He ordered a cup of coffee and a club sandwich, and he got into conversation with Bernice, and told her he worked in insurance. He was divorced and lived in lodgings in downtown Portland. He started coming to the diner every day, and one day he asked her to go to the movies with him. He was fifty years old and she was forty-five.

At this point the sister came into the ward, gave Bernice a withering look, and noisily shifted the trolley of books, so that it stood by the door. Bernice took the hint, and whispered, "I'll go now."

"Come back soon, please."

"I'll do my best."

"I shall soon finish reading these books," said Duibhne hopefully. The real-life drama had captivated her more than anything she read in a book. It was like following a serial in two parts, and she could not wait to hear the next instalment.

"Okay."

When Bernice returned with her trolley on the following day, she was full of excitement. She had asked questions, and found out why Duibhne was in the Infirmary. "You're a heroine," she said. "Everyone is talking about you."

"I am not the heroine. That is Grace – she was very brave. Do you know about Grace?"

"Well, I've heard about her, of course. She's the dame who chopped off a guy's head with a cleaver."

"Goodness," said Duibhne, "I did not know that, but she is a cook, and I suppose it is the sort of weapon she would have to hand."

She hoped Bernice would go on with her story, and the other woman needed no encouragement.

"Charlie asked me to marry him, and I accepted. By this time, he knew all about Mother, and I took him home and introduced them. I thought she would be pleased for me, but she was forever telling me what a lousy job he had, that he did not love me but was just after the house. It was true that we planned to move into the house after we were married; we had Mother to consider and Charlie could not afford to offer us a home. When Mother realised I was serious, she started on a new tack. She maintained she was very ill, although the doctor said her rheumatism and bad heart were the only things wrong with her. She said she could not breathe, that her throat had closed up so that she wasn't able to eat. She moaned and groaned, and made frightening choking sounds, screaming that she was dying. I called the doctor, and he gave her a sedative, but he said her symptoms were psychosomatic."

"What does that mean?" asked Duibhne. She had never heard of such a thing.

"In her mind, that's what it means. It was all in her imagination. She was always saying she hoped to die, that she could not bear the idea of my marrying Charlie. He was everything dreadful in her eyes – mercenary, common and insensitive to her needs. Never, she said, never would she consent to sharing a home with him. I had to take time off work with Mother during her turns, and eventually I was fired. I'll never forget my last day at work. Everyone was kind to me, and the girls clubbed together and bought me a present, a beautiful flower vase. Charlie came to meet me, and we walked back to my house, arm in arm. I was clutching my present, all wrapped in pretty paper and ribbon. I felt desperate, I can tell you, and I didn't know how we were going to manage without my money coming in each week.

That night I was in bed when I heard Mother call

me. I went to her bedside, and she was making the usual strangulated cries. She looked ill because she was not eating properly, and all those 'high strikes', as I called them, must have been a strain on her heart.

I asked her if she had taken the evening pills, and she said 'no', so I went to get them from under the egg-cup. Then I looked under the other egg-cups, and I saw that she had not taken any of her heart pills that day. I took them all in to her, with a glass of water, and I said 'Take these and perhaps you will have a good night's sleep'. She swallowed the three lots of pills without a murmur. One by one, she popped them into her mouth, and gulped them down with water. She was looking at me all the time, over the glass, with her sharp eyes on my face. I swear she knew.

Then I sat in the chair beside her bed, and she went to sleep. I thought she was okay, then I saw she was dribbling from the side of her mouth, and I wiped it away. Suddenly, I realised she was no longer breathing. I called the doctor and when he came I told him what I had done, and do you know what he said? He said, 'I wish you had not told me,' that's what he said, 'Now I shall have to report it.'"

"What happened then?" asked Duibhne.

"Well, it all came out: Charlie and how Mother hated him, and how I lost my job. I had no excuse. I knew she was not supposed to take all those pills in one go. The doctor said he thought they were the cause of her death. It might have been natural causes, but it was unlikely.

You can imagine what conclusions the jury reached. Matricide is a nasty crime. The Judge gave me twenty years."

"What a sad story!" said Duibhne. "Thank you for telling it to me. What happened to Charlie?"

"He visited me for the first year, and then the visits became more infrequent. I was given the job of librarian which meant I was trusted. For some reason, Mrs Stockdale believed in me. I betrayed that trust by doing a bunk, and I went off in search of Charlie. I found him shacked up with a widow who had a bit of cash. I was arrested before I had time to give myself up. Of course I lost all remission for good behaviour, and I thought I would lose my job in the library as well, but Mrs Stockdale talked to me, and decided to give me another chance. She is a saint, that woman."

Duibhne murmured, "I'm sorry."

"Oh, don't feel sorry for me," said Bernice. "It was my own fault, and the funny thing about it is that Mother was right about Charlie. All the things she said about him were true."

Duibhne was afraid she would ask questions about her past history, but she did not. Maybe she had heard it all, together with the saga about Joy and the knife.

"I'm going back to my room tomorrow," she told Bernice on her last day in the Infirmary. "Shall I see you again after that?"

"Probably not," replied Bernice. "I'm in C House and you're in B, so we're unlikely to meet up again."

All Duibhne could do was to wish her luck. Bernice pressed her hand, and they parted.

"It's great to have you back," said Hazel, the next day. "Some of the girls wanted to put up a banner saying 'Welcome back', but the Warden wouldn't allow it!" Their room seemed very small and cramped, and she missed the big window. But that was all she missed. That evening she told Bernice's story to Hazel.

"This is the place for real-life tragedies," was Hazel's comment when Duibhne had finished. "Not all the women here are hardened criminals. Some of them are like us; they made an error of judgement in one frightful moment, and they are made to suffer for it. Poor Bernice, it sounds as if everything was against her. But do not think too much about her, Divvy. You mustn't let her story worry you."

"I don't intend to," Duibhne assured her. "My only worry now is when I shall be allowed to see my son."

"I think it will be soon," said Hazel wisely, "and I am as excited as you are."

CHAPTER TWENTY-THREE

"Today is the day," said Duibhne happily. "Today I am seeing my little boy."

She felt like singing. The day had been a long time coming. Months had elapsed since Duibhne had left the Infirmary, and Bartley was now over two years old. His mother nursed a forlorn hope that she would be able to see him on his second birthday, but it was not to be. She made another request to see the Warden, but this time Mrs Stockdale was almost sharp with her. "Please do not trouble me with this again," she said. "I have already told you arrangements are in hand."

At last, the arrangements had been made for such a simple thing as meeting a child and his carer in the playground. Magda would take him there, and his mother would be escorted to the place.

That morning Duibhne was swilling the blue floor of their room with a mop, which she kept dipping into a plastic bucket and wringing out with her hands. It was Hazel's turn for the bath, and she had just returned, and was sitting on the edge of her bed, drying her wet hair with a towel.

"I must say I envy you," she said. "It must be nice being a mother."

"You will have children of your own one day," said Duibhne comfortably.

"I don't think so," answered Hazel quietly. "I think what I did excludes having children."

"Oh, really!" Duibhne was irritated. It was disturbing when Hazel made remarks of that sort. The fact that she meant every word she said did not make it more acceptable. Hazel took her guilty feelings very seriously, and this often led to deep dejection. On a morning like this, which was full of hope, it created a cloud.

"I'm sorry," said Hazel quickly, recognising the cloud at once, "I'm so selfish. I didn't mean to spoil your joy on a day like this. I am so pleased for you." She squeezed the girl's hand. "Please forgive me."

They had to sit and wait for someone to come and fetch Duibhne.

"Why doesn't she come?"

"She will, it's still early."

Ten minutes passed, and it seemed like an hour. "Has Mrs Stockdale forgotten?"

"No, she has not forgotten."

A long pause, and then Duibhne said, "Oh, why doesn't she come? Is she never coming?"

"She is coming."

They heard the footsteps coming down the corridor, the key in the lock.

"Good luck!" cried Hazel, suddenly apprehensive, although she could not understand the reason for the feeling.

Most of the women guards were hard-faced and tough, the result of years of disciplining people of their own sex and exploiting the power they had over them. The girl who came to fetch Duibhne, however, was young like herself, and displayed none of these characteristics. The system had not had time to work on her.

It was a perfect day in summer, with a deep blue arch of sky, and a few small fluffy clouds scudding across it.

"It is so lovely," said Duibhne to the girl, who had a light step like her own. A little breeze lifted their hair as they walked together across the grass. "This day makes me think of Ireland."

"My great-grandparents came from Ireland. From a place called Tipperary. I'm going to go there one day."

"You'll love it," Duibhne told her. "The grass there is so green, just as everyone says."

"The Emerald Isle . . ."

"When you see Tipperary," said Duibhne, "you will understand why it is called that."

Most of the residents had children, and the playground was provided for them, with swings, a climbing-frame and a sandpit. On visiting days screams and laughter could be heard coming from this part of the grounds. The day of Bartley's visit was not an official visiting day, however, and the playground was quiet.

Bartley was sitting in the sandpit, with a bucket and spade his mother had bought for him for his birthday. Magda was standing close by, anxious, nervous.

As they approached Duibhne felt her heart hammering in her chest. She took a deep breath, and stood still for a moment, watching, without being seen.

The dark curly head was bent down; she had been told about his curls. She could see his little sturdy legs stretched out in front of him, the bucket between them, and one plump hand holding the wooden spade.

As she drew near, he looked up and smiled at her, his all-enveloping smile that was for everyone. Then she knew. She knew that the terrible fear that she had pushed to the back of her mind was, in fact, a reality.

She could not stay in that place, and she ran away from it. She ran away from Magda's shocked face, from the smile of the child, the sweet childish smile with no depth to it. The smile of a child who was always good, who found the world a delightful place with no evil in it, where the face of the loving Magda was his whole universe.

The young guard managed to catch up with her, drew level, and cried, "I'm sorry, I'm sorry." She persuaded Duibhne to walk quietly, taking her arm and leading her back to her room.

"What's happened?" The disbelief in Hazel's voice

made her realise that she had been in ignorance too. No one had seen fit to warn either of them.

Duibhne sobbed and sobbed, and not even Hazel could find words of comfort. She was heartbroken and angry at the same time.

Later in the day she was summoned to Mrs Stockdale's office. The Warden looked sad and concerned when she saw the girl, sitting in front of her, clutching a sodden handkerchief which she had rolled into a tight ball. Her face was swollen and wet with tears.

"Why didn't you tell me?" she shouted.

"We didn't tell you because we didn't know for sure. A great many tests were made before anyone could be certain. I'm afraid he will never be a normal little boy, but he is a very happy one. That should be a comfort to you. Sometimes children with his sort of disability are very unhappy beings, resentful and aggressive. He shows none of these characteristics. Miss Angelo loves him dearly, as you know."

"Miss Angelo thinks he is a normal child," said Duibhne bitterly, remembering countless conversations with Magda when the woman had given no hint of there being anything different about Bartley.

"I don't think you are being fair," replied the Warden gently, "of course she appreciates the situation, but it is hard for her as well, and she is dealing with it in the best way she knows."

She did not mention that Magda had come to see her

after Duibhne had been taken back to her room that morning. She had asked someone in the grounds to direct her to the Warden's office, and she had arrived there, Bartley balanced on one hip, the toy spade still clutched in one fat hand.

Magda shed no tears. Mrs Stockdale, with the perception of a woman with her sort of job, realised that Magda thought herself to be alone now. She stood there, holding the child, and a torrent of words issued from her lips. Without being disloyal to Tom, she managed to convey the difficulties she was experiencing at home. Tom could not relate to Bartley and his solution was to ignore him. He was Magda's problem, and that was that. He had written to his brother, Claw, and explained the situation to him, but Claw had not replied. Magda thought this unnecessarily cruel and callous. What sort of man was Lord Claughessy to take this attitude towards his grandson?

"Please sit down," Mrs Stockdale had said to the harassed woman.

Magda had dropped her handbag and the plastic bucket to the floor, and lowered herself into the chair. Bartley had cuddled close to her, and laid his head on her breast.

"He is a very loving child," commented the Warden.

"Yes, he is, but that is not enough for most people. From what I have seen today it is not enough for Divvy."

"She may come round to it, once she has got over the

initial shock. I think we may have made an error in judgement by not warning her beforehand. I thought if we told her she might imagine it worse than it is, and refuse to see him. Now she has seen him, I think she will begin to get used to the idea."

"I don't think so," said Magda.

"Don't you think that she will eventually feel differently about him?"

"It will be a long time," said Magda, "and we are not going to wait until that happens, Bartley and I. We are going to stay close together."

She sounded so determined that the Warden was anxious about her. "My dear Miss Angelo," she said kindly, "you must be realistic about this. When Miss Shannon is released she will, in all probability, return to Ireland and, of course, she will take the child with her."

"I could never leave Tom," Magda admitted, "so I could not go with them." There was a despairing note to her voice.

"It is very hard for you," said the other woman, "and you have my deepest sympathy, but I think you must prepare yourself for the break. In this case, I fear, it is inevitable."

Magda rose to her feet. "You have been very kind," she said.

Mrs Stockdale did not think she had been at all kind. The sight of the middle-aged woman and the piteous little boy pierced her heart. For once in her life she was at a loss, and did not know what to say or do that would be a help.

"Please come and see me again, if it will do any good," she said lamely.

Magda nodded, and she and Bartley, burdened with a bag and a bucket and spade, left the room.

The Warden remembered them now, as she looked at the weeping Duibhne. She thought, Magda Angelo is the more to be pitied. The girl will soon get over it.

Barbara Mills came to see Duibhne, and told her that Dr Leroy had expressed misgivings about Bartley some months before.

He had said, "Time will tell, and we must watch his development." They had, and the prognosis was not good.

"I'm afraid it is another thing for you to bear," said Barbara, "but you are a brave girl, and you will face this setback as you have faced all the others."

Felix would not have agreed with her. He thought Duibhne would never get over the latest blow that had been dealt to her. She looked strained and ill, and there were smudges under her eyes. He asked Mrs Stockdale to give her time off from the kitchen. He hated to think of her in that steamy hot-house environment, but his request was refused. Politely, the Warden told him that she did not consider a break from work would be beneficial to Duibhne.

It was some weeks before Felix decided he could tell Duibhne what was on his mind.

"I know it is hard for you," he said, "but in a strange way this tragedy may be in your favour." He added hastily, "From a legal point of view, I mean."

The table in the Visitor's Room was a barrier between them, and he longed to take her hand, as he had done in the Infirmary. His love for her made him feel desperate, and he always walked away from these unsatisfactory meetings feeling frustrated and angry.

"How can that be?" she asked, not interested.

"The doctors seem to agree that Bartley's condition is the result of him being mistreated when he was an infant. In other words, a fearful blow to the head. No jury is going to believe you administered that, and I intend to bring it to the notice of the Appeal Court."

Duibhne did not care. She and Hazel had thrashed out the whole sorry saga, night after night, until there was nothing left to dissect and question and, when it became a dried-out husk, they had thrown it away and vowed not to talk about it any more.

She refused to see her son again, although Magda still came to see her, and talked as if they both wanted to believe that the incident in the playground had never taken place.

One day she fished out of her bag a photograph, and handed it to Duibhne. "This is the latest picture of him," she said cautiously. "Do you want it?"

Duibhne studied the photograph of a handsome little boy playing with a wooden train.

"It is very sweet," she said slowly. "Thank you, Magda."

It was make-believe, and they both knew it. Duibhne was well aware that, sooner or later, she would have to acknowledge her commitment to Bartley but, in the meantime, she was not thinking of the future. She was well into her third year now, resigned to the way of life.

When she showed the photograph to Mrs Smythe it was much admired. "Oh, my dear, I had no idea . . . you seem so young to be a mother. Isn't he a perfect love?"

"He is," agreed Duibhne, "and I want to make him a nursery-rhyme book, like the one you showed me when we first met. I know I shall never be able to embroider the pages as beautifully as you, but I would like to try."

She worked with infinite patience, and each minute stitch was an expression of her love for the baby, not the child. In her mind, they were completely separate. Miss Muffet, Jack Horner, Simple Simon . . .

"He is still too young to understand the rhymes," said Mrs Smythe.

Too young. He would always be too young to understand anything.

The nursery-rhyme book was to take many years to complete. In the early stages Mrs Smythe was there to offer encouragement. "Remember, it will be like an heirloom," she said, when Duibhne grew impatient with it. "Your boy will give it to his son, and it will pass down the family."

This sort of dreamy talk suited Duibhne's mood exactly. The work soothed her. Occasionally, her thoughts turned to Magda who faced the difficult task of trying to mete out her love for Tom and Bartley in equal measures and, at the same time, keep them apart as much as possible.

It was not an easy road for her travel, and she had no way of knowing the end was in sight.

CHAPTER TWENTY-FOUR

One morning, when Duibhne was working in the kitchen, Grace came to her side and said, "You'se wanted in the Visitor's Room, honey."

"Who can it be?" She felt herself grow pale with apprehension, and with trembling hands she removed her overall and the white cap from her damp head. Sympathetically, Grace took these from her. They both knew that something must have happened, for no visitors were allowed that day.

Bartley? Her father? Oh, please God, not her father!

The Visitor's Room was a vast empty auditorium on non-visiting days. Somewhere in the middle of the echoing space was Magda, sitting at a table.

"Tom is dead," she said flatly.

She went on to tell Duibhne how she had watched him crossing the yard to tend to one of his precious horses, how he had faltered suddenly, and fallen to the ground.

"It was very quick. A cerebral haemorrhage, the doctor called it, and he said Tom would not have known anything about it. He did not suffer, and I must be thankful for that."

"Oh, I'm so sorry, Magda," said Duibhne, "I know how much you loved him."

"How shall I live without him?" asked Magda, and the tears started coursing down her cheeks. Then, as if answering her own question, she said naively, "He left me all his money and his possessions."

Tom was a rich man, Duibhne knew that. With a painful stab of remorse she felt the sadness of him dying with only his faithful Magda left in his life.

Magda went on, "Of course, I do not care about the money for myself. It means nothing to me, but I am thankful I shall have enough to look after the boy, and see that he has everything he needs."

Duibhne listened to these words with a faint feeling of surprise. Magda, in that stressful moment, was thinking of Bartley as her own child. It was an illusion borne of grief, and she would realise her misconception when she came to her senses. Duibhne was thinking these thoughts, and listening to Magda's voice at the same time.

She was saying, "He understands, you know. I was sad, and he came and put his fat little arms around my neck, as if to comfort me." She went on defensively, "They don't know how much he takes in, but he is smarter than they think."

Duibhne could only sit and hold Magda's hand, until a guard approached and told them the time had come for the bereaved woman to leave, and for her to return to the kitchen.

It was shortly after this that she and Hazel started their campaign for a non-smoking recreational room.

Of course, it was Hazel that got the idea going. "I think there should be a room for non-smokers," she grumbled, thumping the one hard pillow on her bed. "It is not fair that we have to stay in our room all the time. I would like a change of scene occasionally, wouldn't you, Divvy? But neither of us can stand that smoky hole."

"It would be nice to watch the television," agreed Duibhne. "Shall we ask the Warden about it?"

Every request had to be made by filling out a form, and the form took time going through the various channels. Eventually, however, Hazel was summoned to the Warden's office, and she explained the problem, and how a solution could be reached by having a separate room for non-smoking residents.

As always, Mrs Stockdale was a sympathetic listener. "It is a splendid idea," she said, "but, of course, it is a question of space. It would probably mean a new building and that would be very costly. I will mention it to the committee."

"You'll see, nothing will be done," Hazel told Duibhne, and it looked as if she was right when three months passed and they heard nothing. They decided to set up a petition.

Hazel drafted the notice, and asked Duibhne to copy it in her neatest printing. It was important to Hazel that Duibhne play an active part in the project; it was to be a joint enterprise. The notice was headed, *To all Non-Smokers!* in big fat letters, tumbling against each other. Duibhne filled in the letters with a red pen. It reminded her of the painting competition in Limerick, so many years ago. She told Hazel how she had won the prize, and described the ceremony in the cinema when she had gone to collect it. Hazel enjoyed the story.

"My father was so proud," said Duibhne, laughing. "He decided I must have artistic talent."

Privately, Hazel thought Duibhne's father must be the stupidest man alive.

The non-smokers were asked to put their signatures on the petition, and the surprise was that there were so many signatures. Another piece of paper had to be produced and pinned beneath the first, and then another.

The Warden was impressed, and asked to see Hazel again. "We represent nearly half the residents in B House," Hazel told her.

"And we are told every day of the dangers of smoking," said Mrs Stockdale. "That must be an important factor in favour of your request. The only difficulty is that the other houses would have to have a room for non-smokers as well, and I am not sure that the committee would agree to such expenditure."

The campaign became very important to the girls, and they made leaflets and distributed them amongst the women. Gradually, as the months went by, their enthusiasm diminished. Their home-made notice and the papers covered with signatures had long been torn from the board.

"Well, that's that," said Hazel. The campaign had given them an interest, and now that it had come to nothing they felt dull and discouraged.

Then one day they saw workmen in the yard outside, and scaffolding being put up against the walls of the building.

"It can't be!" cried Duibhne.

The rumour spread around the house, and was confirmed: A, B and C Houses were to have extensions, recreational rooms for non-smokers. It was an exciting victory, and Duibhne felt she had contributed to something good. The long empty days in the Correctional Facility had not been completely wasted, and she felt a sense of achievement she had never experienced before, and would never experience again in quite the same way.

"If only we had champagne!" she said on the day of the opening of the new room. For that is what Claw would have provided on such an occasion. Of course, there was no champagne, but a few words of praise from the Warden.

"And Felix," Duibhne told Hazel that evening, "he says we should be proud of ourselves."

She was lying on her bed with her hands behind her head, and Hazel, on the other bed with a book in her hand, looked up and said, "He is a dear man."

It was true. Felix was always ready to listen, and when Duibhne told him about the new recreational room and her involvement in it, he was enchanted to see how a light came into her eyes, replacing the usual sadness. For years he had hoped to wipe the sadness from her face; now a small triumph had done it for him.

"He loves you," went on Hazel. "When you leave here, what will you do about him?"

Duibhne was startled. "What do you mean?"

"Well," said the practical Hazel, "it strikes me that he will want to marry you. He is the sort of man who will want marriage, children, the whole packet. I do not see him happily settling for any other relationship. He belongs to a race imbued with the sense of family. He is a successful lawyer, and absolutely devoted to you. Surely you would consider it?"

Duibhne stared up at the ceiling with its one bare light enclosed in a wire cage. For the first time, she considered the idea of marrying Felix. He would want her to return to Oregon, the place where he worked, and that idea did not appeal to her. There were so many unhappy memories attached to the States, she thought when she was free again she would go as far away from that country as possible. Marrying Felix would create so many problems it did not seem feasible.

"I don't think . . . " she began.

"What don't you think?" asked Hazel sharply.

"I don't think he is the right person for me," said Duibhne slowly.

"You mean you do not love him?"

Oh, she loved Felix all right. She supposed she had known that for a long time now. She thought of his serious brown eyes fixed on her face, listening to every word she said. She thought of his tremendous loyalty to her, and his patience during the long dark days at the Log Cabin. There was no one in the world who had ever given her as much as Felix, and she knew that he loved her with his whole being, that his thoughts were always centred on her. The tedious journeys he had made to the prison to see her, the hours he had spent looking at her across the table in the Visitor's Room were all a testament of his great love for her.

Duibhne met the eyes of Hazel, suddenly directed at her. The expression in them made her feel uneasy. In the years, months and hours they had spent in each other's company, Hazel had never looked at her like that before.

"He is not right, that's it, isn't it? Not quite right. Small, Jewish and a professional man, no wonder your father did not begin to understand such a guy. But then, you should remember that your precious father has not bothered to get in touch with you all the time you have been here!"

Duibhne's eyes filled with tears at the mention of Claw. "I understand him," she whispered.

"Oh, yes, you understand him," said Hazel, "so

much so that his influence has stayed with you during the years you have spent here. You have learnt nothing from the experience, have you? You people," she almost spat out the words, "you people never change. Whatever the circumstances you manage to retain that apartness from ordinary mortals. Even in a stink-hole like this you are still Lady Muck. It is not an enhancement, Divvy, and I feel sorry for you, that you have not been able to break away."

The vehemence of this outburst made Duibhne weep. She did not fully understand what it meant, but it seemed a terrible indictment. Also, she was bitterly aware that it was the first time she and Hazel had quarrelled.

Less than an hour later Hazel was repentant. "Unforgivable," she said. "I'm truly sorry. I don't know what came over me. Put it down to the fact that I don't understand your sort of people."

"What do you mean, my sort of people?"

"Well, your father, stately home and all that. Let's face it, it was only a quirk of fate that brought us together, Divvy. In the ordinary course of events both our lives would have been completely different, and we would never have met."

"But I'm so glad we did meet," said Duibhne.

"So am I," replied Hazel.

"And we are friends, aren't we?" went on Duibhne stubbornly. "Isn't that all that matters?"

"Yes, of course it is," said Hazel, "and I'm sorry I

talked such a lot of hot air, mystifying you completely, I can see that. It's over, and I've said I'm sorry. I can't say more. How did it begin? With Felix, of course. Poor Felix, I suppose I felt sorry for the pathetic little sod. Forget all I said, Divvy. How about we bang on the door, and ask to be taken to our special room to watch the television?"

CHAPTER TWENTY-FIVE

Duibhne decided that Hazel's strange outburst was partly due to her apprehension about leaving the Correctional Facility. Her sentence, with remission for good behaviour, had little more than a month to run, and she was allowed a visit home on parole. She was away for a long weekend, staying with her parents. It was a foretaste of how much Duibhne was going to miss her, and the time passed slowly until her return.

She tried to sound enthusiastic and interested about Hazel's taste of freedom.

"Did you enjoy it? I want to hear everything."

"Enjoy it? I'm not sure about that," was Hazel's reply. "That sounds mean, I know, for Mom and Dad did everything to make it a happy visit for me. Some of my relatives came over, and they were very sweet, wishing me well in the future. But . . . you remember how you felt when you first arrived here? Well, I have to tell you, it's not so different when you leave. There's the same lonely abandoned feeling, and everything seems unnatural, unreal."

Duibhne nodded. She understood perfectly because she too was frightened by the thought of the ordinary world. There was a sameness about life in prison which was almost comforting, and she wondered how she would face up to the problems of the world outside the gates.

Hazel went on, "Of course it was great to sleep in a proper bed again, instead of a metal cot, and not to have those bloody torches shone on you every hour of the night, but I guess I must have missed them, for I couldn't sleep. And when Mom and I went shopping on Saturday morning, I felt as if my being there was against the rules, and I half-expected one of our favourite people to pounce on me, and drag me back here."

"Surely you will soon get over those feelings? It sounds good to me."

"And there's another aspect," said Hazel. "How do I know if I'm forgiven for what I did? The State may have forgiven me, but have I suffered enough to earn God's forgiveness?"

Duibhne always felt slightly uncomfortable when Hazel talked about God. He had featured very little in her upbringing. After renouncing Roman Catholicism there was no God left for Claw and his brother. Lapsed Catholics must become unbelievers; there is no middle way for them. As a child Duibhne had thought about 'her mama in heaven', but when she became more adult it did not make sense. What was this half-remembered being doing in heaven? Galloping after a fox across celestial fields? For that was the activity that gave Kathleen the most happiness, and surely happiness was what heaven was all about?

She found it difficult to understand, and she envied Hazel her uncomplicated view of God. It was strange that such a complex character never wavered in her belief in His existence.

Duibhne could not imagine life without Hazel. It was unthinkable. "They will find someone else to share the room," she said. "It will be a nightmare."

She conveyed her anxieties to the kindly Mrs Smythe who took it upon herself to speak to the Warden, but Mrs Stockdale was her usual fair implacable self, and said, "She must take her chances, like everyone else."

Sitting in the Warden's comfortable office, Mrs Smythe ventured the question, "What was her crime?"

She did not know if it was against the rules of the establishment to give her such information. There were so many rules it was confusing at times. When she had first taken on the task of teaching Duibhne she had assumed it would only be a few months. She could not believe that the girl had committed a serious crime, but as the months became years she began to wonder, and became more and more curious.

Mrs Stockdale had no hesitation in telling her about Duibhne's background. Prisoners have no rights to privacy. She was surprised that the woman had not asked her before, but as this was her first voluntary teaching job she probably did not realise that she was entitled to know everything about her pupil.

Now, Mrs Smythe regarded Duibhne with new eyes. She looked at her sitting so still, engrossed in stitching the nursery-rhyme book. She appeared calm, head bent over her task. There was a glimpse of the exquisite face beneath the long hair, twisted in careless perfection on top of her head. Her hands were steady, one hand holding the small frame on which the linen page was fixed, the other with the needle poised above the work. That hand, Mrs. Smythe now knew, had once held a gun and fired it at a living breathing person, ending a life for ever. She found it utterly incredible.

"There are some terrible people in this place," Duibhne told Felix. "Some of them have committed sex offences against children or are in here for drug-related crimes. Suppose I get someone like that?"

But Felix was in an optimistic mood. He had been busy getting statements from Dr Leroy and the people at the Gibb County Hospital about Bartley's injuries. The damage to the child was of greater significance now it was known that his whole life was to be affected. But was it enough to satisfy the Court of Appeal? Felix could not be sure.

Then the miracle happened.

He received a telephone call in his office from Magda. Would he come and see her? She gave no explanation, but said it was urgent.

As he drove his shiny black limousine through the open gates of Shannon and along the drive, he saw there had been changes since he was last there, nearly three years ago when he had gone to see Tom about the money for Duibhne's bail. At first he did not realise what these were, and then he noticed the lush green paddocks on either side were empty. No inquisitive mares trotted to the fences to watch his arrival. As the car turned into the stable yard, he saw it was deserted, doors shut and no sounds of swishing brooms and rattling buckets. Magda, unable to cope, had sold off the whole of Tom's treasured business. Felix was struck by the sadness, the finality of it all.

Magda opened the door to him, and he saw immediately that she too had changed. The sexuality that had shone through her shyness had gone, and she looked years older. There were grey streaks in her mass of untidy hair. She was dressed as if she no longer cared how she looked. She must miss that funny little man, thought Felix as he followed her into the main room.

The room itself had lost its pristine appearance, the white walls were grubby, and there were newspapers, books, clothes and toys lying untidily on the floor and on the chairs.

"Do you intend to stay on here, Magda?" he asked.

"No, I'm selling it," she replied shortly. "I think someone is interested."

"Good."

With one quick movement, she cleared all the things

on one of the chairs on to the floor. "Please sit down, Felix," she said.

He did so, and suddenly became aware of the child, Duibhne's child, sitting on a rug in front of the empty fire. Bartley was very quiet, surrounded by coloured bricks, but not playing with them. As Felix would have expected, he was a good-looking child with his mother's blue eyes and dark hair.

Magda dropped to her knees beside him, and said, "My treasure and I don't need a big house like this to live in, do we?" She was addressing the little boy, and he responded to the sound of her voice by smiling at her, a sweet wide smile, and putting his little hand on her knee. His eyes seemed to look beyond her, unseeing, a characteristic which Felix found particularly disturbing and, as if to explain it, Magda said, "The doctors have told me he doesn't see clearly, so he will have to wear glasses." She mentioned this quite casually, as if it was his only defect.

Felix sensed that she wished him to relate to the child in the normal adult manner, and so he said, rather too heartily, "Those are great bricks you have there. Are you going to build a tower with them?"

The child silently held out a brick, and Felix took it. "Ask him the colour of it," cried Magda eagerly. "He knows all the colours."

"What colour is this?" said Felix obediently, but Bartley appeared not to know the colour or, if he did, was reluctant to speak. Felix thought it likely that he did not speak at all, and that it was wishful thinking on Magda's part when she spoke of talents he obviously did not possess. Felix didn't know much about children, but his sister had a baby aged fifteen months, and it seemed to him his niece was at about the same stage in development as Bartley, except that she was a great deal livelier.

He wondered when it would be politic to ask Magda to tell him the reason for his visit. He didn't have to because she cleared another chair of all its clutter, and sat down opposite him, immediately embarking on the story she had to tell.

"A young woman came to see me about a week ago. Her name is Holly Maidment, and she used to work in the tavern off the freeway, the place where Bart used to spend his evenings. She is not a bad girl – in her early twenties, I'd say, and has a child to support. No, it is not Bart's child, although, at first, I thought that was what she had come to tell me. The father worked for Tom in the stables, and so far he hasn't been able to find another job. He never paid much maintenance to Holly for the child, and now he is out of work he pays nothing. The baby was a result of a short-term liaison, so she has no claim on the father for herself.

She told me that she and Bart had an affair, but she had learnt her lesson, and was careful. He used to stay at the tavern until closing time, and she took him back to her place. Her mother looked after the child at night. Sometimes Bart stayed until the early hours, sometimes all night. He didn't say much, but she knew that he lived with a girl in an apartment by Lake Trevelyan. He never mentioned a baby. After a time, he became aggressive, and when he hit her on the face, she was frightened. She told him she didn't want to see him again. She threatened to tell Tom what he had done, and asked for money in return for her silence. Bart refused to give her anything." Magda paused, and Felix sensed her embarrassment. "She went to Tom and showed him the injuries his son had inflicted on her. Of course I knew nothing of this, but I believed her when she told me that Tom had called her a liar. He always had a blind spot about Bart. After that, she asked a girlfriend, Mary Jones, to take a photograph of her face before the bruises faded. She gave me the photograph, and here it is."

Felix took the photograph and studied it closely. It was of the front face of a girl, the swelling and bruising around one eye and the swelling along the jawline showing very clearly.

Felix was jubilant. He hardly dared ask Magda the question, "Did you have to pay for this?"

"No," Magda replied. "She wanted money, of course. That is why she came to see me, but I told her she could come and work for me, and get well paid. There is a lot of clearing up to do here before we leave. She is satisfied with this arrangement, especially as she can bring the child here with her. It will be good for Bartley to have the stimulation of the company of another child."

What a clever old girl she is, thought Felix. His heart was so full of gratitude he felt like embracing her, but she was too prickly a character for that sort of demonstrative behaviour.

"I can't tell you what this means," he said slowly. "Well, I can – I think it means freedom for Divvy. It shows that Bart was capable of injuring two women and a child. This evidence, together with a statement from Dr Leroy about Bartley's condition, may tip the balance."

He noticed a change in her rigid expression: an emotion somewhere between joy and relief passed over her face.

"I hope you're right," was all she said.

He left her then, having said goodbye to the child in what he hoped was a sufficiently benevolent manner.

She apologised for not offering him a drink. "Tom always said I had no manners," she said.

What a strange sad woman, thought Felix as he drove away. What will become of her when she is parted from that pathetic child? For he was certain a time would come when the parting was inevitable.

The day of Hazel's release came at last, and she stood in the centre of the room they had shared for so long, dressed in her unfamiliar coat and skirt, quaintly old-fashioned for the hemlines had altered since her arrival at the Correctional Facility. She had been to see Mrs Stockdale. It was a tradition that the Warden said goodbye to the departing ladies. "You did a good job with the non-smoking room," she said. "You will be remembered for that."

"Thank you. You were very helpful and understanding about it," said Hazel.

"Well, I enjoy a challenge."

On the previous evening, their last evening together, Duibhne had said, "We will keep in touch."

But Hazel had other ideas, and had given the matter much thought. She broke the news to Duibhne that she was leaving Oregon, going to the other side of the country, to Harvard to study medicine.

"When you leave here," she said, "you will return to Ireland, that is a certainty. It is unlikely that I shall ever go there and, if I do, you will not want someone like me looking you up, embarrassing you."

"That is not true," cried Duibhne, very distressed. "How can you think such a thing?"

"Embarrassing you," repeated Hazel firmly. "I know it is difficult to imagine now, but you will have to try and forget all this happened to you. Oh, I know you will never forget it, no one could do that, but you can put the remembrance of it at the back of your mind, your own very private memory which you can bring out and examine from time to time. I am positive that this is the right way for you, but do not doubt that I shall always think of you."

Duibhne was heartbroken by this decision, but Hazel was determined. Anticipation of the parting made her unhappy all evening, and unable to sleep that night. Hazel could not sleep either, and the two girls sat up all night, talking.

Now, the moment had come for Hazel to leave, and she was turning to go.

"Give me a hug," said Duibhne brokenly. Words which in the past would never have come to her lips, words which in her future life she would never utter again. "Give me a hug."

Hazel put her arms around her, and held her close. Then she was gone, and Duibhne was left alone, weeping.

Hazel's bed remained unoccupied. Perhaps the Warden took pity on the bereft girl, and decided not to put anyone in Hazel's place for the time being. Perhaps she had been told that there was a chance that Duibhne herself might not be there for very much longer. Whatever the reason, it was a relief to the lonely girl when no stranger came to share her solitude.

CHAPTER TWENTY-SIX

Felix decided to tell Duibhne about his visit to Magda, and the significance of what she had told him. He thought it might buoy up her spirits which were very low. One reason for her depression was that she had half-expected to hear from Hazel – surely she would write to her while she was still in prison? But no communication came from her, not even a message sent through her parents. It was apparent that Hazel had resolved to sever all connections with Duibhne, and she was determined to abide by that decision.

Felix introduced the name of Holly Maidment by telling her that Bart was having an affair with her while they were living in the apartment on Lake Trevelyan.

"Does it upset you to know that?" he asked, beginning to wonder if his revelations would do more harm than good.

She was able to tell him honestly that this

knowledge did not upset her in the slightest. She remembered Florence standing on the steps, shouting, 'Your man is with another woman!'. She had been distressed then, but now it seemed very unimportant.

Encouraged, Felix continued, "He used to visit her at the place where she was living. He met her in the tavern, she had a job there. The affair came to an end when he struck her. She suffered the same sort of injuries as you did when he lashed out at you. Fortunately for us, she got a friend to take a photograph of her showing the facial bruises, so we have some supporting evidence for her story."

"What difference does that make?"

"It shows the true character of Bartley Shannon. That was not apparent at the first hearing of your case. Then, there was nothing to show that he was capable of hurting a woman, let alone injuring his own child. Now, with this new evidence, we can show what sort of person he was."

Duibhne wondered, what was the true character of Bart? She had got it very wrong, that was certain. She remembered him coming to her room at Clonbarron, his naked body pattering along the dark still corridors of the big house, to be with her, and how they had made love in a field under a blue sky with the skylark wheeling above them. She thought of him handing the five-pound note to the tinker, and how she had cut his fingernails for him when they were alone, sitting in front of a peat fire. Their lovemaking had overpowered them both, but never once did he say he loved her. She had longed for him to be what she expected of him, but he had never conformed. Now, when she thought about it, she understood why Tom began to dislike her so much towards the end of her stay at the apartment. Perhaps he was the only person who understood Bart. He, who had been so close to his wild gypsy mother, must have recognised the strange mixture of temperaments that were combined in this human being they had produced together. Tom did not expect Bart to be 'normal', whereas it was all she had ever wanted.

She asked Felix, "If this appeal succeeds – it means that I will be released?"

"Yes."

"Do you think it will succeed?"

"I do."

It was hard for her to realise the implication of his words, but she understood him well enough to know that he believed them to be true.

Before he left her, he warned her that she had to be patient. "These things take time to set in motion," he said. "You will have to be brave and face the loneliness of your life here without Hazel, probably for many months to come, but at least now there is hope."

"Hope," said Duibhne wonderingly. "It means everything in a place like this. Thank you, dear Felix, for giving it to me."

Felix visited her on every day he was allowed. He was aware that he was her only visitor. Magda and

Bartley were living in a flat in Portland, and Magda no longer took advantage of her Visitor's Permit. Duibhne was hurt, and did not understand why she did not come any more. Felix thought he did understand, but it was difficult to explain so he did not attempt it. Magda felt that her intervention would give Duibhne her freedom, and when she had that freedom she would take away from Magda a precious part of her life. She didn't know how she would manage to live without that reason for her whole existence. The future seemed so empty that it terrified her. Of course, she loved Duibhne also, and that is why she had made the sacrifice, but, having made the sacrifice, she felt she could not longer face her.

She had more money than she knew what to do with, and she wrote to Harrods, the prestigious department store in London, and ordered expensive clothes for Bartley. Nothing, in her view, was too good for him. The brown-paper parcels arriving from England were a diversion for her and, opening them, with Bartley looking on, she was momentarily distracted from an ever-present anxiety.

"We must live for the present, my darling," she said, as she buttoned him into a Harris tweed coat with a velvet collar. "That is all we have left."

The weeks passed and became months, and Duibhne almost lost sight of the prospect of an early release. Nothing had changed, and Felix had no news to give her.

"The last appeal failed," she said plaintively.

Felix replied, "But this one will not fail." He was so confident she could not help but believe him.

One day he told her that the date of the appeal had been fixed for a day one month away. Four weeks! In four weeks' time she might be allowed to sleep in a room without a lock on the door. It was hard to take in. She told Grace, "There is a possibility I shall get my release," and Grace replied, "Then you will be with your little boy again." Poor Grace, whose horrific crime meant that she was unlikely to change her present existence. She never complained, and seemed on the surface an amiable creature, fat and comfortable, but at one point in her life she had been provoked to commit a terrible act, and the consequences of that lost moment would be with her for ever.

Mrs Smythe echoed her words when she said, "Oh, my dear, I so hope you will be with your lovely little son again," She knew that she would miss the sessions together. "I envy you going home to Ireland," she said. "My husband will not let me go to England for a visit. He thinks if I set foot on English soil again I will never return. Of course I would, as I keep telling him, America is my country now, and all my family are here. I don't want to live anywhere else." Hazel had been right.

Felix visited her on the day before the appeal. She had made plans which she wished to impart to him.

"Please, will you telephone my father and warn him that I may be coming home?"

He nodded. He had already decided to get in touch

with Claw, now the Earl of Clonbarron. He would telephone him that evening, and hoped that he would not receive a hostile reception.

"And, Felix, will you go and see Magda and tell her what is happening. I want her to know that, if the appeal is successful, she is to come to Ireland with me and Bartley. The three of us will return together, that is my wish. She can take all her bits and pieces out of storage, and ship them to Ireland. Surely she will agree?"

"I think so," said Felix. "She cannot bear the thought of being parted from the child."

"Tell her from me, that will not happen," said Duibhne firmly.

Suddenly, she was absolutely sure that her three years in prison were coming to an end. She envisaged one more night, alone in the cell.

Felix said gravely, "There is something I must say to you."

"Oh," she cried, alarmed, "what is that?"

"Nothing bad, at least I hope it's not bad. It is just that I must tell you how much I love you."

He sat very quietly at the other side of the table, studying her face.

She was confused. She did not know how to reply; her mind was in a turmoil, doubts about what would happen on the following day and plans for the future if everything went well. "I don't know what to say . . ."

"I hope you will say that you will think over what I

have told you, and perhaps agree to marry me one day. Do you think that is possible?"

"I don't know," she said, "I'm very grateful to you." As soon as she uttered the words she realised how insensitive they sounded. She saw the look of disappointment pass over his face. "Please try and understand how I feel," she pleaded, "I can't make up my mind about anything at the moment, least of all getting married. When I said I was grateful, I meant grateful for the love you give me. I expressed it badly. Of course, I know you love me, and I love you too, but, if and when I get out of this place, you must give me time to get used to a new way of life."

"I know," he said, nodding. "Thank you for saying you love me. You make me very happy." He could not help thinking of the thousands of miles that would separate them while she was becoming accustomed to her freedom.

The strident bell was ringing, telling the visitors it was time for them to leave.

Felix got to his feet. "Goodbye, my darling," he said. "If only I could take your hand, and touch your lips, but that is forbidden to me."

"I'll see you tomorrow," she said.

Tomorrow came, and she was taken to the court where she saw many familiar faces in the big panelled room. Barbara Mills, Mrs Smythe, Dr Leroy and, of course, Felix. Was she to leave so many good friends behind her? It seemed she was, for in view of events subsequent to the trial, the evidence of the doctors and Holly's testimony, the Judge granted her instant release. Holly was an excellent witness. She had enjoyed working for Magda, loved the poor little fellow and wanted to help.

After just over three years, Duibhne was free. Felix, who had so often gazed at her beautiful face over the table in the Visitor's Room, was able to put his arm around her and kiss her cheek. It was a victorious day for him, but in his heart he doubted whether he would succeed with Duibhne. His logical lawyer's mind told him that when she left the States he would never see her again. The prospect of life without her was almost more than he could bear, but he forced his mind to concentrate on the present.

She expected the press to be waiting outside the Court House. Felix had warned her that they would be there after the result. But the street was quiet, and there was no sign of reporters. He knew the reason, but said nothing. Instead, he took her in his car to the Gibb Correctional Facility for Women, showing his identity card at the gate, as he had done so many times before, and driving right up to the main entrance of the redbrick building.

Duibhne saw Mrs Stockdale and thanked her, and the Warden wished her well. As she came out, she noticed a new commitment and escort standing outside the door, waiting to go in, and she remembered herself in the same position, sobbing because she thought the world contained nothing but grief.

She went to the desk in the hall and signed for the

return of her few possessions. After signing the form, she looked up and saw the cheeks of the black policewoman behind the desk were wet with tears.

"Why is she crying?" she whispered to Felix as they walked to the door.

"It is the end of a dream," he said, and, when she looked bewildered, "There has been an assassination today."

Duibhne, Magda and Bartley spent the night in Magda's flat, and on the following day Felix went to Portland Station to see the odd little group and their luggage on to the train bound for New York, for Duibhne was to return, as she had come, on the *Queen Mary*. Mr Kendrick had made all the arrangements.

There were no reporters to be seen at the station, and Duibhne did not notice the billboards announcing the death of Martin Luther King. "It's an ill wind . . ." thought Felix.

In the midst of his personal despair he was momentarily diverted by the sight of the bespectacled Bartley, now four years old, dressed like a little English boy in a coat with a velvet collar.

The first-class passengers on the great liner paid little attention to the two women and the child. The Passenger List informed anyone who wanted to know that they were Mrs Angelo, Miss Angelo and Master Angelo. It was April, and the air was still chilly at sea. The women spent most of their time, well wrapped up, sitting in steamer chairs in a sheltered corner of the promenade deck, talking, talking as if they had much to discuss and many plans to make. The little boy sat between them, and perhaps it was because of him that the other passengers avoided getting involved with them. Sometimes the three of them could be seen walking the deck, close together to protect themselves against the wind. But when the child cried, which was unusual, they scurried back to their sheltered place.

When they landed at Southampton five days later, a car was there to meet them. Quietly, it slid away, driven by a chauffeur in uniform. The three of them sat in the back seat, leaning against the soft upholstery. Duibhne, Magda and Christopher.

For, on the journey home, they had decided to change Bartley's name to Christopher.

PART THREE

CHAPTER TWENTY-SEVEN

The editor of *The Daily Graphic* was very pleased with Delphine Blake. It was not every day that a junior reporter managed to ferret out a story about the beautiful wife of a Cabinet Minister. A Cabinet Minister who had recently been in the news himself, whose indiscretions might have led to his resignation. Now a new slant promised to keep the story running, and the fact that the events happened more than thirty years ago made it even more remarkable. It had all the ingredients of real-life drama which would capture the imagination of the typical reader of his newspaper.

Delphs, standing before him, looked very attractive and young, and in the days before sexual harassment became more of a threat to the boss than the worker, he would have been on the other side of the desk, trying to fondle and touch. Delphs would have been well able to deal with that situation. She had already evolved a strategy when dealing with the man: slightly flirtatious, very self-assured and always respectful.

"Well done, sweetie," he said, "all this must have taken place when you were a twinkle in your father's eye."

"Well, no," answered Delphs, "actually it was about the time I was born."

Because of a chance remark of her mother's she had been given this break. She was assigned to interview Mrs Macauley.

"I'm terribly nervous," she confided to Tim when they met for lunch the next day. She told him how, after she left the editor's office, she telephoned Mrs Macauley.

The lady had been cold. "I'm sorry," she said, "I have nothing to say to the press. Surely you have finished with this story?"

"There is a new development, Mrs Macauley, and I think we should talk about it."

"I do not want to talk to you about anything."

"Please remember," said Delphs, "it is the policy of the *Graphic* to treat people with respect. You will not receive this consideration from any other newspaper."

The voice on the other end of the line was icily furious. "As far as I am concerned all newspapers are the same when it comes to printing lies about people. I refuse to see you."

"Everything is in the open, now," Delphs persisted. "There simply isn't any point in being secretive any more."

"I don't know what you mean. I am about to put

down the phone." This she did, and Delphs was obliged to ring her back. There was no answer, so she waited until the evening before calling again.

"Oh! It's you . . ."

"Yes, it is I, Mrs Macauley, Delphine Blake. Please do not hang up on me again. I must see you."

"I have already told you, I refuse to see you."

There was nothing for it but to come out with the truth, which was risky in case she decided to tell her story elsewhere. Delphs did not think she would do that.

"It is about your time in Oregon," she said.

There was a silence, and Delphs could almost feel the blood draining away from the face of the woman at the other end of the line. She hung on, and waited.

"Very well," whispered Mrs Macauley. "When are you coming?"

"Will three o'clock tomorrow afternoon suit you, at your house?"

"Yes."

Delphs drove her own car, a Metro, to Pondings, and Ben Hulton, the photographer, sat beside her, his camera equipment in the back seat. Through the open gate, along a twisty drive, and suddenly the house was in front of them.

"Have a look at that!" said Ben.

"It is impressive," Delphs agreed. She knew that Tim would say that no one should be allowed to live in a house like that. He was left-wing and opposed to the Establishment, and had strong views about the usefulness of the monarchy as well. Of course, Delphs went along with him, but they had to keep their opinions to themselves as Tim worked for *Hey!*, the weekly magazine that concentrated on the lives of the rich and famous, making a special feature of rapturous royals at home playing happy families, while the *Graphic* was staunchly Conservative.

Delphs rang the front-door bell, conscious of a pounding heart and shaking knees. An old man opened the door.

"Delphine Blake. Mrs Macauley is expecting me."

He looked at her, as she thought, reproachfully. "I'll tell her ladyship you are here," he said.

Damn! Mrs Macauley was the daughter of an earl, and therefore had the title of 'Lady'. She thought resentfully, the social rights and wrongs of these bloody people make life so complicated. She sat on a hard uncomfortable settle in the vast hall, surrounded by Ben's paraphernalia, while he hovered in the background examining the pictures on the walls. Pull yourself together, she told herself, you have not done anything wrong. Mrs Macauley, wife of the Minister, is always called Mrs Macauley.

The old man returned and indicated that they should follow him. It was a slow business walking behind him; his poor old legs were bowed like the sides of a viola.

Delphs plunged straight in. "Perhaps I should have

addressed you as Lady Duibhne," she said. "If I have made a mistake, I'm sorry."

"You did not make a mistake," answered the woman. "I am Mrs Macauley. You were right the first time." Then, as if to put the girl at ease, she said, "We have a habit of dispensing with titles in my family."

"Thank you. Mrs Macauley, this is Ben Hutton, photographer for the *Graphic*."

"How do you do, Mr Hutton. Please sit down, both of you."

They sat, and Delphs noticed the elegance of the room, the soft colours, the flowers, the two big dogs adorning the rug in front of the fireplace, their noses on their front paws. As they entered, the dogs had risen in a leisurely way, then settled down again.

It was very quiet, and the woman sitting on the sofa was quiet too. Her hands, holding a tapestry on a circular frame, did not tremble. Delphs wondered whether the work was there to give her confidence.

She said, to break the silence, "I wish I could do that. It is so beautiful."

Mrs Macauley looked up and smiled. She put the canvas away, by the side of the sofa. Her face was so lovely, so serene. Ben was already deciding how to photograph such a remarkable subject. "Strangely enough, I learnt how to do this when I was in prison. A lady called Mrs Smythe taught me. The prisoners were expected to learn something during their sentences. Some of them took courses, but I did not want to learn shorthand and typing or another language, so I said I wanted to learn how to embroider. Mrs Smythe came to teach me once a week, and we became friends. She travelled a long way to come, and the work was voluntary of course. I have always been grateful to her."

Delphs could not help thinking the conversation was taking a rather absurd course. All that stuff about needlework lessons did not sound to her like an American penitentiary, but she was grateful that Mrs Macauley had wasted no time before embarking on her story. Her words came out evenly and factually, as if she was anxious to get the interview over, and behind her.

She carried on, in the same vein, as if addressing a meeting of the Women's Institute.

"Mrs Smythe was extremely kind and, as I said, came a long way in her car. I never knew where she lived. She was English, and missed England very much. She could not get used to the American way of life. I remember at Christmas she got depressed because she could not buy the right ingredients for the Christmas pudding, and she missed Big Ben and English voices reading the news."

"I hope it doesn't distress you talking about your time in prison," said Delphs.

"No, why should it?" answered Mrs Macauley, "It is nice that someone is interested after all this time."

Delphs thought, is she being sarcastic? "It must have been a dreadful experience for you," she said, hoping to steer the conversation away from embroidery lessons.

"Well, it is not one I would like to repeat," the woman

replied, "but, you know, it was light and shade. I had done something very wrong, and I needed a gap in my life to come to terms with it."

"You mean to live with the guilt?"

The blue eyes looked directly at Delphs, "Yes, I suppose I do mean that."

"What was the worst aspect of those three years?"

"Some of the women prisoners were very frightening people. Unexpectedly frightening because they were women. There was drug-taking, stealing and a lot of undercover malice and hate. Many of the women were lesbians, and I had not come across that sort of thing before. In fact, although it is difficult to believe, I'd never even heard of lesbianism, so I did not know how to deal with it. It is real problem in a prison where women are in for a long time. It was important to keep quiet about anything unpleasant that happened, otherwise you were in real trouble. The women formed gangs, and if you got on the wrong side of one of the members of a gang, you had every reason to be afraid."

"Did you ever find yourself in trouble in that way?"

"Yes, once – well, not about lesbianism, but I antagonised a woman called Joy, and she turned nasty. I have hated that name ever since. It was nothing though, and soon blew over. Joy was transferred which was a great relief." She paused, as if trying to bring back to mind the three years. "So much of it was degrading," she said, "as if they were trying to take away our dignity and self-respect."

"What sort of things do you mean?"

"Strip-searches were the worst, every two or three days, and we dreaded them. Then there were urine tests, not so frequent, but necessary because of the drug problem, I suppose. There was no place to be private, although we were allowed to walk around the building and the grounds, quite freely, but aware of being watched all the time. The Warden was a kind woman, though; it's silly but I can't recall her name for the moment. It will come back to me. I remember her saying, 'Come now, it is not as bad as all that'. I had just arrived and was crying my eyes out. She did a nice thing when she arranged for me to share a room with Hazel."

"What was she in for?"

"She ran into a woman and child when she was driving home after a party. They were both killed. Hazel had been drinking, and that went against her."

"My God!" Delphs was shocked. "How could she live with that?"

"Well, she had to live with it, didn't she?" For the first time, Mrs Macauley looked annoyed. "It was done. Regrettable, but done. She had two choices, to kill herself, or to go on living with the terrible realisation of what she had done. I know she contemplated the first course, but she took the harder way which was to live with it. As I said before, the prison provided a watershed between the horror and the reality."

"The cell you and Hazel shared, was it comfortable?"

"Not too bad. But I said we shared a room – we were not allowed to call it a cell."

"It seems a strange mixture," commented Delphs, "the drugs, the aggression, strip-searches and no privacy, and yet the authorities insisted on the cells being called 'rooms'."

"I think it was the Warden who introduced all these newfangled notions. She liked us to speak of the prisoners as 'residents', and Hazel and I used to laugh when sometimes she referred to us as 'ladies'. We were an odd bunch of ladies! The canteen was called 'the dining-room' and the units were called 'houses'."

"Were you given work to do?"

"I worked in the kitchen, boring work at first, and then I progressed to cooking simple things. The residents ate a lot of mince which we cooked in enormous pans, only it was called ground beef, not mince. The vegetables were always overcooked by the time they got to the table."

"Tell me more about Hazel."

"Please do not mention her by name in your article."

"Very well. But tell me more about her."

"We became friends," she said simply. "It was ironic that I had to go to prison to find a friend of about my own age. You see, I had a very happy childhood, but I suppose I lacked companionship, having no brothers or sisters. I had a nanny, and from the time I was seven until I was nearly grown-up I had a governess. She was a wonderful person, and when she left us to get married, I felt deserted. Sadly, she died of cancer, shortly before I finished my sentence, so I did not see her again. I did not go away to school, except for a short time when I went to a school in Ascot to take O-levels. I was not at the school long enough to get to know any of the girls, but I did notice how well they got on with each other, and I thought I had missed out on something. I found out what I had missed when I met Hazel."

"Have you kept up with her, over the years?"

"No, we decided not to do that."

"You both wanted to put the experience behind you, forget it ever happened?"

"Something like that, but, of course, it is impossible to forget those years."

"So you returned home to Ireland to live with your father, and then you met Mr Macauley?"

"He came to Limerick to stay with friends who lived a few miles from Clonbarron. My father and I were invited to dine with them, and he was there."

Duibhne remembered the evening so well. How he had talked! All heads at the dining-table were bent forward to observe better his handsome face, and to hear his words. Claw was bowled over by his brilliance. Afterwards, when she was sitting beside her hostess on a sofa, the lady whispered in her ear, "What a charmer!" Duibhne had looked up quickly, and met his eyes across the room. She felt the magnetism in him, as if he was drawing her away from her stultified existence.

For, although she had her freedom, life in Ireland was as oppressive as it had been before she made her first escape. This time she was certain there was no way she could leave. Felix telephoned her, and wrote numerous letters begging her to join him in the States, but there were obstacles. At last, he told her that he was planning a trip to Ireland, to see her and to try and make peace with the consistently hostile Claw.

Before he booked the tickets he received a letter from Duibhne saying that she was going to be married. He wrote to her, a sad, business-like little letter, wishing her happiness. She never saw him again.

"I met Rod in December," she told Delphs, "and we were married in the spring." Delphine had been bracing herself to ask the important question, and, at last, she said, "When you married, Mrs Macauley, did you tell your husband your experiences in the States, as you have told me today?"

Up to that moment, Mrs Macauley's manner towards her was courteous, agreeable, as if, knowing publicity was inevitable, she wanted to meet it in a gracious way. Now, her body stiffened, and the blue eyes fixed on Delphs like points of steel. "I do not think there is any need to bring my husband into this interview. What I have said to him is a private matter, between us."

"But, of course he knew your past history?"

"I have been very honest with you today, but I have nothing more to say."

"Mrs Macauley, I just want to know . . ."

"Oh! I have just remembered the name of the Warden. Mrs Stockdale. I am so glad it came back to me, as I knew it would."

Delphs knew that it was useless to pursue the

matter. Also she had to admit to a feeling of intimidation, which was unusual for her. "I hope you don't mind if Ben takes a few pictures," she ventured.

"I do mind," said Mrs Macauley, "but I have no option, do I? I hate being photographed." She shrugged her shoulders, and settled herself into the corner of the sofa, her hands fluttering in her lap.

"The needlework, if you please," said Ben.

Obediently, she took the frame, and started stitching. Yes, thought Delphs, visualising the caption, *"I learnt this in prison.'* It was a perfect picture, head bent over the tapestry, hair swirled into an elegant coif surmounting the long thin neck. The finger and thumb of her right hand poised with the needle, the diamond and sapphire rings on the other hand catching the light from a lamp behind the sofa. "Yes, yes!" muttered Ben, darting from side to side.

"Is that all?" sighed Mrs Macauley, as if longing for the ordeal to end.

But Delphs must try another question. "Your husband, did he mind about your son?"

"My son!" the woman cried. "Let's have him in, so that you can photograph him instead of me. He, or rather they, have been waiting all this time to see you. After you have all met, I think we should ask Bell to bring us some tea." She turned to Ben. "Now, at last, you will have a willing subject, Mr Hutton. Christopher adores being photographed."

"And she was right," Delphs told Tim when they met at

her flat the following night. "Christopher was in his element, and Ben took dozens of photographs of him. Will one of them appear in the *Graphic* tomorrow, do you think?"

"It depends," said Tim thoughtfully. "The paper prides itself on its good taste, and, hopefully, they may just print a picture of her. I'm surprised she was so willing for him to be photographed though, you would think she would object to that."

"I agree," said Delphs, "but it was her suggestion. Perhaps she was anxious to prove that she is not ashamed of him."

"What happened next?" asked Tim.

"Well, she pulled a bell-like thing, a long strip of tapestry, no doubt made by her, and the old man tottered in and she asked for tea. There was an awkward silence after he left. I felt I could not ask her any more questions, and Ben had finished taking photographs. The boy, man, whatever you like to call him, sat on the sofa beside his minder, who did not utter a word. She looked like a witch. It was weird, I can tell you. Funnily enough, it was Ben who saved the situation. He sat down on the other side of Christopher and started talking to him, showing him the camera and allowing him to pretend he was taking a photograph. Ben made a comic face, and Christopher laughed and pressed the button. You know, Ben was so sweet with him, and behaved quite naturally, which I found impossible. Afterwards I asked him about it, and he told me he has a nephew who is retarded, and he has got used to talking to him. After a while, to my great relief, the tea arrived. The old chap spread a white cloth on a table, and Mrs Macauley poured out tea into delicate cups. You know, Tim, I sat there watching her, trying to make one person of this distant aloof lady and the young girl who pressed the trigger and, with one bullet, killed a man. I have read the account and there must have been a hell of a lot of blood, and she sat in that flat, with a dead man in the next room, waiting for the police to arrive and arrest her. There was no way I could associate Mrs Macauley with that scenario."

"*Still waters run deep . . .*" said Tim.

"They certainly do, in her case. We drank our tea, ate a piece of cake, thanked her politely and left."

"Sounds as if you did a good job," said Tim.

"Wait until you have read what I have written," said Delphs, "I'm afraid it will pain her dreadfully."

"What have you said?"

"I ask a question. Did he know? Was this a secret she managed to keep from her husband?"

"And was it?"

"Of course not," said Delphs. "How could he have been married to her for all those years, and not known?"

"Yet, if he did know, why did he not divulge it before taking government office? He did not, and that is why he has had to resign."

"I hope they have a strong marriage," she said.

"Ah," said Tim. "I see you don't know they are no longer together. She has gone to Scotland, and he is skulking at the stately home with his daughter. So much for her stand as the long-suffering wife, forgiving him for his affair with Millicent Jones, supporting him at all costs. It looks as though she could take it, and he could not, and the first whiff of publicity about her has put him in a blue funk. I do not believe she would have done a bunk if he had been supportive."

Delphs covered her face with her hands. "What have I done?"

"Nothing, darling." Tim put his arms around her. "You have only brought into the open the inadequacies of a public figure. Perhaps, by doing so, you have done the lady a service."

"She has had enough suffering already."

"Suffering is part of our job, you know that. The public demands a ration of suffering."

"That is why I am going to give up this work," Delphs told him. "Satisfying that demand makes me very unhappy. It is my last story, Tim, I shall never do another."

He was astonished to see tears on her cheeks. She said, "Can we get married, so I can settle down and have babies, and put all this crap behind me?"

"Of course," he said seriously.

"Forget I said that!" She was laughing now. "I'm upset, that's all."

"I'm not going to forget it," he said, "but I am puzzled. Why is this particular story different from any other?"

She tried to explain it to him. Human interest, that is what her work was all about, and his too, in a less aggressive way, for *Hey!* made sure that its intrusion was a sugar-coated pill, harming nobody. Both their jobs relied on the insatiable desire of people to know about their fellow human beings, and the more prominent they were the greater the desire to learn their secrets. Most people in the public eye realised they could not escape the consequences of their actions. The world made judgements, sympathised with the bereaved, berated the sinners and persecuted the liars. The Macauleys got what they deserved, he for a base, empty love affair, she for supporting what was wrong simply to maintain the status quo, both of them regarding themselves as special individuals, set apart from anyone else. All these things Delphs knew in her heart, but it was the face of innocence that altered her viewpoint, and made her question her part in the charade.

She took Tim's hands in her own, and described to him the drawing-room at Pondings, the pictures, the flowers, the dogs lying in front of the fireplace, all the trappings of the rich which he disliked so much. Then she told him about the person sitting on the sofa, the youngish man, his hair streaked with grey, blue eyes (his mother's eyes) staring steadfastly ahead behind spectacles, trusting, and smiling at Ben crouching in front of him, taking photographs.

"He did not understand what was going on," reasoned Tim.

"Don't you see, that is what made it so wrong, the

fact that he did not understand? All the others understood it only too well – Roderick, Duibhne, Millicent, the silly Macauley daughter, her yuppie boyfriend, the boy at school, you and I, we all understood, but he did not, and that is why I want no more of it."

It was not in his best interests to argue with her. She needed comforting, and he comforted her in the best way he knew. In the morning, he got up first, hearing the newspaper being put through the letterbox. He made two mugs of tea, and they sat up in bed, drinking the tea and reading about the ex-Minister and his wife.

"Wow!" said Tim, looking at the picture of Duibhne. "Ben should get an award for this – it's a beautiful portrait, and, please note, no photograph of the dreaded son. There is a heart beating in the *Graphic* office after all."

They decided it was a well-produced story and Delphs could be justifiably proud of it. Then they allowed the newspaper pages to float to the floor, and they held each other close, and made plans for their future.

CHAPTER TWENTY-EIGHT

The first thing Duibhne had done after she received the telephone call from Delphine Blake was to go and look for her daughter. When she found her, she said, "I must warn you that a girl reporter from *The Daily Graphic* is coming to see me tomorrow afternoon."

"But, why? I thought all that business was over."

"Apparently not."

"Is she going to interview you alone? Doesn't she want to see Daddy as well?"

"No, and please, darling, don't mention this to him when he comes home this evening. I'll tell him, in my own way, after dinner."

The three of them sat down to the evening meal, the conversation as uninspiring as the food. Roderick sparkled in company, but made no effort at home. Duibhne was even quieter than usual. I can't stand this much longer, thought Bridget, I'll go back to London.

After dinner, as was his custom when he was at home, Roderick went to his study. This was the time of day when Duibhne and Bridget might have gone to Ma's room to watch television. This evening was different, however, and Duibhne followed her husband, shutting the door behind her.

So Bridget went alone to Ma's room. The study was below, and she could hear the faint murmur of voices when she turned the sound down. Her parents never shouted. They were closeted in the room for so long that she became curious, and went to the top of the stairs and listened. She still could not hear what was being said, but she waited, motionless, ears straining for every sound. At last her mother emerged from the room, and looked up quickly and saw Bridget standing at the top of the stairs. The girl was shocked by her mother's appearance: she looked as if her world had fallen apart. She did not say anything, but hurried up the stairs with her head down, almost brushing past Bridget as she fled to her bedroom, closing the door behind her. After a while, Bridget decided to go to bed too, but she found it difficult to sleep. Had Millicent Jones finally destroyed her parents' marriage? Bridget found herself wishing that Silas was in the big bed in the nursery, waiting for her to come and join him. He was so practical, and would know exactly what to say to her at a time like this.

The following afternoon, from an upstairs window, Bridget watched the arrival of the girl and a photographer. She sat on the window-seat wondering what was going on downstairs. It seemed an eternity before she heard doors being opened and shut, and low voices. She heard a man's voice saying, "Thank you," and then the sound of Bell opening the heavy front door. Peering from behind the curtain, she saw the couple climb into the little car, and drive away.

She came downstairs. Everything was very still, very quiet, and she found her mother in the drawing-room. She was in her usual place in the corner of the sofa, and, to Bridget's surprise, Ma and Christopher were there too. They were all sitting in complete silence, as if recovering from a shock.

"What is happening?" demanded Bridget.

Duibhne looked at her, and the sadness of the night before was still there in her face. "Oh, darling, I don't want you to be bothered with all this," she said.

"Tell her," said Ma fiercely. She got to her feet and grabbed Christopher by the hand. "We'll leave you to it."

"No! Don't go . . ." cried Duibhne, and she began to weep. Bridget was horrified. She had never seen her mother shed tears before. She put her arms around her shoulders. "Surely I can help?"

"Yes," said her mother, stronger now. "Daddy has gone to London. He will be coming back this evening, and I ask you to be here. He will need you. He is resigning from the Cabinet today." She looked at Ma, and said, "We are leaving, as soon as possible."

That was all, a hasty plan was made to go to the

Maiden's Planting, Duibhne's property in Scotland. While Bridget sat with Christopher, the two woman scurried around, packing bags and throwing coats and boots into the back of the estate car. Bridget guessed that all this hurried activity was to avoid seeing her father on his return.

The dogs were shoved into their special space in the boot of the car. Suitcases were piled into the back seat, and somewhere squeezed between them was Christopher. Then, with much hand-waving and blowing of kisses, they were off.

They have not even left me the dogs for company, thought Bridget wryly.

Roderick Macauley returned home two hours later, and he threw on to the hall table a folded copy of the evening paper announcing his resignation from the Cabinet. He kissed Bridget on the cheek, but he said nothing. Nothing was said when they dined together, and Bridget wondered whether to mention the events of the day, but her nerve failed her.

Her father made no comment about the absence of his wife and, after dinner, went to his study, as usual, and Bridget went to Ma's room to watch television, as usual. The next day he was off to London again. She thought, what does it hold for him now? As he was leaving, he pecked her on the cheek, and said, "You'll be here when I get back tonight, darling?"

She detected the note of anxiety, almost pleading in his voice. "Of course, Daddy," she said.

Ma telephoned. They had arrived safely, and her mother was resting. As soon as she put the receiver down, the telephone rang again. This time it was Amanda Rhys telling her she was so overworked she was on the verge of a nervous breakdown.

Breakfast the next day was even more silent than usual. Her father was hidden behind his copy of the *Graphic* – he was completely engrossed in it, and when he had gulped down his coffee, he handed the paper to her. "Goodbye, darling," he said.

"Bye, Daddy." She heard the front door slam as he left the house.

Bell came in to clear the table, and Bridget looked at the newspaper. The photograph of her mother sprang out at her. The situation was so unreal, she could hardly believe it was happening. She forced herself to read the story.

"You must have known about this, Bell," she said.

The old man looked very distressed. "I'd rather not say, Miss, if you don't mind." She wondered if the other servants had been questioning him.

It was astounding to read of events that had happened before she was born. It was difficult for Bridget to believe that her beautiful dignified mother had shot the father of her child, and had spent three years in prison. And the child was Christopher, poor dear Christopher who had been part of her life for as long as she could remember.

She read the article over and over again. It was

written, she noticed, by someone called Delphine Blake. Of course, she must be the girl who came to interview her mother before she went to Scotland. She looked again at the photograph, and saw it was taken by Ben Hutton. It was a remarkable photograph of her mother, looking serene and happy.

Bridget remembered her grandfather in Ireland. She was a little girl when she was taken to Limerick to see him, shortly before he died. He was a very tall old man with a hooked nose, and she had sat on his bony knee. She knew he had once had a brother, Tom, who had died in the States, and Grandfather had inherited the title from him. Uncle Tom, as her mother called him, had seemed a remote character to Bridget, and she had never bothered to ask about him.

Now, she must get used to the idea that Christopher was her half-brother, and that, somehow, her mother and Ma had managed to conceal this fact from her and from Robert, and from everyone else.

Her thoughts turned to Robert, and she wondered if he was having a hard time at school. She telephoned him in the afternoon, and had to wait until someone found him for her. He had been practising cricket in the nets, and was out of breath.

"Would you like to come home for a few days, until this blows over?" she asked, hoping he would welcome the idea.

He did not welcome it – he was enjoying the notoriety too much. "They removed the *Graphic* from the library," he said proudly, "but someone managed to smuggle in a copy."

"Well, you sound more cheerful than I feel," she said.

He asked her, "Do you mind Christopher being our brother?"

"No. I've always loved him."

"I don't mind either . . ."

There was nothing more to say, and she took the newspaper and put it in the top drawer of the chest of drawers in her bedroom. The rest of the day she mooned about the house and the garden, and the next day was the same, and the day after. She saw her father in the evenings, but it was obvious he did not want to discuss anything with her. She retired into a shell of loneliness, and a general feeling of apathy stopped her from seeking help from anyone. She could have turned to Silas, she knew that, but stubborn self-pity held her back.

Amanda Rhys telephoned again, and she marvelled she could be so insensitive. Surely she had read the papers, and must realise this was not the time to worry her with her stupid problems? She managed to cut her short.

Silas had not spoken to Bridget for two weeks, and he felt desperate about it. He tried to telephone her at her flat, but each time the ring had that particular sound when it is ringing in an empty room. In view of what he had read in the *Graphic* he was reluctant to ring

Pondings, but eventually frustration and feelings of rejection made him do so. The telephone was answered at once by Bell.

"Mr Tomalin! How nice to speak to you, sir." Was it is his imagination, or did the old man sound relieved? "I'll fetch Miss Bridget immediately."

He could hear slow footsteps echoing on the hall floor, then lighter hurried steps.

"Hello?" breathed Bridget.

"At last," said Silas. He tried to disguise the joy of hearing her voice by saying casually, "How are things?"

"Bloody," she replied, "just bloody. You know, of course, that Daddy has resigned?"

"Yes, I know that."

"And the rest, all the hidden secrets of my extraordinary family?"

"Yes, I read the article. Has it upset you dreadfully?"

"Let's say it has been a shock. And Daddy resigning as well. I don't understand why he did that, do you? After getting through the business over that woman, why resign now? It doesn't make sense to me."

He agreed it was strange. The latest saga, although unpleasant for the family, did not seem sufficient reason for resignation. After all, something that happened thirty years ago did not affect him personally.

For Bridget's sake, he feigned an interest in Roderick Macauley. "Poor chap," he said, "what a nightmare," thinking all the time, serves the bugger right, it's all he deserves. It was interesting though – why had he thrown the sponge in at this stage? Had that complacent self-confidence finally deserted him? But Silas could not concentrate on Roderick's problems when all he cared about was Bridget, and when he was going to see her again.

"When am I going to see you again?"

"Oh, darling, I want to see you terribly, but I can't come to London. The town rats will be everywhere and I would not feel safe."

He said logically, "Geography does not worry them. If the press want to see you, they will find you wherever you are. Please come back."

"Give me time," she said.

"Is it because you want to be with your mother?"

There was a pause. "Mummy is not here," she told him. "She is at the Maiden's Planting."

He knew about the place called the Maiden's Planting, although he had not been there. It was a strip of land on the Mull of Kintyre, west of Campbeltown. The land sloped steeply to a stony beach with a view across the water to Ailsa Craig and, on a clear day, the Isle of Arran in the far distance. Duibhne had purchased the land herself, some years back, with money inherited from her father. At the time, people were surprised that she did not buy land in Ireland, but Duibhne had no desire to return to Ireland. If there were aspects of that country she missed, this corner of Scotland provided them.

It was a wild deserted spot, and the only inhabitants

along that particular stretch of coast were tinkers who had made an encampment there. Trippers seldom ventured so far; the track was not suitable for cars. There was a narrow bridge over a stream, and beyond that a car could not go. In fact, Campbeltown itself was relatively free of sightseeing drivers, for the long winding road along the Mull of Kintyre ended there, and there was no reasonable quick route back to Lochilphead except by the same road.

Holidaymakers came to Campbeltown for the golf and the beach at Macrihanish, but the Maiden's Planting was hidden from them. With civilisation just around the corner, it remained a rough desolate place until Duibhne purchased it, and gave instructions for a house to be built at the summit of the hill. The tinkers were told they could stay, as the lady from England did not wish them to be moved on.

The house built on the site, at great expense, was of wooden construction in the Scandinavian style with a wide deck looking out to sea. Silas had seen photographs of it, and the name itself was an enchantment. He could understand Duibhne wanting to go there, to get away from perplexities at home, but why go alone?

"Ma and Christopher are with her," said Bridget, as it divining his thoughts over the distance between them.

"Why didn't you go too?"

"I'm staying here because I think Daddy needs me. He's going through a hellish time, you know."

"So I shall not be seeing you?" He could not believe that after waiting so long to speak to her, now he was going to be told that he could not see her.

"Not for a while, darling, but will you be an angel and do me a favour?"

"Of course." He tried to keep the disappointment out of his voice, but in doing so his 'of course' sounded terse and uncooperative.

"Amanda. She is being a real pain because I have not been able to get to Rocket lately. She does nothing but moan, moan. How can she possibly expect me to be there with all this going on? She is so unreasonable. Please, please, dear darling Silas, go and see her, ask her what's bugging her and try and put it right. I can't do anything at this distance."

He promised to go and see Amanda.

"Remember I love you," he said.

"I know." Her voice seemed to fade away. The obvious reply was 'I love you too', but she did not make it. Instead she said, "Thank you, Silas," and click went the telephone, and that was that. He was left feeling empty and unwanted.

CHAPTER TWENTY-NINE

Silas cursed the necessity of having to go and see Amanda Rhys, but, having promised, he knew he must make the effort. He left it until late evening before walking along the London street to the restaurant. It was one of those rare nights when London emulates her sunnier sister cities, and the air was balmy, warm enough to sit outside even at that hour, if only the English habit of mistrusting the weather could have been dispelled. As it was, the customers of Rocket were all inside, in an airless, slightly smoky atmosphere, eating healthy food. When the girls first opened the restaurant they had put a ban on smoking, but lifted it in order to improve the custom.

Amanda was sitting behind the till by the door. Her hair was swept behind her ears, and her face was shiny, damp, devoid of make-up.

"Silas!" she cried, looking pleased to see him.

There was a small queue of people waiting to pay their bills. He stood waiting, feeling resentful against her, which he knew was unreasonable, and against Bridget for giving him this assignment.

Her head was bent. "Come again in three hours' time," she said without looking up.

Three hours! I'll be damned if I'll do that, he thought as he trudged back to his flat. But, in three hours' time he was there again, standing awkwardly at the door. The waiters were preparing for the morrow, whisking the soiled cloths off the tables, polishing the glasses and putting them on shelves, emptying ashtrays and gathering up menus. There was a flurry of activity, everyone wanting to go home.

"I'll be with you in a moment, Silas," said Amanda. She was counting money, recounting and putting it into bags which she placed in a safe. Silas could see it was going to be more than a moment, so he found himself a chair.

At last she was finished, and the waiters collected around her desk, all of them deathly pale and exhausted.

"That's it," she called out to them, and she stood as they filed past her, saying, "Goodnight" to each one. Then, she took keys from a drawer under the till, and said, "Silas, let's go."

He stood on the pavement while she flicked off all the lights, slammed the door and turned the key in the lock, twice.

"I'm so tired," she said, taking Silas's arm. They

walked along the quiet street without speaking. Somewhere, a church clock chimed, once only.

"One o'clock," commented Silas at last. "Do you always finish as late – as early as this?"

"Always," she said, "and I have to be back there by noon today."

"I don't know what will be open at this time," he said. "There must be somewhere we can go to, I suppose."

"We're going home," she said firmly, "to my flat. I do not intend to set foot into a drinking or eating establishment at this hour. I want to go home. I'll cook myself an omelette, and one for you if you're hungry, and I'll pour myself a large drink, and one for you, of course. Then we can talk."

Her flat was in a large Edwardian block with intricate patterned brickwork, and wide steps leading to a massive door. She let herself in with a key, and they crossed a vast empty hall to a lift which took them up to the fifth floor. The building was lit by a few dim lights. It was deadly silent, eerie. "Do you do this by yourself every day?" he asked.

"Of course."

"It's dangerous. Anything could happen."

"I admit, I don't like this bit." Their footsteps resounded on the tiled floor leading to her front door, which she opened with a second key. When she switched on the lights of the flat, he saw that it was nicely furnished, in good taste. "Once I get in here I feel safe," she said.

She was wearing a light linen jacket over a thin straight dress, and she took off the jacket and flung it over the back of an armchair. She kicked off her shoes, and Silas noticed she had slender feet. She padded over to a dresser and found two glasses.

"I am going to have a whisky and ginger ale," she said. "Will that suit you?"

"Sounds good." He was surprised. He thought she would have opened a bottle of wine.

"We can have wine with the omelettes," she said.

"I thought you said you felt tired?"

"No longer. It passes off. When I leave Rocket, I'm knackered, but by the time I get home I'm wide awake, and then I can't sleep."

He sat on a kitchen stool, drink in hand, watching her make the omelettes. She was not particularly pretty, but there was something attractive about her. He had only met her a few times, but had noticed the attractive qualities each time. He was a bit put off by her slightly brusque manner. He thought it might be a cover–up for feelings of inadequacy, very understandable when dealing with the Macauleys. She had a good body, and her face was natural, a pleasant lived-in face. He wondered if she felt jealous of Bridget who was so beautiful.

"You live here alone?" he asked.

"Yes, I don't like the idea of sharing. I manage all right without anyone." She was whisking the eggs in a bowl, and taking an occasional slurp of her drink. "Talking of sharing," she said, "isn't it time Bridget did something with her share of the business we are supposed to be running together, instead of leaving it all to me?"

"She has an awful lot on her plate at the moment," he said loyally. "This last bit of publicity involving the family has hit them all very hard." He spoke proudly, as a person close to the family, on intimate terms with them all, Duibhne, Bridget, Robert and, God forbid, Roderick himself.

"Are you engaged to Bridget?" she asked.

"No."

"I wondered . . ." She flipped the omelettes on to two plates. Then she cut wedges of wholemeal bread, and said to Silas, "Knives and forks are in the top left-hand drawer."

They sat at the small kitchen table, opposite each other. By this time they had finished the first drink, and had moved on to a bottle of red wine which Silas had opened at her command.

"I have never been an 'Atlas' fan myself," she told him. "There is something about him that curls me up, and once, when I was sitting next to him at dinner at Pondings, I thought he rubbed his leg against mine." She glanced at Silas, as if to ascertain how he would take criticism of the great man. "Perhaps I was mistaken," she said.

"Probably not."

Encouraged she went on, "He must have known his wife had been in prison for three years. I thought the woman who wrote the article in the *Graphic* rather implied that he did not know." She looked deeply into the contents of her glass. "Of course he knew. He chose to remain silent about it, that's all. When you become a Cabinet Minister everything about you or anyone close to you has to be revealed. No secrets, or you are in trouble. He took a risk, and was found out. That's why he had to resign."

"Perhaps he did not know," suggested Silas. "Perhaps she never told him."

"What sort of marriage would that be?" demanded Amanda. "They may have drifted apart now, but it must have been all right in the beginning. She would have told him then, surely?"

Silas thought of Duibhne, the lovely face, aloof, untouchable, gliding through life like a majestic swan on a calm lake. She would be good at keeping a secret. He enjoyed discussing the Macauleys with Amanda; it was an indulgence talking about them.

"Of course, Roderick was very generous putting up the money for Rocket," she went on. "It was such an exciting project at the time, but now . . ." In the manner of females she changed to another tack, and said, "Where is Bridget's mother now?"

He told her about the Maiden's Planting, as much as he knew about it.

"It sounds a wonderful place," she said, "the way you describe it. Good luck to Duibhne, I say. She deserves some peace and happiness."

"I've never been there," he said, "but I'd like to see it very much." He was quite sure he would see it, one day. Perhaps if Bridget decided to join the little party in Scotland he could get time off work and go with her.

They carried the dirty dishes to the sink. "Leave them," instructed Amanda, "I'm not doing them now." They went into the sitting-room, taking with them their glasses and the nearly empty bottle of wine.

"I have to go," said Silas. He realised he had not done as he had set out to do which was to try and ease the situation for Bridget. He tried to make amends by saying, "I know it is hard work on your own, but do you think you could stick it out until this wretched business has blown over?"

Her reaction to this question astonished him. She was sitting on the sofa, clasping her glass of red wine, when she burst into floods of tears.

"I can't," she sobbed. "I'm tired. I'm too bloody tired. Can't you see that? How can I make you understand? Day after day, night after night I work at that place, and I have no time for anything else. No time to live a normal life, no time to go out, no time for sex. All I do is work, work, while your precious Bridget does absolutely nothing."

He did not like the way she said 'your precious Bridget', but he knew that she spoke the truth. "You could always leave the job," he said reasonably.

"That would be like admitting defeat," she said. "Why should I leave? I have done nothing wrong. Roderick is a rich man, so why doesn't his daughter suggest they employ someone to help me with the management? Most restaurants have a deputy manager. I'll tell you why that does not happen. It is because Bridget likes to have a finger in the pie. She doesn't want to give up her role in the running of the place, but neither does she want to do anything. She is bored with it already, that's the trouble."

Her voice was getting higher and higher, and he thought there was going to be another paroxysm of weeping. He handed her a clean white handkerchief from his pocket.

They were both a little drunk, so it seemed perfectly natural for him to put his arms around her hunched shoulders. "Come on!" he said in what he hoped was a comforting but authoritative voice.

She was a pathetic creature, and put her head on his shoulder. "Let's go to bed," she said, head hidden. "I'd like that. Please, please!"

He found himself in a ludicrous situation. He had never envisaged such a thing happening. He was acutely embarrassed. He got to his feet, rather unsteadily, intending to make a getaway.

Suddenly, incongruously, he recalled the words he had uttered hours before to Bridget, when he had said, "Remember I love you." If she had replied, "I love you too," he would have left Amanda's flat immediately, but she had not said it, and it was that non-reply that made him stay. At least, that is what he told himself, later.

It was all a bit unreal because they had both been drinking and were suffering from lack of sleep, but they came together as two people bowed down by problems and uncertainties.

"You needn't worry," she assured him, "no one will know." He was surprised by her common-sense approach, but he believed in her integrity. Despite the faint ringing in his ears and a slight feeling of imbalance, it all worked amazingly well.

He got up before her, leaving her sleeping as she did not have to get up as early as he did. He tiptoed around her room looking for his clothes. He was anxious not to waken her because he thought she needed as much sleep as she could get. He felt a deep sense of gratitude towards her.

During the day Bridget telephoned him at his office and, for the first time in his relationship with her, he was overcome by guilt and fear for the future, a dread that he would be betrayed. He thought of Roderick and his long-term liaison with Millicent Jones. He had been found out in the end. His conversation with Bridget ended abruptly. She put the phone down on him, something she had never done before. Although he knew it to be impossible, he felt she had an insight into what he had done.

To reassure himself, he walked to Rocket that evening. As soon as he saw Amanda, sitting at the till brows furrowed in concentration, he knew, without any doubt, that she would never tell anyone what had happened.

He said, "Everything all right?"

"Fine," she replied, giving him a wide smile. And, as if understanding his anxieties, "Don't worry, Silas. Everything is fine."

He did not see her or get in touch with her for a week after that, a whole week. Neither did he hear from Bridget. One evening he went to the restaurant to collect Amanda after she had finished work. The weather had changed, and he told himself that he did not like the idea of her walking back to her flat, alone, in the pouring rain. When she saw him standing in the doorway, she looked startled, then pleased. They walked along the deserted street, close together, huddled under his big umbrella. They spent the night together, a night not stimulated by alcohol or preceded by storms of tears and feelings of resentment.

It was hard for him to leave her in the morning. He sat in his car in a traffic jam, bemused, wondering. It was the same when he got to the office. After some deliberation, he telephoned Amanda and asked if he could see her again that night. She would never refuse him, and her voice on the telephone was eager, expectant. He knew that she was undemanding, but she loved him.

As he put the receiver down, conscious that he was longing to see her again, he came to a decision. To tell Bridget how he felt.

CHAPTER THIRTY

Amanda was nervous about Silas meeting her parents. She didn't know how anyone who had once aspired to becoming a member of the Macauley family could readily accept a publican and his wife as future in-laws. So anxious was she that she lapsed into complete silence during the journey by car to the village in the Cotswolds where her parents' public house was the focal point of the community.

Silas, noticing that she did not put her hand on his knee when he was driving as she usually did, understood how she felt. He tried to think of helpful words to say to her, but he did not want to sound patronising or as if he considered a problem existed. He loved her, but he had to admit to a slight apprehension himself. He did not know what to expect.

He had not completely thrown off his old life, and the memory of going to Pondings to see Bridget was still in his mind. It had a way of returning to him at odd quiet moments, such as this one, and he wished the past could be wiped away as if it had never happened. He found himself thinking, perhaps that is how Duibhne wanted it and then realised, as he had, that it could not be done.

Bridget had been surprised to see him. Surprised and happy, and he was disconcerted by the enthusiasm of her welcome. When she learnt of the reason for his visit, she had been sweet and understanding. "I'm very happy for you," she said. He drove back to London, his mind in a turmoil, thinking of all the years he had known and loved Bridget. Years which he would never forget, as he now knew for certain, although he suspected she was untouched by them.

The countryside was beautiful, unspoilt. No ugly electricity pylons stalking across the fields – somehow this bit of England had been protected and preserved.

"There is nothing in the world to beat it," he said. "It's a pity that when people visit this country they seldom see this side to it." He stopped the car so that they could look at the view, without worrying about sharp bends and hedges obscuring the road.

"We're nearly there," she said. They were the first words she had uttered for miles and miles, so he grasped at them. "Which way?" he asked eagerly.

"Over there," she pointed to a cluster of houses and a church spire. "That's our village."

The car turned into a lane approaching the village.

Here there were modern houses, square boxes, which had been constructed in material to tone in with the old Cotswold stone cottages in the centre of the village. They passed the school, surrounded by fields, and then a park with swings and a climbing-frame. Now they were coming into the old part, and on their left was a War Memorial. Silas had been told this was a landmark, and Amanda indicated a lane for him to go down and, ahead of him, he saw the cricket pitch. He had been told about this also, and he had informed Amanda that in the days before he became a high-powered businessman, he had played cricket for the team in his father's parish. He noticed the smart pavilion and, standing back at the far side of the pitch, the pub.

It was called The Beetle. As Amanda explained, nothing to do with the insect, and the picture of the mallet on the swinging sign indicated its origin. The pub had the lot as far as tourist attraction was concerned: the famous Cotswold stone, uneven roof and a giant mulberry tree growing in front of it. When they got out of the car, Silas noticed a sign warning customers not to sit under the tree during the month of August, as the falling fruit would damage their clothes.

Like most pubs it was dark inside, and Amanda made the introductions in the dim narrow hall.

"Reg and Linda, if you please," said her father. "No standing on ceremony, Silas."

He led the way up the stairs to their living quarters, private rooms which looked out on to the back garden.

Silas could hear water running, and realised there was a small stream at the bottom of it. There were extensions on either side, built at the back of the building so as not to spoil the charm of the front aspect, and these contained a few rooms for guests.

Silas received a cordial welcome, and he soon perceived that Reg and Linda had no misgivings about him: he was their daughter's choice, and they were confident it was the right one.

"For God's sake, relax," he whispered to Amanda, and she gave him a grateful smile.

He warmed to her parents. They were such genuine unpretentious people. If they had put a show on for him he would have felt uncomfortable, but they did not. Reg was the head of his small kingdom; the pub had been in his family for generations and he was as proud of it as if it had been the most stately home in the land.

"It has to go," he explained to Silas. "I'm putting it on the market, and Linda and I are retiring to one of those new houses at the edge of the village. It's been hard work for both of us, and we have had enough. I hoped my son would want to take it on, but he's not interested."

That evening, almost apologetically, he asked Silas if he would go into the bar for a drink. "While the ladies are preparing our supper." The bar was manned by Charlie, who came in to help when Reg was not available. Silas was impressed that The Beetle had kept its image as 'the local'. All the regulars were there, propping up the bar, and stopping their conversation to look at him with interest when he came in with the landlord.

"So often these lovely old places have changed in order to cater for people coming from London," said Silas. "Once a place gets a recommendation from Egon Ronay the locals are squeezed out."

"That's right," Reg nodded. "I was determined that would not happen. This pub belonged to my father, and his father before him, and so on. It hasn't changed much over the years. Oh, I have built on rooms and made improvements, but I hope the character of the place hasn't altered."

They went upstairs to have the evening meal, prepared by Linda with the help of her daughter. Reg produced a bottle of the best champagne to toast the happy couple. They sat at a table overlooking the darkening garden, and they could hear the noise of the stream. "I hope it won't keep you awake, Silas," said Linda. "We're so used to it, we don't hear it any more."

They toasted each other, and then raised their glasses to Amanda's brother who was absent. He was at university training to be an architect. "It's a shame Bob isn't here," said Linda, and explained, "He's taking exams at present, but you'll meet him soon enough, Silas."

Later, much later, Silas went to his room, accompanied by Reg who had something to impart. "You are not with our girl," he said, "although I'm sure you share a room in London. I know how things are these days, but Mother . . ." he smiled, "she wouldn't understand, so you will have to be separate while you are here, until you are wed, of course."

"I understand," said Silas.

When he was alone, he leaned out of the bedroom window. It was very quiet except for the stream chattering on the stones, and the air smelled sweet and fresh.

Presently, there was a knock on the door, and Amanda was there. "Darling," she said, and she pressed her body against his. The longing was so intense, he almost gave way to it, and asked her to stay, but he knew it would be wrong. His thoughts turned to two mothers, Duibhne and Linda, and the different attitudes they adopted. Duibhne had always been happy to allow Silas and her daughter to share the nursery together. He thought there were anomalies in her character he would never fully understand. Perhaps they were explained by the recent revelations. He forced his mind away from thoughts of Duibhne, which were irrelevant in his present situation.

It was a comfort to know that Amanda was weak in her love for him, and would have thrown away all good intentions if he had asked her. They kissed and parted. She told him that she was in the next room and knocked on the wall to prove it. When he climbed into the narrow bed the sheets felt crisp and cool. He slept deeply until Reg came to waken him with a cup of tea.

They insisted on giving him a large breakfast, even though he told them he was used to a slice of toast and a snatched cup of coffee. Linda was a woman with fixed ideas, and one of them was that a man should start the day with a breakfast of egg, bacon and sausage. She and Reg were a very relaxed couple, apparently not given to violent opinions or arguments. They were united in wanting to please Silas and, as Charlie had been given the running of the pub during his visit, they had time to entertain him.

Reg was a very likable man, with a down-to-earth approach to life, and Silas wondered what it was that imbued this straightforward character with such serenity and good will. Then he found out the secret. Reg took him to an outbuilding at the rear of the car park, and Silas was told that it had once been a stable but was now used as a place for Reg to make his pots. The unfinished, unglazed ones, all shapes and sizes, stood in rows, waiting to be put in the kiln.

"Do you sell them?" asked Silas.

"Indeed I do," replied Reg. "You wouldn't be able to move in here if I didn't sell them. As well as being a hobby, it's a nice little earner, and I hope to get the odd penny from it when I retire."

"It is going to be quite a job moving all this," commented Silas, looking at the paraphernalia.

"I'd like to keep it here," Reg admitted, "so I can come back and do my work. The kiln is here, and I don't fancy moving that. Surely, I'll be able to come to some arrangement with the new owner?"

Silas was doubtful. "It would be complicated," he said, "and would mean separating one portion of the property from the rest." It was apparent that dear old

Reg knew nothing of the complexities of buying and selling. He looked a bit downcast for a moment, and Silas hastened to offer encouragement. "You may be able to sell to a local," he said, "who will understand and be willing to cooperate."

"Charlie has said he would like to buy," said Reg, "but I doubt as how he could raise the cash."

"There is always a way of raising money if the project has potential, " said Silas wisely, "and certainly The Beetle is a good investment."

On the drive back to London, Amanda chatted happily all the way. Everything had worked out well, far better than she had expected. Now, she had to meet his parents, the canon and his wife, and she was going to do that very soon. They were going to drive to the Midlands on the following weekend. "We'll be in separate rooms there too," Silas told her.

"Did you hear me knock on the wall?" she asked, "Mother said we could have shared a double room as far as she was concerned, but Dad would not have approved. He's old-fashioned in his outlook."

"They are very nice people," he said.

They were entering the suburbs when Silas decided to ask the question which was on his mind. "Shall we buy the pub, Amanda, and move out of London?"

She made no reply.

"I could do it, you know," he said. "I could sell my flat, and I have some money invested. I think we could make a go of it, between us."

"I knew you were going to suggest that," said Amanda. "Suddenly, this morning, I knew what was going through your mind."

"At some stage you and your brother decided you wanted to leave it," said Silas thoughtfully. "Perhaps you don't want to return to it?"

"I remember when I was a little girl," she told him, "Dad used to carry me into the saloon bar, and all the customers would make cooing noises at me."

"Was that bad?"

"No, I loved it."

"But not what you want for a child we may have?"

She thought about this for a moment, then she said, "I think our child would attend the village school, as I did, and as he or she grew older would want to escape, as I did. Surely, isn't that how every growing child feels? A child brought up in London would probably feel the same way."

"I'm sure you are right," he said, "and we have to think of ourselves, what we want to get out of life."

"I know I long to leave Rocket," she said, "and it is very exciting to think of running a place of our own, just the two of us. Would you miss your job?"

"I'd miss the money I make," he admitted, "but I've known for a long time that I'm not completely happy about it being a lifelong commitment. If we do this, and I'm beginning to think we will, it will not be a doddle. You realise that, don't you?"

"Yes, of course I realise what is involved," she assured

him, "but nothing could be worse, or as demeaning, as working for Rocket. And you don't need to worry about Dad interfering, it is not his style. He would leave everything to us."

"I shall need his advice," said Silas, "and I like to think of him being able to work in that pottery of his."

He spent the rest of the journey telling her of the plans he had made while lying in bed on the previous night. "That dark saloon is wasted, and we could enlarge it and build a conservatory, looking out at the garden and the stream. People could eat in there all the year round, and in the summer we could put more tables and chairs in the garden. I don't want to change the atmosphere in the pub; the locals must not be frightened away. No exotic expensive meals. Grilled veal with a hint of garlic served with wild mushrooms gathered from the fields, none of that crap! Neither do we want chips with everything. No chips! There must be a middle way."

"There is," said Amanda confidently, "and I know what it is. There is one thing working at Rocket has taught me: people do not want giant helpings heaped on a plate. They want simple healthy food, and I know of dozens of delicious recipes we can use."

They talked in this delightful way, wonderfully stimulating for both of them, until they got to Amanda's flat. Then they sat in her little kitchen, and continued talking. Of course Silas stayed, and rose early the next morning to go to work. He left Amanda sleeping, and he kissed the small portion of her cheek which was visible, and left a note on the hump in the bed, telling her he would pick her up at Rocket at one o'clock the following morning. As he let himself out of the flat, he thought that with luck this ridiculous caper would soon be a thing of the past.

During the day he had moments of abstraction, so many thoughts tumbling about in his head. It was hard to concentrate and, in a quiet moment, he found a scrap of paper and made a rough sketch of the conservatory he envisaged at The Beetle. Amanda, sitting at the till in the restaurant, was dreaming also, and she doodled on the back of one of the menus. It was not a conservatory she drew, but the outline of a female figure, an egg for a head, sticks for arms, a bouquet which was just a scribble, and the flowing lines of the basic design for a wedding dress.

CHAPTER THIRTY-ONE

As soon as it was done, Bridget regretted hanging up on Silas. It was just that the conversation she had with him irritated her, as everything seemed to irritate her these days. She had telephoned him, and plunged straight into the conversation by demanding, "Well, did you see Amanda?"

"Yes, last night."

"How did it go?"

"She is fed up," he told her, "and, quite honestly, I don't blame her. It is damned hard managing on her own, working all hours day and night. Perhaps you could find someone to help her?"

"Can't afford it," replied Bridget decidedly. "We're just beginning, you know."

"Don't you think that is a good reason to be there yourself?"

"I've told you, I can't go to London. I'm needed here.

Heavens, Daddy put up all the money for Rocket, it's a chance in a lifetime for her. I hope you told her to stop whinging."

"I don't believe I did . . ."

"That's what I asked you to do, Silas." That was the moment when she slammed down the receiver. She knew it was an unforgivable thing to do, especially when he had gone to see Amanda for her sake. Immediately, she felt sorry for what she had done, and almost rang back to apologise, but then thought: I can't be bothered. He'll understand.

The trouble was that she could not be bothered to do anything, and felt increasingly lonely and neglected. Every day was the same, her father going to London in the morning, returning in the evening. They dined together, he making light conversation for her benefit, she mostly silent because she could not rid her mind of the idea that there was so much they ought to be saying to each other. The unsaid words were like a barrier between them, and she wondered what would happen if she opened the subject herself, if she asked him, for instance, if he expected her mother to return.

Ma sent her a postcard from Campbeltown, and she showed it to him. He glanced at it quickly, and then handed it back to her.

"I was thinking," she said tentatively, "that I might join them."

For the first time he showed some emotion, and seemed genuinely upset by the suggestion. "I hope you don't mean that, my darling," he said. "You are the only bright thing in my universe at present, everything else is very black."

She had no idea he was depressed, and felt a wave of pity for him. "Oh, Daddy, I'm so sorry . . ."

"I don't know what I shall do if you leave me," he went on, a note of self-pity in his voice, "although I can see there is no reason for you to stay."

She tried to explain to him how she was feeling. "It is just that I am not as bright as you say. In fact, I am very dull, and I suppose that is because I have not enough to do here."

"What about getting in touch with your friends? They could come and visit you during the day when I am not here. I'm afraid I am not anxious to have anyone to stay at present, and I like to keep the evenings free for us to be on our own. I value the time we spend together so much. But, please, do ask anyone you like to come and see you while I am in London."

"I can't be bothered," she said.

After that, she did not mention going away again, and tried to settle back into the usual routine. Sometimes she picked flowers in the garden, and arranged them in vases, as she had seen her mother do, but if her father noticed them he made no comment.

From time to time, as the days passed slowly, she wondered idly why Silas did not telephone her. No doubt he was annoyed because she had hung up on him, but it was unlike Silas to stay annoyed for very long. She hoped he would soon get over it because she would like to talk to him.

She spent a great deal of time in Ma's room, watching the television or reading Ma's books. She longed for the holidays when Robert would come home. Surely, her mother, Ma and Christopher would return then?

Then one day, from Ma's window, she saw Silas's car coming up the drive. She ran downstairs, opening the front door, and down the wide stone steps as fast as she could go. When he got out of his car, she threw her arms around his neck. Immediately she knew something had changed. The joy of seeing his dear familiar face was clouded by his evident embarrassment. In a world where nothing was right for her, the realisation that something else had gone wrong was almost unbearable.

"Shall we walk around the garden for a while?" he suggested. He did not want to go into the house. They circled the lawn, and soon she understood the reason for his discomfiture: he had come with a purpose other than to see her. He had come to tell her he was in love with Amanda Rhys.

She heard herself saying, "Oh, that's lovely, Silas. I am so happy for you."

She endeavoured to keep her voice level, so that he got the impression she was almost relieved. No doubt, his devotion, unwavering as she thought, had become irksome, and she was glad to be free of the burden. He had rehearsed what he would say to her, but the warmth of her welcome surprised and unnerved him. The subsequent equanimity she displayed, after he had blurted out the reason for his visit, eased his pain at having to wipe the trust and love from her face.

Politely, he asked about her family. She told him that her mother, Ma and Christopher were still at the Maiden's Planting.

"How long are they going to stay there?" he asked.

"I don't know. I may join them or go back to London. I haven't made up my mind yet." And it is nothing to do with you any more, she thought.

Like strangers they walked back to his car. He caught a glimpse of her exquisite profile as he started the engine. Her head was turned away from him, as if she was anxious to get away. As he drove off, she directed an icy blue stare at him, and raised one hand.

That afternoon, she stumped over to Ma's cottage, just to peer through the windows at the dust and untidiness within. Even the garden had become a mess, the lawn shaggy with buttercups and daisies. She walked alongside the flowerbeds, and plucked out a few weeds which she threw on the heap at the bottom of the garden. She decided she would help Ma by doing some proper weeding, and went in search of a trowel. The shed where all the tools were kept was locked. They have even stopped me from doing that, she thought. Being in the garden made her think of Christopher and his love of flowers. Memories of her childhood flooded back to her as she walked back to the house, her throat constricted in an effort to hold back the tears.

In Ma's room she pulled down the bulky photograph albums from one of the shelves. Ma had always been punctilious about putting photographs into books. She found an early one which she had not seen before. It concerned America, so she went to get the newspaper cutting from her bedroom, and laid it alongside the album, so that she could remind herself of the story the reporter of the *Graphic* had told. There was a photograph of a stout little man standing in a stable-yard, and she thought that must be the person her mother referred to as Uncle Tom. There were photographs of a white house, very square and modern, and many of horses, either standing in the yard or in fields. In another photograph of Uncle Tom he was accompanied by a young man, a young man who wore spectacles, and reminded her of someone.

She turned the pages until she came to what she was looking for, pictures of her mother. There were many of them, and in most of them she was holding a baby. Under one of the photographs Ma had written the words, Divvy and Bartley. Bridget kept referring to the article the girl had written, so that she could make sense of it all. The photographs of the baby kept appearing, and there were ones of him when he was a little boy, looking more like the Christopher she knew. Under one of him playing with a wooden train, his face turned slightly so that he looked normal, Ma had written, *Bartley, given to his mother*.

Why had her mother kept all this from her children? Bridget felt it was a betrayal of trust. She heaved the album back on to the shelf, and took another one down. This contained more familiar images. Herself and Robert when they were little children, and later photographs of herself and Silas. Silas with his hair cut like a pageboy which was the fashion of the time when they were both teenagers. Pages and pages of photographs of herself and Silas growing up together. Amanda Rhys has not got those memories, she thought resentfully, they belong to me, and nothing can take them away from me.

That evening, after dinner, she went to see her father in his study. She thought she would find him writing at his desk, but he was sitting in the armchair, reading *The Times*. He put it down when he saw her come into the room, and looked at her seriously. "Is something the matter?" He thought she had been very silent during dinner.

"Silas is going to marry Amanda Rhys," she said.

"Really?" He tried to sound interested, but it was difficult when he had so much on his mind. His sad little sigh conveyed his preoccupation.

"He came to tell me today." The tears were at the back of her eyes, ready to spill out at the slightest provocation, and she made an effort to hold them back.

He must have noticed something in her face, for he looked at her sharply over his spectacles. "You don't mind too much, do you, darling? Property rights and all that?"

She did not understand what he meant. "Well, old Silas was always around, wasn't he?" he said by way of explanation. "You must have got used to him."

"I don't mind," she told him, "I'm happy for them both." She wondered why she kept saying she was happy about something that was making her so unhappy.

"He was not right for you," her father continued. "A very limited character, in my opinion. As for her, she does not appreciate what we have done for her."

He was merely echoing her own complaints about Amanda. "She's welcome to him," she murmured, and the unworthiness of the remark only added to her grief.

"That's the spirit," said Roderick. "You have known Silas for so long, it is bound to feel strange when the relationship comes to an end."

"Yes, I know."

"It always feels strange," said her father, "but life goes on and, believe me, in time you will meet someone more suit – more right for you." He gave her hand a little squeeze.

"All right, Daddy," she said hastily, suddenly longing to get away because she knew he was wrong. They were both wrong. She had missed out on something good, she had let it slip away from her, and there was no way she could retrieve it.

She fled to her bedroom and allowed the tears to gush from her eyes. She lay face down on the top of her bed, and wept. She prayed and railed against Amanda Rhys at the same time. She did not think her prayers would be answered. In the great scheme of things God would not be concerned with her small grief, and He would probably think, as she did, that she had got what she deserved.

CHAPTER THIRTY-TWO

Silas was driving to the Cotswolds from London, feeling delicate after a farewell party his colleagues at the office had given him the night before. He had crawled into bed at two o'clock in the morning, rising at nine in order to be on his way. He was tempted to stay in bed until noon, but he knew how disappointed Amanda would be if he did not turn up until the late afternoon. She would pretend she did not mind, but the disappointment would be there in her voice if he telephoned and said he would be arriving later than expected.

At the party a good friend had made a short speech, pointing out that Silas was the perfect name for someone who was intending to become a country bumpkin. A white smock was produced, the sort that farmers wore in olden times, and Silas had good-humouredly held it against himself, saying, "Thank'ee kindly, sir." He knew that most of the people there thought he was mad, giving up a good job for an uncertain future in the sticks. And the girl he was going to marry, although attractive, was not a patch on his old love, Bridget.

He stretched his arms, hands still firmly holding the steering wheel. He knew that this movement was an indication of fatigue, that he ought to stop and rest. He decided to press on because he wanted to see Amanda; they had been parted for a week. They had stayed a weekend with his parents in the Midlands, and he thought that had been a success, although it was hard to tell, as his mother and particularly his father never revealed their true feelings, except to each other. Whatever their verdict on the girl their son was to marry, they would share it. Silas thought that Amanda had been constrained during the visit, not completely natural, on the defensive as if she half-expected criticism. Whereas with her parents he had felt completely at ease from the first.

She was staying in the new house which Reg and Linda had bought for their retirement. She had sold her flat in London without any trouble; as soon as it came on the market a buyer was found. Silas was not so lucky, and his flat remained unsold. Amanda thought he was asking too much for it and he should come down in price. He reflected that this was probably one of the first things she would say to him and he decided not to tell her that the estate agent had telephoned him and suggested the same thing. Until the flat was sold they could not start negotiations for the purchase of The

Beetle, which Reg still managed, although not living in the rooms above any more. He had been very taken with the idea of his daughter and future son-in-law running the family pub, but he tended to damp down any ambitious schemes they had for improving the place. Silas remembered Amanda telling him her father would not interfere, but Reg was already interfering. It was not going to be plain sailing.

Driving through the countryside, listening to music and trying to stave off the desire to sleep, he found his thoughts turning to Bridget. Most of the time he managed to forget her; he forced himself to forget her because he thought remembering was a dangerous pastime. But at times like this, when he was alone, he thought of her.

After Amanda had left her job at Rocket and had gone to live with her parents, he found himself walking to the restaurant. He told himself he was interested to see if it was still operating. It was closed. A sign on the front of the building announced that it would be opening shortly, under new management.

It was as if the Macauleys no longer existed. When Silas made tentative enquiries about them to mutual friends he was told that no one had news of them. The newspapers did not feature them any more. A tiny item in the *Graphic* predicted, as Silas had once done, that Roderick would enter the House of Lords, but it was only an idle assumption in a gossip column.

Once, he said to Amanda, "I would like to know what happens to them all," and she had made the crisp reply, "Well, we're not likely to hear, are we?" He kept quiet after that because he knew she hated Bridget, and he did not like having to listen to her saying bad things about her. It was true that when he severed connection with the Macauley family he had not appreciated that they would be lost to him for ever.

Amanda had arranged to meet him at The Beetle. As he turned his car into the car park, she ran out to meet him. She put her arms around him, and he pressed his face into her soft neck. "Ah-h!" it was wonderful to see her. They walked into The Beetle, hand in hand.

"Dave's in the bar," she said.

"Spare me Dave today," he pleaded.

Dave was a regular of ten years' standing, a humorist whose jokes and quips had amused Silas, still did, but now he thought he was the last person he wanted to see.

"You look so tired," said Amanda.

"Well, I didn't get much sleep last night," he told her. He described the party. He promised to show her the farmer's smock, later on when he unpacked his case. "It's great to be free of that job," he said. "Just think, darling, this is my first day of freedom."

"No regrets?"

"No regrets. Let's have a drink and a sandwich in the garden," he suggested. "I'll wait there for you, and you go and order a gin and tonic and a bacon sarnie for me, please, and anything you want for yourself." He passed two tenners over to her. "That way, I'll avoid Dave."

"I thought you liked him!"

"I do, but I can't face his particular brand of comedy today. Don't forget, I shall probably be enjoying his company for the next twenty years." For some reason he found this a sobering thought.

They sat on wooden benches with the drinks and the food on the table between them. It was chilly in the garden, so everyone else was staying inside. They were alone, and he held her hand across the table. "I wish we could stay here," he said.

He hated having to stay in the new house, in the spare bedroom which was papered with pink roses, and had a thin wall separating him from Amanda. Silas preferred the cramped living quarters at The Beetle, comfortably shabby, but he soon realised that in moving into her new house Linda had achieved a long-time ambition. It was exactly as she wanted it, clean and tidy, and completely devoid of character and good taste.

Amanda, fiercely loyal to her mother, did not criticise the décor, but she knew, without him saying a word, what Silas thought of it.

"At least there are no flying ducks," she said to him, on the defensive as usual. When he took time to consider it, he thought her defensiveness a distinct disadvantage in their relationship.

"What about the flat?" she asked him, "anyone interested?"

"No."

"Have you thought about bringing down the price?"

"I've thought about it, of course, but I'm not sure if it is the right thing to do."

"We've got to sell it," she said impatiently, "otherwise we won't achieve anything."

His head ached, and he could not put his mind to solving problems. "Let's leave it for today."

"Perhaps I should have stayed at Rocket," she said plaintively, not prepared to leave it. "At least I'd still be earning."

"It's shut down," he told her.

"How do you know?"

"I walked over there one day, to see if it was still open."

"How funny," she said.

"Why funny?"

"Well, I think it is funny that you are still interested. Interested enough to walk all that way. Were you hoping to see Bridget there?"

"Of course not." He felt the course the conversation was taking was leading him into a trap, and he took steps to avoid it. "You know only too well she was hardly ever there."

"Where is she now?"

"I have no idea."

"I thought one of your friends last night would have been able to give you news of her."

"Not at all," he said.

A warning voice in Amanda's head told her it was time she stopped talking about Bridget. "I'm sorry, darling," she said. "We have to go to the house as I'm having a fitting for my dress."

"Fine," he said happily. As a gesture of good will, he poked his head around the door of the saloon bar as they passed. "Hi, Dave!"

"Silas! Can you stop for a chat and a beer?"

"No chance," said Silas. "Wedding plans are top of the agenda for today."

There was a concrete path leading to the front door of the new house, with rough ground on either side. In a few years' time Reg would have changed it into a neat garden. The hall smelled of new paint and the staircase was still uncarpeted, but Linda had put her pictures on the walls and the furniture had been moved from their rooms at The Beetle.

As Silas entered the sitting-room they were met by a tidal wave of salmon-pink satin. It flowed towards them, cascading in folds, and Silas jumped to one side as if to avoid getting his feet wet.

"Don't step on it!" shrieked Linda. Two girls in the background collapsed into giggles.

"You should not be here," Linda told Silas reprovingly, as she gathered yards and yards of material over her arm. "The bridegroom shouldn't see this."

"It's only the stuff for the bridesmaid's dresses, Mother," Amanda protested. "Surely Silas doesn't have to stay away?"

But Linda was insistent: Silas must leave. Amanda came to the door with him. "I'm so sorry, darling."

"Weddings are always a pain in the neck," he said and, as he walked away, he remembered Bridget saying, 'I want the works, fantastic wedding, bridesmaids . . .' He had hoped Amanda might settle for a registry-office marriage, but apparently that was not to be. His father had agreed to officiate at their wedding, so it was going to be almost as Silas had imagined.

He had the rest of the afternoon to himself and, feeling as he did, he could not face dear old Reg and plans. Desperately he desired sleep, but that meant returning to the house which was out of the question. He did the next best thing, and went to his car. He sank into the soft leather of the driver's seat, and thought how he was going to miss this, a most treasured possession, his cherished motor car which was soon to be exchanged for something more economical and practical.

He slept deeply and without dreams. He awoke with a start when the far-side door was opened. Amanda slipped quietly into the seat beside him. For a moment he did not know where he was, and was only conscious of a stiff neck which he moved experimentally from side to side. It was not yet dark in the car park, but the afternoon had gone while he had been sleeping.

"It's not going to work, is it?" said Amanda abruptly.

"What?" He could not imagine what she was talking about.

"In taking on me and my family you are not being

true to yourself," she said. It was so like her to plunge into a contentious exchange of views without giving him any warning. He wondered if she had been brewing up this argument while having her dress fitted, and whether their earlier conversation about Bridget had sparked it off.

"The Macauleys are in your soul, and you will never be free of them," she went on dramatically.

He was awake now, and angry. "That's balls," he retorted. "Roderick is a Macauley and you know my opinion of him."

"He is only a part of the whole concept," she said. "You met the Macauleys when you were an impressionable schoolboy, and you have been in their thrall ever since. I thought when we were together you had broken away from them, but I was wrong. For years you have been influenced by them, and your own family became nothing to you because of these people."

"My family gave me nothing," he said. "You have met them, and you know what they are like. There was never any jealousy about my friendship with the Macauleys; they were only too happy for me to spend most of my holidays with another family. You don't understand about my parents, they are so close there is no room for anyone else. They should never have had a child. They had one son, me, and they didn't know how to treat me, what to do with me. I'm sure it was a relief to them when I found my own level."

"It wasn't your level though, was it?" Amanda

snapped. "It was a level just out of your reach and, therefore, an enchantment."

"What does all this mean?" demanded Silas. "When you talk of enchantment, do you mean Bridget? I think it is not the Macauleys that worry you, but just one of them – Bridget."

"Yes, you're right," she said, "and I can't live with the knowledge that she is on your mind. Admit it, you still think of her."

He did not deny it. "Give it a chance," he pleaded. "I have known her for ten years. You cannot throw away ten years without a backward glance."

"You will get dissatisfied with everything here," she said, "my parents, the pub, and, in time, me. I am not prepared to inflict such pain on myself."

"I love you," he said.

"I know you do, now."

"And you are going to chuck it all in, everything we mean to each other?"

"Yes, I am giving up what I want most in the world, but I'm sure it's the right thing to do." She wrenched the ring off her finger and gave it to him.

The events that followed were a nightmare for Silas. Reg's rage knew no bounds, and Linda became hysterical. Two people he respected and admired became like avenging furies. Amanda stood on the sideline and wept. During the furore he heard her say, "Dad, Mum, I broke it off, not Silas."

They did not listen to their daughter – they were

determined that it was his fault and not hers. Reg said, "It's a pity your public-school education has not taught you how to behave like a gentleman," and, at this point, Silas decided to leave.

He walked back to his car, hardly able to breathe, his heart thumping in his chest. "Oh, God," he muttered as he started the engine, "God help me . . ."

On the journey back to London, when he had calmed down, he tried to analyse what had happened. He accepted that Amanda had a clearer understanding about his feelings than he had himself, but she had given up very easily. He had been happy with her, and when he needed someone to care about him she had been there. He liked her mother and father, Reg working on his pots, Linda so bright and welcoming to the people in the pub. He had admired them for being worthwhile real people. Lately, they had begun to irritate him, but that must be the way with all future in-laws, especially when there is a wedding to plan and organise. Perhaps it would have been better if he and Amanda had stayed in London, apart from both sets of parents.

Then he dismissed Reg and Linda from his mind, for he could not accept they were the reason for everything breaking up. Amanda had said, 'The Macauleys are in your soul' but he knew that it was Bridget that was in his soul. He thought, I have always loved her, and I can't change that. It is the reason for all this.

The thought comforted him, for other explanations

were base compared with the simple fact that he still loved Bridget. He had not behaved dishonourably. It was not his decision to break off the engagement. By the time he reached the outskirts of London he was beginning to think it was not such a bad decision after all.

CHAPTER THIRTY-THREE

One morning, as he was crossing the hall before leaving the house to go to London, Roderick was waylaid by Bell.

"May I speak to you, sir?"

Roderick stopped short. "Of course. Is anything wrong?"

"Miss Bridget, sir. I'm worried about her, and I'm sure her mother would be worried too if she knew."

Roderick experienced a moment of panic. "Knew what?" he asked sharply.

"She just doesn't look well, sir, and anyone can see she is unhappy. I don't like to see a sad expression on that pretty face."

Roderick clasped the old man's hand. "Thank you for telling me," he said.

That evening, while they were dining together, he observed his daughter closely. It was true, she did look thinner, and there were smudges under eyes, as if she had not slept. He watched her toying with the food on the plate in front of her, and he experienced a resurgence of the panic he had felt that morning. The word anorexia came to his mind, and he was sure there were other nameless horrors to which young women were prone.

"I am not going to my study this evening, " he said. "I'd rather sit in the drawing-room. Will you join me, darling? There is nothing special you want to watch, is there?"

"Of course not."

He turned to Bell. "Will you bring us a bottle of the red wine I ordered last week, and the opener. Don't open it yourself, there's a good man, I'll do that myself."

Bridget sat in her mother's usual place in the corner of the sofa, and her father sat in an armchair opposite her. They waited for what seemed an interminable time for Bell to return.

"He's getting so old," said Bridget despondently, as if she knew that another part of her childhood would soon be snatched away from her.

At last he returned with a tray holding the bottle of wine, a silver corkscrew and two glasses.

"You go off to bed now," said Roderick kindly, "no need to wait up for us. I'll put these in the kitchen when we have finished."

The old man left them.

"Speaking of Bell," said Roderick, "he is worried

about you. He thinks you have something on your mind. Is that true?"

She found it hard to believe he could be so insensitive. "I have you and my mother on my mind," she said, "wondering all the time if you are going to stay together."

He was taken aback. "I hope so," he said. "I would not like to think anything different. Whatever gave you that idea?"

She lost her temper then, and shouted at him, "Why do you treat me like a child? Mummy is in Scotland and you are here. I don't think that in view of everything that has happened lately it is an unreasonable question to ask."

He pulled the cork from the bottle and filled the two glasses. "Of course it is a reasonable question," he said calmly, "and the answer is that we are staying together always."

The relief was so great she felt like bursting into tears. Tears were very near the surface these days, and she had learnt how to hold them back. "I'm glad," she said.

"I have spoken to your mother several times, and they are returning shortly after Robert comes home for the holidays. Divvy needed the rest, a chance to recover after what has been a difficult time for both of us."

Bridget began to feel more relaxed; sitting in her mother's beautiful room with all the familiar objects around her, the world seemed less of a terrible place.

"Do you miss your old life?" she asked.

He thought for a second, and then said, "I can honestly say I do not miss it. There are other things I can do, you know, and, strange as it may seem, probably just as useful as the work I was doing before I resigned. I feel very positive about the future."

"Silas and I could never understand why you did resign," said Bridget. It was a luxury, just saying his name as if they were still together.

"I resigned because I did not want any more questions to be asked. I wanted to put an end to all the press interference. I could bear it for myself, it is unavoidable when one is a public figure, but I could not bear it for your mother."

"And Millicent Jones? That woman who started it all, what was the attraction there?" The fact that they were talking together like civilised people had made her bold.

Before, he would have evaded such a direct question, but this evening he met it straight on. "I don't know," he said slowly. "I did not love her, like I love your mother. In fact I did not love her at all."

"And you lived with a woman for six years without loving her?" said his daughter sharply.

"I did not live with her. Sometimes weeks went by without my seeing her. I suppose I liked being with her because she was so ordinary. It was relaxing for me to just sit and listen to her chatter. Not politics, she had no interest in that direction. She had a sharp tongue, and we had rows, and, you know, that was a relief as well. I made the mistake of thinking it was a relationship with no complications. She seemed so content, having her little house and seeing me from time to time. One thing I can tell you, Bridget, there is no such thing as an uncomplicated relationship. It may appear that way, but sooner or later, one side of the partnership starts making demands." He looked at her sadly. "I know it was wrong of me."

She noticed that under the light of the lamp behind his head he looked quite old. The years are not kind to faces of handsome men. When the skin begins to sag there are no individual features to disguise the ageing process. The slight puffiness around the eyes and the lines around the mouth only emphasise the loss of perfection that had once been there.

"It was very wrong of me," he said.

"And you are wrong about something else as well," said Bridget. "About Silas. You said he was a limited character and I would meet someone else. He is not a limited character, he is a marvellous person, and I love him more than words can say. Of course, I will meet someone else, but I know it will not be the same. I can never love anyone as I love Silas, and because of my stupidity I have lost him to Amanda Rhys. I had something good, and I threw it away. Like you with Mummy, I suppose, but you have been given a second chance."

"I'm so sorry," he said, "I did not realise . . ."

The tears did come now, and it was a relief to weep openly. He handed her a crisp white handkerchief and, when she had recovered, she smiled at him. "Do you know that this is the first time in my whole life I have had a serious conversation with you?"

"I hope it is the beginning of something good," he said seriously.

"And Mummy, when she returns, I suppose she will expect us all to say nothing and pretend all this never happened."

"I'm sorry," said Roderick, "that you find both your parents so uncommunicative. There is no excuse for me. I had the most carefree childhood. My mother was a teacher and my father was a clergyman . . ."

"Like Silas," interrupted Bridget.

"Yes, like Silas. We have that in common. I had a brother and sister, and we talked and argued about everything. We shared an ambition to succeed. As you know, we managed that; your uncle is a judge and your Aunt Jean is a doctor. There were never any secrets between us, we were open about everything. I think the political life destroys openness, and I blame my own failings on that. Perhaps now I have left it behind I will do better by my children. Your mother, however, had a very different upbringing. I don't know if you remember her father; Claw they called him. He was a very odd fish, and when your grandmother died he was left to bring up his little girl. Divvy had a nanny and an old-maid governess, and those two, and her father, made up her family. It is no wonder that she is reserved, and finds it hard to show her emotions."

Bridget was interested to hear about her mother's life in Ireland. Duibhne had never talked to her about it. "That is where I met her," her father told her. "She and her father and Ma and the boy were rattling around together in this vast mansion which was rapidly falling into the most terrible state of disrepair. Claw did not seem capable of doing anything about it. Now it has been completely renovated, and is a very magnificent hotel."

"And you met her, and fell in love with her at once?"

"Yes, I did. I thought she was the most beautiful person I had ever seen, and I still do. I made up my mind to marry her, and she needed to be rescued."

"It is very romantic," sighed Bridget.

"I am very sorry about you and Silas," said her father. "I wish I could help you, but of course there is no way I can. You will get used to the idea of being without him in time – that is the only comfort I can give you. It will get better."

"Thank you, Daddy," said Bridget. She changed the subject. "Are you going to London tomorrow?"

"Well, I was, but I can cancel it if you would prefer me to stay here."

"No, don't do that. But, would you mind very much if I go to Scotland to be with Mummy during the last few days she is there? I stayed here because I thought you were depressed, but I don't think that is the case now. If you can spare me I would like to go to the Maiden's Planting."

For a moment Roderick reverted to his old self. "I rather hoped you would come with me when I go to collect Robert," he said, managing to inject a little pathos in his voice.

"I think you should meet Robert on your own," said Bridget decidedly. "Then you can talk to him, as you have talked to me this evening. He doesn't know what is happening either, you know, and may be more worried than he shows."

"You will be going by train?" he enquired anxiously.

"No, I shall drive. Mother has done that drive many times and, if she can do it, so can I. I'll leave you now, darling, so I can pack my bag, and make an early start in the morning." She picked up the tray. "I'll leave this in the kitchen on my way. Goodnight, Daddy, and thank you for everything. I love you."

"I love you too," he said.

The next day, when she came downstairs, he had already left for London. She told Bell that she intended driving to Scotland.

The old man became flustered and worried, as he did not think she should drive so far on her own. "Your mother would not like it," he said.

"I'm not a baby, you know," she told him, "although everyone treats me like one. I'll be perfectly all right."

He insisted on giving her a packet of sandwiches and a thermos of coffee. "It will be dark before you get there," he grumbled. "Why not stop on the way?"

"I want to get there as soon as possible. I'll only have a few days there, as it is, and then we will all be coming home for Robert's holidays."

"I'm glad to hear that, Miss Bridget, but I'm afraid you will be so tired after so much driving, and I don't think you have looked well lately."

His sympathy made the tears start to her eyes again. He noticed them at once. "Something is wrong," he said, "I'm listening."

She kissed his cheek. "I know you are," she said, "but I shall feel better when I get there, I promise."

It was many hours before she crossed the border, but at least while she was in England the rain kept off. She turned on the wipers at Scotch Corner. After that, a mist descended and she had to peer through the windscreen to see the road ahead. On the outskirts of Dumfries she was stopped by a policeman. She turned down the music blaring on the radio, and wound down the side window. She looked into his rain-soaked young face. "I'm sorry if I was driving too fast," she said.

His expression was the same as Bell's had been earlier in the day. "Are you all right, Miss?"

"Perfectly fine, thank you." He let her go, with a warning.

From Inverary the road seemed interminable. She felt tired and hungry, so she stopped in a lay-by and drank some of Bell's coffee and started eating the sandwiches. A pantechnicon drew in behind her, and she saw the bright headlights in her mirror. She had a moment of fear, and started the engine. She finished the sandwich as she was driving the car. She passed the lights of Tarbert, and the little boats bobbing on the sparkling water, then on to a twisting turning road that seemed to go on for ever.

It became increasingly difficult to see through the mist and the rain, and her eyes were dimmed with tears. Weariness and depression took hold of her now, and she wallowed in self-pity, driving too fast around the sharp corners. They were right, she thought, the people who thought she was too young and silly to attempt such a long drive. She had been young and silly in her attitude towards Silas, and now all she could remember about him were the good things, what a marvellous lover, friend and loyal supporter he had always been, not appreciated by her until he was lost to her for ever. "I'll never get there," she said aloud, and wondered what would happen if her car broke down on this lonely road.

At last, pinpricks of light told her that she was nearly there. She had reached the sleeping town of Campbeltown. She drove alongside the loch which was still and flat, and she noticed the rain had ceased. She drove to the little bridge, and stopped the car when she knew she could go no further. The door of the house on the hill was thrown open, and a shaft of light illuminated the path.

Bridget stepped out of the car, as her mother, warned by Bell of her arrival, ran down the slope and gathered her in her arms.

CHAPTER THIRTY-FOUR

Silas took his flat off the market, locked it up, and went to stay with his parents. "It is lovely for us to have you," said his mother, "but won't you be terribly bored?" Silas tried to explain to her that boredom was what he most desired at present.

They lived amazingly full lives, and were out most of the day. Cold ham and salad, under a covered plate, was left in the refrigerator for Silas's lunch each day. It never varied. In the evening the three of them met for a glass of sherry before sitting down with supper on trays, to watch the television. They were happy to watch anything that happened to be on at the time, soaps and programmes about vets and doctors as well as political discussions and the news.

The modern house was run very efficiently; he had a comfortable bed and there was always hot water for a bath. A cleaning lady came in twice a week. His mother used a small car to get her to her many functions: she was a Justice of the Peace, Governor of the local school and sat on numerous committees as well as her other duties, arranging flowers in the church and visiting her husband's parishioners. The canon generously allowed his wife to have the car, and went everywhere on a bicycle, black robes flapping dangerously near the spokes of the wheels.

Silas went for long walks with the dog, a Labrador, grown stout through lack of exercise. The two of them shed pounds. He stayed a fortnight, and at the end of that time, decided he did not know his parents any better, but at least understood how they regulated their lives. They had created a pattern for living which suited them very well. He got the distinct impression that they were pleased he had come, especially his father who was the softer character.

The canon took a holiday on Silas's last day, and went fishing with his son. While they were sitting silently by the river (fear of disturbing the fish was a reason for not talking) Silas ventured to say, "Thank you, Father, for this break. It was just what I needed."

There was a long pause, and he feared he had overstepped the boundary of sentimentality. Then the canon said gruffly, "I was sorry things did not work out with that girl."

Silas muttered a few banal words to the effect that perhaps he and Amanda were not right for each other after all, and his father replied, "Oh, I did not mean that girl."

When he got back to London, he telephoned Pondings.

It was gratifying that Bell was always so pleased to speak to him.

"Are you well, sir? Mr Macauley is in London at present, and the other members of the family are in Scotland still."

"Do you know when they are returning?"

"Not before the beginning of the school holidays, sir, when Master Robert comes home."

Silas drove to a small village just across the border into Scotland. He sat in a gloomy single hotel bedroom, looking at the telephone and trying to summon up the courage to lift the receiver. Bell had given him the number of the Maiden's Planting, and eventually he dialled it. Duibhne answered it, and she expressed no surprise, just pleasure at hearing his voice. Yes, she would be delighted to see him the next day. Well, they would all be delighted. Was Amanda with him? When he said, "No," she did not ask questions, but quickly passed on to the business of giving him directions.

It was a very beautiful drive, the road twisting and turning across heather-covered country where shadowy hills cut off the glowering sky, and bright silver cascades of water tumbled perpendicularly from the rocks. Although it was still daylight, the sky was dark, and gentle rain pattered on the roof of the car.

When he reached Campbeltown everything was grey and covered in mist. The houses had a Spartan look about them, those on the edge of the loch fronted by gardens where the flowers battled with the wind and the stinging rain. As he had been instructed, he bumped along the rough cart-track which came to a sudden stop just before the narrow footbridge.

The house stood on the top of the hill, a tall wooden construction with a large expanse of sloping roof. It was a stiff climb, and he paused at the top to stand and look at the spectacular view. There was a rough sea, beating on the shingle, but through the mist, Ailsa Craig, the bleak remote island of the birds, could be seen quite clearly. Beyond, the Isle of Arran was hidden by clouds.

What a magical place, thought Silas, I wonder if Duibhne is at peace here? Suddenly, she was there to greet him, and he was astounded by her appearance. She was dressed in trousers and a big shirt, like a man's shirt. Her hair was tied back in a tight little knot, and her skin was taut and tanned. The brightness of the blue eyes showed most vividly against the brown unmade-up face. She seemed genuinely pleased to see him.

"You have come so far!" she cried. Then, "Oh, dear, you have not got your case. Now you will have to climb the hill again."

"I didn't know I was staying . . ."

"Get it, you foolish fellow. You don't expect us to allow you to drive back along that road tonight, do you? I hope you will stay several days."

He fetched his case, and when he joined her again at the top of the hill, she said, "How well you look, Silas. Quite different."

"I left my old job," he told her, "and I've been on holiday."

She showed him his room: small, white walls and pine furniture. He heard her clattering down the uncarpeted stairs. In the adjoining bathroom, washing his hands in the basin, he stared at his reflection in the mirror, and asked it a question: What am I doing here? His practical self told him he had probably made a disastrous error of judgement, but another voice came in triumphantly and said: I'm back.

When he went downstairs he found Duibhne in the kitchen, filling an electric kettle from the tap. "I thought we would have tea," she said. "Ma, Bridget and Christopher are not here, as you see. They have gone for a walk along the seashore." She paused. "I did not tell them you were coming. It will be a surprise for them."

He said awkwardly, "I expect you realise by now that Amanda and I are not going to be married."

"Yes, I imagined that must be the case. I'm very sorry for you both."

"It was my fault," he told her. "She is a wonderful girl. I have been a fool. It seemed so right, but I did not foresee that there was a whole chunk of my life I could not cast aside in such a hurry. I needed time, but she could not understand that. How could she?"

"Perhaps it was for the best," she said gently.

He looked about him at the very modern kitchen with white and steel surfaces. In the centre was a large pine table with high-backed latticed chairs grouped around it.

"I like this room very much," said Duibhne. "When I had the house built, I decided to dispense with a dining-room, and had another room instead which doubles as my study and a television room. Christopher loves watching television."

"So do my parents," said Silas.

She put a teapot, cups and saucers, all the bits and pieces for tea on to a tray. It was strange watching her do domestic tasks, out of character. She took a cake from a tin, and placed it on a plate.

"Chocolate cake!" said Silas.

"Made by Ma. She is a marvellous cake-maker. I am hopeless. I hope they will be back soon to help us eat it. There is a lot of driftwood on the beach, and they collect it for firewood. And talking of fire . . . I wonder how it is doing?"

Silas walked ahead with the tray, and he put it on a low table in front of the fire which was burning brightly in an enormous stone fireplace. The room, so understated and with the minimum of furnishings, was charming, as Duibhne's room at Pondings was charming, except that this room had a light feel about it, despite the dark sky outside.

Instead of portraits on the walls, as at Pondings, here there were a few abstract paintings, muted shades merging into one another, and in one corner of the room was a slim streamlined bronze sculpture standing on a plinth, curving to a sharp gleaming point culminating just below the ceiling.

Silas was astonished and approving at the same time. The chairs made of soft grey leather were wonderfully comfortable and, as he sank into one of them, he said, "This is such a beautiful room."

"My Uncle Tom had a room like this in his house in Oregon," said Duibhne. "I suppose I remembered it when I decided how I wanted this to look." She added inconsequently, "Ma is very fond of this room."

He thought he owed it to her to explain, "I have not come here with any hope. I'm afraid Bridget will not be pleased to see me, but I had to see her. I wanted to see you as well."

"I'm sure that is not true," she replied, "although it is nice of you to say it. As for Bridget, I cannot predict what her reaction will be. She is stubborn, as you know, and does not give much away. She is my daughter, after all." She smiled as she poured the tea, and cut them both a slice of cake.

"It is true that I wanted to see you," Silas insisted. "I thought of you all through that terrible business which must have hurt you very much."

"In a way I feel a sense of release," she said, "all that silly secrecy is ended, and I am free at last. Can you understand that?"

"I think so," replied Silas, "but I wish it had not been one of those damned reporters who gave you this freedom."

"Delphine Blake who wrote the story is a good person," she told him, almost reprovingly. "Delphine! What a name that girl has, it is worse than my own. She was very kind, very discreet, and I thought she wrote an excellent article about me. Didn't you think so?"

"I must say the *Graphic* is one of our more civilised newspapers."

"You see, when I returned to Ireland after I had been in prison," she went on, "my father wanted the whole episode to be forgotten, as if it had never happened."

He was rather shocked to hear her use the word 'prison' in relation to herself.

"I loved my father dearly, but we were never very good at communicating with each other about important things and, at the time, it seemed the right thing to do, for everyone's sake, to cut out completely those years I spent in the States."

But there were reminders, thought Silas, and it looks as though she dealt with those. Had she been able to manipulate Roderick Macauley as well? Surely, that would have been impossible? Or, perhaps she had just been unlucky in the two most important men in her life, a father whose intellect did not extend beyond hunting and the form book and whose paramount emotion was pride, and a husband whose wife and family fitted into a slot for furthering his ambition, who could not see beyond his handsome face in the mirror.

Silas recalled how Delphine Blake had asked her readers whether they could believe that Roderick

Macauley was ignorant of his wife's past. He longed to ask Duibhne the same question, and he searched his mind for the right words.

She anticipated him by saying, "It was terrible that poor Rod had to resign because of me. You see, you have to reveal all the family skeletons when you become a Member of the Cabinet. If he said he did not know they would never believe him. How could they believe such a thing?" She twisted the gold band on her left hand, as if reminding herself of the reality of the situation. "I destroyed his career more effectively than that Jones woman," she said bitterly.

He realised she had not told him what he wanted to know, and he was certain she never would. He sensed by the expression on her face that she knew what he was thinking, and he became confused. "I don't want you to think I am prying," he mumbled.

She leaned back in her chair. "Dear Silas, I know you are just interested. We are old friends."

"Thank you."

"I said it was a relief to talk openly about my years in prison, and I meant it. There are not many people like me who have had that unique experience, and I am mindful of the reason for it. It is a fearful thing to destroy a life, to cut short an existence that might have proved valuable and worthwhile. Who was I to snatch all those years in one frightened angry moment? I must live with the shame of it, always. I left out so many details when I was talking to Delphine Blake. Perhaps, one day, I will come here, where there is peace and tranquillity, and write down all I remember."

"What a marvellous idea," said Silas.

"I was talking to Delphine about my friendship with Hazel Chamberlain," she went on. "She was the girl I shared a room with at the Correctional Facility. We became very close. She knew me better than I knew myself. I could have learned so much from her – proper values and how to judge people for what they are, rather than who they are. I'm afraid I was a poor pupil, and I know she found my narrow restricted view on life very irritating, but it did not affect her liking for me. Also, I think she blamed my attitude on the way I had been brought up and, as I did not know any better, I was forgiven." She leaned forward and poured out more tea for them, glancing at the window as she did so. "Talking to Delphine about her after so many years made me determined to get in touch with her. I found out that she died fifteen years ago. I could not get any information about the reason for her death, just that she died. She became a doctor, as she hoped, but she never married." Duibhne's hand went to her face, and she covered her eyes. "I felt so awful when I heard that. I know that we agreed we would not keep in touch, but it was a wrong decision. I have made so many mistakes, but that is the one I regret the most. She died, perhaps alone, fifteen years ago."

"I'm sorry."

"It is I who should be sorry, Silas, for talking so

much, but it is such a relief to talk about it, and for that I am grateful to Delphine Blake. I owe so much to her, but I know she imagines my feelings to be just the opposite. She was upset, I sensed it, and I am going to write to her and tell her she must not be worried."

"I shouldn't bother," he said shortly. "It is all in a day's work for someone like her."

"I don't think so," said Duibhne firmly. "She is different." She allowed herself a faint irony when she added, "I don't think she will publish my letter." She went on, "It was Christopher who touched her soul. The hardest of hearts could not fail to be affected by the sheer futility of Christopher's life. We have our pathetic little stories to tell, but my poor Christopher's story is a book with blank pages. Christopher's story is no story at all."

"You care for him, don't you?" Silas found himself asking the question, fearing the rebuff it might evoke.

But she answered him readily enough, as if she wanted him to know the truth. "Oh, yes, I care for Christopher. I always have, you know. Even in my darkest moments, when I could not face up to what had happened to him, I still loved him. I was a coward when it came to the difficult part and, fortunately for me, there was someone who wanted to take that on. I have been blessed in so many ways." She got up and walked to the window. "I can't think why they are so long," she said restlessly. "They should have been back ages ago. Ma is to blame. She walks too far. Christopher will be exhausted."

"Does Ma like it here?" he asked.

She turned away from the window, and sat down again. "We all love this place. But Ma has her cottage and her precious possessions. She will be glad to return to them. We all have to pick up the threads again, Silas, after what has happened."

Suddenly he realised there had never been any question of her not going back. He had mistakenly thought she would cut adrift from the old unsatisfactory arrangement, that she would carve a new independent life for herself. But this was not to be, for she loved Roderick Macauley, the man himself as well as all he represented, position, home and family. She would never be able to acknowledge that this part of her life was as much a failure as the rest had been. She was determined to make a success of it. She had grasped what she needed, a respite from it all, a time to take stock, to weigh the advantages against the disadvantages and to realise the importance of forgiveness.

"It is the same for me," he said slowly. "I have to start looking for a new job."

He saw that she was watching him closely, as if trying to decide what she would say next. "I have talked so much," she said at last, "and you have listened patiently. There is something else I have to tell you. Not about me this time, but about my daughter."

He had the uneasy feeling that she was going to tell him that his coming to Scotland was a mistake. He felt that during their talk that afternoon he had come closer to this remote woman than he had ever thought possible. He sensed with this new bond between them she would be completely honest with him, and he dreaded her honesty.

He had misread the situation, for she started to describe to him Bridget's arrival at the Maiden's Planting. How shocked her mother had been to see the woeful tearstained face. How the girl had sobbed in her arms. Duibhne was alarmed because she did not know the cause for such an outpouring of grief. She knew that it was more than just the strain of a long arduous drive. Later, Bridget told her mother the reason.

Silas could hardly take it in. He stared at a patch of carpet beneath his feet, unable to meet Duibhne's eyes.

"She did not look in the least pretty," she went on. "She just looked like a girl who has been hurt."

"Because of me? Are you saying she is unhappy because of me?"

"Don't imagine she will not get over it," said Duibhne more briskly. "Girls recover from lost love, you know, remarkably quickly. Already, she is happier than when she first came, going for walks on the beach every day. This is a wonderful place for forgetting."

"I don't want her to forget," said Silas fiercely. "I won't allow her to forget."

"I'm afraid it may be you who will have to keep reminding yourself how she felt when you were no longer around," said Duibhne smiling, "when she is being tiresome and unreasonable. You know her character very well, Silas." Her eyes turned once more to the window. "Look at the weather outside and it is getting dark. I am beginning to worry and I think we should go and look for them."

By the front door there was a line of heavy raincoats on pegs, and she took one down and handed it to him, then put one on herself. She tied a scarf over her hair. When they were outside the force of the wind almost unbalanced them, gusting in from the sea, stinging their faces.

There was a strange configuration of black cloud on the horizon, like a square block of rain moving towards the west. "It is exciting here in a storm," she told him, "but better to be inside, away from it."

As they slithered down the hill, Silas noticed other signs of life, on a strip of land almost hidden from view. Shadowy figures darted here and there, covering a makeshift dwelling with a tarpaulin, preparing for bad weather. "Who are they?" he asked.

"Tinkers. I haven't the heart to move them on, they remind me of my childhood. Anyway, they guard the place for me."

When they reached the stony beach, the wind was so strong she had to shout at him over the noise of it. "Can you see the walkers?"

He strained his eyes, and thought he saw three figures in the mist. They were the length of the beach away, but as they got nearer he could see them more clearly. Then he could make out the shapes of the two dogs, bounding backwards and forwards in front of them.

Duibhne had seen them too. "You go ahead," she cried. "I'll wait here."

Silas started to run, buffeted by the savage wind and the driving rain. As he drew near, he heard Ma's voice, "It's Silas!" When he reached them he could hardly breathe, partly from running so fast and partly from the joy of seeing Bridget again.

She said, "You're back!" and he kissed her face which was smiling and wet with rain.

Then he noticed Christopher who seemed to have lost all impetus to move, and stood like a rag-doll, legs buckled, hair blowing across his face. Strands of hair flicked across his misted-up spectacles. Silas felt a surge of compassion for this sad man who had been dealt a rotten hand in life, and who was now plainly terrified by elements he could not begin to understand.

Silas took his arm, and pressed it close to his side, and he saw Bridget take the other arm. Magda was behind them, waving to the indistinct figure of Duibhne.

"Come on, Christopher," said Silas, "we're going home."

THE END